SWEPT AWAY BY
HER WAYWARD HEART . . .

Juliette lay gazing up at the ceiling, wide awake and far from sleep. She had never dreamed it was possible to yearn so strongly for one man's arms, never suspected that love could come without invitation or welcome, defying all reason, rejecting all logic . . . It was not enough to want a man whose heart had long since died with the only woman he'd ever loved and lost, but did he have to be the brother of the man she was to wed?

The
Frenchwoman

Barbara Paul

GOLDEN APPLE PUBLISHERS

THE FRENCHWOMAN

*A Golden Apple Publication / published by arrangement with
St. Martin's Press, Inc.*

Golden Apple edition / January 1984

Golden Apple is a trademark of Golden Apple Publishers

ISBN 0-553-19754-1

Published simultaneously in the United States and Canada

PRINTED IN THE UNITED STATES OF AMERICA

To Jessie

Chapter One

She moved silently about her bedroom with its high, flower-painted ceiling and old, pine-paneled walls, a shaded candle giving her a glimmer of light. One drawer and then another was opened as Juliette Delahousse hastily selected the garments she needed to take with her in her flight from the house and she turned resolutely from anything that was frivolous or unnecessary in the different life she was soon to lead. Her hands shook with tension, and she started violently whenever a floorboard creaked underfoot or a drawer handle rattled under her touch. Now and again she paused by the communicating door into the next room where her chaperone, Mademoiselle Rousseau, was sleeping, intent on making sure that there was no break in the rhythmic, muffled snoring. To be thwarted of escape in the last hour would be beyond endurance, for the penalty would be a marriage of convenience to an Englishman whom she had never seen.

A shudder went through her again at the thought. With fresh anxiety that nothing should turn against her she went across to the window and held back the curtain to peer out at the weather, wanting to make sure that it was not going to play any last minute tricks on her. One could never tell with the tail end of the winter in Sweden. A blinding snowstorm could sweep in without warning off the Baltic to envelop Stockholm, making it difficult to get through the streets on foot and virtually impossible to cover any distance at speed on horseback along the country roads beyond the city's boundaries.

With relief she saw that the night was as clear and still as when she had last looked out. Under a starry sky and beyond the snow tops of the trees in the grounds below, Stockholm looked as though it might have been carved out of ice itself with its delicate spires and copper roofs glinting in the moonlight and set on a carpet of snow renewed that day, which was surely winter's final swirl of its cloak to keep approaching spring at bay. In those same streets on a day bitter with savage frost more than a year ago her father, Henri Delahousse, who had fought valiantly for Napoleon in many fields of battle and survived unscathed, contracted a fatal chill through his own conceit, so typical of him, while riding in a royal procession as escort to the new Swedish Regent, Jean Bernadotte, formerly Marshal of France and one of the French Emperor's most noted generals. Henri had been proud to be numbered with the French officers chosen by Bernadotte to be with him in Stockholm after he had accepted the invitation of the old and enfeebled King Carl of Sweden to become heir to the throne, the Crown Prince having died suddenly, leaving none of Swedish blood suitable to take his place. Not only was it a great honor to join Bernadotte's entourage, but Henri shared the new Regent's growing distrust of Napoleon, whose grandiose ambitions had extended beyond the bounds of all reason, and he was less sorry to leave France than he might have been. Yet he loved his country dearly, and being freshly come to Sweden he underestimated the insidious cold of the new climate and dispensed with his cloak when he rode in the procession, not wanting to hide his broad-shouldered splendor in the uniform of the *Chasseurs à Cheval* of the Guard in a last public showing of French military glory before he followed the example of his fellow officers in Bernadotte's retinue and adopted permanently the blue and gold of the Swedish army.

He was dead when the ship bringing Juliette and her stepmother, Marianne, docked in Stockholm harbor, his merry and immoral and generous natured existence snuffed out by a fiery fever of the lungs. They were just in time for the funeral.

Juliette stepped away from the window and let the curtain fall back into place. At times tears of grief still assailed her without warning, and she must not let them occur now, especially when she knew that her father would be encouraging her rebellion against a loveless match, he who had reveled in the force of love and passion like the true Frenchman that he was. He had married again only a matter of months before leaving for Sweden, and it was sad and ironic that after years of being a widower, with many lovely women passing in and out of his life, he had made an error of his own in finally taking Marianne as his second wife, a widow of rare, porcelain beauty, distantly related to the Bonapartes, who had proved herself hard and mercenary, bartering her body for his ring and having no heart to match his. To add to his disappointment, Marianne showed that she had taken a strong dislike to his daughter, his only child whose mother had died at her birth, upon their first meeting on the eve of his departure for Sweden. Juliette, released from her convent school in Rouen to be with Marianne until they should also leave some weeks later, had been bewildered by the marked hostility, never having known anything but love from her father and gentleness and kindness from the convent nuns.

Opening the closet door Juliette surveyed her dresses to see which she should take, and a mirror near at hand reflected the candlelight and held her slender image within its frame, making an aura of her ivory-fair hair, which she wore parted in the middle and drawn up in a topknot, curling tendrils lying against the nape of her graceful neck. Her looks were piquant and gamine, with a short, pert nose, firm rounded chin, and a full-lipped, generous mouth, outcome of her French ancestry, but the gentle, lustrous eyes under the arched brows came from her English mother as did the cream and roses complexion with its bloom that had paled at the news of the impending marriage of convenience received only that morning, her face still holding the stress and strain.

Half a dozen black mourning gowns hung side by side, reminders of a year of virtual isolation, a period of conventional retreat from society, which had borne no relation to her own deeply private sorrow. Marianne, having fallen out with the Bonapartes before leaving Paris, had had no desire to return there, con-

sidering the Swedish court circle to be acceptable under
the new French influence, and in addition she liked
the grand residence that Henri had purchased in readiness for the coming of his wife and daughter to Stockholm.

Eleven months to the day of their arrival in Sweden
Juliette had reached her seventeenth natal day, still
wearing only deepest black, her bonnets heavily veiled,
and forbidden to don the transitional colors of lilac or
gray normally worn towards the end of a mourning
year, although Marianne had ventured long since into
rich purples and palest heliotrope and wore her black
with such dash and flair that it was possible to forget
it was the color of death. She had also relaxed the
social rules in her own case while keeping Juliette seg-
regated from all that was gay and festive and entertaining in the outside world; Marianne went out in the
evenings or held small dinner parties at home; sometimes she gave cozier suppers for a single guest, but
who any of these people were, Juliette did not know
for certain, since she was never included and spent the
evenings in her own rooms, dining alone with Mademoiselle. Occasionally from her bed she would hear
noisy chatter in the hall when the guests departed, but
her apartments were too far away on an upper floor
for her to make more than a guess at whom they might
be. As for the guests who came singly, she never heard
when they left, but she thought they must stay until
the early hours, having once heard a man cough when
it was almost four o'clock, and Marianne always lay
abed the next day and did not rise at her usual time.

Next to the black garments hung a simple evening
gown of gossamer muslin over almond pink silk, and
the sight of it stirred in Juliette such tender, romantic
thoughts that it was heartbreaking for her to consider
leaving it behind. She reached in and took it down to
hold it against herself, turning toward the mirror. In
this gown she had met Nicolaus. She had worn it on
that first evening out of mourning at a gala performance at the Opera House when he had fallen in love
with her, and she never tired of hearing him tell

again and again of how she had looked to him on that
never to be forgotten occasion.

The invitation to go to the opera had come from
General de Marquet, a more senior member of the
Regent's French entourage; otherwise it was doubtful
whether Marianne would have allowed her to accept.
Never would she forget the wonder of it all! The glitter of the chandeliers. The ladies of fashion with gold-
en filets or tall plumes in their hair. Gentlemen with
collar points as high as their cheekbones, nearly all in
formal, tight knee breeches, their coats of plum, emerald, azure, or midnight black. The richness of gold
brading on dress uniforms. The mingled fragrances of
perfumes and pomades. She had felt like a butterfly
emerging from a chrysalis into a world that had been
long awaiting her.

On all sides heads had turned as the General had
escorted her with Marianne up the wide staircase, and
Juliette had seen nothing unusual in it, being well used
to the impact that her stepmother's beauty could make
on those unprepared for it. It was not until they were
settled in their seats in the box that she realized that
a fair share of the male glances were concentrated on
her. In an agony of delight and embarrassment she
pretended not to notice the glint of opera glasses
turned in her direction, and it was a relief to her when
the arrival of the Regent in the Royal box diverted
everyone's attention as they all stood, and afterwards
the auditorium was dimmed by the snuffing of candles and the performance began.

In the interval people came to pay their respects
to the General and the ladies with him, and again
Juliette could not help noticing how looks came twice
in her direction. Marianne, used to holding all attention, noticed it too, and her smile was fixed and taut.
Had Juliette been left in any doubt that during her
year of hibernation she had developed into a degree
of attractiveness that she had not suspected, it would
have been dispelled for her by all she saw in the wickedly flirtatious eyes of Nicolaus Nilsson. Young and
dashing in his dress uniform of the Swedish Royal

Guards, courier to the Regent, he had come to pay court to her stepmother, but stared instead at her, his glance returning to her constantly until Marianne, losing patience, two high spots of color burning through the powder on her cheeks, dealt him a stinging rap with the edge of her fan.

He was undaunted. "I must see you again, Juliette," he had whispered behind Marianne's back when taking his leave from the box as the lights dimmed for the second act. "It was Destiny that brought us both to the Opera House this evening. I know it!" After the performance was over one of the bewigged and liveried attendants of the Opera House had passed a love note to her secretly on his behalf, but not until Mademoiselle's snores resounded from the adjoining bedroom did she dare to relight the candle and read it through, putting her hand to her throat, a blush rising at his ardent protestation of having fallen in love with her on sight.

Somewhere in the depths of the sleeping house a clock struck the quarter hour, reminding Juliette that time was passing swiftly, and returning the evening gown to the closet she frowned on the memory of the hysterical, fault-finding scene that Marianne had created upon their return from the opera. After that, out of all the invitations that flowed into the house, none was accepted by Marianne on Juliette's behalf for any gathering to which they were invited together. Never again was Marianne to risk her stepdaughter's younger face holding a candle to her age. Their relationship, always painfully uneasy, went into a sharp decline.

Juliette's movement in stretching out her arm to the closet caused the golden locket she wore on a chain around her neck to swing against her breasts within the highwaisted bodice of her gown, and she drew it out, putting its warmth against her cheek, smiling over the knowledge that it contained a miniature of Nicolaus, able to see in her mind's eye his chiseled good looks, the narrow, dancing eyes that begged unthinkable favors from her, and the soft fairness of his fronded hair. He alone had made her life bearable under Marianne's nagging, complaining rule, which never eased, never ceased to deal out punishments in the shape of privileges withdrawn, and treated her as though she were a wilful child instead of the young, clearheaded adult that she was.

The morning after the opera she had taken a stroll in the autumnal-hued grounds of the house, and in a daydream over the wonder of the evening before she had leaned on the parapet at the end of the garden, which overlooked the green waters spanned by the many bridges that linked the islands on which Stockholm was built. She paid no heed to the traffic of carriages, wagons, pedestrians, and equestrians passing across them, lost in her own blissful thoughts. Then, when she turned to retrace her steps, the crunch of gravel underfoot on a nearby path had made her turn her head sharply. There she saw Nicolaus dressed for riding. He doffed his tall hat and held it.

"What are you doing here?" she exclaimed in incredulous delight.

He laughed softly and reached out quickly to draw her to him within the shelter of the trees where there was no danger of their being seen from the house. "I told you I had to see you again—and here I am. By chance I happened to sight you leaning on the parapet as I came riding over the bridge." He gestured in its direction. "Hoping you would not have moved away I left my horse by the side gate and came into the grounds that way."

"The side gate! It's never used. Hardly anybody knows it's there."

"Ah!" He grinned conspiratorially. "I quickly scouted around."

"You could have knocked on the door of the house and asked for me," she teased provocatively.

His eyes danced dangerously at her. "Would I have been allowed to be alone with you, do you think?"

She shook her head merrily, amused by his audaciousness. "Mademoiselle would have chaperoned us all the time and looked at you like this." She had difficulty in composing her happy face into a scowl, and he took advantage of their joint burst of laughter at her somewhat unsuccessful effort to put his arm about her waist and press her hard against him.

"There! You see! Much better for me to seek you out in the garden." He was looking down into her face and his expression became serious in its ardor. "You are bewitching, Juliette. I'd seen you before our meeting yesterday evening, but always you were heavily veiled. I should have known your features would match the perfection of your figure."

Color suffused her cheeks. "You pay bold compliments. How did you know it was I?"

"By the carriage you rode in. By the chaperone who never left you. By the way you trailed after Madame Delahousse into the dressmaker's or the milliner's, always a slim, black shadow in her wake. Then at the Opera House I could scarcely believe my eyes when I looked upon your face at last."

"So you said in that note you had sent to me." She tried to sound reproving, but it was impossible, so overwhelming was his amorous approach, so throbbing his voice.

He touched her cheek with his ungloved fingertips, his gaze dropping lingeringly to her lips and then meeting her eyes again. "I bless my good fortune in finding you on your own today. Say that I may see you often. Do not deny me your company."

Painfully she remembered Marianne's displeasure at having to share his and everybody else's attention with her at the opera. "Somehow I do not think my stepmother would allow it."

"She need not know. You would prefer that, wouldn't you?"

"I must admit I'm heartily tired of having my days pressed into the dullest of routine with no freedom to do as I please." A sense of mischief took over, and she felt ready to outwit her chaperone and Marianne at every turn. "I go twice a week to the park near the Palace with Mademoiselle for a walk. I always climb the hillock there to the copse of fir trees on the summit, but she never comes with me, and waits below. It's a safe meeting place."

"But that's a chill one, my love. Surely we have mutual acquaintances at whose houses our visits can be planned to coincide?"

"I'm not on calling terms with anybody. I've not been allowed to go anywhere or do anything during the past year."

"But your time of mourning is over. Invitations will flood into your home, especially after the sensation you caused yesterday evening. I wasn't alone in being lost in admiration. Is there a maid you can send with messages to me at the officers' quarters in the east wing of the Vasa Barracks and who can be trusted to receive them from my manservant in return?"

She shook her head. "I cannot think of one." With the exception of the lowliest kitchen staff, whom Juliette had never seen, all the domestic staff, including the two chefs and the pastry-cook, had been brought from Paris by Marianne, and there was not one who would risk his or her livelihood in such foolhardiness.

He smiled at her. "I refuse to be discouraged. Nothing shall stop my seeing you. In the meantime there is our next meeting to look forward to. Tell me the days when I may find you at the park."

"On Thursday and Saturday mornings."

"Watch out for me. I hope soon to have solved the matter of a better trysting-place."

"I must go." Their talk of time had reminded her that she should be back at the house and she became agitated, fearing that at any moment Mademoiselle might appear in search of her; if they were discovered together it would be an end of any further meetings. "I promised not to be late returning indoors."

He bent his head swiftly and would have taken her lips, but she turned her face from him as she slipped from his arms, not with any deliberate intention of being coquettish, although all that was feminine in her told her instinctively it would make him more her slave to yearn after that kiss until she chose the moment to bestow it. He showed his disappointment, but he smiled and moved to watch her as she ran from him in haste along the path, leaving him to depart the way he had come.

There then began for her the most enchanting period of her life, even surpassing those times she had
spent with her father before Marianne had crossed his
path when, between service in Napoleon's campaigns,
he had come to the convent at Rouen and taken her
away to their country home in the district, the home
which later he had had to sell in favor of an elegant
Parisian residence for Marianne; there they had
walked and talked, ridden through the forests and
fished in the rivers, passing countless contented hours
in each other's company. Nicolaus gave her back with
a new and haunting sweetness the rare happiness she
had known then. She was sure that first snowflakes
would always remind her of their park meetings in a
copse of firs on a hillock in the park.

He was often away for weeks at a time bearing
despatches in the service of the Regent, but he made
up for his enforced absences by appearing wherever
she went when he was in the city. All the invitations
that came to the house, no matter if they were addressed to her personally, were—together with any
other mail sent to her—opened by her stepmother,
who accepted or declined the invitations on her behalf
depending on whether or not Marianne wished to shine
alone at any particular occasion. Never did they go
anywhere together. It pruned down drastically the
events Juliette was able to attend, but the presence of
Nicolaus lifted each one into the category of a grand
occasion, and he kept her heart light. At balls and
parties he danced with her. He enveigled a seat near
hers at concerts and plays and musical evenings, making the nape of her neck tingle with the intensity of his
gaze. Into her hand at every opportunity he pressed
love notes and poems, which she kept locked in her
jewel casket and read through over and over again
whenever Mademoiselle was not around.

It was in the copse with the soft snow underfoot
and the tall pines a magic ring about them, making a
shield against all alien gazes, that she succumbed at
last to his kisses, his mouth warm and moist and eager,
his arms hard about her. It marked a subtle but determined change in his attitude towards her, and in

the weeks that followed he became more ardent, more desirous that their time together should not be snatched and brief.

One morning there, when the sun was making pale patterns on the soft snow, she could tell he was restless and ill at ease, his yearning for her transparent in the tautness of his face, and he spoke with a desperate brusqueness.

"Since I am not allowed to call on you with Madame Delahousse's permission—"

She showed confusion, torn between pleasure that his feelings should be strong enough for him to take such a step as to wish to present himself as a serious suitor, and dismay mingled with anger that Marianne should have thrown out his request without any consultation with herself about what her feelings might be.

"Has she quite forbidden you?"

"In no uncertain terms." His gaze shifted, not quite meeting her eyes, and he took one of her hands into his, tracing abstractedly the intricate stitching on her glove with a forefinger. "I am desolate."

She was touched and moved. "I will speak to her—"

"No, no." Startled and anxious, his eyes became wide. "I implore you not to mention anything to Madame Delahousse, or else she might use her influence with General de Marquet to get me posted away from Stockholm, and then we should never see each other again."

She clutched at him. "That must not happen."

"Dearest, it must not. How could I live without seeing you?" He gazed down into her face, absorbing all he saw there, his own expression tender. "No one has any right to stand in the path of true love. There must be a dozen ways out of that large house in which you live. Cannot you find some safe route to take which would enable you to slip out by night to meet me? I'd have a closed sleigh waiting, and we could go to the abode of some friends of mine who would welcome the chance to offer us a trysting-place under their roof."

Although her mind innocently went no further than

the expectations of a few sweet and passionate kisses taken and given in such surroundings, there was something indefinable underlying his words that went against her own natural honesty, making her sense that the standards she lived by had been somehow assailed, as when a strong tide flows in against the struts of a quay below a deceptively tranquil surface. From earliest childhood she had taken through filial love and admiration the high standards of her father in matters of honor. Without it one could not be true to oneself or one's fellow men. One gave one's word and kept it. One followed an honorable course and did not stray from it. Not for nothing was she the daughter of Colonel Henri Delahousse, who had galloped first of all the rest into the bloody battles of Austerlitz, Auerstadt, and Jena. But weighing against the instinct that cautioned her not to be swayed by Nicolaus with his passionate eagerness was the romantic spell he had cast over her, the excitement he promised, the opening up of the wonder and fun and ecstatic joy that falling deeply in love would be if she let him show the way for her.

"I'm not sure," she answered evasively, trying not to be dazzled.

His lips came within brushing distance of hers. "Tomorrow I leave Stockholm with despatches for Pomerania. Think about what I have asked you while I'm gone, and when I return before the month is out, have the answer ready that I long for." On the last word of his heart-turning appeal his lips took hers, and the kiss bound them until they broke apart, she to go running down the snowy slope back to Mademoiselle, he to watch her for a few minutes before turning to go the other way.

When she arrived home, her coat and skirt hems damp from that same snow, she had no time to change, being told that Madame Delahousse wanted to see her immediately upon her return. Removing her bonnet and dangling it by its ribbons, her coat unbuttoned, she went at once to her stepmother's salon. She found Marianne seated on the striped sofa sorting through some fashion plates newly arrived from Paris.

"You wished to see me, Madame?"

Marianne nodded, setting aside the fashion plates and leaning languidly back against the cushions, elegant in crimson silk, her fingers full of rings. With one graceful hand she motioned for Juliette to take the chair opposite her, and when her instruction was obeyed she said without expression, "I have a pleasant surprise for you. You are going to England."

Juliette, completely taken aback, stared at her incredulously and said the first thing that came into her head. "But we are at war with England, Madame!"

"Nonsense! The Regent made a declaration of war against England on Sweden's behalf simply to pacify Napoleon, but it is tacitly understood by the Swedish and English governments that not a shot will be fired between the two countries and trade is being carried on as before. I have been in correspondence with your English aunt, Mrs. Phoebe Colingridge, your late mother's only sister, who lives in London."

"Am I to visit her?" Juliette's tone was deeply apprehensive.

Marianne's narrow smile was not reflected in her eyes. "Yes, in a way, but it is to be more than that. Between us your aunt and I have arranged a fine marriage for you. To an Englishman of property."

"No!" Juliette's voice seemed to have strangled in her throat and every vestige of color drained from her face. She knew Marianne had every legal right to choose a husband for her. Several girls at the convent had left to enter marriage of convenience with partners selected by their parents, and she had pitied them, confident that her father would allow her to make a love match when the time came for her to marry, but now she found herself in the same dreadful predicament. "No!" she cried again, her hands outthrust protestingly.

Marianne was undisturbed. "Come, come. You know it is my responsibility to choose a husband for you, and you are no longer a child, but a woman ready for marriage. I should be failing in my duty to your father if I did not see you well settled. I will remind you that I have absolute authority in this matter and none can go against me."

"My father and mother married for love. They would have wished the same for me." After the initial shock defiance was rising in her. "You cannot make me go to England! You cannot force me to marry!"

"That is true." Marianne inclined her head sagely. "Unfortunately it would mean you had become too strong-willed for me to harbor in my house. I should have to find you other accommodation in the care of those able to manage you. Rebellion against my authority is something I could not deal with indefinitely."

"You would have me incarcerated!" Juliette was aghast, comprehending fully the extent of her stepmother's loathing for her.

"La! How you do exaggerate! I was thinking more on the lines of another convent—not the one at Rouen, needless to say, but another of a stricter order where your dowry would be eagerly received and put to good use."

"That would leave me penniless!"

"It would indeed, but that need not worry you, surely?" Sarcasm edged the steely words. "Without a franc to your name you could be certain it would be for love alone should any man desire to marry you. Of course, the confines of a convent are not conducive to romantic meetings, and I fear you could not count on seeing or being seen by any prospective husband. A pity, but there it is." She made a graceful gesture of appeasement. "Be advised by me and put aside that alternative to the future that has been arranged for you. Your aunt is convinced you will be well suited to the gentleman concerned—"

"What does my aunt know of me?" Juliette retorted hotly. "She has never written to me. Never shown the slightest interest. That is how much she understands my likes and dislikes."

"Don't be so ungrateful. When it would have been easier for her to find an older man, even an elderly widower, to marry you, she has taken time and trouble to find a young husband for you."

"I imagine the huge dowry my father settled on me

is bait enough for any man, whatever his age." Juliette retorted bitterly.

Marianne continued as if there had been no interruption. "He is the younger son of a most noble family and resides at West Thorpeby Hall on the east coast in the county of Norfolk. His name is Gregory Lockington." She touched lightly with an almond-nailed forefinger a thick wad of papers lying on the round-topped table beside the sofa arm. "The marriage contract has been duly signed and sealed and was delivered into my hands early today by the captain of an English ship. I took this opportunity to secure passages on his vessel for you and Mademoiselle, who will stay with you until your wedding day. You will sail for London with the *Fair Venture* when it leaves again tomorrow."

"Never!" Juliette leapt to her feet, tears springing from her eyes. "I'll never marry this man whom you and my aunt have picked out for me!"

"Hush, hush." Marianne held up both hands, showing a disdainful abhorrence at the prospect of a temperamental scene. "I mentioned my duty to your father, but you have a duty too, and in all honor you cannot deny your own mother's last wish."

Puzzled, Juliette looked at her warily. "My mother? I don't understand."

"Why do you think that, from the earliest age, you were taught English and encouraged to become bilingual? For what special reason was a tutor of English allowed thrice weekly into the convent to give you private lessons and not the other pupils? Have you never given the matter any thought?"

"I know my father wanted me to speak the language well for my mother's sake."

"It was more than that. Far more. With her dying breath your mother expressed the hope that one day you would marry in England and settle there. Your Aunt Phoebe knew of it and that is how I secured her cooperation. If you have any reverence for your mother's memory I cannot see how you can refuse to go through with this marriage, which has been arranged to fulfill that last wish of Charlotte Delahousse and to bring you all the benefits entailed."

Juliette clenched her fists. Was it true about her mother's last wish? She could not doubt it. She knew well enough that her mother had never been happy in France, her father had sometimes talked about it, although he had blamed it on the national characteristic of the English to think no land compared with their own, refusing to accept that his wife had never forgiven the bloodshed she had seen during the early days of the Revolution, nor had she forgotten the awful occasion when, newly come as a bride to Paris, she witnessed the storming of the Bastille. France to her was not the country that her daughter thought of with loyalty and affection, no matter that, in this new year of 1812, it was rumored that Napoleon was planning a new campaign and bringing more Frenchmen under arms for further conquests. It was impossible not to accept that her mother had cherished hopes and dreams that one day her child would find happiness in marriage amid the peaceful green hills and dales of England.

Resolutely she drew in her breath, her voice shaky with emotion. "I cannot marry a man whose company I might not find—agreeable. My mother would not have wished that for me."

Marianne frowned with impatience at her continued stubbornness. "Of course you will find him agreeable. He is twenty-six years old, strong and healthy and well-educated. It is a great pity that the portrait of him, sent when negotiations were first begun, was badly damaged by sea water when the ship almost foundered in a storm, and the features quite obliterated. Therefore I have no likeness of him to show you, but he was well pleased with the miniature he received of you. Now be sensible, Juliette—"

"I will not marry him!"

Marianne's face hardened, matching the harsh tones that made every word snap forth. "I have done all that is humanly possible to secure your future in a favorable marriage, but if you choose to reject it the only alternative is a convent life for the rest of your days. I give you until nine o'clock tomorrow morning to make up your mind. Do not imagine that choosing the latter course will delay your time in Sweden, because a ship leaves for France an hour after the *Fair Venture*'s departure at noon, and you shall be on it. In the meantime you will remain in your bedroom under Mademoiselle's eye and she will see to your packing after your decision is made. Now go! I am wearied by the sight of your mulish face."

Juliette flew from the room, the door slamming behind her. In her bedroom she paced up and down in mingled despair and fury, clenching and unclenching her hands, and she reached the decision that was not either one of the alternatives that Marianne had given her. She would run away, and while there was still time. But where? She had no traveling papers to see her out of Sweden or get her on a boat to cross the stretch of the Öresund into Denmark. She had no money either for that matter, at least not enough to go any distance, but Nicolaus, dear, dear Nicolaus would help her. He would be able to get her a traveling-pass of some kind, and with his knowledge of frontier formalities he would know how to get through. But time was so short, and with Mademoiselle posted by Marianne to keep an eye on her to make sure she stayed in her room she could neither go herself to tell him of her predicament, nor was there anyone she could trust to take a message without reporting back to Marianne.

Finally she decided there was only one course open to her. She must wait until the whole house was asleep and then, all bridges burned behind her, she would fly to Nicolaus, who would welcome this chance to aid her. Desperate as she was to escape, common sense told her it would be madness to venture abroad in the midnight streets when other kinds of danger would lie in wait for a female on her own, and if she did arrive at the barracks at such an hour she would most surely be turned away by the sentries as a draggle-tail. Better to wait until early morning when the streets were still lamp-lit but the whole city was astir. Then she could request to see Nicolaus with an air of authority

and full propriety. She would wear traveling clothes
and take a single piece of hand-baggage with all she
could pack into it. As long as Nicolaus could get her
out of Sweden, she would be content to stay in any
town of notable size where she could obtain employ-
ment as a governess or companion or music teacher.
In no way would she propel Nicolaus into marriage
with her no matter how eager he might be with the
way clear at last. That must wait until the time was
right. Indeed, since Marianne's announcement, marriage was the last state of affairs she wished to contemplate for the time being. She was young and she wanted
to taste liberty. This was the first chance she had ever
had of being truly free, and her appetite was whetted
for it. Impatiently she waited through the day for darkness to fall.

Night finally descended, but although she rested she
had not slept, lying awake and waiting eagerly for the
moment when she might rise and commence preparations for her flight. It came at last. She had completed
her *toilette* and dressed before setting an opened valise
on the bed. Now, having packed undergarments, a
shawl, a spare pair of boots and another of shoes, she
was faced with having to decide which dress to take,
there being no room for more than one. Reluctantly,
after pressing her cheek once against the softness of
the almond pink evening gown, she returned it to the
closet and took out instead a more practical day dress,
which she folded as she returned to the bedside where
she packed it down. The clasp of the valise snapped
as she closed it, making her freeze at the exaggerated
loudness of the sound in the silent room, but the
rhythm of Mademoiselle's snores did not change pattern.

Her sigh of relief came in a little gust. She was
trembling violently, but it was as much with excitement
as it was with nervousness and suspense. Before long
she would be speeding with Nicolaus through the
snow-white landscape in a carriage sleigh with a whip
cracking and flying hooves creating sparks on the icy
surface. Or, if he was to travel in the saddle, she
would ride at his side, wildly happy, matching the

pace of her horse to his. What an adventure! And at the end of the journey lay freedom and independence. Only for love would she surrender it, and it could be that she would find her life so inextricably bound to Nicolaus after this flight with him that a wedding ring would come to symbolize that same freedom and not the prison of despair that a marriage of convenience would have been.

The clock struck again. It was time to leave. Outside in the city tradesmen would be beginning to stir in the darkness before dawn. Daily servants would be making their way through the streets to their place of work, and at the quayside fishermen would be unloading the night's catch. All dangers of the night would be banished before the birth of the commercial day, and she need have no fear for her safety in the streets. Quickly she put on a fur-lined cloak with a hood over the woolen dress she was wearing with a matching pélisse for extra warmth. When she was ready, she pulled a spare pillow down under the bedclothes, which she had humped to make it appear that she was still lying there should Mademoiselle take one of her looks into the room before calling her at the usual hour of eight o'clock, by which time she hoped to be safely with Nicolaus. The last thing she did was to blow out the candle before going from the room and closing the door without a sound behind her.

She waited a few moments to let her eyes become accustomed to the darkness. Ahead of her lay a considerable distance before she reached the way out of the house for which she was aiming. She had decided it was too risky to leave by the main door, and never having been down into the kitchen regions she had no knowledge of that part of the house where already the more humble members of the servants' hierarchy would be starting on the first tasks of the day, which left her with the only safe route: a door on the first floor that led out to a flight of stone steps down to the garden. From there she would be able to slip through the cover of the trees to the side gate unobserved should anyone happen to glance down from a window. Unfortunately she had to pass by Marianne's bedroom and she hoped desperately that no creaking floorboard would give her presence away, her step-mother being a far lighter sleeper than Mademoiselle, but that was a hazard she had to face.

Like a dark shadow in the deeper darkness she made her way with extreme caution. A lamp left burning all night in the hall made a pale well of it as she traversed the head of the stairs, and she had cause to draw back sharply, her heart hammering, when a yawning servant-lad came from the direction of the kitchens in soft felt shoes, carrying an armload of logs. She saw the boy's sleepy face held in an aura of rosy firelight as he opened the grill of the tall porcelain stove in the hall and thrust in the fuel. Then he shuffled back the way he had come, still yawning and scratching an armpit.

Relaxing a little, she released a little pent-up sigh of relief and, tightening her grip on the handle of the valise, she continued on through another branched corridor into the wing where Marianne's bedroom was situated. She soon caught the sheen of the door, which was heavily ornamented with gilded carving like all the other doorways on the upper and lower floors. Instinctively she kept as much of the width of the corridor as was possible between it and her as she went slowly by it, taking one cautious step after another. Then, after what seemed like eons of time, she was past it! Marianne had not heard the faint rustle of her skirt, the whisk of her trailing cloak, or the barest slither of leather sole on the wooden floor. Ahead, obscured from view by a handwoven tapestry curtain, lay the glass-paneled door that led to liberty!

In her eagerness to reach it she increased her pace swiftly as though her heels had taken wings, and with one swift movement she shot back the curtain with a tinkling of rings. Snow and ice had made a lacelike pattern on the outside of the glass and some of it flaked away delicately as she exerted more pressure than was needed to turn the key, her fingers trembling violently. In exultation she put her hand on the knob to turn it. Then suddenly, without the least warning, Marianne's door opened wide and a stream of can-

dlelight from the bedroom within fell full upon her, il-
lumining her from head to foot. With a gasp she
wheeled about, the valise in her hand swinging out, to
knock accidentally against a lacquered pedestal that
had been brought from Paris. The Sèvres vase that
topped it tottered and fell, smashing to smithereens at
her feet.

She made no move. It was as if she had not
heard the crash. She was staring with growing distress
and heartwrenching despair at Nicolaus, who stood silhouetted in the doorway, as dismayed as she at the
unexpected encounter, his cloak over his arm, his gloves
in his hand, about to make his departure from the
house. Behind him Marianne's languorous voice in the
direction of her exquisitely draped bed spoke to him
on a rising note of anxious inquisitiveness in her own
tongue.

"What on earth was that, *mon amour?*"

In the first few seconds of seeing Juliette he had
had the grace to look shamefaced at her discovery of
the double game he had been playing, but seeing by
her eyes that he had lost his chances with her beyond
recall, the cynicism that was natural to him took over,
spiked with a vicious displeasure at the turn events
had taken. Where Juliette was going in outdoor clothes
and with a piece of hand-baggage at such an hour he
had no idea, but that was not his concern. A bitter
smile twisted his mouth and his glance mocked her as
he answered Marianne over his shoulder in French,
his Swedish accent rasping.

"You had better come and see for yourself."

It was the final betrayal. Had he chosen to shield
her, it being obvious to him that she would not want
her stepmother to know she was there any more than
he had chosen to be seen by her, Juliette could have
found it in her heart to forgive him for his deceit and
duplicity even though her romantic illusions had been
completely shattered, but with his words he had heaped
his own anger and humiliation upon her, making her
his scapegoat, and she was numbed by it.

In a floating *peignoir* that created a soft aura about
her body, Marianne appeared languidly in the door-

way, and abruptly she pulled its ruffled folds across
her when she saw Juliette. Wrath and outrage twisted
her features, but she did not address her stepdaughter,
turning instead to Nicolaus and giving him a little
push.

"Go!"

"Very well. What about—?" He shot a quick look
in Juliette's direction.

"I'll deal with her. *Au revoir*. Safe journey, *chéri*."

He left Marianne's side and strode towards the door
by which Juliette was standing. She watched him
dumbly, but he avoided her eyes and not knowing
she had unlocked the door he inadvertently locked it
again when he turned the key. Swearing under his
breath, he rectified his mistake and wrenched the door
open, to disappear into the dark morning, his foot-
prints swiftly covering the trail on the snow-covered
steps that he had made earlier upon his arrival at the
house, and reaching the side gate that was so familiar
to him. Juliette and her stepmother were left facing
each other.

Imperiously Marianne beckoned her into the bedroom and when the girl had entered she rounded on
her furiously. "What are you doing in outdoor clothes
at this hour?"

Juliette was whitefaced, the skin drawn tight over
the fine cheekbones. She felt suffocated by the per-
fumed atmosphere of the room and stood with her
back to the rumpled bed, not wishing to look upon it.
"I was running away."

For a few moments Marianne stared at her and
then she laughed shrilly and without humor, lifting her
chin and revealing the length of her white throat.
"How absurd! How childish! I declare you're more fit
for a convent than for marriage!" She crossed to the
stool in front of her toilet table and sat down on it, the
back of her curly head reflected in the oval looking
glass, as she continued to regard her stepdaughter with
undisguised contempt. "How far do you think you
would have gone before being discovered and brought
back? A word to General de Marquet and he would
have had half a regiment stopping every equipage on

the highway and searching every wood and forest."
She let her hands rise and fall in a gesture of relief. "Thank heaven the scandal that would have resulted has been avoided." Her eyes narrowed. "Since
your wicked act of defiance has come to nothing I
suggest you make the decision about your future without further delay. Which is it to be? A nun's habit or
a bridal veil?"

Juliette's trembling lips moved twice before she managed to speak. "I could never bring myself to accept
the life of a nun. I have no vocation."

Marianne was without mercy. "Then let me hear
your acceptance of the alternative."

Juliette tilted her chin, not knowing how sharply
she reminded Marianne of Henri Delahousse at that
moment, and she spoke with quiet resolution. "I will
marry Mr. Lockington. You need not fear that I might
go back on my word. I shall honor all that has been
promised on my behalf."

"Good." Marianne rose and went to the tasseled
bell pull, which she jerked once. "I am sending for
Mademoiselle. She will see you back to your room. The
packing of your baggage can begin. The sooner you
are on board the *Fair Venture* the better."

Juliette and Mademoiselle boarded the English ship
while the cargo was still being stowed aboard and a
full two hours before any of the other passengers arrived on the quayside. When the *Fair Venture* set sail,
nosing its way out of Stockholm harbor, Juliette went
up on deck from the cabin she was to share with
Mademoiselle, and watched the city slip away, the sun
glittering on the thawing snow. Never again would she
listen to love lies, never more would she be the innocent
following blindly along the path to seduction. Nicolaus's betrayal had jerked her out of girlhood into a
maturity beyond her years.

Turning away from the rails she went forward and
gazed bleakly seaward. Heaven alone knew what fate
awaited her as Gregory Lockington's bride, or what
sort of home awaited her at West Thorpeby Hall on a
wild and windswept alien coast. A sense of foreboding
filled her as dark as the clouds gathering on the hori-

zon. She stayed on deck until the biting wind forced
her at last to huddle into her cloak and go below.
With tawny sails billowing taut and with ropes strain-
ing the ship's bow cut through the heaving water.

Chapter Two

It was a distance of some miles from the quayside where the *Fair Venture* docked to Mrs. Phoebe Colingridge's house. Juliette sat stiff with dread in a corner seat of the musty smelling carriage, expecting no welcome from the aunt who had all but ignored her existence throughout the years, and experiencing a feeling close to panic at the approaching meeting with the unknown man she was to marry. On the opposite seat Mademoiselle, always a dull companion with whom Juliette had never had anything in common, lay with her feet up, still weak from the seasickness that had kept her on her bunk throughout the voyage, and paying no heed to the confusion of traffic around them and the noisy shouting of hawkers and pedlars.

Guardedly, interested in spite of herself, Juliette watched the streets and buildings go rolling by, observing the tree-filled squares with bright patches of early flowers, the busy market places, and the endless rows of bow windowed shops and emporia. It was the first day of March and with no trace of the snow they had left behind in Sweden it was as if spring had already arrived. She thought London impressive and crowded and dirty, but not without elegance. It was not like Paris—no city in the world could be like Paris!—but architecturally it had much to commend it.

"Are we nearly there, do you think?" Mademoiselle asked weakly, holding a lavender-scented handkerchief to her nose. The swaying of the badly-sprung carriage was not unlike the motion of the ship. Why she ever left France in the first place she did not know. She had hated living in Sweden, loathed traveling, and the last place she wanted to be was in England, the old enemy of her beloved country.

"I should imagine so," Juliette answered her, low-voiced. "We seem to have entered a district of elegant private residences."

Even as she spoke the carriage began to slow down. It drew up in front of a house that was one of a dozen that made up a remarkably fine, curved terrace, pillared and porticoed with lacelike wrought-iron balconies and imposing doors adorned with shining brass knockers, which faced a wide, green park. Without doubt these were the houses of persons of wealth and good taste and position in society. Mademoiselle, sitting up, eyed the shining white row with suspicion. She was prepared to dislike everything in England.

The coachman sprang down to help them out of the vehicle, and after they had alighted he turned to unload their boxes. Mademoiselle, unfailingly conscientious in her duties, gathered up her strength and advanced a trifle shakily up the steps into the portico ahead of Juliette, where she hammered the brass knocker, which was shaped like a lion's head. The door was opened at once by a white-wigged and green-liveried footman. Her English tended to be faulty, her accent atrocious, but she spoke with dignity.

"Miss Delahousse and Miss Rousseau 'ave arrived," she said to him as she entered, Juliette following. "Tell your mistress that we are 'ere."

The footman summoned two other servants to carry in the baggage, but he himself got no farther than the foot of the staircase, which dominated the damask-paneled hall with its graceful lines and gleam of gilt, when Aunt Phoebe Colingridge, having caught the sound of the visitors' arrival, emerged from an upper drawing room. Her heels tapped towards the head of the flight and Juliette, standing neat and chilled and full of trepidation, raised her head slowly, her bonnet brim clearing a first view of her mother's sister from whom she expected not a vestige of goodwill. Then her eyes widened. The plump and pretty middle-aged face looking down at her was suffused with joy and excitement. To Juliette it was as though the sun had suddenly and unexpectedly parted the clouds. Aunt Phoebe was glad to see her!

"Dearest Juliette! Darling child! Sweet offspring of

kind and gentle Charlotte, my own dear sister!" Already Aunt Phoebe was hurrying down the stairs, half crying, half laughing, her dainty hands lifted and dancing, her bracelets jingling. She was overweight and voluptuous, her gold pendant and her strings of pearls bouncing over her full bosom, and her hair, which was dressed in the highly fashionable style of careful dishevelment, was a vivid red, far brighter than anything nature could have contrived.

"She's painted!" Mademoiselle exclaimed with dismay under her breath to Juliette, reverting to her native tongue. "Painted like a trollop. Look at the amount of rouge on her cheeks. And her hair is—*dyed.*"

But Juliette had moved forward, drawn by the warmth and sincerity of her aunt's words. She had recognized instantly a natural generosity of spirit, a true goodness of heart.

"Oh, Aunt Phoebe!" she exclaimed huskily, scarcely able to believe her good fortune. "I was afraid you wouldn't want me here."

"Not want you? I've been counting the days, the hours, the minutes." Aunt Phoebe stepped from the last tread and held out her arms to her niece. Juliette flew into them and was engulfed in a soft and fragrant embrace, she hugging her aunt in turn. When they drew apart, each with the emotional glitter of tears, Aunt Phoebe tilted her parrot-bright head to hold her niece at arm's length and study her.

"How lovely you are, child! Your miniature did not do you full justice. You have your mother's eyes and her roses and cream complexion. Yet there is a likeness to your father, too. His classic bones, but softer and gentler as they should be. What of his charm? His irresistible, Gallic charm? I think you have been blessed with that as well, but in you it has turned into a power to bewitch every young man who looks at you, I know it!"

Mademoiselle gave a little cough to interrupt the flow. "Your pardon, Mrs. Colingridge," she said with a nervous flutter of her hands, "but Madame Delahousse was of the view that no good could come of encouraging a young girl to 'old an inflated opinion of 'erself. It can only lead 'er into flighty ways along the path to immodesty."

Aunt Phoebe looked at her with surprise, plucked eyebrows delicately raised, and a glint showed in the round, china blue eyes that denounced Mademoiselle as a fool and a busybody. "Mademoiselle Rousseau, of course," she said courteously, but without pleasure. "I was amiss in not addressing you before, but I was quite overwhelmed at seeing my own dear sister's child for the first time. From letters exchanged with Madame Delahousse I gained much from reading *between* the lines, and with regard to Juliette I know I hold different ideas from hers in many ways. I think it best that my niece severs all ties with the past. She is my responsibility now, and I shall see to her chaperonage in the future."

"But I am to stay with Juliette and chaperone 'er in London and in Norfolk until 'er wedding day! Those were Madame Delahousse's instructions."

"I will watch over her here, never fear, and at West Thorpeby Hall there is a widowed lady who is companion to a young invalid in the house, and will chaperone Juliette too. So you see, you are no longer needed." Aunt Phoebe smiled charmingly to take the sting out of the dismissal. "You may stay a day or two and rest with every comfort to enable you to recover from your long journey, and then a passage shall be obtained for you on a ship back to Sweden."

Mademoiselle looked frantic, alarmed as much by the prospect of a return voyage on that dreadful North Sea as facing her employer after having failed to carry out her orders. *"Non, non!* There is no future for me there."

Juliette intervened quickly on her behalf. "Mademoiselle has long been homesick for France."

Aunt Phoebe's face softened in sympathy. "I've only been homesick once in my life, and it's an affliction I would not wish on Napoleon himself." Again she smiled at Mademoiselle. "You may take passage on any foreign ship that is able to convey you to your homeland with which we are at war. I'll pay all your expenses to your ultimate destination. You have brought my niece safely to me and that must be rewarded."

Mademoiselle looked half-faint with relief. *"Merci, madame."*

Happily Aunt Phoebe put an arm about Juliette's waist and chatted to her as they turned towards the staircase together, Mademoiselle being conducted by the footman to another part of the house. "I've had a bedroom prepared for you which overlooks the park, child," she said. "It gets all the sunshine, even at this time of year. Are you very tired after your voyage? No! That's good! I'm eager to talk. I've never liked the sea myself, but that's not the reason why I never crossed the Channel to visit your Mama in France after she became Henri's wife. You see, there was that dreadful Revolution and then the war, and by the time the truce was signed she had been dead long since. Now we are plunged deeper than ever into war with France again, and although our late lamented hero, Nelson, defeated Napoleon's fleet at Trafalgar almost seven years ago there is still no sign of hostilities coming to an end."

She put her hand on the newel post to take the first stair, but Juliette paused, unable to hold back any longer the question that was uppermost in her mind. "Is Mr. Lockington here?" she asked tremulously.

Immediately Aunt Phoebe's expressive face showed her compassion and understanding. "No, he's not, child. His elder brother, who is Master of West Thorpeby Hall, agreed with me that you would need some time to become accustomed to living in a new country and that it would be best if you were adjusted to everything before journeying to Norfolk."

"How thoughtful of you," Juliette exclaimed huskily on a grateful note. It was like a reprieve; she felt quite dizzy with it.

Her aunt's smile was wise. "I knew also that you would not want to meet your future husband when feeling travel stained and weary, but would want to look your most radiant. As it happens, you look as fresh

as a daisy, but I was not to know that. I cannot say
the same of Mademoiselle, poor soul. The sea air put
no bloom into her cheeks."

Still Juliette made no move to ascend the stairs.
"What is he like, Aunt? What is Mr. Lockington like?"

"The portrait sent to you was a good likeness."

"I never saw it." There was despair and fear in her
face. "It was damaged at sea on the way to Sweden.
I knew nothing of this marriage of convenience until
the very last minute. Why didn't you write to me?
Why didn't you ever write to me?" Her cry was full
of anguish.

Her aunt showed confusion, her soft mouth quivering as if it went hard with her to face up to her fail-
ings, and she slipped her plump arm through Juliette's
as they began to mount the stairs slowly. "I was wrong
not to correspond with you, I see that now, but there
are always reasons, special reasons, why people act
in ways that are inexplicable to others. Mine were
very private, very personal ones, and—strange as it
may seem—it does not come easy for me to reveal
them even after all these years—"

"I have no wish to pry."

"I know that, child." A wispy smile showed absently and went again, the blue eyes distant, all thought
concentrated on a particular line. "But you have a
right to know. You see, I fell in love with Henri
Delahousse while staying with friends in Paris when
I was a young girl, and he was attracted to me until
your Mama arrived to join me there. After that he had
eyes only for her and she for him. The following June
he came to England and they were wed. Troubled
times had come to France then, but I doubt if even he
had any idea how terrible it was to be."

"I know he didn't. He used to talk about it all to
me sometimes."

The two footmen who had carried Juliette's boxes
up two flights of the grand staircase to her room reappeared, and Aunt Phoebe waited until they had passed
and left the hall before she continued.

"Your parents left England after the marriage ceremony, and I never saw them again. The Revolution in France made travel impossible, but letters did sometimes get through. Then your Mama died. Henri wrote to me of her last hours and of the daughter she had borne him. Memories were still painful to me, and I put away that part of my life as if it had never been." She gave a little sigh. "I never married, but I have loved other men and they have loved me." The faraway look faded from her eyes and she came to a standstill to face her niece. "Then, when I was asked to arrange a marriage for you, I gained an insight through your stepmother's letters into the animosity with which she regarded you, and realized what misery you must have known since Henri's death. From that moment I could not do enough for you. I wanted to sweep away the years of my neglect and make amends, realizing what I had missed all these years in not knowing the child of my dear sister and my greatest love." A ring of vehemence came into her voice. "I had no cause to suspect from Marianne Delahousse's letters that you were not being kept informed of all the marriage arrangements, otherwise I would then have written to you direct, do believe me."

"I do, Aunt! Although with Marianne having laid her plans for me in such secrecy I doubt that I would have received your letters even if you had written."

"What a shock it must have been for you when you learned where your future was to lie."

Juliette smiled a trifle wryly. "I must confess to being still afraid of whatever lies in store for me in this forthcoming marriage, and yet I know I should put fear from me, because common sense tells me that someone as kindhearted as you would most surely have chosen well and carefully on my behalf."

"I have, child! Not for you the rakehells of London, the lechers with distinguished names, the fortune hunters, and the debauchees! On the highest recommendation I selected a gentleman who has sown his wild oats and put them behind him—those reckless days normal and natural to any young man of spirit—and who was on the lookout for a beautiful wife on whom he could lavish his love and attention. I tell you, Gregory Lockington is a catch, my girl! Rich in his own right and unbelievably handsome!"

Juliette's eyebrows shot up in astonishment. "Is he really? In truth, I expected him to be quite ugly and a pauper. I believed it was his lack of looks that was the cause of my stepmother disposing of his portrait without showing me whatever trace of it was left. Describe him to me, do!"

Aunt Phoebe gurgled excitedly, thankful to be free of the unhappiness that had dogged the earlier turn of their conversation. She liked life to be kept on a contented and frothy level, and did not care to consider sad or serious matters. Although she allowed her cook to give food to those who begged at the kitchen door, set aside bundles of warm clothing for distribution to the needy when winter came, and never turned out a pregnant servant girl without aid or money, she chose to ignore the black tide of the poor and homeless and destitute that swarmed like a dismal sea through the city, and always averted her eyes when she dropped a silver coin into a ragamuffin's thin and wasted hand. To talk of a beautiful man was a delight and she gave herself up to it with pleasure.

"He is tall, well-built, and something of a dandy in his dress, although," she added hastily, not wanting to mar him in Juliette's eyes in any way, "none can blame him for that when he looks so grand in all he wears. He has piercing, dark eyes and a splendid smile, his teeth very white. His voice is deep, and he has slim, strong horseman's hands, which is not surprising, seeing how well he hunts and rides. Altogether he is a most fascinating young man!"

"You make him sound a positive paragon," Juliette said faintly, trying to crush down the memory that persisted of another whose good looks had been comparable with those that had just been described to her. But not all men were deceitful. Not all men were totally self-centered. A man such as Gregory Lockington could have married almost any heiress if he had had a mind to, so there must have been something about her likeness in the miniature that had captured his interest. There must be. There had to be!

As if her thoughts had been read, Aunt Phoebe gave her hand a little press of reassurance. "Put away your fears. One look at your miniature and he was won. He is eager for the marriage, but I insisted on a betrothal of three months from the day of your meeting. By the time your wedding day dawns you'll not be marrying a stranger."

"You've considered everything," Juliette said on a wave of thankfulness. "If there can be liking and respect between Gregory and me, then I know we shall have the basis for a good relationship, and—" determinedly she thrust Nicolaus from her mind— "we may come to love each other dearly."

Impulsively she leaned forward and kissed the round, rouged cheek, unaware that she was seeking to put some seal of conviction on to her own declaration, and she did not see the start of uncertainty that had been kindled in her aunt's eyes at her words.

"Yes, yes," Aunt Phoebe agreed a trifle quickly. "After all, you won't be long together in that gloomy old house."

"Gloomy?" Juliette questioned, matching her pace to her aunt's plodding steps.

"Well, Gregory doesn't think it is gloomy, and neither does his brother. They are both enamored with its stones and mortar, but I think it's far too large for comfort and it stands on a lonely site, within earshot of waves breaking constantly against the cliffs. Fortunately you will only be there for three months until your marriage, and then a gracious home will be awaiting you some miles away in the vicinity of the market town of East Thorpeby, which is a lively hub in the community. I have a sketch of the Lockingtons' ancestral home somewhere, which was sent to me when the marriage negotiations first began."

"Please show it to me," Juliette requested, turning with her aunt along the gallery.

"Willingly, my dear."

It struck Juliette that Aunt Phoebe was trying to play down her earlier disparaging remark about the place, but at that point they reached the bedroom which had been allotted to her for the duration of her stay in London, and she expressed her admiration of it. The walls were hung with palest yellow silk and the furniture was in the Chinese style, something she had not seen before, and the circular carpet almost covered the floor in a spread of dancing dragons. Her two boxes had been set down by the wall, and Aunt Phoebe remarked on their modest size.

"Even if they are crammed tight you cannot possibly have enough clothes in them to make up the wardrobe you are going to need in your new life as Mrs. Gregory Lockington."

"I do have a number of books in them." Juliette had removed her coat and bonnet to lay them on the bed.

"Books! Mercy me!" Aunt Phoebe lifted her hands, her rings flashing, her bracelets clicking. "You'll have other things to think about besides books once you're wed. We'll have a great deal of shopping to do. Madame Delahousse was willing enough for me to take on the responsibility of fitting you out. There's your wedding dress, too—unless you wish to have your mother's gown remodeled."

"You have it?" Juliette gasped, a glow of pleasure in her face.

There was a nod of the bright curls. "After the marriage ceremony she left it with our Mama—your grandmother. It was packed away and when I was turning out the old home, a long time ago now, I came across it and kept it. I suppose I had the thought at the back of my mind that one day it would be handed over to you."

"There's nothing I should like better than to wear it!" Then the significance of what she had said went home to her, the animation faded from her face, and she clasped her hands together nervously. "After all, I'm carrying out my mother's most heartfelt desire that I should wed one of her own countrymen, so it would, perhaps, have brought extra joy to her had she known I'd be wearing her own gown." There was a trembling pause. "Marianne told me that it was my mother's last wish that I should marry in the country of her birth. Did my father write of it to you at the time?"

Aunt Phoebe looked incredulous. "Madame Delahousse told you that? Your father did not mention it, and I find it hard to believe that your mother, who loved him as she did, would ever have expressed what amounted to regret at their marriage with her last breath. I fear your stepmother has played you false all along."

Juliette gave a sad smile. "Whether she spoke the truth on that particular matter or not—and I cannot now believe in view of what you have said that she did—I have given my word on this marriage, and I would be failing both my parents if I did not keep the vow I have made."

Aunt Phoebe answered her emotionally. "You are Henri's daughter indeed. That you are like him would have pleased your dear mother more than anything else could have done."

At that point a lady's maid made her appearance, putting an end to their private talk, but they smiled at each other in affectionate communication before Aunt Phoebe turned to address the servant by her surname of Cobbett, instructing her to unpack Juliette's baggage and to wait on the guest at all times.

Later in the drawing room after they had dined together, Aunt Phoebe plying her with questions, Juliette asked if she might see the picture of West Thorpeby Hall. Her aunt went to an *escritoire* and rummaged about in a drawer before finally producing it.

Holding the ink sketch with both hands Juliette studied it. She saw a grand mansion, but a strangely forbidding one, in spite of its many windows and gracious lines. A flight of steps with delicately-fashioned, wrought-iron balustrades swept up to the entrance, the doorway flanked by Ionic columns of some proportion, which in turn supported a fine stone pediment surmounted by the Lockington coat of arms. Splendidly proportioned domes rose at each of the four corners of the house, one of them crowned by a huge clock set within a temple-like cupola, its hands stand-

ing at the hour of noon or midnight. Altogether it
was a competently executed drawing, but Juliette, who
was something of an artist herself, had the impression
that the hand which had held the pen had emphasized
lines and angles and shadows to bring out a sinister
aspect to West Thorpeby Hall. Had it been done unconsciously through a personal dislike of the place?
She looked at the signature.

"Who is Caroline Hazlett?" she asked.

"That's the widow I mentioned to Mademoiselle
Rousseau, the lady who will act as your chaperone.
She was a Lockington before she married, a cousin
of the brothers."

"And the invalid she chaperones?"

"That is Venetia, Blake Lockington's ward." Aunt
Phoebe plumped up a cushion and set it against the
small of her back in the chair where she had reseated
herself. She gave a little sigh of resignation. "Well, I
suppose you have to know all the circumstances sooner or later. I must tell you that the Lockington brothers
have been somewhat reckless and undisciplined in
their time and they gained reputations for themselves
that stick like mud to them yet."

"You did speak in passing of Gregory's past, making light of it. Do not hide anything from me, Aunt."

"There's nothing to hide," Aunt Phoebe assured her
hastily. "What has gone before is over and done with.
Both brothers have retreated into Norfolk and are
leading the lives of sober country squires."

"What brought about the change in them?"

"Ah! With Blake Lockington it was a final tragedy
after a series of questionable escapades." Although
they were alone Aunt Phoebe instinctively lowered her
voice. "He was in his cups, which foxed his judgement,
and he failed to prevent a driving accident in which
Elizabeth Rose-Marshall, the girl to whom he was betrothed, was killed. At the same time his ward, also a
passenger, was badly injured and will never walk
again. That is Venetia, the invalid of West Thorpeby
Hall. Since that terrible day he has become a changed
man. The ballrooms and clubs and gaming halls of
London see him no more."

"And Gregory?"

"His was the natural exuberance of youth that has now been channeled into a desire for marriage and a family."

Her aunt's words should have quietened her doubts, but a feeling of unease persisted, no matter how hard she tried to suppress it. "On whose recommendation did you select Gregory for me?" she asked.

"I have a dear friend, Sir Duncan Barry. He knew their late parents and admired both the father, a fine gentleman, and the mother, a most gentle lady, so naturally he is well acquainted with the Lockington family history. Some great men have borne the name of the Norfolk Lockingtons, and out of such breeding comes good stock. Sir Duncan assured me there is no trace of madness or sickliness or any other afflictions that can crop up in generation after generation in some noble families. It was he who said I could do no better for you than to settle on the younger brother, seeing that the elder was set against marriage since his bereavement. I left it to Sir Duncan to make all the preliminary enquiries and arrangements, and then I traveled to West Thorpeby Hall myself, taking your miniature with me. That's when everything was finally settled."

"I see."

"There. Now you are in possession of all the facts." Aunt Phoebe perked up as if all had been dealt with satisfactorily. "Do you like to play cards, my dear? I thought we might have a hand or two of piquet if you're not too tired."

There was no more talk about the Lockington brothers that night, and for the next few weeks Juliette kept them out of her thoughts as much as possible, giving herself up to a social whirl which proved to be hectic by day and night. In spite of being at war with Napoleon there was a spirit of gaiety and optimism prevailing throughout the land, which—according to Aunt Phoebe, who was a staunch royalist—had much to do with the Prince Regent, that pleasure-loving gentleman, having had the power of the Throne put into his hands during January of the previous year, when it became apparent to all that the King had become incurably mad and could never make a decision of importance again.

Juliette could not help but contrast what she heard of the Prince Regent with all she knew of the austere Bernadotte, who could not have been better matched to the northern people that he ruled had he been Swedish born. In no way could the two regencies be compared. Neither was there any likeness between her aunt and Marianne, although Juliette soon learned that Sir Duncan was her aunt's lover, but whereas Marianne's amorous adventures had been sly affairs with men much younger than herself, Aunt Phoebe's gallant was a man of her own age, gray-haired, raffish, and distinguished, who came openly to the house, their relationship being of long standing, and neither of them hid the genuine regard and respect that each held for the other. Since his shrew of a half-mad wife kept to her Scottish castle there was a lack of embarrassment all round, and in the present social climate, which had eased away from the rigors of convention upheld by the old King, he was able to escort Aunt Phoebe wherever they wished to go, no doors being barred to them, her niche in society unaffected by public knowledge that she was his mistress.

It being the height of the London season Sir Duncan took Aunt Phoebe and Juliette to many of the brilliant events to which they were invited, and Aunt Phoebe—unlike Marianne—delighted in her company and everywhere spoke of her as "my dearest niece." Juliette found male admirers seeking her out wherever she went, their intentions honorable or otherwise, but she had become wiser and more discerning and felt years older than the naive girl who, although she had not been in love, had allowed herself to be taken in by a smooth tongue and wooing compliments in a snow-covered city far away. She lost count of the number of pairs of dancing slippers she wore through, and fell into bed each night in a state of blissful exhaustion, slipping at once into untroubled sleep.

Now and again, when people heard she had come to England to marry into the Lockington family, she was aware of receiving wryly amused and curious looks, many feminine ones more than a little tinged with envy. Armed with the knowledge that Aunt Phoebe had given her, Juliette outwardly kept her composure, holding to herself the torment of trepidation that engulfed her without fail whenever the Lockington name was mentioned, and crushing down all thought of the day when eventually she must come face to face with Gregory.

By day, when not attending tea parties or whist parties or paying calls, Juliette and her aunt spent their time shopping or at the milliner's or dressmaker's. Her trousseau grew daily, and it was a poignant moment for her when she handled her mother's wedding gown after Aunt Phoebe had produced it, wrapped in layers of white linen, and laid it out for her. It was made of yards of silk gauze embroidered with roses and pearls, filmy as spiders' webs, over underskirts of peach-pink satin, sashed in the same color and with a draped fichu, all in a bouffant fashion long since discarded for the slim and elegant line that had evolved from the days of the Directoire. After she had selected a new design, there being enough material in the two upper layers alone, the gown was handed over to expert seamstresses to be unpicked, washed, and remade.

It was finished and ready, together with the veiled and silk rose-trimmed bonnet to go with it, when a letter came from Norfolk to Aunt Phoebe, giving the date of Gregory's intended arrival in London to meet his future bride. Juliette, receiving the news, blanched. It had come! The event she had kept thrust from her mind in order to enjoy the few short weeks of liberation that had been allotted to her. Reality swept in to engulf her. The dream was over. The bubble burst.

Aunt Phoebe showed her practical side again. "I shall give a supper party here on the eve of his arrival," she said firmly, folding up the letter and pretending not to notice how tense the girl had become, how hollow her cheeks, how troubled her eyes. "I'll invite all the people you have met whose company you enjoy best. It's better for you to drink champagne and be madly flirtatious and dance half the night away than to lie sleepless, worrying unnecessarily about the morrow."

Leave the worrying to me, Phoebe Colingridge added silently to herself. Oh, let me have done the right thing! I was so sure at first, but why hasn't he written to her? Not a word. Not a note. Not a gift. Not a bouquet sent on his behalf. Even this letter comes from Mr. Blake Lockington and not in his younger brother's hand. Has Juliette thought about Gregory's lack of ardor? Has it worried her? I believe not. It has been a comfort to her not to have to think about him or the future, for she has a streak of maturity in her, unlike most girls of her age, and showed that she knew enough not to be swept along by a mere description of him as the handsome devil that he was. But they were a strange family altogether, the Lockingtons. Stranger than she had realized when she brought Juliette to their notice. But it was too late to draw back now.

"How wise you are, Aunt," Juliette was saying, attempting a smile that failed to banish the anxiety in her eyes. "I'm going to miss you when I'm living in Norfolk. You will visit me sometimes, won't you?"

Aunt Phoebe almost hesitated, but it was no time to confess to not being able to abide the countryside or to admit that to her Norfolk with its bad roads and eerie marshes and rough winds seemed as distant as the moon. Her one trip to West Thorpeby Hall had been enough, but she would at least attend the wedding and any christenings that—pray God!—would follow. Her answer came readily and with her plumply dimpled smile.

"Yes, but I shall want you and Gregory to come often to London and visit me, too." In that way she would be able to keep an eye on the girl. If things did not work out, after all, she would enlist Sir Duncan's aid and get him to pull every string available to get Juliette out of England and back to France and away from danger. Danger? Merciful heaven! Whatever put the thought of danger into her head! She, more than the bride herself, was giving way to nerves.

On the evening of the supper party Juliette went through her wardrobe carefully, Cobbett taking out one gown and then another to assist her in reaching a decision, but she had worn them all many times over the past weeks, and even the pink gown worn on that fateful evening at Stockholm's Opera House had been aired on more than one occasion. None seemed quite suitable for this last night of freedom, and Cobbett's garrulous flow of advice confused more than it helped.

"This azure silk is elegant, miss. Why not the sprigged green muslin? You always look as pretty as a picture in the heliotrope."

"I don't think any of them will do," Juliette said at last. Leaving the bedroom she went into another where a large, brass-cornered imperial, specially purchased to hold her extensive trousseau, stood against the wall, its lid open. From it she unfolded one of the loveliest of all the new evening gowns that had been made for her, and knew she would look no further.

When her hair had been dressed by Cobbett and she stood ready in her gown, her reflection told her she had made the right choice. No other garment could have boosted her morale to such an extent, for it suited her better than anything else she had ever worn, the gold-shot silk gauze setting off the expanse of creamy bosom revealed by its extreme décolletage and touching with highlights the echoing gold of her own tresses. With a wheel-shaped fan in hand, her white gloves high to within an inch of the short, puffed sleeves, she went downstairs to join her aunt and Sir Duncan awaiting the guests in the large drawing room where later doors would be opened into the super room.

"A vision, indeed!" declared Sir Duncan at the sight, an appreciative glint in his eyes.

"Enchanting!" Aunt Phoebe exclaimed proudly, giving her a kiss on the cheek. Then there came the sound of hooves and slowing carriage wheels drawing up outside.

The party was destined to be a success from the moment the first guests stepped over the threshold. Aunt Phoebe was a superb hostess, and the evening sparkled like the champagne in the crystal glasses. Juliette gave

herself up to the enjoyment of the evening, laughing
and chatting and flirting gaily. If she drank a little
more champagne than she would normally have done
she was not aware of it and only thought that never had
her new-made London friends been more entertaining
or amusing. It was just before supper that through
the buzz of conversation and above the accompanying
music being played by a quintet in the hall, that she
heard the butler announce the name of a guest who
had come later than all the rest.

"Mr. Lockington!"

Gregory had come! Unable to wait until morning
to see her, he had come on a romantic impulse to meet
her ahead of the allotted time. Slowly she swiveled
round, holding her breath, her lips slightly parted,
and with wide eyes she looked towards the silk-draped
archway that led in from the hall beyond. There he
stood, a man of wild and vigorous height, lean and
vital and splendidly made, elegant in full evening dress
of deepest black. He was all that had been described
to her, his features strong and striking, the cheekbones
jutting, the brow wide, the nose highbridged to the
point of arrogance, the experienced worldly mouth
blatantly sensual, and his dark head well-groomed with
fashionably brushed forward sidelocks holding the
line of the thrusting jaw. Yet in spite of his impec-
cable appearance, his stillness of stance, there was
about him a curious air of turbulence that made him
seem too powerful for the fragile setting of gilt and
ormolu and satin-striped walls, almost as if he had
brought with him a breath of the storm-fraught coast
of Norfolk where the marshes and the crying sea birds
and the tormented waves made up the habitat that
was his own. He was scanning the room, searching for
his hostess, and then, even as Juliette stared at him,
his heavy-lidded, greenish eyes met hers.

She stood motionless, unable to take her eyes from
his, held gloriously captive by his clamping gaze. Her
heart leapt with a curious and joyous violence. It was
unlike anything she had ever experienced before, all
her senses thrown into a turmoil, her young body

quickened and awakened and committed by an intangible look from across a room. The sweet, romantic impact that Nicolaus had made upon her could not be compared with it in any way, and it was as if she were sinking wonderfully into an unknown, half terrifying, half glorious abyss from which there was no return.

A slight commotion near at hand caused her to break their locked gaze with a little start, lowering her lashes. Her aunt had been informed of his arrival and people were parting with a rustle to let her through. Catching sight of Juliette through a gap, Aunt Phoebe beckoned to her excitedly with both hands in a sparkle of rings, indicating that they should meet the newcomer together. Almost automatically Juliette obeyed the summons, her feet seeming to glide across the floor, and she and her aunt arrived at the same time in front of him. Not yet daring to meet his eyes again so soon, she kept her lashes downwards, and under their long protective fans she looked no higher than his chin, which dominated the pristine whiteness of his plain cravat folded about his high pointed collar.

"What a delightful surprise, Mr. Lockington," Aunt Phoebe said warmly, extending her bracelet encrusted hand to him.

He took it and bowed. "The honor is mine, Mrs. Colingridge. Forgive my untimely intrusion, but I reached London earlier than I had anticipated and after settling some business I decided to call without delay."

"It's not an intrusion at all. Indeed not. You could not have come at a better time. Now you shall meet Juliette, who is everything—oh, everything!—that we hoped for and expected."

"I can indeed see that," he said slowly in his deep, firm voice, regarding her once more.

"Juliette, my dear," Aunt Phoebe turned to her happily. "Let me present to you Mr. Blake Lockington, your betrothed's elder brother."

She thought her heart stopped. All she knew was that she felt such a physical blow of disappointment that had her lashes not been lowered her eyes would most certainly have given away the shock that her aunt's words had dealt her. For a few magical moments in the belief that he was Gregory she had known the beginnings of hope, the first dawnings of a tender anticipation that had promised the eventual banishment of memories of Nicolaus's betrayal with all its attendant shadows of misery and pain. Instead, nothing had changed for the better. Only a greater darkness had gathered about her, and she dared not probe the reason why.

"Your most devoted servant, ma'am." He bowed to her as to her aunt, and she dipped in a curtsy. "I trust I may be allowed to call you by your Christian name, seeing that you are to be my brother's wife."

"By all means, sir." There was a slight tremor in her voice, but nothing that could not be put down to a natural nervousness at meeting the first of the family into which she was to wed. "Is—is my betrothed not with you?"

Before he could make an answer Aunt Phoebe added her own question somewhat anxiously. "Yes, where is your brother? Why is he not with you? There was no need for him to wait until tomorrow before meeting Juliette simply because that date was set. Where are you staying? I'll send a servant to fetch him—"

Blake interrupted her. "He hasn't traveled with me. I came alone from Norfolk."

"Is he ill?" Doubts were flooding back into Phoebe Colingridge's mind with a fresh torment. Only if the young man were at death's door could he be excused from not coming to London to meet his bride.

"I assure you he is in perfect health and bitterly disappointed that circumstances prevented him from making the journey. If he could see Juliette as I see her now his disappointment would be increased a thousandfold."

The rose color ran along Juliette's cheekbones. She wanted no compliments from Blake Lockington, whose searing look had momentarily suspended time for her when their eyes had met with that first sight of each other. It was her own folly that she had mistaken an open assessment of her physical charms, such as Nicolaus must have made on the night of the opera, for a betrothed's welcoming of the woman of his choice, but out of the old hurt Blake had unwittingly renewed she could not hold back some retaliation.

"It seems to me that my meeting him is a pleasure he is content enough to postpone."

Blake regarded her with studied thoughtfulness for a second longer than necessary before replying, which made the color run deeper in her face. "It was not his wish that I should come in his place, I do assure you. I have his message and his reason for having to remain at home, which I'm ready to pass on to you if we may retreat to a more secluded place for a little while." He switched his gaze to glance inquiringly at her aunt.

"Yes, of course." She turned to her niece, telling herself that there was surely nothing to worry about when Blake Lockington seemed so relaxed and undisturbed, but—oh! oh!—how she wished she had settled on somebody else than his brother for the girl she had come to love as though she were her own child. "Take Mr. Lockington to the upper drawing room, Juliette. It will be quiet there. I'll have some champagne sent up right away."

The upper drawing room was Juliette's favorite room in the house. It was small and rose colored, and on this night it was illumined by a cozy fire and the flicker of a single candle in a tall silver stick. Too late Juliette wished she had ignored her aunt's suggestion and taken him to one of the larger, less secluded rooms where the atmosphere would have been less intimate, the surroundings less confined. It seemed to throw the two of them together as if they were lovers who had sought a private rendezvous, and she could not believe that he did not feel it too. She sat down on the rollended couch, her face turned towards the flames, but he remained standing, the firelight sending his shadow dancing over the walls. The pur-

plewood clock on the Cressent cabinet seemed to tick
with unusual loudness for several seconds before he
spoke on an assessing note.

"Gregory is a very lucky man. You're a beautiful
young woman."

Her pulse beat wildly in her throat and she rested
her fan against it, inclining her head in acknowledge-
ment of the compliment. Over the past weeks she had
become more than used to male flattery and been unmoved by it, Nicolaus's deceit raw and vivid in her
mind, but however desperately she might wish it to
be otherwise, this man's low spoken words of restrained
admiration plunged her deeper into a state of confusion that threatened to undermine her carefully main-
tained poise.

At that moment the door opened and a footman
appeared with the champagne. He would have served
it, but Blake dismissed him and poured the champagne himself. When he had handed her a glass, which
she sipped and put to one side, he sat down beside
her.

"Gregory sends his compliments and his most abject
apologies," he began, crossing one long leg over the
other. "Since long before the signing of the final draft
of the marriage contract he had set in motion the
redecorating of Ravensworth Hall, the mansion he inherited a while ago, all with your comfort and pleasure
in mind. There have also been extensive alterations to
the property. It will be a fine home for you when
you are wed."

"I was told that," Juliette answered, almost inaudibly.

"Unfortunately there have been delays and hold ups
of every kind, trouble with the delivery of materials
needed, always difficult in a far distant area, and sick-
ness among the workmen. Then, when he was about
to leave for London, a hitch more serious than all
the rest forced him to take up residence and remain
in the property, preventing his journeying to fetch you,
but at least under his personal supervision the final
stages of the work going on there will be completed

in time for your inspection after your arrival at West Thorpeby Hall."

She turned and gave him a clear, straight look. "I'm not a fool. If he were truly as glad about this marriage of convenience as others would have me believe, nothing would have kept him away."

He regarded her thoughtfully. "I would not insult you with a lie to spare your feelings. I have told you the truth. He could not come. Matters were beyond his control."

She bit her lip. "I can think of only one reason that prevents a man leaving his own property when he is in good health and his own master."

"Yes?"

She looked at him again with a challenge that showed she would tolerate no prevaricating of any kind, wanting an answer as straightforward as before. "Is he in debt and keeping the bailiff at bay?"

He raised an eyebrow at her shrewdness, finished the last of the champagne that he held at a single gulp, and reached out to set the emptied glass back on the tray. Only then did he answer her and with some hesitation. "That is the predicament, I regret to say."

"How did he incur this debt of such magnitude? By gaming, perhaps?"

"Debts of honor have to be settled before all else."

"I'm aware of that. My father lived by such a code, but never once was the roof over his head put in jeopardy."

"It is only a temporary state of affairs in Gregory's case. Had I known about it in time I dare say something could have been done about it and he would have been here to meet you. Nevertheless, it will soon be cleared up and put right now."

An answering riposte burst from her before she could moderate her words. "You mean that when he's married to me and possessed of my dowry, his financial difficulties will be at an end! No wonder he is so eager for the wedding day!" She pressed shaking fingertips over her eyes, shrinking inside herself at the awfulness of the situation in which she had been landed.

By his slight movement on the couch she knew he leaned towards her, and he addressed her evenly and frankly. "No, I don't mean that at all. When I arrived in London this afternoon I went straight to my lawyers to arrange an advance to be paid to Gregory from a large inheritance that will be his on the day he marries. He has had his choice of many young women and could have his choice again, but he wants to marry *you*, Juliette. He is set on it. Even before he saw your portrait everything he heard about you enticed him, and after he had clapped eyes on your likeness he could not wait to put his signature to the contract. But all that will be nothing to his feelings when he sees you in person. That I know."

It was like hearing the last bolts shot on a prison door between her and freedom. The faint, faint hope that she had cherished deep inside herself that Gregory might have lost enthusiasm for the match, a hope fed on his failure to correspond in any way from Norfolk since her arrival in London, died completely. But at the same time Blake's calm attitude steadied her and she lowered her hands, forcing herself to reason logically. So Gregory was rich in his own right after all, not that she cared anything about money, having been willing to let it all go when she had plotted her escape from Sweden. She knew it was common enough for a younger son's allowance to fall short of what he needed for the pastimes of bachelorhood and she wouldn't hold that against him, but she could not have endured under any circumstances the thought that she had been virtually bought and sold to settle losses at a gaming table! It would have been the final humiliation to crown the distress that was already hers.

He rose to his feet and took a few steps across the carpet where he stood looking down at her. "Will you be ready to leave for Norfolk tomorrow morning? It's a long journey, and we'll have to stay overnight at inns along the way."

She nodded, rising too. "Almost everything is packed and waiting."

"Good." He went to the door and held it open for her, but she shook her head.

"I'll not go down to the party again. With so much traveling ahead of me it would be better if I retired now. Already the hour is late."

"Shall I tell your aunt for you?"

"If you would be so kind."

"Then I'll bid you good night, Juliette."

"Good night—Blake."

His eyes rested on her for a fraction of a second longer and then he left the room, closing the door quietly after him.

Reaction set in with such a shuddering that she rested one hand on the end of the couch and leaned on it for support, her head drooping on the graceful stem of her neck, and she could not control the quivering of her lips. Everything about him touched her heart and she could no longer deny it: the velvet deepness of his voice, the little creases that had appeared on either side of his mouth when his lips had twisted into a shadow of a smile at her, and the latent strength of his well-shaped hands. Her attention had been caught by the unusual ruby ring he wore on his left hand, the stone set in claws of gold fashioned like those of an eagle, and throughout the time they had been talking it had seemed to her that it glowed at her like a warning, reminding her that soon she would be wearing another kind of ring, which would bind her for the rest of her life to his brother, who waited for her in the shadows of the sinister and gloomy West Thorpeby Hall.

Chapter Three

Dressed for traveling, Juliette came to the head of
the stairs and looked down into the sun-splashed hall
where Aunt Phoebe was talking to Blake, who had
arrived in good time, standing with his beaver hat in
his hand. Neither had noticed her yet, and she started
down the flight, able to see through the open door the
waiting chariot into the back of which her baggage
had already been stowed. Cobbett, who was to accompany her, had gone ahead some few minutes before to settle herself in the dickey-seat at the rear of
the chariot. Ah! She had been sighted. Both Blake
and her aunt turned simultaneously, and he greeted
her.

"Good day, Juliette."

His tone was courteous, but laced with impatience.
She knew she had kept him waiting, having taken more
time than she had needed, but a natural reluctance to
leave the home that had become a haven to her had
been more than matched by a desire to postpone their
meeting again, which she could see was of little importance to him. Indeed, his frown had deepened more
than it had lifted. In spite of his politeness over the
matter the previous evening it was not hard to guess
that the whole business of coming to London on such an
errand on his brother's behalf had caused him much
irritation and displeasure, seeing that the city no
longer held any attraction for him, which was the trouble with people who mended their ways, for they became obsessional in their reform. Or was he reformed?
She could not believe there was anything of the saint in
Blake Lockington, but without doubt he had been
heavily marked by the tragedy for which he had been
responsible.

Aunt Phoebe came to her. "I'm going to miss

you, child," she said emotionally. They embraced in a poignant silence and then drew apart, hands holding. Juliette's throat was full.

"Thank you for all you've done for me. These days in London have been wonderful."

"Tush! I've done little enough. All I want is your happiness." Slipping an arm about her waist almost protectively, Aunt Phoebe turned to address Blake with unaccustomed fierceness. "Take good care of her. Let no harm come to her in that grim old house of yours."

He jerked his head at her words. "Ma'am! Why should it? There's nothing to hold against West Thorpeby Hall except its isolation."

"Hmm. You showed me gracious hospitality when I visited you there, and every comfort was mine, but that did not make me less uneasy of all its dark nooks and crannies. My niece is young and far from friends and—"

"—and not lacking in courage," he interrupted abruptly, "but to set your mind at rest I guarantee her protection with my life if need be." He looked from her to Juliette. "I should like to cover as many miles as possible before night falls, so if you've nothing more to keep you here we'll be getting on our way."

Juliette nodded and spoke again to her aunt. "You will come to my wedding, won't you?" she implored, suddenly afraid that dislike of the Lockington residence might sway her only relative from her original intention to attend the ceremony. It had not taken her long to discover how important it was to her aunt that life should be placid and comfortable and kept from any unpleasantness.

"Don't fret, my dear. I'll by there." The promise was freely given and with vehemence. "Nothing shall keep me away."

A last kiss on the round, rouged cheek. *"Au revoir,* Aunt Phoebe."

Blake held out a hand to her and slowly she put hers into it and let him lead her out of the house. She held her head very high and her step did not falter.

Outside, the traveling chariot shone in the morning

sun, every speck of the previous day's journeying
wiped and polished from the dark blue paintwork
with its gold border, and two postilions in buff livery
stood ready to mount two of the four black horses which
clopped their hooves on the cobbles, tossing their
heads impatiently. Blake's valet, who was to ride beside her maid, whipped open the emblazoned chariot
door. Inside it was upholstered in *petit point* with brocade blinds and a ceiling of padded silk. All this she
noticed in a glance as she stepped into it and sat
down, Blake following to take a seat beside her.
The door was closed. The postilions swung themselves
into their saddles, a whip snapped, and the horses
lunged forward, setting the wheels in motion. Juliette,
pressing her face to the window, saw her aunt give one
wave with a wispy lace handkerchief and then, in tears,
dart back into the house as though unable to bear
watching her out of sight, but she continued to gaze
out at the house until the whole terrace curved away
and the green park where she had often strolled between the flower beds could be seen no more. Only
then did she sink back against the cushioned softness,
drawing a long draught of breath and releasing it
again on the faintest of sighs.

He heard it and gave her a sidelong glance. "You're
close to your aunt, are you not?"

"Next to my father she's the dearest person I've
ever known, and she has made sure that I've been
everywhere and seen everything since I arrived on her
doorstep."

"How did the pleasures of London compare with
those of Paris in your opinion?"

She smiled quietly, shaking her head. "I never had
the opportunity to sample the gaiety of Parisian circles.
Have you never been to France?"

"Oh yes. Several times during the truce, but God
alone knows when the opportunity will present itself
again. Are you not torn by conflicting loyalties? Your
stepmother wrote that you considered yourself a
Frenchwoman, but your ties to England were equally
strong."

She thought how cleverly Marianne had phrased

it, putting nothing forward to turn a patriotic Englishman, such as Gregory Lockington would be, from the match. But she decided she would have to clarify her position, no matter if it did offend her listener's sensibilities.

"Those are her words, not mine. Apart from an interest in becoming bilingual because of my mother being an Englishwoman, I must admit to giving no thought of loyalty to the country, which—apart from a brief respite—has been at war with France for the whole of my life."

"But what of your feelings now?" he persisted, twisting his body round to look directly into her face within its azure bonnet brim. "Now that you've seen England?"

She met his gaze clearly. "All I have seen of its people and its gracious architecture and its tranquil countryside has endeared it to me, and I hope, as the years go by, to learn to love England as I love France, but in my heart I am French, in my attitudes I am French, and although my father said often that I have much of my mother's looks and ways I have yet to learn what is English enough in me to combat my emotional temperament, which I recognize as characteristic of those whom I will always think of as my fellow countrymen."

He was studying her. "In spite of the fact you are shortly to marry an Englishman?"

"In spite of that."

"So although your father joined forces with Bernadotte you still consider yourself to be subject to the Emperor of France."

She was angered. "No! I'm a Frenchwoman, sir— but not a Bonapartist!"

To her surprise he threw his head back and laughed, not at her, but with a rich appreciation of her declaration. His mirth made him look more approachable, less stern, and his mouth remained tilted in a smile as he said, "I put it to you that it is your Englishness that abhors the tyrant in Napoleon Bonaparte."

The chariot swayed as the horses turned into Piccadilly and she caught at the silken strap hanging by the window beside her, tilting her head to answer, her mouth slipping into a serious smile. "That could be. During my days at the convent I was alone in seeing no glory in Napoleon's endless marching into other lands, his conquering of all he surveyed, and for a long time I thought myself odd to doubt and question so powerful a leader, whom all else regarded as the personification of the glory of France. It was a wondrous relief to me when I discovered that my father and other men of conscience like him, including Bernadotte, not only shared my opinion, but wanted to withdraw their support, seeing certain changes of character in the Emperor, which they considered meant doom for France through that now insatiable lust for power. There was no truer patriot anywhere than my father, indeed no braver soldier in the service of France, but he had come to the point when in all honor he felt he could no longer lift his sword under the *Tricolore* when it meant furthering Napoleon's aim of world domination."

"It is said that Bernadotte's hatred of Napoleon stems from his own thwarted ambition to be ruler of France himself."

She gave a little nod. "That's one side of the coin, I do not doubt, but remember that concern for France itself lies behind it. My father had the greatest respect for Bernadotte and believed he had the power and the wisdom to make a great ruler. France's loss was Sweden's gain, and it was from Sweden that my father hoped to work with Bernadotte towards a lessening of the Emperor's iron hold on Europe."

"Bernadotte has done nothing yet, and Napoleon's power grows."

"Give Bernadotte time. He will show his hand when the moment is right."

"I trust your faith in him will be rewarded."

There was as element of doubt in his tone that displeased her and she decided to change the subject. "Tell me something about Norfolk," she requested. "I could gather little enough from my aunt, who visited your home once only during the marriage negotiations and loves London better than any other place. You mentioned the isolation of West Thorpeby Hall—have you no neighbors?"

"None of any consequence for five miles. The Hall's land is bordered by the sea to the east and by marshes to the north. The market town of East Thorpeby is reached by a lane that follows a ridge of land that cuts across the marshes."

"Is there no town called West Thorpeby?"

"There was once a hamlet bearing that name and it was sheltered by the same strip of land that I've just mentioned, but it vanished without trace centuries ago, and only the house remains as a reminder of its existence. Legend has it that it was lost—sinking down into the sodden ground—when the sea invaded on the strength of a great storm. It is certainly true that now and again ancient artifacts come to light on the marshes—pots and pans, a cart and once a spinning wheel. Fishermen who ply their trade along the coast and those who till my land avoid that place, saying that it's possible at times to hear the cries of those who once lived there in their last hours."

She shivered. "What a grim tale."

"It is, but I can assure you that those cries are made only by the sea birds and wild fowl that haunt the marshes. Pheasants are so common that they're known locally as the Norfolk sparrow, and you will see flights of wild geese that come from the far north as well as others with feathers of every hue."

"Is it safe to walk across the marshes?"

"You must take care. Much of it is swampland, but there are paths. I'll show them to you."

She looked out at the passing traffic, her bonnet brim hiding her face from him. No, she could plan no expedition with him. After this journey was over she would take care never to be alone with him again. "Where is Ravensworth Hall situated? Shall I be able to see the marshes or the sea from its windows?"

"No, you won't I'm afraid. Gregory's house lies close to the market town. You'll not be isolated there. Among those who live in the district there is a regular interchange of social events—balls and garden parties and all the rest of it. You may find that you don't miss London at all."

"Everything except the Prince Regent," she said lightly.

"You'll have Gregory."

She closed her eyes briefly on the pain inflicted by his words. She would have Gregory. Oh dear, yes. She would have Gregory.

The chariot bore them through the crush of post-chaises and coaches and gigs and every kind of commercial vehicle until eventually they were out of the heart of London and bearing along the Bishopsgate street, passing Spital Fields, into Shoreditch and the green countryside.

He was a considerate traveling companion and guide, pointing out places of interest to her along the route and enlightening her as to the importance of each in his country's history. The postilions kept up a good pace and when at midday the horses were changed at a coaching inn, she and Blake ate together in its taproom, and later, when dusk fell, they put up for the night at another hostelry of grander proportions where every comfort was provided for the weary travelers who entered its welcoming doors. In the private parlor, which he had reserved in advance for their own use, they sat for an hour by the fire after supper, he with a glass of port, and she relaxed against the chair's cushions, her feet upon a footstool. For the first time he mentioned his ward, Venetia.

"West Thorpeby Hall has over a hundred rooms, but don't imagine you will be lonely there whenever Gregory is absent from your side. Venetia, my ward, is apt to gather company around her as thick as bees to honey." The wing of the chair held his face in shadow and she sensed rather than saw the more serious set of his expression when he added: "I suppose you have heard that she has been unable to walk since there was—an accident. It happened just a year ago."

"Aunt Phoebe told me."

He must have guessed that she had been told the rest of it. She had been given more garbled accounts by the gossipy tongues of people who had thought to inform her once they had heard she was to marry into the family, but she had learned to rebuff them coolly and turn away, having quickly acquired the poise to cope with the unexpected or the unpleasant in a way that she would have previously deemed impossible. Nevertheless, there was no denying the sad and sordid facts of what had occurred, and she could understand how harshly he must suffer for it. What had she been like, the girl who had died? Elizabeth Rose-Marshall. It was a pretty name.

"I hope that Venetia and I may become friends," she said, breaking into the little silence that had fallen.

"I should be glad of that. She finds her condition hard to endure. There's so much denied to her that previously she enjoyed. For example, she was a superb horsewoman, but these days she will not have riding mentioned in her hearing."

She was filled with compassion, understanding what it must mean to the girl. "It's not so very long since she became incapacitated. Surely there's some hope that one day she'll learn to walk again."

He gave his head a doubtful shake. "I've had the best physicians available to give their opinions. One of them suggested that she imagines the excruciating pain that she declares she feels if she puts her foot to the ground."

"Imagines it! I've never heard such an extraordinary theory! Did he carry out tests to prove this claim of his?"

"Yes, but without success. Venetia became so distressed that she was ill again for weeks afterwards."

"I will do anything I can to help her."

"You're most kind. She has a companion, who is a distant cousin, but at times poor Caroline gets on Venetia's nerves and then there is little harmony between them. Caroline's husband was killed in a battle against the French on the Spanish Peninsula. Unfortunately he left her less than provided for, and she has made her home at West Thorpeby Hall."

She comprehended the situation. Most large house-
holds included one poor relative or another—the pre-
text of giving them a post of some standing saved
their pride and dismissed all suggestion of charity.

"Does Venetia enjoy reading?" she asked. "I have
a large number of both English and French books in
my baggage that she might enjoy."

He seemed doubtful. "Not many books interest her,
although she does like to be read to on occasions. Tell
me what you have brought with you."

She listed on her fingers all the titles she could recall
immediately and could tell he was surprised by the
wide range of her interests, but her father had always
encouraged her to read, often providing her with litera-
ture of which the nuns did not wholly approve, and
her attitude to life was far broader than average as a
result of it. Much of her criticism of Napoleon had
sprung from her having learned early to question and
probe all angles of a subject.

"I should like to read those three volumes on
France's early history that you mentioned first," he
said keenly. "Would you loan them to me?"

"With pleasure. You're welcome to any of them."

"There was another title that you mentioned. Er—
which one was it now?"

She went over the list again, and he lifted a hand
at a certain title.

"That's the one you should lend Gregory," he said.
"French politics fascinate him. We have had many a
discussion—and many an argument—over them. He
feels we have much to learn from France."

"And you think not?" She realized that her tone was
on the defensive.

"In music and the arts and in culinary concoctions,
but not, my dear Juliette, in government." His English stubbornness showed through on that point, and
she could not blame him for it. The land of her birth
had a sorry record in the past few decades.

"Surely it is dangerous to express any admiration
for France—be it politics past or present—at this time
of war against Napoleon?" she questioned.

"Gregory keeps his opinions to himself outside the

walls of my study or his own rooms at West Thorpeby
Hall, otherwise he would be liable to have his carriage
windows smashed with a brick or see an effigy of himself being burned on a bonfire by the local riffraff,
which would be a most disagreeable experience, being
only one step away from an attack on his own person."
He hoped he had not alarmed her and leaned forward
in his chair. "You have nothing to fear from anybody.
The fact that you are half English will outweigh your
French links, and all are used to the presence of
émigrés in this country from the time of the Revolution.
It is my own countrymen suspected of being traitors
who have something to fear, and Gregory, for all his
talk, does not come into that category, thank God!"

"What has inspired this interest of his in the politics
of France?"

Blake shrugged on a sigh. "It's the culmination of
many things. When he was young, he had a tutor who
made a great impression upon him with certain revo-
lutionary ideas until my father discovered what was
being instructed and threw the fellow out. Although
nobody realized it at the time, much of what had
been instilled stayed with him, and then when we
went to France together during the truce he was at an
impressionable age and all he saw there seemed superior in every way to anything in his own country,
a quite natural reaction of youth and inexperience on a
first sortie abroad. Last but not least, he is a younger
son, and in this country where the first-born son in-
herits the family seat, land, and whatever riches there
happen to be in the coffers, it can go extremely hard
with other male offspring, who are usually left nothing
and must resort to the Army or the Church for a livelihood. Gregory was fortunate in being left heir to
another inheritance from a great-uncle without issue,
but he cares for West Thorpeby Hall as much as I do,
and he must live with the knowledge that it can never
be his through an accident of birth that made me three
years his senior. It can be a bitter pill to a proud man,
and Gregory is a true Lockington in that respect."

She was quiet for a few moments, thinking over
all he had said. "I am glad you have told me all this,

because it will help me to know and understand him better."

"You mean to do well by him, don't you? I can see it."

She gave a nod. "I shall do my best. How soon after my arrival at West Thorpeby Hall shall I meet him?"

"I expect him to be there when we arrive. The lawyers were sending a messenger on horseback with a letter to placate the bailiff, which should at least enable Gregory to come and go with freedom until the money comes through." He must have seen how she bit into her lip. "Does the prospect make you nervous?"

She looked away from him. "I fear so."

"There's no need to be. You are beautiful, you are intelligent, and you are French by birth, fulfilling all my brother's desires. It is he who must look to please you, and make you happy and content in your new surroundings."

She managed a smile, rising then to retire. Little did Blake know that it was he himself who had destroyed what little chance there had been of her finding true happiness with his brother. He walked with her to the door of her room.

"Good night," he said, "I hope you will sleep well."

Inside her room she closed the door and leaned against it, listening to his footsteps going away down the corridor. What was happening to her? Why could she not crush down the feelings that soared in her whenever he was near? His attitude towards her had certainly given no encouragement along those lines, for at their first meeting he had assessed her like merchandise, and afterwards in no way had his behavior toward her lapsed from the friendly, but slightly impersonal courtesy that any gentleman would show towards his brother's future wife. She could only conclude that she was suffering from some curious reaction through Nicolaus's betrayal. It was the only explanation for such madness of the heart, for that was all it could be. She must not allow herself to think even for a second that it was a more tender emotion that afflicted her.

The door opened against her and she moved away

from it sharply. Cobbett had come to help her undress.

The day broke clouded and overcast, but for the
first stage of their journey after leaving the inn the rain
held off and the going was brisk. It was shortly after
they had crossed the boundary into Norfolk that the
downpour came and there were times when heavy rain
reduced the highway to a morass of mud that hampered
the horses and clogged the elegant wheels. She collected visual impressions of Norfolk along the way,
discovering that it was not entirely as flat as a table-
top, which she had been told by those who must
have known little about it, but at times was softly
undulating, its colors pasteled into misty blues, greens,
ochres, and burnt sienna, making her fingers itch for
her water-color box. She enjoyed painting and longed
to set down all she was seeing on paper. There were
other stages of the journey when vast areas of reeds and
grasses stretched away as far as the eye could see and
it was not uncommon anywhere to cover miles without
seeing any sign of habitation. In the market towns the
wheels rattled over round cobbles of local flint, the
material with which most of the buildings were made,
and the tiled roofs toned from vermilion to crimson
and deepest plum in the changing pattern of sunlight
and shade, adding to the color of the busy street.

At Norwich, where they were to stay overnight, he
escorted her round the cathedral, and afterwards they
climbed the Mound to the old, gray castle where the
wind played havoc with her hair and bonnet strings,
the ends of her silken scarf whipping out as though it
had taken on life of its own, but she was refreshed
and exhilarated by the blustery tussle after long hours
in the chariot. When his hat went bowling away they
chased it together, both laughing, but it was caught
for them in the niche of a ruined wall. She dusted it
off for him, picking off the pieces of dry grass that
clung to the nap, and when she handed it to him her
heart almost stopped, for he was looking at her with
pain behind his eyes as if he were seeing, not her, but
someone like her, and she could only suppose that
unwittingly she had reminded him of some past hap-

piness shared with the girl he had lost. She was deeply moved, and any last doubts she had about the nature of her feelings for him were swept away.

His mood remained subdued from that moment, his lighter spirits of the previous and greater part of the journey quite vanished, leaving him once again the guarded, brooding man who had appeared in her aunt's drawing room like a breath of the wild and turbulent Norfolk weather which she was now encountering. Yet with the good manners that were natural to him he gave thought to her entertainment and took her that evening to the Theater Royal where they watched a competently enacted performance of a drama entitled *The Wanderer's Return,* for he had earlier in the day discovered that they shared an interest in the theater that matched their enjoyment of music, which they had discussed at length during the first day's journey. A passion for the countryside was something else they both knew and understood and had talked about, she recalling the long rambles she had taken with her father. She could not help wondering whether she and Gregory would have as much in common.

When they had returned from the theater and after Cobbett had seen her into bed, Juliette lay gazing up at the ceiling, wide awake and far from sleep. She had never dreamed it was possible to yearn so strongly for one man's arms, never suspected that love could come without invitation or welcome, defying all reason, rejecting all logic, and could be so completely one-sided. The irony of the situation was almost beyond endurance: it was not enough to love a man whose heart had died long since with the one woman he had ever cared for, but he must needs be the brother of the man she was to marry. She rolled over and buried her tormented face in the pillow.

The next morning saw the start of the final stage of their journey. At first they talked as on other days, but gradually as morning became afternoon he was silent for an hour or more at a stretch and she, in turn, could no longer turn her mind to conversation, such a high-pitched tension taking hold of her at the way the distance was at last running out between her and her

betrothed that, with every milestone passed, it was as
though a key was being turned in her back, tightening
every nerve in her body to breaking point.

Through the windows she saw that the countryside
had become wilder and more bleak, any beauty there
was snatched from it by the bitter light of an approaching storm, which rumbled and rolled ominously, its
lightning flickering. Stretches of oak woods made dark
smudges as though a giant thumb had daubed itself
on an artist's palette and scored the somber hues
across the landscape. Dusk fell early, the heavy clouds
pressing out the light of day, and when they reached
the market town of East Thorpeby lights were twinkling. Yet Juliette could see little of what it was like,
except that there was a wide square with a timbered
market cross in the middle of it, a church with a
tower, and the ruins of an abbey that loomed above
the shops and cottages. Once the town had been left
behind and the chariot was alone in the dusk again,
the storm, which had remained in the distance for
several hours, burst forth in forked lightning that split
the sky, and the thunder roared and crashed about
them.

She saw they were following the road along the ridge
of land that Blake had told her about and below,
sweeping away into the darkness, were the marshes
and swamps that had once claimed a long-forgotten
village. The grass bent under the force of the wind
and where water gleamed the bulrushes twisted and
whirled, merging with storm-tossed ferns of monstrous
size, which shimmered in the blue glow of the lightning, for all the world like tormented beings raising
their arms in a wordless plea for help.

Then the marshes were left out of sight and trees
gave some shelter to the road. The land was climbing,
not steeply, but enough to prepare her for the approach of West Thorpeby Hall, which she knew could
not be far away, but although she watched for the
first gleam of lighted windows nothing showed in the
blackness ahead. She glanced across at Blake, but he
was sunk in the corner seat on the far side from her, his
back to the direction they were following, his elbow

on the armrest under the window, his chin in hand, his gaze through the glass unseeing and distant as though it were entirely his own thoughts that held him preoccupied and he saw nothing of the passing woodland with gentler meadows beyond. Had he not spoken with a deep-rooted sense of pride in his house she would have thought he dreaded this moment of return. Or was it that everything about it reminded him of Elizabeth and the life he might have lived there with her, temporarily overshadowing all else for him at this journey's end?

A flash of lightning gave her a first glimpse of West Thorpeby Hall as the chariot raced through the huge, open gates and took the graceful sweep of the drive. In the eerie light she saw the great house appear suddenly and unexpectedly as though it had risen out of the ground, the four slated domes at the corners holding a strange, black-pearl luster, the clock showing its face like a pale moon. Then the whole building was gone again, blotted out by the engulfing darkness, and as she continued to peer ahead through the window only the chariot lamps offered a faint glimmer, which washed over in turn the trunks of the tall trees that bordered the drive.

"Why are there no lights in the house?" she demanded unsteadily. "It seems that Gregory is not at home after all."

He jerked his head round towards her, broken from his private reverie, and frowned incredulously. "No lights? That's impossible. Even if he has not been able to leave Ravensworth Hall there are others in the house."

"Pray see for yourself." She pressed the fingertips of both hands against her face as if to still her torn nerves. To have the meeting delayed yet again was no longer a relief. Until she had met Gregory and could concentrate her thoughts on him, she could not hope to start untangling herself from the loving bonds that had created a cage of her own making.

He had sprung up, let down the window, and leaned out, heedless of the rain beating into his face. A great roll of thunder set the sky atremble.

"Good God!" he exclaimed with great concern. "There must be something seriously amiss!"

He did not close the window or return to his seat, but stayed where he was, one hand outside on the handle, which he turned to half open the door in readiness for the moment when the chariot started to slow up in front of the broad flight of steps that swept up to the grand entrance. Before the wheels came to a halt he was out of the equipage and taking the flight at a leaping run of three or more steps at a time. Juliette saw him thrust open the immense door between the Ionic pillars and enter, shouting for his servants. But none could have come to answer his call, for he reappeared shortly afterwards and came running down the steps again, issuing orders to the two postilions as well as to his valet, who had climbed down from the rear seat.

"Get round to the kitchens! See if you can find anyone there!" He had descended the flight as quickly as he had gone up it. "The whole place appears to be deserted." He reached the chariot where Juliette stood framed in the doorway, ready to alight, and put both hands on her waist to lift her out swiftly and set her feet to the ground. "Come with me. I intend to get to the bottom of this mystery and I don't want to let you out of my sight in case there's any danger involved."

On the rear seat Cobbett, who had been folding back the covers that had shielded her from the weather, uttered a dismayed shriek, her face drained white within the dripping brim of her sodden bonnet.

"Danger! Mercy! What have we come to?" But she was given no time to get down, the valet swinging himself on to the footplate and hanging on as the postilions sent the horses galloping through the archway in the direction of the stables, disgruntled and more than a little alarmed themselves that no grooms, usually so disciplined, had come running to ease them from their duties by taking the bridles at the end of their long and exhausting ride.

With Juliette's hand in his, Blake rushed her up into the house, her bonnet flying from her head to dance down her back on its ribbons. Once inside, he pulled the door closed after them and swiftly lighted the wicks of a tall candelabrum, one of a pair that stood on a sidetable. Then he took from the pocket of his greatcoat a traveling pistol of the kind kept at hand in case of highwaymen, and checked it. Picking up the candelabrum in his left hand, the pistol ready in his right, he gave her a hard, searching look.

"We're ready to investigate. You're not afraid, are you?"

"No," she answered truthfully. Not afraid of anything with him. Not afraid of anything any more except the way she loved him, which he must never, never know.

"Let us go then. Keep close to me. I'm making first for Venetia's apartments. If there are thieves in the house that is where they would expect to find jewelry."

She looked about her as she followed hard on his heels towards the staircase. Green marble columns supported the gallery that encircled the hall and in tall niches statues of ormolu gleamed against flake-white walls picked out in gold. As they mounted the stairs several opposing pier glasses reflected into endless distances the bright points of the candleflames that streamed from the candelabrum he held high above their heads.

It seemed an incredibly long way to Venetia's apartments, even though they moved with speed down the long corridors. When finally they reached the double doors that led into his ward's suite of rooms, Blake handed her the candelabrum to hold, indicating with a wary nod of his head that there was someone within. Then, setting his wrists on the handles he pressed them down together and flung them wide into the room, his pistol cocked and ready.

Juliette gave a cry. The most amazing sight met their eyes and Blake lowered his pistol almost in disbelief. Venetia, ethereal, almost ghostly in a diaphanous dressing robe over silk, her soft, abundant hair a cloud of reddish-gold about her slim, finely-boned face, her eyes huge and blinking brownish-amber like a cat's in the sudden candlelight, was supporting herself by strained and frantic hands on the backs of two chairs, one on either side of her, and was trying to put one foot in front of the other in a desperate attempt to walk. Taken completely by surprise, the fine nostrils of her short nose almost translucent in their flaring, she echoed Juliette's cry with a sharp, high-pitched scream, which she emitted involuntarily, and at the same time she released her white-knuckled grip on the backs of the chairs, all strength seeming to ebb from her. In the crash of one fallen chair, the other also tilting away from her to land with a thud, she crumpled to the floor.

Blake rushed to her. Thrusting aside the clutter of chairs, he scooped her up in his arms and held her, she pressing her face away from the light into his shoulder. "Why on earth are you alone here? What is the reason for everything being in darkness?" His harsh anger was not directed at her and she must have known it, but still she did not answer. "Where are all the servants? Why isn't your maid with you? And where in God's name is that companion of yours? Caroline Hazlett has no right to desert you in my absence! I'll have someone's blood for this stupid trick!"

With Juliette following him he carried the girl into an adjoining bedroom and laid her on the silk-draped bed where she rolled on to her side and put her arms over her head. Seizing a taper he lighted other candles in the room from the candelabrum that Juliette held, fuming as he did so, and when the room was aglow he turned back to the bed, concern for his ward deep in his voice, and he sat down on the edge of it, putting a hand on her shoulder. "Venetia! You must answer me! Who is responsible for leaving you unattended and the house empty?"

Her reply at first was a sheer physical demand for comfort. She hurled herself about and threw her arms about his neck, crowding herself against him, and her voice came muffled and plaintive. "After Caroline went to town shopping I sent my maid down to the kitchen quarters to be with the rest of the servantry. I dared any of them—indoor servants and outdoor alike—to step out of their quarters on the pain of instant dismissal until I rang my bell."

"For what reason?" he persisted, keeping one arm about her while he leaned over and reached out to give the bell pull by her bed a tug to release those in the depths of the house and in the stables from the constriction of the order she had given. "And why no lights?"

"They've been down there since before it was time to light the lamps. That's why. It took me hours—or it seemed like hours—to crawl from my couch to the two chairs and haul myself to my feet. I wanted to see if I could learn to walk again—and I didn't want any of the servants spying on me!"

"Such elaborate precautions weren't necessary. Not a servant would have intruded. You could have kept your maid within call."

"No! No!" Her head dropped back as she looked up into his face and she hammered one fist against his chest, her voice rising on a note of near despair. "I didn't want anyone to know about my attempt. Not even you. No, you least of all. It was to be a surprise if I could manage it. And then you had to come bursting in on me with—" she swung her head round in a toss of flame-gold tresses to glare at Juliette, her face contorted with fury, her eyes blazing with venom, and the words were ground out between her set teeth "—her! That *creature!* Gregory's betrothed. To gape at me. Me! Get out of my room, you hateful wretch! Get out!"

Her voice reached a vibrating shriek of loathing and she tore herself from Blake's arms, lurching towards the end of the bed as if she might fly for the girl who stood at the foot of it.

Juliette fled. Overcome with dismay, she dashed out of the apartments and away down the corridor, embarrassed and shocked that she should have inadvertently started out on the wrong foot with Venetia, for whom she'd had such plans for friendship and for help. She was angry with herself, too, for having remained at the bedside after lighting the way for Blake with the candelabrum, which she still held. But the whole scene had happened so quickly and unexpectedly, and somehow it had not occurred to her to withdraw immediately, perhaps having some thought at the back of her mind that she might be able to give assistance should the girl have harmed herself in any way in that fall to the floor. She could understand that injured pride and humiliation had spiked the ugly words screamed at her, and all she could hope for was that, when Venetia's rage had subsided, it would become clear to the girl that she had felt only admiration for that courageous effort to learn to walk again—and not pity.

Another point stood out: Venetia had been making the attempt as much for Blake's sake as her own. Was it possible that she was in love with him? There was certainly a closeness between them. Had his bereavement and her tragic circumstances drawn them together? It was often out of adversity that love came. Juliette knew that whatever his feelings were for another it was no concern of hers, but although she wished him well and wanted happiness to be his after all he had gone through, it tore at her that she was not the one in whose arms he would find it.

Engrossed in her thoughts, she had paid little attention to the route she was following, believing herself to be retracing her steps, but now she came to a halt, holding the candle flames high. She had come to the end of a corridor, but instead of finding herself at the head of the grand staircase down to the hall as she had expected, she was in a part of the house that she knew she had not been in before, having passed through an archway into a strange, octagonal room of considerable size. Moving to the center of the carpet, which must have been specially woven to fit exactly the odd shape of the eight-sided room, she rotated slowly and saw that there was an archway set into each plane and she had no idea through which she had entered, for beyond every one lay blackness, untouched by the candlelight she held, the flickering glow passing over the vivid murals on the walls. She had the uncanny impression of holding the wick of a gigantic lantern and viewing through its glass the exquisitely painted scenes that seemed almost to revolve around her, for such an optical illusion did the room conjure up. On all sides the murals, executed in miniscule detail, showed the countryside lashed by weather similar to the storm that she knew to be still raging overhead, although there was a kind of suffocating silence in the room in which she stood, as if it were blanketed against all outside disturbances, and the rolls of thunder seemed far away.

How accurately had the artist captured local pastoral vistas in wintertime! On some panels rain pelted down, throwing patterns across ponds and pools while in other scenes blizzards were caking the landscape white and ice glinted amid reeds and bulrushes frozen to a delicate brittleness. Two-thirds of the space was given up to a wild insweep of sea across the marshes, and the glaze, moving with the flicker of the candles, gave life to the rolling waves. It was an eerie room, chill and desolate in spite of the richness of the mouldings and the unlit, ornate corona suspended from the ceiling.

Suddenly her attention was caught by a tiny detail in the scene of the swamped marshes and she moved across to peer closer at it. She saw it was a tiny hand, showing pale above the dark sea water in a last, desperate clutch at the air before vanishing for ever out of sight. Near it on the surface of the water bobbed an upended cot among floating rafters. Cold horror swept over her and she held the candelabrum close as she went from one muraled panel to the next, seeing captured there the whole grisly story of the last hours of the hamlet of West Thorpeby before it was swallowed up by swamp and sea.

With a violent shudder she drew back into the middle of the room again. What a macabre theme some long ago artist had chosen to ornament what would otherwise have been an intriguing if not entirely comfortable room. What was it that made her reluctant to try each of those black archways in turn to find her way back into the corridor along which she had come? Was it the optical illusion that beyond each of them lay endless darkness that no lamp could light? Or was it that she no longer believed herself to be alone?

Fiercely she told herself there was nothing to be nervous of, but she was alerted as if to danger, fear seeping through to the very marrow of her bones. In the candleglow she knew herself to be bathed in brightness amid the dancing shadows, vulnerable and exposed to the sight of anyone lurking in the darkness.

It was then that she heard a whisper of sound somewhere beyond one of the archways that she could not define. Had it been a trick of draught? The swish of a skirt? The brush of a silk-clad shoulder against a wall? Her heart, already thumping, quickened its pace.

"Who's there?" she demanded in as strong a voice as she could muster, but although she listened intently, only her own tones echoed back to her from every archway, each overlapping the other as though eight voices instead of one had called out. Then there came to her, so strong that it seemed to beat against her eyes, fill her ears, and penetrate her nostrils, the knowledge of an alien presence. A chill presence. Steeped in time. And an indefinable part of the room itself. Even as she strained every nerve to decipher what it could be she saw to her dismay the flames of the candelabrum begin to stream out in a draught which she herself could not feel. As she put up her hand quickly to shield them, registering the not unsurprising fact that she was trembling, each flame—to her intense alarm—spluttered wildly for a few seconds in the hot wax and went out. The total blackness of the windowless room enveloped her like a velvet pall.

She screamed. Hysterically and without reason and with a complete loss of all her level-headed common sense. She knew only that she was more afraid than she had ever been in her whole life before, and somewhere in the blackness surrounding her was—something! Terrified that whatever it was would close in to touch her with limp, icy fingers, she lashed out blindly with the candelabrum, and then screamed again when the candles tumbled from their sockets to the floor, creating a fresh clatter close to her feet. She swept back instinctively, uttering another scream more piercing than the first.

Then from somewhere in the distance lamplight was

coming, but although she knew there was no longer any cause for her to be afraid, she could not bring herself to go and meet it, but remained as though still trapped by terror, her breath coming in dry, sobbing gulps, and listened to the approach of hurrying feet. The lamplight swelled out, showing her the corridor down which she had come, and racing along it towards her with several servants in his wake was Blake. As he entered the octagonal room she found the strength to break the spell that seemed to hold her, and letting the candelabrum drop from her nerveless fingers she flew without thought into his arms.

He held her hard about her shoulders, one hand cupping the back of her head. "What is it? What has frightened you?"

She wanted to stay there in the sanctuary of his embrace for ever, but already, with the room now fully illuminated by the lamps held by the staring servants, she felt foolish at the fuss she had created and withdrew a step, causing his hands to slip down her arms and cup her elbows instead of releasing her as she had expected.

"The candles blew out," she stammered. "It was stupid of me to scream, but I must have taken a wrong turning after leaving Venetia's apartments and completely lost all sense of direction. Being left in total darkness was the last straw."

"It wasn't stupid at all," he contradicted kindly, bending his head to look into her fear-pinched face with a gaze that told her he was not entirely satisfied with her explanation, although she sensed a lessening of tension in him as though he were relieved to find that, in spite of her alarming screams, she had come to no harm. "To stumble about in the darkness in an unfamiliar house could be dangerous. There are plenty of steps to sprain an unwary ankle, and I wouldn't want you to spend these first weeks at West Thorpeby Hall with your foot propped on a footstool like some old gentleman with gout."

She forced a smile, aware that he was trying to put her at her ease, and she wished she could tell him about the eerie noise she had heard, for to talk about it would lessen the impact it had made on her and soothe away that terrible fright she had endured, but then he really would think her half-witted and empty-headed. She must accept that it had been no more than a trick of her heightened imagination. But it wasn't just the sound. What of that suffocating sensation of a chill and alien presence being near at hand? That had been so real. So very real.

He was dismissing the servants. "Leave one of those two lamps you have on the table there. That's right. You may tell anybody else who heard the screams that Miss Delahousse has come to no harm and had merely lost her way. Return to your duties."

The larger lamp was left and the servants went off down the corridor, leaving them alone. She spoke breathily. "I'm sure I'm the first guest to end up in a far end of the house."

He gave a little laugh. "Not by any manner of means! This isn't the first time it's happened, I assure you. It's as easy for newcomers to get lost in the corridors of West Thorpeby Hall as it is when they step into the maze that was planted in the grounds years ago in my great-grandfather's time."

She was regaining her courage and she took another step from him, which left him no alternative but to release his light hold on her. "How is Venetia now?" she asked.

"Somewhat calmer. That was a most unfortunate introduction for you to have. She is temperamental, but I trust you will have patience with her. Making that supreme effort to walk again is proof enough of her courage."

"I agree." Then she shook her head gently. "Never fear that I'll hold her angry words to me against her. I hold myself to blame for not withdrawing instantly."

"You're most understanding. I'm sure you'll find as time goes on that she will be extremely glad of your company. There are so many hours after visitors have departed when she sinks into deep depression, thinking of all the social occasions she is missing. Often, as

I said, she finds Caroline's presence irksome, and I'm not always there when she needs to be cheered and comforted."

She looked puzzled. "But surely she goes out a great deal? You said she had many friends—"

"Acquaintances, but not friends. Venetia doesn't make friends easily, and now it is more difficult for her than before. To someone as beautiful—and as graceful as she was before the accident—who always loved to dance and make an entrance and be the vivacious center of any gathering she attended, it comes excruciatingly hard for her to see others of her own age shine in the place that should have been hers."

"Doesn't she go anywhere?"

"Not to balls or parties where there'll be dancing. She selects her invitations carefully and will go only where I'm able to carry her in my arms."

So, Juliette reflected, Venetia can still enjoy making an entrance. She could imagine the effect it would have on any gathering to see Blake, tall and dramatically arresting with those fine looks of his, arriving with the lovely invalid in his arms, her gown a flow of silk and lace. The more she put together all she had gathered about Venetia, the more it seemed obvious that the girl was in love with him. Deliberately, as though shaking the thought from her, she made a sweeping little gesture to indicate the room in which they were standing.

"This is a most unusual salon. I've never seen one like it before."

"There are four of these Octagon Rooms in the house." He moved into the middle of the floor, where he stood with feet apart, his hands resting on his hips. "One under each of the stone domes that rise from the corners of it, which is the reason for their peculiar shape. The ceilings and murals were painted over three hundred years ago. This is the North Octagon Room." He picked up the lamp and lifted it high at arm's length to enable her to view the ceiling in greater detail. "See how the paintings carry the theme. Those four figures are Wind, Frost, Ice, and Snow."

She stared upwards at them and thought how sinister those sharp faces were, how evil the eyes, but then the scenes of destruction in the surrounding wall murals echoed the power of those elements to crush and destroy when unleashed, like dogs of war.

"Did Aunt Phoebe see this room?" she questioned, wondering if these same paintings had given her aunt such an aversion to the house.

He lowered the lamp and held the base in both his hands. "No, I don't think so. In fact, I'm sure she didn't. This part of the house isn't used often, and guests are never accommodated here. Gregory has his own apartments in the North wing, which runs from this room through the third archway into a corridor similar to the one that you turned into by error and which brought you here."

"Are the other three Octagon Rooms painted with so grim a theme?" she queried with a slight shiver.

"No, indeed. All have pastoral scenes, although these—" he gave not a nod towards the murals "—carry the dark side of what life can be like in this area. The sea has invaded many times throughout the centuries."

"Surely this room tells the end of the village of West Thorpeby?"

"It does, and a sad time it must have been, too. It is possible that the artist commissioned to do the work was himself a survivor from that particular tragedy. The date certainly tallies, and there are certain small details that suggest he was an eyewitness, but no one can be sure." He smiled at her. "You will like the other three Octagon Rooms, I know. The one under the East dome has the rising sun and scenes of spring, the South has the full midday sun and high summer, and the West, which shows autumn, is perhaps the most beautiful of them all, everything seeming to be bathed in a red-gold light. I'd show them to you now, but you're surely too tired to go through a conducted tour of the house at this late hour."

"What of Gregory?" she asked falteringly. Through all that had happened since her arrival at West

Thorpeby he had not been banished from her mind. "Where am I to meet him? Here or at Ravensworth Hall?"

"I'm not sure yet. I have despatched a servant with a message to tell him you have arrived." He raised the lamp to show her the way through to the corridor again, but she paused under the archway, able to see now that a windowless passageway, paneled with black oak, appeared completely to encircle the North Octagon Room, which explained the curious echoes as well as the odd insulation against outside sounds. It did not, however, offer any explanation for all else she had experienced there.

"Do all the Octagon Rooms have a passageway encircling them?" she asked.

Blake nodded and swung the lamp out to reveal, a few feet away, an ancient door, previously hidden by the darkness, which was recessed deep into the curved wall. "There's such a door in each, which gives access to the domes. Above this one is the clock set in the cupola above it."

"I haven't heard the clock strike."

"You won't. The hands stand permanently together at the hour of twelve. They have done ever since the clock was first put up there by an ancestor of mine over a hundred years ago. There's nothing fundamentally wrong with the clock. If started, it will tick and strike the hours round until it comes to twelve again —then it stops. Not even the clockmaker himself, who considered it one of the finest clocks he had ever made, was able to put it right, and the general opinion is that there is something in the cupola itself that isn't true and it's this architectural error that throws the clock off balance."

She refrained from saying that the whole North Octagon Room and everything connected with it was of the stuff of which nightmares were made. Instinctively she kept close to his side within the safe radius of the lamplight as she passed with him out into the passageway, thankful to know that at least the guest-room that awaited her would be far from this part of the house where she would be reluctant ever to set foot again. But before they reached the corridor she turned her head sharply and looked back over her shoulder into the inky darkness.

"What is it?" he asked, half turning to follow her gaze.

"Er—nothing," she said. "Nothing at all."

It was nothing, she told herself. Only her imagination. But why then did she have that awful sensation that whatever was dark and evil in that curious room had come rippling silently after her as if to seek out the place where she would be?

Chapter Four

In the suite that had been prepared for her Juliette found Cobbett unpacking her boxes. At her entrance the maid straightened up and hurried across to her.

"Let me take your coat and bonnet, madam. Mercy! What a weird house this is! We found every servant in the household—every manjack of them!—sittin' about in the kitchens. Some were dozin', some quarrelin', some playin' cards, and so on. Wouldn't have done for Mrs. Colingridge, I can tell you. But it appears that Mr. Lockington's ward ordered them to stay down there on pain of instant dismissal. We wouldn't have stood for that in London, I told them. Boxed up for hours like monkeys in a cage. It was the same in the stables. The postilions had to unharness the horses and lead them in before the grooms would take over."

"Thank you, Cobbett," Juliette said quietly. She could have been thanking her merely for taking her coat and bonnet from her, but Cobbett reluctantly accepted that her young mistress would prefer peace to her chatter, and merely mentioned that she had ordered bath water to be sent up. Not being country-bred, Cobbett had not liked the idea of leaving London to wait upon the French girl in the wilds of Norfolk for an indefinite period, and whether the West Thorpe-by Hall household would prove too much in every way she had yet to see. She would certainly have no compunction in taking the next stagecoach back to the metropolis should there be any more crazy goings-on such as had greeted her—and Miss Juliette—upon their arrival that evening.

Juliette, going on a tour of the suite of rooms allotted to her, was surprised at the size of it. The long, columned salon must surely be comparable in spaciousness to others in general use on the lower floors. She

could tell at once that it had been redecorated and re-
furbished for her coming, for there was a newness to
the pale gray paintwork and a brightness to the
gilded pelmets, the gold paneling, and the gilt
torchères. The delicate apple-green silk of the upholstered chairs and sofas was echoed in the striped wall-
paper and in the rugs spread on the polished boards
of rosy wood. An anteroom led into her bedroom
where again all the furniture was new and in the current fashion of bamboo, but upon closer inspection
revealed itself to be not the cheap wood at all, but
imitated in costly satinwood, thus reaching the heights
of sophistication. Setting off the lightness of this elegance the curtains of the bed and the swags and dra-
peries at the windows shimmered in shades of lilac. A
bell pull would summon Cobbett from her accommodation some distance away in a less exalted part of
the wing, and leading off the bedroom were two other
rooms, a dressing room with paneled cupboards in
which all clothes could be hung away, and the other
contained a washstand, wooden rails hung with snowy
towels, and a large, rose-patterned hipbath.

As Juliette inspected the dressing room a string of
maids entered by a door that gave access from the
corridor without encroachment on the main rooms of
the suite, each woman carrying a copper jug filled
with steaming water, and they filed past her with re-
spectful bobs into the adjoining room where each in
turn emptied the contents into the hipbath. One by one
they glided out again as quietly as they had come, the
last maid closing the door after her.

The hot bath soothed away Juliette's travel aches
and weariness, but did nothing to ease her mental tension. She sat at the toilet table while Cobbett deftly
brushed and combed her hair, thinking how the strain
of knowing that at any time Gregory could arrive in
answer to Blake's message was showing in her
features, making her eyes appear to be all pupils and
her face pinched. It was not a face with which to greet
one's future bridegroom, who might even now be waiting in the salon downstairs. Should he not be there
she must still steel herself into coming face to face

with Venetia again, who would be dining with her and
Blake, although there was no reason to suppose that
there would be a repeat of any of the unpleasantness
she had been subjected to previously, but at best Venetia would only be adopting a frigid civility, which
could not possibly be conducive to a harmonious dining hour.

Wearing a soft, blue-gray gown that suited her, she
emerged from her suite to find that, in contrast to the
darkness upon her arrival, the house now blazed with
lights, and there was the silent-footed movement of
servants everywhere. Had she needed to ask the way to
the salon where her host awaited her, there would
have been plenty of opportunities, but as it was she
located it without any difficulty. Just before passing
through the open doorway she paused with the deliberate intention of calming herself, and then with
dignity she entered the salon.

Venetia was not there. Neither was Gregory. Blake
was alone in the room and he turned at the sound of her
footsteps, giving her a smile. Her heart was not calmed
enough to meet his presence, and it soared anew like
any captive bird set free, causing joy and despair to
mingle within her.

"Venetia is not joining us," he said. "She has retired to bed. Neither need we expect Gregory before
tomorrow. The servant has returned after delivering
the message. Apparently my brother still has company
in the house, friends who have been helping him to
hold the fort."

She held out her hands to the fire, feeling chilly in
spite of the warmth of the room. Was it possible that,
in spite of what everybody had said, Gregory was as
nervous of meeting her as she was of meeting him? It
was certainly obvious that Venetia was not ready to see
her again yet. That was natural. After all, she herself
had experienced similar misgivings about their meeting again. All she could hope for was that she hadn't
made a permanent enemy where she had hoped to
make a friend.

"I would like to talk about Venetia's efforts to walk
again," she said. "When you flung open the doors and

we saw her in the first flood of light she was standing
well, straight-backed and poised, but her full weight
was not on her feet, because she was half suspended by
her own grip on the chairs, and all the tension seemed
concentrated in the leg and foot she was trying to thrust
forward into a step. My father observed how fear
would paralyze men in battle, and who's to say it's not
a similar kind of panic-stricken terror affecting Venetia, which is preventing her from taking up life again
as she knew it before?"

"I don't deny that real fear can play havoc with
anybody's behavior."

"Maybe if you talked to her and tried to find out—"

He shook his head with some exasperation. "Do you
think I haven't? My God! If it weren't for me she'd be
the same lively girl who first came to reside here when
her days of schooling were at an end! I'm a daily reminder to her of what happened."

"What exactly *did* happen? I've had only my aunt's
version, but for all I know it could be as garbled as
all else that London society gossips about."

His face closed against her, his eyes darkening, his
brows drawing into a frown. "I don't doubt you heard
the basic truth of it whether through gossip or otherwise. If there's any more talking to Venetia that has
to be done, you'd better be the one to do it. Discover
and sort out what you will. No greater harm can come
than that which has been done already."

A voice, unfamiliar to Juliette's ears, broke in shrilly
from the doorway. "I disagree! If a distortion of the
mind exists it can be only one step from madness! I
think you, Blake, have lost your wits yourself to give
this stranger *carte blanche* to take matters into her
own hands. And you, ma'am—Juliette Delahousse, I
presume you to be—will be advised to leave all interference well alone. I'll not see Venetia end up in Bedlam or anywhere like it!"

Juliette, startled by the unexpected interruption,
stared at the young woman who stood on the threshold
of the room. She was slender to the point of thinness,
fragile and diminutive, with a haughty, well-bred look
to her high-browed face, which was pale-complex-

ioned, the cheeks peach-toned, the mouth thin-lipped
but rosy. Her air of neatness was accentuated by the
polished gleam of her chestnut brown hair, which she
wore scraped mercilessly into a beribboned topknot.
In the lobes of her small ears she wore garnet bobs,
which matched exactly the color of her gown.

Blake suppressed a kind of angry sigh. "This was a
private conversation, Caroline, but since you have seen
fit to join in I'll remind you that everyone else—even
yourself—has failed to do anything practical to help
Venetia, and if Juliette should find a way we must
both support her all we can."

Caroline Hazlett came forward into the room and
fixed a glacial gaze on Juliette. "I can see you are
more French than English. You have the look of the
Parisian about you."

Juliette raised her eyebrows slightly. "Have I? Yet
I have spent so little time there—days I can count on
the fingers of both hands. I'm flattered—"

Caroline raised a hand sharply. "I didn't mean it as
a compliment. There's nothing honorable in being a
Parisian or looking like one. I despise France and all
it stands for! Tyranny and murder and oppression!
You'll find that everyone else around here feels the
same."

"Caroline!" Blake thundered. "We're not bringing
Napoleon's war into this house! You forget yourself—"

Quickly Juliette touched him on the sleeve. "Please,
Blake. Say no more." The color burned in her cheeks,
but she addressed Caroline evenly. "In times of con-
flict between countries feelings run high. I met those
in London who chose to turn away from me at social
gatherings rather than acknowledge someone known
to be half French. You have been more forthright in
speaking your thoughts outright, but do not expect me
to deny my love for France to make myself more
acceptable to the community. That I cannot do."

"My husband was killed by the French at Torres
Vedras!"

"You have my most sincere sympathy."

Caroline caught her breath. There was no doubting
that Juliette, whose clear gaze had not left hers, had

meant those gently spoken words, but it did nothing
to ease the bitterness and resentment she had felt ever
since she had heard that a Frenchwoman was to be received into the house. Not a refugee like those who
had fled from the Revolutionaries years ago, people of
aristocratic lineage forced to seek exile or face the guillotine, but the daughter of a French officer who had
fought for Napoleon! Boney! The Corsican! The little Emperor! By whose orders the French had at-
tacked Wellington's lines of defense and taken the
life of the man she loved! Reducing her to the state
of widowhood, which she loathed. She was not suited
to a single state or for impoverished circumstances,
which made her dependent upon Blake's charity, her
Lockington pride as fierce as that of her benefactor,
as indeed it ran in the veins of all those who came of
that ancient lineage. But her troubles did not end there.
Until the marriage of convenience between Juliette and
Gregory had been arranged there had been a chance
—just a chance—that he would have looked seriously enough in her direction to have rescued her
from her widowhood. She had had it all worked out.
It would enable him to draw on his inheritance and
she would enjoy the status of a married woman once
again, turning a blind eye to his extramarital amours,
for she knew she could not keep a man like Gregory
faithful to her. Nor would she have wanted to. She did
not love him, but she had needed him. And this hateful creature standing in front of her had ruined everything!

Blake had put a hand on her arm. "Come now,"
he said compassionately. "We understand the bitterness you feel over your bereavement, but I beg you
not to lay the crimes of others at the feet of the innocent. Juliette is shortly to become your third cousin by
marriage when she is wed to Gregory. This house has
had enough torment to contend with. Let's not add any
more trouble to it."

His appeal, although it did not pacify her, at least
appeared to touch her, for she gave a reluctant nod,
biting deep into her lower lip. She spoke shakily to
Juliette, keeping a tight control on herself.

"It's true what Blake says. We are to be related shortly. I will try to remember that your mother was Phoebe Colingridge's sister."

It was as far as she was able to go towards any kind of truce between them, and Juliette realized it. "At least we have common ground in our concern for Venetia," she said. "I see no reason why we shouldn't try together to help her. Since you know all about her case, perhaps you will advise me."

Caroline looked at her uncertainly. There was no mockery, no veiled contempt, no hint of a jibe. French or not, she seemed genuinely concerned for Venetia. Better to advise her than let untold harm be done. Better to hold one's tongue temporarily on other matters. Nothing could change her own personal attitude towards the Frenchwoman. Nothing.

"I'll do what I can," she conceded grudgingly.

The butler appeared at the door. "Dinner is served, sir."

Blake, who had thought for a while that he was to have Caroline refusing to sit at the same table as Juliette for the rest of her stay in his house, escorted them both through to the dining room.

When Juliette finally tumbled into bed she felt as physically and emotionally exhausted as if ten times as many hours had gone by since she had last risen from rest to face that last stage of the journey to West Thorpeby Hall. To crown everything that had happened, there had been Caroline's hostility to face. At the dinner table the widow had been polite enough, but Juliette had not been deceived, able to judge that Blake's words had had little real effect. In Caroline's eyes she knew herself to be as darkened by Napoleon's shadow as if he had been sitting beside her in the neighboring chair.

Sleep took her unawares. It came upon her with a sudden closing of lids and loss of consciousness before she could reach to extinguish the lamp by her bed, and she slept deep in her pillows within the shadows of the lilac silken hangings of the four-poster in which she lay. When there came some commotion away down the corridor outside her room she was not at first disturbed by it, but when it did not abate, culminating in the protest of a servant being thrust aside at a stumble, she did roll over restlessly and throw an arm above her head. Then hurrying footsteps approached her door and after the barest preliminary of one heavy blow of a fist against the panel, it was thrown open and swung back with a crash.

She sat bolt upright in bed, sleep dashed from her, and snatched up the bedclothes to her chin as she stared at the intruder, who had already closed the door and was leaning back against it, his arms folded. He was tall, about the same height as Blake, and the family resemblance was there in build and features, the face handsome and boyish, the eyes dark and brightly alert under strong brows, the nose high-bridged with splendidly curved nostrils, the mouth wide and firm-lipped, and his hair, wind-blown and tousled, was extremely black. This, then, was Gregory Lockington!

"I've come to see my bride-to-be," he announced challengingly. It was easy to see he had been drinking, but he was by no means intoxicated.

His brashness in intruding in such a manner after all the tension she had been through was the final outrage. "Since you have waited this long, it would have been better to have left our meeting until the morning instead of choosing this late hour!" she retorted fiercely.

"It's not long past midnight."

"I was sleeping!"

"Your lighted window led me to believe otherwise." He treated her to a wide, white-toothed smile of dashing Lockington charm. "Have I let my eagerness run away with me?"

"I had begun to wonder if we should ever meet," she replied coldly.

He gave a half-laugh and came exuberantly across to the bed. Before she could make any move he had set one knee on it, seized her by the shoulders with both hands and jerked her forward, so that the light of the lamp fell fully on both their faces. He caught his breath and his eyes narrowed at her.

"You're far lovelier even than your portrait led me to expect!" he exclaimed hoarsely. "I did not dare hope you would be so fair. Do I please you? I *hope* I do, seeing that we are to spend the rest of our lives together."

She lowered her lids and turned her face away from him. The rest of their lives! How final it sounded. She was enervated by it, all her courage seeming to have ebbed away, and she was at a loss to know how to answer him.

He took her reaction for shyness and modesty and, sitting on the bed, he drew his hands down from her shoulders and over the soft cambric of her nightgown sleeves to her hands, which he caught and held. "Look at me," he coaxed, bending his head to try to catch her glance. "I've ridden like the wind to come to you and yet now you fall silent and sit with your face turned away. It was no choice of mine that Blake had to play escort on my behalf." His voice took on a more persistent note. "Come, Juliette. You torment me."

Still she kept her face averted from him, forcing herself to come to terms with the situation. Only when she could be sure that nothing of the despair she felt showed in her eyes would she be able to meet his gaze with any confidence. If he thought she failed to find him attractive his pride would be offended, his male ego severely wounded, and she would not willingly cause him any hurt or embarrassment. As he had said, they were destined to live out the rest of their lives together as husband and wife, and it was only sensible to gather the shreds of herself together and make the best of things. Sensible—but nigh impossible. Her head dipped lower away from him.

"Please go now," she begged. "We can talk in the morning."

"I can't believe you're as heartless as you pretend." The phrase came softly. "Let me stay for a while longer. There's nobody else to disturb in this part of the house. We have it to ourselves." He reached out as he spoke, taking her chin between finger and thumb and turning her face towards him. Mercifully, as she considered later, she reacted again with anger and her eyes flashed, her chin jerking free of his touch.

"It appears I'm out of touch yet with Norfolk ways! They are more unconventional than I imagined possible. If this were France—"

"Ah, if it were! I'm an ardent admirer of France and all things French. Your country leads the world in intellect and art."

"It truly gladdens me to hear you say that," she admitted freely, always warmed by praise for the France that was dear to her. It had not been easy in London where she had been emotionally on the defensive, having been exposed to hearing many just and unjust accusations hurled against France during talk in which she had been involved or forced by chance to overhear at various social gatherings; often these remarks had been uttered by people not at first aware that she was French born, and bitter in their condemnation of her country, which she considered to be as much under the heel of Napoleon as any of the foreign lands that he had conquered, no matter that the French had not yet discovered the truth of it for themselves.

His hand, which had hovered since she had jerked her chin free of his touch, now settled lightly but surely upon her waist. "Didn't you know that it was the fact that I knew you to be French—and undeniably more French than English, seeing you had lived all your life there—which first made me consider this marriage of convenience that has been arranged for us?"

"Not until I reached England. Before that I was kept in the dark about everything. Aunt Phoebe told me all she knew about the Lockington family, and later Blake told me something of your interests."

"But you still have much to learn about me. It will enchant me to be your tutor."

On the surface his words were innocent enough, but it was apparent to her that he was entertaining voluptuous thoughts about her, the intense intimacy of the present atmosphere created by the bed, her almost transparent night attire, the quietness of the rest of the house, and their being alone together, all encouraging him to a boldness of attitude—and action—that she must put a halt to at all costs. With an outward show

of calmness that she did not feel, she turned back the
bedclothes on the side of the bed opposite to that on
which he was sitting, and reached for her satin peignoir, which she slipped on, covering her nightgown,
only too aware of the open admiration with which
his gaze swept her.

"Since we are becoming acquainted while the rest of
the house sleeps," she said, thrusting her feet into
slippers, "the least I can do is to summon my maid
and have a glass of wine served for us to toast the future together."

She went towards the bell pull, intent on summoning Cobbett, thankful she had thought of an excuse
to bring an end to their being alone for the time being.
When they were wed she would have no choice in the
matter, but the right to freedom was still hers and
he knew as well as she did that he had broken convention outrageously by invading the privacy of her
bedroom. Curiosity and not ardor had provoked it,
but desire was making him stay.

She did not hear him rise from the bed after her,
but he moved with a panther-like swiftness and as she
stretched out her hand to take the bell pull he seized
her wrist and held it. "Not yet!"

Even as she turned her head sharply to him, startled
by his action, he slid on to the third finger of her captive hand a betrothal ring of diamonds and emeralds.
She stared numbly at its sparkling magnificence, prism
arrows reflected from it across the room in the lamplight. She knew she should be flattered that he had
chosen to lavish a fortune on such a ring for her, but
there was something so final and sealing about seeing
it on her finger that it was as though the slam of a
prison door resounded in her ears, making her already
his.

"It's—a beautiful ring," she managed to say, her
throat choked.

"Now we are truly betrothed!"

He swiveled her round towards him, taking her into
his arms, and his mouth came down on hers. He kissed
her hard and lustfully, but instinctively she remained
stiff and unyielding in his embrace, and when he re-

leased her it was with a sigh of stifled impatience as if he thought her cold and unawakened to the senses of womanhood. Had it been Blake who had held her in his arms nothing could have stopped her kissing him back with all the fervor of her deeply passionate nature. But to think of Blake was madness. With a trembling hand she reached again for the bell pull and tugged it. Only when she turned again did she see that he was observing her closely.

"Is there someone else?" he questioned shrewdly, leaning an arm along the marble mantel and tapping his fingers lightly on it, the thumb of his other hand looped in his waistcoat pocket. So he was not to be fooled. She might have guessed that to a man of experience her lack of response denoted more than a virginal reticence. But before she had a chance to say anything, he added: "Don't be afraid to speak frankly. There need be no pretense between us on any score. Our names being put to a document of agreement wasn't tantamount to a declaration of love from that moment forth."

She hugged her peignoir about her and took a few slow steps away from him until she reached the sofa, where she sat down. "I'm aware of that. I would go further and call all marriages of convenience nothing more than cold-blooded transactions. In our case I bring you my dowry and you give me your proud and honorable name. I intend to be an amiable and faithful wife to you, but—" she raised her gaze from her hands folded in front of her and met his eyes—"I can promise nothing more."

Immediately, and with sadness that she could not control her errant heart, she saw that she had disappointed him, but he hid it quickly behind a cheerful, cynical grin. "I expect nothing more." He looked down at the embers of the fire, to push with the toe of his boot a crumbling log back farther into the grate, and spoke sardonically. "Love is a transient emotion, a period of temporary insanity that does nobody any good. Fortunately—or otherwise, according to the circumstances—it never lasts, and only fools expect it to, but our marriage will endure until death comes to

one or other of us. Yes, it will be like a rock, Juliette."
His voice turned crisp with emphasis and all mockery
had gone from him. "On that I am determined. If you
gave your heart to someone you left behind in France
or Sweden it will give me no concern. It's not your
love I want from you, but an heir to inherit West
Thorpeby Hall. For this purpose I had to look for a
wife who would have all the virtues needed to ensure
that no doubt could be cast on the paternity of any
son born. You have those virtues. The most careful
check was made upon your character. I could not risk
endless lawsuits in a battle to establish rights to inherit."

He was being as frank with her as she had been
with him, almost in retaliation, but she liked him for it,
thinking that it was as well everything was out in the
open. She concentrated on his extraordinary statement,
which caused her much bewilderment.

"Your brother is the head of the family. The house
is his and will go to his children after him—not to
any son of yours." She could not bring herself to say
"ours," afraid that the word would stick in her throat.

He gave an odd, triumphant laugh. "He'll never have
a son! At least, not one born in wedlock. He killed
the only woman he would have married as surely as
if he had broken her neck with his own hands. The
shock of it will remain with him for the rest of his life.
He'll never put another in the place he had planned
for her as his wife and mistress of West Thorpeby
Hall."

"You can't be sure of that!"

He surveyed her with mild surprise that she should
contradict him. "So sure that I would wager my life on
it. I know my brother. He loved Elizabeth Rose-Marshall as he loved no other woman, and there have been
plenty in his life." Tilting his head to one side he regarded her thoughtfully. "In a way you remind me of
Elizabeth. I find that strange, almost uncanny, but it is
intended as a compliment, believe me. She was one
of the most fêted young women in Norfolk. Venetia
boasts that she can take Elizabeth's place with Blake,

but she is deceiving herself. He feels nothing more for her than compassion."

Juliette seemed to hear what he was saying from far off. Only his remark comparing her with Elizabeth stood out, searing itself on her mind. She was recalling how Blake had looked at her on their day in Norwich when she had brushed the grass from his hat. It was not anything in the past he had been remembering with pain in his eyes, but Elizabeth herself. She had reminded him of Elizabeth and therein lay the reason for any special consideration and gentleness he had already shown towards her and might still show in time to come. With difficulty she forced herself to answer without expression Gregory's comment on the relationship between Venetia and Blake.

"Love takes many forms. Perhaps he does not recognize the true nature of the regard he has for her. I only saw them together for a short while, but it seemed to me there was a closeness between them."

He shook his head dismissively. "His responsibility towards her has increased tenfold since the accident. But he'll not marry her."

"How did she come to be his ward in the first place?"

"She's our late second cousin's child. Charles Lockington was a widower, and when he fell ill with lungfever he had no one to name as guardian other than Blake. It was as simple as that."

He turned his head sharply, Cobbett having opened the door and entered, clad from throat to ankle in a dark red wrapper. Sleepy-eyed, she blinked at the sight of a stranger in the young mistress's bedroom, guessed immediately who he was, and clamped her mouth down in disapproval. In heaven's name, what was Miss Juliette thinking of! Receiving her intended at such an hour!

"Bring a bottle of that special wine I brought with me, Cobbett," Juliette requested quietly. "You know where it is, don't you?"

"Yes, Miss Juliette. I put it in the cabinet in your drawing room."

Cobbett's face relaxed, for she had caught the look of appeal in the girl's eyes and understood the situation. Demanded to see her, had he? Hmm. One look at that handsome devil was enough to tell any woman, whatever her age, that he was one to get his way with whomever he wished. Two of a kind, those Lockington brothers. Dear me, yes. Two of a kind.

She made haste to fetch the wine, which had come originally from a cellar stocked by Miss Juliette's own father, one of a score of crates that the girl had been allowed to bring from Sweden. Wine was wine as far as Cobbett was concerned, but she realized that this one must be for the connoisseur's palate, and with some reverence she carried it with the two crystal goblets on a silver tray from the salon and through the connecting anteroom back into the bedroom.

"I'll wait within call, Miss Juliette," she said, setting the tray down on a side table, "in case you should want me again."

"Thank you, Cobbett." Juliette's glance showed her relief, even though her voice did not betray her. She watched the maid leave and saw that the door was left ajar.

When the wine was poured Gregory raised his glass. "To you and your beauty, Juliette! May West Thorpeby Hall be a better place for your coming into it!"

She thought it a strange toast, but she acknowledged the compliment by inclining her head before taking a sip from her own glass to his good health. His eyebrows lifted appreciatively when he had tasted the wine and he inhaled its delicate bouquet again before holding it to the light to admire its rich color. "This is superb! If it weren't for the smuggling that goes on these days there would be no French wines getting through the commercial blockade set against this country by Napoleon and his allies. But even through these underground channels it's almost impossible for a wine as rare as this one to get through."

"I have several crates of it for you. It's a betrothal gift."

"I'm overwhelmed!" He took another mouthful and

savored it, giving her a sideways glance. "Tell me, what is your opinion of this house?"

"It's very grand and gracious," she said carefully, "but for my part, seeing it first in the darkness, it looked awesome, even menacing."

His face tightened. "Who's been dealing out tales of its horrors to you? That dimwitted aunt of yours?"

She gasped indignantly. "Don't dare to speak so of her! She spoke only kindly to me of this house and those who live in it, and the only criticism of it that I ever heard her utter was when she told Blake that she thought it was a grim place."

"That didn't please him, I'll be bound!"

"If it didn't, he was too gentlemanly to show it."

Gregory shrugged a trifle too carelessly. "Tales get about, you know. There are always eerie stories told about old houses and past generations who lived in them. The Lockingtons have had their fair share of the ups and downs of fortune in the three hundred years or so since they first built a house on this site, but nothing that need worry you."

His casual, throwaway air, in spite of coming so hard on the heels of his slip about the house's horrors, was convincing and would have soothed any anxieties she might have gathered about the place if she had not been through that strange experience in the North Octagon Room; as yet he knew nothing about that, and for the time being she did not feel inclined to tell him of it.

"As you say," she remarked, putting down her glass and linking her hands, "I need not concern myself with West Thorpeby Hall. What of our future home? I trust that Ravensworth Hall has no ghosts in it?"

He opened his mouth as if he would have snapped a question at her, but he appeared to think better of it, his gaze shifting to a further study of the wine, albeit a trifle absently as though his thoughts were otherwise engaged. She had the feeling he had been about to ask her how she knew there were any ghosts at West Thorpeby Hall, but that could be a fanciful assumption on her part. Had it been a ghost whose presence she had sensed in that curious room? She did not doubt it, not even now that she was away from the eerie atmosphere of the North Octagon Room. Often she had heard it said that disquiet souls wandered endlessly on an eternal quest for peace and rest. And who could deny such a possibility?

"There are no ghosts at Ravensworth Hall," he stated flatly. "But I did not say you need not concern yourself about West Thorpeby Hall. I simply said that nothing about it need worry you."

She eyed him thoughtfully. "What are you trying to tell me? Why not come straight out with whatever it is? You said we were to be frank with each other." A moment of hesitation. "Would it help if I tell you that I know the bailiffs have been dunning you?"

His reaction was explosive. He slammed down the glass with such force that the stem cracked. "Damnation to that brother of mine! He had no right to tell you!"

"Don't blame him. I guessed. It wasn't difficult."

He flung himself away from the fireplace and took a few angry paces one way and then the other across the carpet, one arm with fist clenched behind his back. "Since you know the worst, there remains little to tell you. Debts of long standing have swallowed up the mansion that should have been our home. I was playing cards with some acquaintances at Ravensworth Hall when word came that you had arrived here. I would have come sooner, but luck was going my way and for another hour or two it looked as though I might recoup enough to quieten my debtors for a while longer. Unfortunately luck deserted me once again. I handed the key over to the bailiff when I left to ride to my future bride." He had stopped his pacing and gave her an ironic bow. "I fear you must resign yourself to living at West Thorpeby Hall for longer than you had anticipated."

"But your debts are to be settled by an advance Blake has arranged on the inheritance that is due to you on our wedding day," she said, relieved that the situation was not as bad as he imagined it to be. "The lawyers sent a letter direct to the bailiff. Isn't

that how you were able to come away from Ravensworth tonight?"

"That letter wasn't worth the paper it was written
on, but the lawyers did not know that. I do not doubt
that one or other of my debtors will hasten to inform
them now that my house has fallen to the bailiff. You
see, the inheritance is there, but any advance is ac-
counted for before it can reach me. I've gained credit
on the strength of that inheritance ever since other
funds ran out. It is, one might say, mortgaged to the
hilt. Not a penny of it will be left over to jingle in my
pocket." To illustrate his point, he pulled out the lin-
ings of his pockets and thrust them in again, giving a
wry laugh. "So much for my wealth. I'd have told you
none of this until after our wedding day if you hadn't
forced the issue. But don't think you'll be marrying a
pauper. Other monies will be coming in to me. Money
and power. As my wife you'll have all the jewels and
furs and carriages you could wish for, and it will be
sooner than you think. Much sooner! The only difference you'll notice is that for the time being we'll be
living in this house instead of another of our own."

She stood up in agitation. "We can't live here after
we're married! I don't want to!" The thought of seeing
Blake daily after she had become another man's wife
was too much to bear.

His expression remained hard, although a concilia-
tory smile parted his lips as he reached out to take
both her hands into his, compelling her to draw closer
to him. "There'll be no interference in our private life
by anyone else in the house. It is large enough to house
a dozen families separately. Blake and the others will
go their way, and we'll go ours."

Still she protested. "You'll have my dowry when
we're married. More than enough to buy a splendid
house anywhere you wish. We needn't stay in Norfolk
if you've a mind to live elsewhere." She seized on the
idea. "Let's go away from the east coast. It's rough
here, and wild. I've heard that Oxfordshire is a fine
county and that Surrey and Sussex have rolling hills—"

He interrupted her firmly. "Norfolk is the place for
us, and West Thorpeby Hall the house where we shall

live. Your dowry is not to be used to set a roof over
our heads."

"Better that than to gamble it away!" she cried
heatedly.

He jerked up her hands, bringing her forearms
hard against his chest, and enfolded her in an envelop-
ing embrace, his face lowered close to hers. "I've been
reckless at the tables in my time, but no more so than
any free man with money to stake. I've had my winning streaks and it's only over the past twelve months
that fortune has turned her face consistently against
me. You're going to change my luck again! I promise
you that, the sooner you marry me, the sooner you
shall have a country house to call your own, as well as
a London residence where you may entertain to your
heart's content! With you at my side I'm going to play
for the highest stakes in a different kind of gaming.
Not at the tables. Not with cards or dice or horses,
but in a political game of chance that will bring me
power and make a royal princess of you, my beautiful
Frenchwoman!"

"I don't understand you. You talk in riddles."

"Less of a riddle than it sounds! But something to
explain in detail when we've had more time together."
His embrace tightened about her and his voice thick-
ened. "This will be a partnership without equal. The
past left behind by both of us. A new beginning.
Somehow I knew it when I first heard your name—
Juliette, daughter of Colonel Henri Delahousse, hero of
Austerlitz, Auerstadt, and Jena!"

She was grateful that he, an Englishman, should call
her father a hero, but then she believed it would have
been the same even if he had not shared her love for
France for the English were singularly fair-minded,
being as quick to acknowledge courage in the enemy as
they were to condemn tyranny and treachery wherever
it was found.

"My father never thought of himself as a hero, but
he was a very brave man. The Emperor gave him
special honors."

"And you have his same courage, I can tell."

Blake had mentioned belief in her courage too, but

that had been in connection with the house and the future life that awaited her; Gregory's remark had a different ring to it, almost as if he believed she would be willing to take up arms and fight in battle as women had done in skirmishes during the Revolution.

"You flatter me unduly, I do assure you." She tried to ease herself from his arms, alarmed by the blatant lustfulness that vibrated in him. The mere fact that she was French born and, through her very connections with the enemy forces ranged against his country, linked with Napoleon, seemed to excite and inflame him in a manner that disturbed her. In marrying her, in conquering her, in possessing her, did he see his actions as his own recapturing of the true and gracious France that he and she and others like them longed to see restored to its former glory?

"I happen to think otherwise," he answered her, keeping a tight hold about her waist while he cupped his other hand against her face and with the ball of his thumb tilted her chin upwards to bring her lips nearer his own. "You are the woman for me in every way!"

She shut her eyes as his lips descended, not in any kind of amorous anticipation, but with her heart aching with love for Blake she needed to shut out the sight of his elated, eager face and his parted mouth about to sweep down on hers. Whatever happened, she must not hurt him again, for he wanted only good to come of this marriage, and so did she. Then, even as the kiss came, away in the salon beyond the anteroom Cobbett screamed. Gregory startled, lifted his head, releasing her from his hold. "In the Devil's name, what's that about?"

Juliette's first reaction was one of relief mingled with anger, for it seemed to her that Cobbett must have been eavesdropping and chosen an opportune moment to intervene, and the thought that their conversation had been overheard by an inquisitive servant who had overstepped the limits of her silently invited chaperonage was not to be suffered. But when she followed Gregory through into the salon she saw at once that she had misjudged the maid, who lay huddled on the floor in the light that came from a single candlestick, well beyond the doors of the intervening anteroom and quite out of earshot. Gregory dropped to one knee and with both hands he turned the woman's head. A redness showed with increasing vividness on her brow.

"She's only fainted," he said impatiently.

"What is that mark on her forehead? Has she received some kind of blow?" Juliette hovered over the maid, deeply anxious.

"It's only where she hit the floor when she fell. She must have been sitting in that winged chair and tipped forward out of it when she lost consciousness."

"I'll get my vinaigrette." She ran back into the bedroom and across to the toilet table. As she pulled open a drawer and searched among her ribbons and handkerchiefs, which earlier Cobbett had so carefully folded away, she had the extraordinary feeling that she was not alone in the room. Her hand fastened on the phial, and holding it she swung about abruptly to let her gaze travel round the room. Nothing was different. Nothing was out of place. And yet—And yet—

Gregory's voice called from the salon. "Can't you find it?"

Upbraiding herself for dallying, Juliette rushed back through the anteroom and found him slapping Cobbett's wrists in an effort to bring her round.

"Why on earth do you think she screamed out like that?" she asked, kneeling to wave the vinaigrette under her maid's nose.

"The Devil knows! Unless—" he stopped what he had been about to say and his eyes fell away from hers.

"Yes?" she prompted.

"I've really no idea," he stated flatly, refusing to be drawn. "Anyway—" he frowned wrathfully "—it sounds as though she's managed to awaken the whole house with her maniacal shriek."

Footsteps were coming along the corridor outside at a run. A tapping of knuckles sounded urgently. "Miss Delahousse! Are you all right?"

"Yes, yes," she answered, continuing to wave the

vinaigrette and concerned that Cobbett did not respond, so deep was her swoon. "You may come in."

The door opened and the footman on duty entered breathlessly. His fresh, young country face set in thinly-veiled sullenness when he saw that his master's brother was still in the apartments. He liked Mr. Gregory as little as everyone else in the servants' quarters, the spoiled younger son with his unpredictable moods and his free hands with any of the prettier maidservants. Not quickly forgotten would be that push aside Mr. Gregory had given him when he had attempted to stop him blundering his way into the young Frenchwoman's suite by explaining that she had gone to bed long since and would most surely be asleep. Mr. Gregory never showed when he was in drink, but in drink he was and always quick-tempered with it if crossed. Maybe a good wife would settle him down and make him more like his brother, who had been a real lad in his time if a quarter of the tales were true.

"What's wrong, sir?" he asked. "I heard a scream—" He broke off, seeing the figure lying prone on the floor.

Gregory answered abruptly, drawing back from the woman and rising to his feet. "Miss Delahousse's maid has fainted and isn't coming round. Fetch the housekeeper."

Juliette looked up over her shoulder. "There's no need." Cobbett's eyes were fluttering and she had started to gasp at the pungent aroma of the vinaigrette.

Without being asked, the footman hurried across to assist Juliette in helping the maid to sit up. Then putting two strong arms about her he lifted Cobbett on to the sofa, which Juliette, having jumped to her feet, pushed forward to make it easier for him.

"That's right," she said gratefully, plumping up a cushion and putting it behind her maid's head. "Thank you so much. Put her feet up. Splendid! Now she will be comfortable."

Gregory balled his fists in exasperation. He would have preferred not to have had anybody else's intrusion on this annoying little scene, but the untimely appearance of the footman had meant it was not to be avoided, in which case it must be closed as quickly as possible.

"You heard what I said!" he growled at the footman. "Miss Delahousse is not to be troubled at this hour of the night with a sick servant. Put a taper to a few more wicks in this room and then get the housekeeper here without further delay."

"Yes, sir." The footman did as he was instructed, setting a brighter glow to the room and then departed, but he had not gone any great distance when he realized that the scream must have echoed far in the night silence of the house and it appeared that half the household had been awakened.

The master appeared in a crimson dressing robe tied with a silken, tasseled cord, and after being given a brief word of explanation he hurried on in the direction of the young Frenchwoman's suite. Shortly afterwards Mrs. Hazlett put her head round the door and, wide-eyed, wanted to know who it was who had been screeching.

The footman was beginning to enjoy himself. The night watch was always monotonous and nothing ever happened. Nothing that a finger could be put on, that is. He had had the creeps many a time, which was the reason why he kept good candlelight at hand whenever he was on duty in the dark hours, and he took care never to peer too closely into the shadows in case *she* took it into her head to appear to him, trailing her wet robes and with her ghastly, drowned face framed in weed-entangled tresses. Good God, no! He never wanted to see *her!* Neither did the master or the rest of 'em above stairs. Not that anything was ever said about it, but it was the conclusion drawn below in the servants' quarters, where everyone went in fear of *her* by day and night in certain parts of the house, even though *she* was said to make her presence known only when any disaster was about to befall the family. It was a pity *she* hadn't been able to foresee her own gruesome end those three centuries ago, because then *she* would have ended up decently dead and buried in the churchyard instead of always being a threat to a person's peace of mind when the old house creaked and groaned in the long hours of darkness.

A shiver passed down the footman's spine and he increased his pace, his footsteps clacking noisily. When he reached the housekeeper's room he had to knock on her door several times before her snores ended on a grunt and she stirred. He guessed she had had her usual nightcap of hot toddy laced with brandy that was kept for medicinal purposes. Medicinal purposes! The footman grinned to himself and knocked on the door with his knuckles again.

"Mrs. Harman!" he called. "Are you awake? You're wanted in Miss Delahousse's suite. That maid she brought with her has been in a swoon and got a biff on the nut."

There came the protesting creak of a bed. Then a few moments later the flap of slippered feet hastened towards the door.

Blake arrived in Juliette's drawing room to find her seeking to calm her maid, who was sitting up on the sofa in a state of distress, hands shaking and teeth chattering, in spite of being wrapped in a blanket from her mistress's own bed. Unable to hold a glass, she was taking the last sips of wine from a goblet that Juliette was putting to her lips. Standing a little distance from them, looking anything but pleased, was his brother, who greeted him with a glare.

"My God, Blake, you too! Is the whole household to gather because this wretched creature nods off to sleep and has a nightmare?"

"The scream was loud enough to waken the dead," Blake answered crisply. "I was reading in bed, but had I been sleeping it would have most certainly awakened me. What has been going on here?"

Cobbett's eyes were red-rimmed in her blotchy face, a bruise showing dark on her forehead, but she addressed him strongly. "I w-wasn't d-dreaming, sir. I admit I was almost n-nodding off to s-sleep when I heard an awful h-hissing sound like b-breath b-being drawn in through clenched t-teeth. And there was s-something—I don't know what!—moving in the s-shadows

over there!" She flung out an arm and pointed to a
distant corner of the room beyond the columns, which
was shrouded in darkness, unreached by the candlelight.

Her words chilled Juliette, who was reminded of
that strange, inexplicable sound she had heard in the
North Octagon Room. Had that been a hiss? The faintest intake of breath between set teeth? And what of
that odd impression of not being alone when she had
returned to her bedroom to fetch the vinaigrette? Had
some eerie manifestation drifted in there after making itself known to her unfortunate maid? But at all
costs she must allay Cobbett's immediate fears.

"Old houses are full of strange sounds at night,"
she said, trying to convince herself as much as Cobbett
that it was nothing to be concerned about.

"You don't have to tell me that, Miss J-Juliette.
I've worked in h-houses older than t-this one in my
t-time. B-But that sound w-wasn't like anything else
I've ever h-heard afore *and* whatever made it was here
in t-this room with me!"

"Are you saying that it was a ghost?" Juliette questioned on a light tone chosen to soothe with the suggestion that it was a complete improbability.

Tears brimmed over in Cobbett's eyes. "I t-think
it was."

Juliette, overcome with sympathy for her, wrapped
her arms around her maid to comfort her. As she did
so, she happened to see the two Lockington brothers
exchange glances. They believe Cobbett! she thought
incredulously. They *know* she saw something spectral!
In spite of what Gregory had said, he hadn't thought
for a moment that the woman had had a nightmare
and dreamed that terrifying experience.

Cobbett clutched at her. "Suppose it's still in this
room, w-watching us?"

In that instant Juliette knew she must show fearless-
ness, not only to dispel her poor maid's terror, the
shock of which could damage her nervous state permanently if nothing was done about it, but because she
must assert herself, project her own personality against
that unknown quality, and show that, however long

she might be compelled to live at West Thorpeby Hall, nothing—living or spectral—was going to crush down her spirit. She could love in the secret places of her heart, for that was her own private anguish and she would let it harm no one, but in turn, she would not be harmed by whatever force it was in the house that had bestirred itself in the North Octagon Room and penetrated this suite, which lay the length of the house away from that place.

"I'll show you there isn't anything to be afraid of now!" she declared, springing to her feet. Snatching up the candlestick she ran lightly with it down the length of the long, elegant room, dispelling the shadows as she went, the gilt-framed looking glasses throwing back her image. At the far end she paused, holding the candle first to the right and then to the left, illuminating the corners before whirling about again. Back she came in a soft flutter of silk and lace, her peignoir billowing out, her silvery-fair hair an aura about her face.

"There, Cobbett!" she declared, handing the candlestick to Gregory, who replaced it for her. "Nothing watching us! Nothing there!"

For the first time she saw uncertainty on the maid's face, doubt springing up to cloud that earlier conviction that it had been no nightmare that had terrified her, no split-second dream that had conjured up that terrifying experience. At that moment Mrs. Harman entered, a black silk robe over her night attire, a frilled, white nightcap framing her round face, which was still flushed from being awakened with something of a start from deep oblivion. With her head cocked in keen attention she listened to Cobbett's own account of how she had had "a bit of a start" and fallen from her chair in a faint. No mention now of a ghost, and Juliette breathed a sigh of thankfulness. Better for Cobbett to have doubts than to walk in terror with shattered nerves.

"I'll help you back to your room," Mrs. Harman said kindly to Cobbett. "Put your arm through mine. I'll treat that bruise for you. It will be much better in the morning."

Blake was quick to assist the housekeeper in raising the maid to her feet and walked with them as far as the door when it became apparent that Cobbett could manage well enough by taking her companion's arm. Nevertheless, he saw them safely on their way along the corridor before coming back into the room.

"Well," he said, "it seems that everything can settle down now." His look at Juliette sharpened. "Are you nervous to be on your own? I can post the footman outside your door—"

"There's no need," she insisted vehemently. "I shall go back to sleep with a quiet mind. I feel extremely tired."

"Then I'll bid you good night." He moved to the door and waited, showing he did not intend to leave without seeing that his brother departed, too.

Gregory, as though to let Blake know that he had put a seal of approval on his future bride, kissed her on the cheek. "Good night, Juliette. I'll see you in the morning."

The door closed after them. For a few seconds Juliette stayed where she was, her expression deeply thoughtful, and then almost automatically she gathered up the blanket that had been left on the sofa. Hugging its softness to her she went on slow steps through the anteroom into her bedroom. Sitting down on the bed and drawing her feet under her she closed her eyes, remembering the faces of the two Lockington brothers when she had turned at the end of the long room and retraced her steps at a light-footed run, her nightclothes wafting about her. Caught off guard, forgetful of everything but the almost ethereal and misty sight she must have presented in the pale candleglow, they had both stared at her, but each with a different look in his eyes.

Gregory showed he was struck afresh by her looks, the appealing curves of her figure, his eyes lustful and his greedy mouth parted. It had been easy to tell he was congratulating himself anew on the choice that he had made. But it had been Blake's gaze on her that had almost stopped her in her tracks and made her long to hold out her arms to him. His velvet stare had been both tender and violently passionate, the look of a man appraising the woman he loves, and at the same time so blended with pain that she had wanted to cry out to him. Once again she had reminded him of his lost love. All she could hope for was that he would not come to hate her for it.

With a moan she spread her fingers wide and clasped her bowed head despairingly.

Chapter Five

In the morning Juliette found Caroline Hazlett alone at the breakfast table in the morning room. Blake had already eaten and gone out; of Gregory there was no sign, and she supposed that Venetia breakfasted in her own rooms. This proved to be correct.

"Good morning," Caroline said stiffly. "I'm the only company you'll have at breakfast most mornings. Venetia never appears until eleven o'clock when she's either brought downstairs to take a ride in her carriage, or carries out any other plans she has made. Have you quite recovered from the disturbance that your maid created last night?" She put a thin-fingered hand to her brow. "I couldn't get to sleep again afterwards. I feel quite exhausted this morning."

"I'm sorry to hear it," Juliette said sincerely, helping herself to a portion of fish fricassée from one of the many silver-covered dishes ranged the length of the tulipwood sideboard table. "Perhaps you would take a walk with me later. It's a fine day after yesterday evening's storm. I'm eager to see the exterior of the house and the grounds in daylight. You could fill in details about its history if you feel so inclined." She took her plate to the table and sat down opposite Caroline. A parlormaid poured her a cup of coffee and then departed, leaving them alone.

Caroline's face was twisted with indecision. Juliette guessed that hostility towards herself was vying with a natural desire for discourse and company, perhaps even curiosity to discover more about last night's events. To be an appointed companion could be a lonely business in spite of the social implications of the post, for invariably there was friction. In her own case Mademoiselle had been weak and self-centered, repulsing friendship, and had thus created abject loneliness for both of them. As for Caroline and Venetia, it was difficult to imagine two more opposing personalities, one flamboyant and excessively temperamental, the other mouselike in appearance, but possessed of a defiant will that made her want to pick up metaphorically the banner that her fallen husband had fought under and continue the battle on his behalf within the confines of the drawing room and even, if her present mood swayed her against the proffered olive branch in a Frenchwoman's hand, in this very morning room.

"What sort of details?" Caroline asked suspiciously.

Juliette pursed her lips slightly, not rushing into anything, and stirred her coffee. "Well, Blake told me a great deal about West Thorpeby Hall on the journey from London, but then I hadn't seen the house, except in your inksketch, and had no idea what an unusual house it would prove to be. Unusual with its four Octagon Rooms—and eerie."

"It's certainly eerie," Caroline commented bluntly. Then she bit her lip as if wishing she had not made the remark.

Juliette made no show of noticing her reaction. "I know that this land has belonged to the Lockington family since Norman times, and that they have suffered the buffeting of changing fortunes under one king and then another as the years have gone by. I also learned that somewhere in the grounds are the ruins of the castle that was the home of the first Lockingtons." Her lashes swept upwards and she regarded Caroline steadily across the table. "A place so old must be steeped in legend. I would like to have those legends recounted to me. As you were a Lockington before your marriage, albeit a distant cousin, you must have heard them from early childhood. Is that not so?"

Caroline, having finished the selection of cold meats on her plate, set down her knife and fork and patted a little grease from the corner of her mouth with her crackling linen napkin, her expression withdrawn and evasive. "I know them. Why should they be of interest to a *foreigner?*" Emphasis had been put on the word. The olive branch had been thrown aside and stepped on.

Juliette's expression did not change. "Since West Thorpeby Hall is to be my home for an indefinite period it is surely most natural that I wish to know all there is to know about it."

"I thought the wedding day had been fixed for some time towards the end of the summer."

"That's when it's to be, but Gregory has decided that we will continue to live under this roof for a while after that."

Caroline gave a contemptuous little snort. "So the bailiff has taken over Ravensworth Hall after all. Gregory's fortunes have always fluctuated. Don't despair. He could be as rich as Midas again with a turn of the cards. He has always retreated to West Thorpeby Hall when luck has gone against him, because here he can continue to live in style at his brother's expense until his pockets are full again. Anyway, he'll be flush enough when his inheritance comes in on the day he marries you."

Now that all chance of getting Gregory for herself had gone, Caroline felt free to release her venom against those very faults of his which she had previously been prepared to overlook.

In spite of her offensive tone Juliette chose once more to turn the other cheek, having no intention of enlightening her as to the true state of Gregory's financial affairs over that mortgaged inheritance.

"I hope to persuade Gregory to look for another residence, but if I fail I will certainly make sure that the household accounts do not suffer because of our presence here at West Thorpeby Hall."

Caroline smirked. "Nobody can turn Gregory from any path he has chosen to follow. You'll soon find that out." She showed satisfaction in anticipating the thwarting by the younger Lockington brother of any futile attempts to change him that the Frenchwoman might make. She put her neat head on one side, a gleam appearing in her light gray eyes. "So you want to know the legends of West Thorpeby Hall? Very well.

I'll take a stroll with you in the grounds. I'll tell you whatever you want to know." She rose from the table, pushing back her chair. "I'll meet you in the hall in half an hour. First I have to see Venetia to find out what she has made up her mind to do today."

Before donning her bonnet and coat Juliette went along to her maid's room; she had been sleeping when Juliette had made enquiries before breakfast, but now she was awake, propped against pillows, and there was little to be seen of the bruise on her forehead, which had almost faded away. A tray on a chair by the bed showed that she had eaten all that had been brought to her.

"How are you feeling this morning?" Juliette asked solicitously.

"Better, thank you, but lying here I've had time to think things over. I had a real fright last night and that's the truth. Even if I did nod off and dream the whole thing—and I'm not saying I did, mind!—there must be something right evil in this house to put such a dream in my head. I couldn't go through an experience like that again. I really couldn't."

"What are you trying to tell me?"

Cobbett sat forward, dragging into place the shawl about her shoulders. "I'm giving in my notice. Oh, I'll not leave you until another can fill my place, but Norfolk ain't for me. I'll take the first coach back to London as soon as you have a new lady's maid to attend you."

Juliette had mixed feelings. Cobbett had proved herself capable and attentive, but she had had the feeling that the maid had been instructed to report back to Aunt Phoebe on all developments that took place. The last thing she wanted was for her aunt to worry unnecessarily about her or to come hurrying to Norfolk to intervene on her behalf. She had had enough interference in her life and wanted no more of it, however good intentioned and kindly meant.

"I understand perfectly. I'll speak to Mrs. Harman without delay. A replacement shall be found as soon as possible."

"That's good of you, miss."

Juliette made to leave, but paused by the door, looking back at the woman in the bed. "There's something you can do for me in return."

"Yes?"

"Tell my aunt what you have just told me. Norfolk isn't for you. Those were your words. I don't want her driven frantic by any lurid descriptions of last night's interlude."

Cobbett considered the request, turning it over in her mind. The young mistress could have made a nasty fuss about being let down by her giving notice so soon after their arrival, but had chosen not to—a point to be appreciated. On the other hand, Mrs. Colingridge had wanted to know all that happened at West Thorpeby Hall in relation to her niece, being anxious about how she would fare. But that meant there could be trouble for herself if Mrs. Colingridge thought she had run out on Miss Juliette because there was something scary about the house, and there *was,* dream or no dream. She reached a decision.

"I'll not mention the matter," she declared blandly, placing one hand over the other on the sheet in front of her and leaning back again. "After all, it happened to me—not to you."

Outside the maid's closed door Juliette heaved a thankful sigh. At least she could be sure that Aunt Phoebe would be kept out of it. As she retraced her steps towards her own suite she realized she still had time in hand before meeting Caroline, and could discuss the engaging of a new lady's maid with the housekeeper.

Mrs. Harman answered the summons promptly, rustling into the drawing room where Juliette was taking a look out of the window, already clad in bonnet and coat, but wondering if she should take a parasol. It was certainly a brilliant day. She turned with a smile to bid the housekeeper good morning and tell her what the situation was.

A somewhat weary look showed in Mrs. Harman's eyes. "I'll do my best, but I've had great difficulty in finding ladies' maids for Miss Venetia. Being an invalid she does not seem able to tolerate the attentions of one servant for any length of time."

It was a charitable way of saying that Venetia was impossible to please, and Juliette guessed it. "Do you have to send to London?" she enquired.

"On occasion, but it is my experience that London ladies' maids will not stay in the country for any length of time. At least, not in a house as isolated as this one. Therefore, I am not surprised by Cobbett's wish to return. Usually I send to Norwich, and sometimes it's possible to get a trained girl from one of the great houses around East Thorpeby. Naturally for you I will send only to London, because being used to Paris you will want one who is exceptionally skilled with the dressing of hair and with a needle. No doubt Mr. Gregory will be taking you to London for the Season once you are married, and this will be an incentive to offer."

"A carrot for the donkey?" Juliette said, amused.

"Fair means or foul," Mrs. Harman answered dryly on a note of levity unusual for her. Then she became formal again. "In the meantime there are three girls in the house well trained enough to wait on you for the time being. All three were Miss Venetia's ladies' maids at different times—the last one until a month ago. I've kept them on, all being Norfolk girls and content to do other work, but eager to be called upon when extra assistance is needed in their favored field on occasions when the house is full of guests. Will you leave the choice to me, or do you wish to see them first for yourself?"

"I'll speak to all three in turn after luncheon, Mrs. Harman. I see no reason to send to London if I find one of them completely suitable. It will solve the whole problem." She tilted her head in interest. "Tell me, is the house often full of guests?"

The housekeeper hesitated. "Not these days. Not since the big house party that was being held when the tragedy of the fatal accident occurred. The master has never entertained on a grand scale since then. It was a terrible blow to him, and indeed everyone. Miss

Rose-Marshall was a lovely young lady. I know I speak for every member of the staff when I say we had all looked forward to her becoming mistress of West Thorpeby Hall."

"Had Mr. Lockington and Miss Rose-Marshall known each other long?"

"The Lockingtons and the Rose-Marshalls are local families and have always known each other. Sir Alex, the only son of the family and head of the house since his father died a few years ago, was at school with the master. Some say it was only the fact that they were old and close friends that enabled Sir Alex to forgive the master for anything he might have done that caused the death of his sister. Anyway, his and Miss Lucy's standing by the master did a lot to save him from being cut by half the county, because the Rose-Marshalls are highly respected everywhere."

"Who is Miss Lucy?" Juliette asked with interest.

"She's the eldest sister, not that there was much difference in age between the three girls, and Miss Elizabeth was the youngest—about Miss Venetia's age. The two girls were friends. That's how they happened to be together in the same vehicle when it crashed and overturned."

"What a dreadful time for everybody!"

Mrs. Harman nodded sadly. "I wouldn't like to live through it all again, and yet I was merely a bystander, so to speak. The master was distraught. Then there was the funeral with half the county attending, and many looking askance at him already because of the news flying around that it was his fault it had all happened. As if he hadn't enough to bear losing the girl he loved!" Her tone was indignant, her loyalty to the man who employed her beyond question. "Accidents can't always be avoided. The circumstances were unfortunate, but he was the last man—in his cups or sober—to wish to cause harm to anyone."

"How long was it before it became apparent that Miss Venetia would not walk again?"

Mrs. Harman's face hardened, revealing a certain lack of sympathy toward the young woman in question. "She was unconscious for at least a week after the accident, and then she should have pulled herself together and recovered, instead of resigning herself to an invalid's life."

"Perhaps that wasn't possible, Mrs. Harman."

"Why wasn't it? Admittedly one leg was broken, but it was set skillfully and healed without complications."

Juliette realized it would be useless to put forward the obscure theory that mentally the girl was not ready to walk again, for that would be beyond the housekeeper's comprehension. It was almost beyond her own, but she had come to accept that it was possible. She was even hoping that, armed with this new knowledge, she might work out a way to break down that barrier for Venetia.

"We must trust that one day she will recover completely," Juliette said, intending to close the conversation.

"I endorse that hope most sincerely," Mrs. Harman added, nodding. "She has cost the master a fortune in physicians' fees, you know. A fortune!" She threw up her hands expressively.

"I think he would spend his last penny if it could restore her to full health again," Juliette declared judiciously.

"Oh, I agree, Miss Delahousse. I agree." Mrs. Harman was intent on making her see that she had never thought otherwise.

Juliette moved across and picked up the parasol from the chair seat where she had placed it, having decided to take it with her after all. "I'm going out for a walk in the grounds now if anyone should ask for me," she said, thinking that Gregory might come looking for her.

"Yes, Miss Delahousse. It's a beautiful day. I hope you will enjoy your constitutional."

Caroline was not in the hall when Juliette went downstairs, but she appeared a few minutes later. "I can't spare you much time," she said distantly. "Venetia is expecting company for morning chocolate, and she wants me to be there."

"By all means. We'll walk together as far as you can go, and then I'll continue by myself."

Side by side they went out into the morning sun. Both snapped up their parasols, Juliette's of tawny silk with a swinging fringe, and Caroline's a ruffled affair of dark green muslin. Down the sweeping steps they went and, upon reaching the flagged forecourt, Juliette drew back to look up at the house. In the morning sunshine it no longer looked as sinister as it had the night before when it had seemed to rear up out of the darkness: and there was mellowness in the ancient walls that gave depths of rich color to the stonework, which was veiled in places by creeper, the leaves showing green and shiny, all on the move in a wind that was blowing from the direction of the sea some distance away.

"Although you may not realize it," Caroline said on the slightly pompous note sometimes adopted by those imparting information, "the house is built at an angle to the lines of a compass, which means that from here we can see the south and east domes at either end of the front of the house, while at the back are the west and north domes."

"I've been in the North Octagon Room," Juliette remarked, still studying the splendid frontage, "but not the others."

"Have you?" A flicker of surprise passed over Caroline's features. "What did you think of it?"

"I thought it was an intensely dramatic room. The murals are exquisitely painted, but horribly macabre."

"Anything else?"

"It has an oppressive atmosphere."

"You felt that, did you? That's interesting. Others have said the same. When I used to visit here as a child I would never go near it. I still keep away from it."

"Blake told me about the clock above it that always stops at the hour of twelve."

"That's the oddest thing, isn't it? My father, who was a Norfolk man, used to say it should never have been put there in the first place. Let's take this path." She indicated one leading away through the yew box hedges towards the flower gardens, and as Juliette drew level with her she continued: "Apparently before the clock was set in that cupola all those years ago there was a weathervane that never worked. It always turned to the North, and no matter how hard the wind blew from any other direction it made no difference to it."

"What was the explanation for that?"

"Something to do with currents of air under the cupola roof, I suppose, but the legend is that the Devil pinched it between finger and thumb. Needless to say, that legend was passed on to the clock, and it is said that it is the Devil's touch that stops the hands at twelve."

Juliette looked back over her shoulder at the house. They had walked sufficient distance from it for her to be able to glimpse the north dome with the pale gleam of the clock's face. The Devil's touch. Not hard to believe on a wild night with the wind howling through the trees, but much less alarming on a fine spring morning with birds singing and the surrounding flower beds a riot of early color. Caroline went on talking.

"When we get a little further on you'll see a grassy mound and a few ruined walls, which is all that remains of the old castle. It was never as large as the Norman castle at Norwich, but it dates from the same period, and from it Blake's and Gregory's forebears kept guard over a wide area. It will give you a good view of the marshes if you have the energy to climb up the mound to the walls, and it's easy to sight from there the dikes that Blake has had dug to drain some part of the swampy land."

"I went up the Castle Mound at Norwich. This one will be of even greater interest to me. Are there any legends about the ruins?"

"Not that I know of. It's the house—or rather the north dome of West Thorpeby Hall—that holds the legends."

"You told me about the clock. What else is there?"

From under the parasol ruffles Caroline gave her a sly, sideways glance. "If you've a nervous disposition

you won't thank me for telling you, but historical fact
and legend are blended together in the tale of the
North Octagon Room."

"Go on, please," Juliette insisted.

"Early in the sixteenth century the lord of West
Thorpeby Hall, a certain Thomas Lockington, with
grown sons who had left home, married for the second
time, taking to wife a woman many years younger than
himself, a beautiful, flighty creature with whom he
was besotted. When the King summoned him to London, Thomas did not dare to allow his wife, whose
name was Isabelle, to accompany him, because he
feared the advances that would be made to her by the
lecherous gallants at Court, who would have all the
time in the world on their hands while he would be
engaged on Royal matters that would entail hours of
solitary work. So he left her at home, much to her
chagrin, and some weeks later she—either to punish
him for leaving her behind or because she was bored
and lonely—took into the house a whole band of
strolling players, most of them as young as herself, to
entertain her and her household with masques and
plays and music. You can imagine the riotous behavior of all concerned and the junketing that went
on." Caroline compressed her lips primly, rolling up
her eyes censoriously as if the house still rang with the
laughter and scampering feet and the singing of
bawdy songs.

Juliette, although knowing that the whole façade of
West Thorpeby Hall and much of the interior had
been structurally altered since that time when Isabelle had held a court of her own, turned again to
look towards it and was able to picture with ease
how it must have looked in early Tudor times. Then,
out of the corner of her eye, she happened to glimpse,
beyond the distant trees that lined the mile-long drive,
the sparkle of harness. A carriage was approaching
the house. It sprang a thought into her mind.

"Did Thomas return in the midst of it all?" she
asked.

Caroline gave a sharp nod. "He came home late one

night with his retinue of horsemen and servants and flew in a rage at the sight that met his eyes. The play for the evening was over, and entertainers and members of the household were dancing and merrymaking in the great hall, well flown on his wine. But Isabelle was nowhere to be seen. He discovered her in another room alone with a lute player. Thomas went berserk. He lifted up the youth bodily and hurled him from the window to his death below. Isabelle, screaming and crying, was dragged down to a dungeon under the house. As for the rest of the strolling players, they were used so brutally by Thomas's men-at-arms that many crawled away with broken limbs and made for the village where some of them had made friends. No doubt Isabelle would have ended her days in the dungeon, because Thomas swore that he would never set eyes on her again, but two or three of the players who had escaped injury did not desert her. They delayed their flight and with the aid of one of the household they rescued her. But that was the night of the great storm. They caught up with the rest, but none had gone far when the sea swept in, bursting through banks, flooding the land, and Isabelle and the players and all the village were lost."

"How tragic!"

"That's not the end of it. Thomas never spoke her name again—at least, not until he was on his deathbed many years later in the North Octagon Room. Then he cried out her name with his last breath. So great was his cry that she heard him in her watery grave, and came back to the house trailing mud and weeds from her garments. Others saw her—or so they said. It's certainly recorded that one manservant suffered an apoplectic fit and died instantly on the stairs near the room, and a maid completely lost her wits with fright the same night. Isabelle is said still to haunt the house. She appears whenever misfortune threatens. She, wanton creature that she was, wants to gloat over the sufferings of those descended from the Lockington who inadvertently sent her to her death."

"I've never heard a more hideous tale," Juliette said

faintly. She could tell that Caroline had relished the recounting of it. "But perhaps Thomas misjudged her. Perhaps she was innocent."

"She couldn't have been." Caroline's attention was distracted by the sight of the carriage and horses coming into view near the forecourt. "I must go! There are Venetia's visitors!"

Juliette called after Caroline's swiftly departing figure. "Why are you so certain that Isabelle betrayed Thomas?"

Caroline flung her answer malevolently over her shoulder. "She was French. Like you. Everybody knows the French are not to be trusted."

It was a vindictive and totally unnecessary jibe. Juliette, an angry flush dying her cheeks, bit back a retort, reminding herself that she had been forewarned that Caroline had intended no friendship in telling her the legends of West Thorpeby Hall.

Turning her back to shut out the sight of Caroline and the young ladies she was already greeting, the air filled with chatter and little high squeals of laughter, Juliette continued at a brisker pace on through the garden; it was sheltered from the wind by hedges which were grown specially tall to give protection, at least ten feet, and kept clipped and trimmed by the gardeners to a velvet-like appearance. At the end of the path she happened to be following she saw ahead, rising above some woodland, the castle ruins, and set off towards them.

It took her longer than she had estimated to reach them, but it was well worth the walk, even though the wind, given free rein when the protective hedges were left behind, strongly buffeted her parasol and sent the fringe swirling. Climbing up a worn flight of ancient steps she reached some castellated battlements, and standing there she thought how right Caroline had been in saying that the view was something to be seen, no matter that much else she had said had been laced with spite and a desire to cause fright. Northwards the boundary wall of the grounds lay many acres distant, showing itself between copses of trees like a thin, flint-stoned snake, and beyond it the land dipped gradual-

ly at an incline to become flat, spongy marshland
stretching away as far as the eye could see; a place
of coarse grasses, bog pimpernel, watermint, and marsh
violets, broken by the silver glint of mud-banked dikes
and natural pools. A way to the east, able to be viewed
from the clifftops of the high and dry Lockington
land on this stretch of changeable coastline, lay the
waiting sea, white-tipped waves curling like fingers
ready to snatch again at the low-lying ground that had
long since become a morass, water-sodden and unar-
able, but curiously beautiful in its barrenness under the
flicker of seabirds' wings.

In the brightness of the day she could see over to
the west the road along which she had traveled with
Blake, the hard escarpment that had withstood the onslaught of the sea and havened the good Lockington farmland on the far side of it.

Something in her went out to this wild and blustery
part of England. The weather was not kind to it. The
sea was both enemy and friend. And some of its
landscapes were so harsh and forbidding that it would
be easy to forget that others were lush and gentle. Yet
she had the feeling that she could put roots down and
become part of it, a conviction that had never assailed
her in any other place where she had ever been. Had
she been waiting all her life for a true homecoming?
But how could any homecoming be true without love
being given and reciprocated by a man and a woman
sharing the same abode?

Tears threatened, but she could not—would not!—
let them come. Slowly she turned until she had viewed
from all directions the great, green parkland in which
West Thorpeby Hall stood like a huge, square jewel,
the windows its many facets catching the sunlight.
Had Isabelle, new to England and to her husband's
bed, stood on these same battlements, which even three
centuries ago would be scarcely less ruined than they
were now, and gazed at the surrounding countryside?
What sort of person had she been? An unhappy girl
compelled by parental authority to marry a much
older man and live away from her native France? On
that level Juliette could draw a comparison to herself,

even though Gregory was only nine years her senior.
Had Isabelle cared for Thomas or had she not? A
flighty creature, Caroline had said. That suggested
shallowness of character and a selfish trait bent on the
satisfaction of her own desires. Had an inherent wan-
tonness turned to evil, an evil so great that because of
the manner of her death her soul knew no peace and
gloated over every misfortune that befell the house of
Lockington? Was Isabelle waiting for some dread and
final act of vengeance?

A cloud passed over the sun. Juliette shivered, deciding to stay no longer on the windy battlements
and at the same time making up her mind to return
again at the first opportunity to the North Octagon
Room and study the murals closer than she had done
before. Blake had mentioned that they were believed
to have been painted by an eyewitness. In that case
she might find a likeness of Isabelle among the figures
fleeing from the rising waters. If there should come
again that eerie sensation of a spectral presence being
at hand, she would at least have some idea what Isabelle looked like—or had looked like before her
drowned state!

As she turned about to take the steps down again, a
flashing in one of the windows on the side of the
house in the shade attracted her attention. It had
showed for a second and was gone. Was it a hand glass
catching the light? There it was again! A tiny sun itself
pressed against one of the panes. It was a spyglass!

She turned her head away, making no show of having seen she was being spied upon. When she drew
near to the house again she looked up at the windows,
but whoever had been there had gone and she was
not entirely sure at which of them the unknown person had been standing, but it had been among three on
the second floor not far from the east dome.

She had almost reached her suite when she met
Gregory, who greeted her with a grin. "You've been
out walking, I can see. I was looking everywhere for
you."

"I left a message with the housekeeper."

He gestured impatiently. "I haven't seen her. Why didn't you join the ladies drinking chocolate? I met the parlormaid fetching another potful and she told me you weren't there."

"I was not invited."

His face darkened and his mouth tightened ominously. "Were you not? But surely you met Venetia when you arrived yesterday evening?"

"Er—only briefly."

"Did she not dine with you?"

"I dined with Blake and Caroline. Venetia didn't come down to dinner."

"She always does! Giving you the cold shoulder, is she?"

"She and I are strangers yet. With time we shall become better acquainted. Today she is entertaining people whom I don't know."

"But whom you should know!" He seized her by the wrist. "We'll amend that state of affairs without delay."

He began to hurry her along with him and she protested, hanging back at arm's length. "No! No! I will not intrude."

He did not as much as glance back at her, his grip vicelike. "You won't be intruding. Not you, Juliette. Not my future wife. I'll not have you snubbed in this house!"

He was racing with her, causing her almost to stumble at the speed, and realizing that it was useless to try to wrench herself from his powerful hold she tried another tactic, clutching at his sleeve.

"Look at me! I'm wind-blown from my walk in the grounds. Let me tidy myself. Allow me to put my appearance to rights before a looking glass."

Her ruse to make him halt his headlong rush worked. He knew women often better than they knew themselves and the importance to them of looking immaculate before the critical eyes of their own sex was familiar enough to him. For himself he liked slight disarray in an attractive woman. The unbuttoned glove, the slipped bonnet ribbon, or the peep of lace at bosom level hinting at further and more intriguing déshabillé.

Juliette with her hair within her bonnet brim tumbled by the wind and her coat skirt dusty and stained green where she must have brushed against some lichen-covered stonework, was more beguiling to him than if she had stood there with a sterile, out of a bandbox look. Last night, coming upon her unannounced, she had stirred him dangerously in her warm and tousled state, her intensely feminine fragrance an invitation to his manhood, but he had shown restraint and he had not alarmed her, and she in turn had behaved with a remarkable calmness and treated the unconventional hour of his call with an air of considerable common sense.

She was all he wanted in a wife. In his bed she would pleasure him. In his own game of political intrigue she, being French, was the partner he needed. Her dowry, nothing less than a small fortune, would set him back on his feet and gild the path to the power that would be his when the right moment came. Damnation to the three months that had been set down as the waiting period before their wedding day! It would not be his fault if he could not persuade her that the date should be brought forward. It hadn't happened yet that he had failed to persuade a woman to do whatever it was he desired of her.

"Tidy yourself if you must," he said amiably, but he gave her no chance to move towards a looking glass, slipping his arms hard about her waist and drawing her amorously in to him. "If you went among those girls in sackcloth and ashes not one could hold a candle to your beauty."

"I have no comb with me—" she began.

Near at hand a pair of double doors opened. A buzz of chatter was suddenly hushed. Within the circle of Gregory's arms Juliette saw the five members of Venetia's morning party staring at them from the doorway, faces framed in a multicolored selection of bonnets, ribbon- and feather-trimmed.

"What's the matter?" Venetia's voice asked from within the room. "Why are you all struck dumb?"

One of the girls turned and answered in a whisper behind her hand, but the sibilant sound penetrated in the silence. "It's Gregory. He's cuddling her—that French girl you told us about. At this hour of the day!"

All but one of the girls tittered. The exception, a serene-faced girl with wide, dark eyes under fine brows, her complexion creamy, her pink mouth gentle, came forward, extending both her hands towards Juliette, whom Gregory had released without haste, more amused than annoyed at the interruption.

"I've been looking forward to meeting you, Mademoiselle Delahousse," the girl said warmly in a singularly sweet voice. "I'm Lucy Rose-Marshall."

Juliette caught her breath unconsciously. This was Elizabeth's sister! "I use only the English prefix to my name now I'm in England," she replied, "but do call me Juliette." She felt her hands gripped with a quick pressure that denoted welcome—and reassurance?

"How kind of you. I hope we are going to be good friends." She let go of Juliette's hands only to slip an arm through hers. "Come and meet everyone else." She cast an inquiring look at Gregory. "Unless the only gentleman present prefers to do the honors?"

He gave her a little bow. "You would do it more charmingly, my dear Lucy."

The flicker of her lashes showed she was well used to his compliments and set no high store on them. Quietly she introduced Juliette to the girls. Jane Durward. Sarah Brymble-Keane. Charlotte Crowhurst. Mary Whitmore. Juliette saw curiosity and inquisitiveness in their eyes, but no maliciousness. It had obviously impressed them that Lucy had made overtures of friendship to the newcomer, and this more than outweighed anything against her that Venetia might have said. Yet there was an inevitable undercurrent of jealousy, too. Apart from Blake Lockington, who everybody knew would remain a bachelor now that Elizabeth had been taken from him, Gregory was one of the county's most eligible bachelors, and to lose him to a girl whom nobody had clapped eyes on before—and a Frenchwoman by birth at that!—was the rubbing of salt in the wound.

The four girls had formed themselves into a semicircle just inside the doorway during the presentation of the newcomer, almost without being aware of it, and now, behind them in the room, Venetia spoke again, but sharply and rudely.

"You said you were all leaving. Either come back into the room or go. Nobody has given a thought to the fact that I happen to be in a draught."

The girls exchanged glances, but turned contritely, parting as they did so, one going forward and the others stepping aside. Juliette, still with Lucy, saw Venetia lying against cushions on a chaise longue and was filled with admiration at her appearance. Her glorious, burnished hair, brushed and topknotted like coiled satin, was set off by the emerald green of her morning gown, which was fashionably elegant, the sleeves puffed at the top, but continuing tight down the rest of the arm, the creamy lace at the cuffs matching the shawl that was draped with careful ease over one shoulder. But her face, clamped into an ugly scowl, ruined the picture she presented.

"Good day to you, Venetia," Juliette said.

Now it was Gregory who came across to tuck her arm in his, drawing her away from Lucy and well into the room. "You have met my betrothed, I hear."

Venetia went pale, nervously clutching at the shawl, and she answered him harshly. "She's told you!"

Juliette understood instantly that Venetia believed she had recounted to Gregory a description of that attempt to walk, and she spoke quickly before he could reply. "I explained that we met for a matter of minutes yesterday evening. I was quick to take my leave, but everything was a little bewildering for me. I even lost my way afterwards! I found myself in the North Octagon Room."

Venetia flashed her a glance that showed a boiling fury at being compelled to be under an obligation to her, even though it meant the keeping of her secret. "So Blake informed me," she said through clenched teeth.

Then the girls made their farewells again to Venetia, who suffered herself to be kissed on the cheek by each of them, and chattering together they left the room.

Only Lucy took longer to leave, having a final word with her.

"I hope we haven't tired you. We were a noisy gathering."

"Not at all. Come again soon, Lucy."

"I will."

Juliette withdrew outside the door, but Gregory waited to fall into step at Lucy's side as they emerged from the room. "I'll see you to your carriage." He held out a hand to Juliette. "Come with me to wave your new acquaintances on their way."

"Yes, please, do," Lucy endorsed. On their way down the grand staircase she said, "I've left an invitation for you both as well as one each for Blake and Venetia, although she's certain to refuse, no matter how hard I try to persuade her otherwise. Alex is giving a ball for me. You must promise that you'll be there."

"A ball! How delightful!" Juliette said. But Blake would be there. Looking as he did on the night she first saw him. Somehow she must get used to seeing him constantly, even though it caused her such joy and anguish.

"You're giving me my first opportunity to show Juliette off to the county," Gregory declared.

Lucy smiled. "Every man present will envy you. Make sure that no one among them spirits her away from you."

"Let anyone dare to try!" he laughed.

"With your reputation for pistols and swords I think you need have no fear on that score."

They reached the steps. Juliette remained at the head of them while Gregory went down to hand Lucy into the carriage. She waved in answer to the flutter of gloved hands as the carriage drew away. Then, seeing Gregory come towards the steps again, she turned to go indoors and came face to face with Blake.

For her it was an unnerving moment. With her thoughts being full of him she was afraid she had given herself away. She had looked straight into his eyes as he had looked down into hers, and the throb of excitement deep in the pit of her stomach leapt as it always did at the sight of him, shooting its fireworks through her veins, making her heart pound.

"You're making friends already, I see," he said, nodding with a smile in the direction of the departing carriage.

"I found Lucy Rose-Marshall most agreeable," she replied.

"She is a very fine person. Her late sister was the same."

"I can believe that."

"But I digress. How are you today? You had two alarming experiences within hours of arriving at West Thorpeby Hall."

She thought of the spyglass turned on her at the castle ruins and, although not frightening, it was a third experience to cause her some unease. "I have suffered no ill effects," she assured him.

"What of your maid?"

She thought it considerate of him to inquire. The head of a great household did not normally concern himself with the well-being of underlings. "Quite recovered, except for her bruised forehead. However, she is set on returning to London."

Gregory had joined them. "Who's set on going back to London?" he inquired jovially.

Blake gave her no time to answer and gave his brother a hard glance. "If Juliette will be good enough to excuse us we'll go to my study. A letter has just been delivered by post to me from that same city. There is something we have to discuss."

Gregory's expression became truculent and he took up a stubborn stance, shoving his hands deep into his pockets. "No more discussions! I had more than enough talk to fill my head when I told you this morning that I had lost Ravensworth Hall."

"I consider this matter to be a deal more serious even than that. Had you explained why you surrendered the key to the bailiff without waiting a little longer for the money to come through, I should have been prepared for the lawyer's extraordinary statement now received!"

Juliette, aware that a quarrel was brewing, made to

retreat, but Gregory caught her arm above the elbow and jerked her to his side. "Juliette knows my financial straits—and she knows also that it's only a temporary state of affairs."

"I hope she shares your eternal optimism!" Blake was heated, but he did not shout. "Now let us go into my study. This is no place to discuss private matters."

"Very well." Sullenly Gregory acquiesced. Juliette, seeing them move shoulder to shoulder across the hall together, thought what a handsome pair they were, and yet, in the way they walked the difference in their characters was revealed, Blake's stride being purposeful, Gregory's more buoyant, but both stepping with that arrogance inherent in them from the long line of their ancestry that had ruled these wide acres of wind-blown Norfolk since the time of William the Conqueror. On this line of thought she raised her eyes to look at the portraits of some of their distinguished forebears, which hung on the wall above the staircase. As she did so there was the faintest change between light and shade across the glaze of the one nearest the head of the stairs. Somebody—or something—had moved to avoid detection.

Without hesitation she gathered up her skirts and ran up the staircase to investigate. On the landing she looked to the right and to the left, but the area was deserted as were the corridors that branched away from it. She was certain she had not been mistaken.

"Whoever you are, I swear to bring you into the open before long," she said aloud, knowing her quiet but clear tones would reach a wide radius in that silent place. Then she caught her breath, realizing she had thrown down the gauntlet to who knew what evil force contained in West Thorpeby Hall!

Chapter Six

Juliette turned from the window when the third girl sent by the housekeeper entered the room. Cobbett had risen from her bed with alacrity when she had heard that not only was she about to be replaced without delay, but that a stagecoach for London passed through East Thorpeby during the afternoon. She had departed with her belongings in an equipage from the house in haste. Juliette had been quite thankful to see her go, and was determined that her next maid should not have an endlessly clacking tongue. Both the girls she had already interviewed had been excellent applicants, but she felt duty-bound to give the third one a hearing. She sat down on the sofa and the girl stood before her.

"What is your name?" she asked.

"Sorrel Askeby, ma'am."

"That's a very pretty name and a most unusual one," Juliette remarked, thinking that the girl was unusual, too. Had the voice not been unmistakably of Norfolk origin she would have been inclined to believe the girl had been transplanted—like herself—from some foreign shore. Not pretty. Not beautiful. Almost ugly with those tip-tilted elfin eyes, dark olive skin, and sharp bones. Her hair, judging from her brows, could be black, but it was completely hidden under the white cap.

"My Pa was a wandering man who could never abide a roof over his head and preferred a hedgerow. He chose my name before he left my Ma to fend for herself—with me only six days old."

A frank admission, but said with a certain pride, implying that she and her mother had managed quite well without him. It suggested to Juliette that this girl would be capable at all she turned her hands to, and there was an intelligent look about her that surpassed the two previous girls.

"What is your present post in the house?"

"I'm the head linen-maid. I have been for the past three months, ever since Miss Venetia decided she could no longer do with me about her. Nobody can stitch better than me."

Again that frank declaration of fact with no intention of conceit. "Did your mother teach you to sew?"

"No, it was my Grandma. My Ma could dig and hoe and plant and sow on the strip of land that was ours, taking help from nobody, but her hands were too rough and gnarled to use a needle well. She died when she was thirty, and she looked older than my Grandma did when she passed on."

"What age were you when you went into service?"

"Thirteen. I soon made up my mind to be a lady's maid, and I worked my way up to it."

Juliette could imagine the determination that had carried through that ambition. "How old are you now?"

"Nineteen."

"What experience have you had as a lady's maid?"

"I was with Miss Venetia for six days—"

"Six days!"

"Nothing I did pleased her." Bluntly and without evasion. "Before that I was at Hetherham House, home of the Rose-Marshalls. That's where I was trained."

"Were you with Miss Elizabeth or Miss Lucy?"

"Neither, ma'am. There was a third sister, who married and went to India. She would have taken me with her, but I didn't want to go. That's when I came to West Thorpeby Hall, just over three months ago."

"Did you see much of Miss Elizabeth while you were at her home?"

"Yes, ma'am. She used to think I was better at dressing hair than her own lady's maid, and I did it for her sometimes when she was going somewhere really special. I dressed it for her on the evening she was killed."

Juliette was moved by this information that in a way Sorrel Askeby was the last person to be in close contact with Elizabeth, and because of it she felt herself persuaded to make this girl her choice. What was more, there was a certain aloofness about the girl which made her feel she would keep her distance and take no advantage, perhaps even the reverse, avoiding anything that remotely amounted to a favor.

"Mrs. Harman has already recommended you to me, and you may start at once. My own maid has left and is on her way back to London."

"Yes, ma'am." No word of thanks, no sign of gratitude. Only a thin compression of the lips that showed satisfaction. Whence did the girl get her stiff-necked pride? From some Romany streak inherited from her wayward father? Or was it more likely that it came from her peasant mother, who had rooted out a living on some small, arable patch, abhorring charity? Either way it did not matter. What was important was that perhaps sometimes Sorrel Askeby might talk about Elizabeth, and she did want to know more about the girl Blake had loved. Through knowing more about Elizabeth she might come to learn more about Blake himself.

"I shall call you by your Christian name, Sorrel. It makes me think of the English countryside."

"As you wish, ma'am."

"I've been told that there are to be guests for dinner this evening. I'll wear the powder-blue velvet."

"It shall be ready, ma'am."

The interview was over, and Sorrel departed to tell Mrs. Harman of her promotion. Juliette, having decided she would spend the afternoon exploring the house on her own and locate that part of it from which she had been spied upon, went to the head of the grand staircase and stood there for a moment, trying to gain a full sense of direction. Blake, sighting her from the hall, came to the foot of the flight and set one foot on the last tread. He was dressed for riding.

"What are you about?" he inquired with interest.

She smiled down at him. "I'm trying to get my bearings. I don't want to get lost again."

He came up the stairs towards her, tucking his riding crop under his arm. "I'll take you round the house," he announced chivalrously. "I promised I would."

Here she was getting involved with him again! "No, please. I can see you're about to go out. Don't let me hinder you."

"I'd be a poor host if I let my future sister-in-law wander about until she ended up in the attics or the old dungeons," he said, the little creases showing on either side of his mouth as he smiled.

She relaxed with a little laugh. It would be all right. All the time he reminded her, however casually, that she was his brother's future wife she could keep her head and it would be all right. "The dungeons sound as grim as the North Octagon Room!"

"Worse! They're dank and even darker."

"I don't think I care to see them."

"Never fear! They've been locked up for many years. Nobody ever goes down there. They're part of the house's old foundations." He drew off his gloves and put them with his crop on a side table. "We'll start with the East Octagon Room and go on from there."

Although it was windowless, as all four of the octagonal rooms were, with the same encircling passageway and the inset door to the dome above, the East Octagon Room created no feeling of claustrophobia and was not sinister in any way. As he had said to her previously, it was a room of great beauty. It glowed with the rising sun. The artist had captured the first pale tints of dawn, which increased with bold brushstrokes to a crescendo of light. The murals around the walls showed the beginning of earth's life again as well as the birth of a new day. There was the sowing of the land, new lambs gamboling, and banks full of spring flowers; in others an orchard shimmered with blossom, and the first green shoots of the corn showed. All of them were peopled with children and farmworkers and ladies and gentlemen in quaint Tudor clothing, on horseback and in carriages. Excitedly she located West Thorpeby Hall.

"There's your house!" she exclaimed merrily.

He bent his head close to hers. "That's right. See the castle ruins over there by the trees?"

She moved away from him, too conscious of his nearness, every nerve in her body vibrating, and spun round in the middle of the room. "I suppose it's the lack of exposure to daylight which has preserved the richness of color in these rooms." She looked up at the heavy iron candleholder. "The artist must have had more candlelight than that corona could have provided to do such intricate work."

"I'm sure he did, but even then it must have been a strain on his eyes to paint without daylight."

"Does anyone know the artist's name?"

"Unfortunately it was never recorded. All we know is that the work was carried out by the orders of a certain Thomas Lockington who lived here at that time."

She looked over her shoulder at him. "Isabelle's husband?"

He stared at her for a few moments. "Who has told you the tale? Gregory?"

It struck her that both brothers, hearing that she knew the tale, had immediately suspected the other of telling it to her and had reacted with a flash of displeasure. Each in his own way had wanted to protect her from it. She recalled the glances they had exchanged the previous night when Cobbett had declared she had seen the ghost. The legend was as real to them as if it had all happened yesterday—and Isabelle in her watery guise a vivid part of their background and their lives.

"No, I heard it from another source," she said, not elaborating.

"You must not let your mind dwell on the miseries of that tale," he insisted. "This house has known much joy in its time as well as sorrow. There have been many good marriages, many happy brides who have found love and happiness at West Thorpeby Hall —as I trust you will as wife to Gregory."

She hardly knew how to answer him, her voice strangled in her throat, but she managed it somehow. "None of us knows what the future will bring, but to find love in marriage is surely a blessing surpassing all else."

From the East Octagon Room they went into the adjoining wing and she saw drawing rooms and salons that presented grand views from the windows, the color and magnificence of the furnishings a rivaling delight to the eye. The South and West Octagon Rooms when they reached them were no less glorious than the one she had already seen that afternoon. The South Octagon Room carried the theme of full summer with the ceiling an azure blue with small, white puffball clouds and the pastoral scenes captured in the murals showed stretches of golden corn, buttercup-spattered meadows, and cows grazing. In the West Octagon Room the painted setting sun filled it with a red-gold splendor that seemed to reflect from the walls. Here was harvest time with much of the corn already gathered in and women gleaning in the fields. Where autumn shaded the woodland a hunt was in full gallop and on West Thorpeby Hall the brilliance of the sun's fading rays touched the mullioned windows as much as she had seen the light reflected when she had stood on the castle ruins. She gave a backward glance as they passed through the passageway that enclosed the room.

"What are the domes above the octagonal rooms used for?" she inquired.

"From them one of my ancestors, who was an astronomer, used to view the stars, but that was a long time ago. All four doors up into the domes are kept locked to keep children who sometimes come to the house from going up there. That was a precaution taken years ago by my father when Gregory and I were boys—we had risked breaking our necks by climbing up on the roof of the clock cupola for a dare."

"It sounds as though you were an adventurous pair!" she exclaimed, amused.

His eyes danced. "What one of us didn't think of, the other did. No wonder my father was prematurely gray! That's when we first became known throughout the county as 'those wild Lockington boys.' "

"So the room above the North Octagon Room has been locked up ever since?"

"Yes." He could tell there was something else she wanted to ask him.

"I've been thinking about the hand showing above the water in the winter mural. Surely it is Isabelle's?"

"It is said to be hers."

"A macabre detail indeed." She gave a shiver.

"I agree."

They continued the tour of the house, but spoke no more about the gruesome North Octagon Room. When they came to the part of the house from which she had been spied upon, Juliette noted with interest that it was no more than a stretch of corridor along which anyone could have paused to set a spyglass on her. Caroline's rooms were near at hand and not far distant was Venetia's own suite. Had one of the girls at the chocolate party slipped out to eye her? Or had two or three come, handing the spyglass on to each other? At least she could be sure that Lucy would not have been among their number.

A few yards farther on Blake showed her into the Music Room. Her interest was caught by a prettily ornamented harpsichord, and after trying a few notes and finding it perfectly in tune she sat down and played him a merry little piece. He leaned against the harpsichord and watched her, chuckling with her at its impish rhythm. He applauded when she finished the piece and let her hands fall into her lap.

"Well done! Promise you'll play for us after dinner this evening. There's a fine pianoforte in the White Drawing Room."

"Have I seen that room yet?" She put her head on one side inquiringly.

"Not yet. It's one of those on the ground floor. Well? Will you play? I'd like to hear that tune again."

"I'll play," she promised.

"What may I have for an encore now?"

She gave him a twinkling glance and commenced a piece of appalling solemnity to tease him, not expecting him to halt her as he did, his hands coming down on both of hers. His physical touch, cool, firm, capturing her fingers so unaware, made her start and look at him as though lost beyond her depth, the discord created by the flattened notes seeming to ring in her ears.

"Nothing sad from you!" he said huskily. "Not from you!"

Instantly she realized the terrible mistake she had made. Unwittingly, reminding him of Elizabeth as she did, she had probed his innermost sorrow. He released her hands and she bent her head, biting her lip, and her fingers leapt into a lilting tune, but nervousness prevented her touch from being as light as before and although she played adequately she knew it was not as it should have been. This time he did not lean against the instrument to watch her, but moved to stand a little to the side of the stool and whether he looked at her or away she could not tell.

He did not applaud again when she came to the end of the piece, but then their mood was not as gaily carefree as it had been before, although he thanked her and asked her who the composer was and where she had learned to play so well. Still discussing music, they kept to the topic throughout the rooms that remained for her to see, except when she commented on anything that caught her eye and he took pains to explain whatever was of interest about it. In the library, after he had shown her how the books were listed and catalogued in order that she might find whatever she wanted at any time, he faced her with a look that showed his pride in all she had seen.

"West Thorpeby Hall has now made itself known to you," he said, lifting his hands from his sides and spreading them wide to indicate the surroundings, and the rest of the house beyond.

"I'll not be able to lose my way again," she answered, a smile touching her lips. "Thanks to you I have the layout of the house firmly fixed in my mind."

He immediately smiled back at her. "Then no afternoon could have been better spent."

"I've delayed your ride by far too long."

"It's of no importance and can wait until tomorrow. I had intended to ride out and view some of the digging being done on a new dike." He glanced at the library clock, frowned in disbelief, and then took from his waistcoat pocket his gold watch, which he snapped open to check the time. "It's almost five o'clock! I suggest we join Venetia for afternoon tea."

Juliette shook her head firmly. "Not today. I invaded her morning party through Gregory's wish that I should meet those gathered there. I mustn't press my company on her again so soon. If I'm to do anything at all to help her—and I pray that I'll be able to!—I must give her time to forgive me for my earlier intrusion on her private struggle to walk. At least she learned today that I kept what I saw to myself and that I'm not given to gossip." Her voice took on an insistent note. "But don't let me keep you from her. We'll meet again at dinner." She set a hand on one of the library shelves by which they were standing. "I'm going to browse through some of the books here. This is one part of the house where I can find my own path through all it contains."

After he had gone she did take a book of prints down from the shelves and sat with it in a chair, intending to look through it, but instead she leaned back, leaving it open on her lap, and gazed unseeingly before her. She was remembering the touch of his hands on hers, the bite of his great ruby ring as it bit into her flesh in his lack of awareness at the amount of pressure he exerted. Such a longing had possessed her to feel those same hands on her body that a tremor had passed through her, setting up such an ache in her breasts that she could feel it still. In a way she could be considered as wanton as Isabelle, for she was exultant and shameless in that yearning. The only difference was that Isabelle had taken what she wanted from life, not caring whom she hurt and trampled upon. With herself there could be no taking or giving, no betrayal of a match that would be forever loveless.

When Juliette eventually left the library and went upstairs she found Sorrel waiting to help her change out of her dayclothes. Across a chair lay fresh underwear. The powder-blue velvet gown had been skillfully steamed to bring up the pile, and for her hair a small bunch of newly-gathered spring violets, still damp from the undergrowth, was being kept fresh in a glass on the toilet table. Beside them was a heap of carefully selected ribbons shading from the hue of the violets to the color of her gown, which were to be plaited to adorn her tresses and set off the tiny blossoms. Silken shoes stood ready with the cross-tie straps newly ironed, and everything from a lace-trimmed handkerchief to a small pocket looking glass had been placed ready in a beaded evening reticule.

When she went downstairs again, arrayed in her finery, Juliette felt she had found a "treasure," which was the term she had always heard used to describe that rare being, the loyal and dedicated servant, but how she would ever reward such service she had no idea. Her appreciation of the violets, which must have meant careful searching, perhaps for an hour or more, had been treated with complete indifference, and her praise in the manner in which everything had been made ready greeted by a stare that showed the girl took high standards of work as a matter of course and could have done it no other way.

Juliette was conscious of making an entrance when she came in the salon where Blake and his guests were gathered. Heads turned and fans were stilled. Gregory, swinging round from chatting to the prettiest woman present, grinned and raised his eyebrows admiringly.

"Our guest of honor," Blake said in greeting to her, reaching her first. Gregory took his place at her side as Blake conducted her round the room, making the presentations. All there were polite and gracious to her, but that was as far as it went. She did not expect more, realizing that these people, like Caroline, who had given her a wintry smile for the sake of appearances, thought of her yet as being more French than English. It would take time for her to become established in the community. During the presentations they came to Lucy and her brother, Blake's old friend, Sir Alex Rose-Marshall, a bluff, portly young man with a big, square face much weathered by the Norfolk sun and wind. He greeted her with an appreciative twinkle and a broad smile.

"I'm greatly privileged. Your servant for all time, ma'am."

She liked him immediately, deciding he was as good-hearted as his sister, who greeted her warmly, saying that she was looking forward to a talk with her later. To Juliette her friendliness shone out like a sun's ray.

Although the entrance Juliette had made into that room had been eye-catching, it paled before that made a little later by Venetia, who had waited until she could be sure that she would be the last to make an appearance before coming downstairs. It would have done credit to Queen Charlotte herself.

The double doors, which had been closed after Juliette's entrance, were suddenly opened wide by the two footmen in attendance, and two more stood revealed, each standing with a hand on the back of the chair in which Venetia was sitting. It was no ordinary elbow chair that had been set on low wheels, but a carved and silvered dragon of a chair, more ornate than anything that might grace the Regent's Royal Pavilion at Brighton, which gloried in Chinese art. The arms of it were snarling, fire-spitting monsters with jeweled eyes, the back formed by their spreading wings, and her feet rested on their coiled and spike-ended tails. She herself was in white, the stark simplicity of the classical gown in marked contrast to the flamboyant setting of the chair, her hair dressed in curls, but unadorned, the stole looped over her arms of the same silk as her gown and trimmed with a silver fringe.

As the footmen pushed the chair forward Blake went to take it from them, first leaning towards her to pay some compliment that set her sparkling at him, and he propelled her the rest of the way into the room. She greeted everyone effusively and was immediately surrounded. Only Juliette was ignored by her and found herself left with Gregory, who had turned his back on Venetia either by accident or design, on the outskirts of those who had clustered forward. There were several who had made no move to join the throng, and they continued conversing with each other or with Juliette and Gregory, but the subject of the magnificent chair was on everyone's lips.

"Blake sent to China for it," Gregory said with faint contempt in reply to someone's query as to where such a rare chair was to be found. "Venetia's extravagant tastes could beggar my unfortunate brother in the end."

There was an uncomfortable silence among those listening to him, and Juliette could tell that it was passing through all their minds that Blake, since he was responsible for the girl becoming immobile in the first place, was surely obliged to do anything in his power to make up for it, even if it did set him back a few thousand guineas now and again.

For the first time Juliette realized that Gregory did not like Venetia, although the girl had greeted him even more extravagantly than she had done everyone else. It also came back to her that Gregory had exchanged no direct word with Venetia that morning, and it now seemed possible that his outrage at the apparent slight against herself, his betrothed, had had its roots in his personal dislike of Blake's ward, which made him see offense in all she did. Was jealousy partly the cause? Did he begrudge her being showered with gifts paid for out of the family fortunes when he, the younger son, had empty pockets, no matter that he had no one but himself to blame for his impoverished state?

Venetia, having made herself the center of attraction, proceeded to hold the floor for the rest of the evening. At the long table her conversation and witty repartee sent ripples of modulated laughter in both directions. Gregory never so much as glanced in her direction, but he shared his attention between Juliette, who was seated beside him, and the pretty woman with whom he had been talking earlier, who sat almost opposite him. Twice Juliette noticed him raise his glass and drink to her, almost in invitation, but no doubt there were other times as well that she did not see, when the gentleman on her other side was engaging her in conversation. Unbidden, Nicolaus came into her mind. He, like Gregory, had known how to charm women with looks that made them feel they alone were desirable above all others, they alone more beautiful, more tempting. She had not loved Nicolaus, but he had scarred her. Like a moth drawn to a flame she had been singed. Did moth wings ever heal?

When the ladies withdrew to the White Drawing Room, leaving the gentlemen to their port, Lucy invited Juliette to sit with her and they were joined by several others. With the gentlemen absent it was noticeable that Venetia received less attention than before, but she still dominated the company with her presence. Later, when the gentlemen had rejoined them and tea was being served, Blake stood with a cup and saucer in his hand and bent his tall head the better to catch what Lucy had just said to him in the buzz of conversation.

"The Chinese chair? You heard nothing about it? Venetia can certainly keep a secret. It was delivered at least a month ago, but she wanted to surprise everyone with it on a special occasion, such as this."

Beside Juliette a certain Mrs. Campbell, her round face flushed either with heat or wine to a bright pinkness, spoke to her behind her fan. "The minx made sure of eclipsing *you,* my dear. This should have been *your* evening."

It was a chance remark, but it made Juliette see that her first unfortunate encounter with Venetia could have made little difference to their relationship, for the girl had made up her mind long since to put her in her place and make sure she stayed there.

Before the evening came to a close, Juliette, to please Blake more than anyone else, played several pieces on the pianoforte and was warmly applauded. But it was Venetia's achievement afterwards that must have remained uppermost in everyone's mind when the company dispersed and went home, for she recited with a wealth of expression, which showed she would have made an excellent actress, a most moving poem about a girl waiting in vain for her sweetheart's return. Only in the last few lines of the final verse was it revealed that he had given his life for his country, leading a cavalry charge against Napoleon's forces. The patriotic fervor of it brought thunderous applause, except from the two Lockington brothers; Blake's face went taut, the bones showing through his skin, at his ward's tactless choice of poem, which could only cause embarrassment to the newcomer in their midst, and Gregory showed real anger, glowering at Venetia as if it was all he could do to refrain from striding across and hitting her. Lucy's hands also remained without movement out of deference to Juliette's finer feelings until she saw she was clapping with the rest.

"You're applauding?" she gasped.

Juliette raised an eyebrow at her. "No slant was cast against French honor, and the poem was well-delivered and well-acted. I would consider myself meanminded not to acknowledge talent when it is presented with such gusto."

Lucy laughed and broke into applause, too. Juliette felt Mrs. Campbell's folded fan prodding her in the ribs. "Well done, my dear. That's taken the sting out of the recitationist's tail! She wanted to see you reduced to discomfiture."

Venetia, obviously expecting recriminations for her behavior, made a retreat through a side door in the room, being pushed away by a footman who had answered her signal from his post at the double doors when the guests began to move through them, making their departure. Juliette saw her go as she and Gregory exchanged farewells with the guests, but not until the room was emptied, Blake himself seeing everyone off, was her absence obvious.

"She did as well to sneak away!" Gregory stormed. "Hell's devilment! I could throttle her!"

"No harm was done," Juliette said placatingly.

"It's filthy propaganda!" he exclaimed, refusing to listen. "Those poems are churned out by the hundreds for foolish creatures like Venetia to spout out at gatherings and inflame misguided patriotism."

She stared at him, amazed that he should have allowed himself to become so upset. That he should be dedicated wholly to the cause of peace would have made her feel a respect for him that had been lacking before, except that there was something curiously fanatical in his declaration, which sounded too violent to be in harmony with the high principle involved.

"I'm not sure I understand you," she said uncertainly.

Again he did not appear in his temper to be aware of what she had said, but only that she had spoken. He took hold of her by the shoulders, almost shaking her in his forceful agitation. "We'll put an end to it, you and I! Nobody shall stop us!"

So brutally did he kiss her then that she felt suffocated, her lips wrenched open, his mouth seeming to cover half her face. Out of wrath against others had his lust flared for her, and when he let her draw breath it was only to keep her captive in his arms and make a request to her that she was at a loss to know how to answer.

"Let's get married soon! Next week. Next month, if you must. But don't make me wait until the summer is almost over!" He put trembling fingertips against her throat and trailed them down to the cleavage of her breasts revealed by the lowcut scoop of her bodice, ignoring her attempt to draw back from him, his arm strong about her waist, and his voice dropped a note, becoming tender and persuasive, a look of such ardency glowing in his eyes that she could see how easily he could coax any woman to his will. Any woman not in love with another man. Any woman but her. "We're bound to each other by more than a contract to marry," he urged. "We share the same views, the same ideals, the same love for France." His touch became bolder and more explanatory as if of its own volition, his gaze following. "I'd marry you this night if a priest could be roused from his slumbers and fetched to us."

Blake's voice spoke levelly from the doorway. "Your ardor is not to be wondered at, but a betrothment period of three months was agreed upon and cannot be altered."

Juliette did not look towards him, standing still and pensive, but Gregory, his good humor quite restored, turned languidly, still keeping an arm about her waist. "On the contrary. If both parties are willing, there's no need to keep to the time stipulated."

Blake came to stand within a few feet of them, and he addressed her in a peremptory manner. "Are you willing, Juliette?"

In her heart she was anything but willing, yet the thought came that since she had to build a life with Gregory it would be fairer to him and even to herself to cut short the intervening time and make an end to her helpless longing for Blake in total commitment to their marriage. She saw it as the only way open to her.

She tilted her chin a little higher, and now she did turn to face Blake, answering him clearly. "I see no reason to wait longer than necessary. Six weeks should be time enough for the invitations to be sent out and all preparations made."

He looked askance at her through strong-lashed lids brought close together, the glint in his eyes hard and disconcerting, almost as if he thought to challenge her on the wisdom of the decision she had made, but he gave a nod. "So be it."

Gregory was jubilant. He had champagne brought in, and watching him pour it she was reminded of the evening when she and Blake had drunk champagne together on the occasion of their first meeting. She took the tall, thin glass that Gregory handed to her and watched Blake take his.

"To our marriage!" Gregory declared, raising his glass to her.

Blake chose his own toast. "To your happiness, Juliette!" He tossed back the champagne without taking the glass from his lips and with a sweep of his arm he hurled it into the embers of the fire where it shattered into a shower of crystal shards. Then he went from the room without a backward glance.

Juliette watched him go and then became aware that Gregory's gaze was fixed on her. "You haven't touched your champagne in the toast I gave you," he said, an edge to his voice.

With a quake of misgiving she noticed that there

was a glittering look that came perilously close to suspicion in his eyes, and with it a dangerous set to his mouth that boded ill for Blake or for anyone else who might happen to divert her wholehearted attention at a serious level, however innocently, from him!

Chapter Seven

In the morning light Juliette did not regret the decision she had made, but it lay heavy upon her. Sitting on the stool by the toilet table, one foot extended as Sorrel knelt, crisscrossing her shoe ribbons to tie them in a bow above the ankle, she found she had to force herself to tell her maid the news that had to be told. Last night, the hour being late, she had spoken little as Sorrel had helped her to bed and folded and hung away her evening clothes, and she had been thankful not to have the garrulous Cobbett about her any longer.

"My wedding day has been brought forward," she said.

The proud head in the frilled, white mobcap did not lift, the quick fingers busy with their task. "So I heard below stairs this morning, ma'am."

That eternal grapevine, which spread information from servant to servant and to the lower quarters of one great house and then another, had been more than active. She must write to Aunt Phoebe this very morning or else, distant as London was from West Thorpeby Hall, there was always the possibility that she might hear the news from another source of the change in the marriage date.

She spent the best part of the morning at the bureau in her salon, writing long letters to her aunt and to an old convent friend who was married and lived in Provence. A note of acceptance to Lucy's ball was also penned, and when she had dashed sand on it to dry the ink and had sealed it with a blob of sealing wax she felt well pleased with all she had done.

With a little time to spare before luncheon she decided to go along to the North Octagon Room and take another look at the murals in the light of all she had learned of Isabelle and her dreadful hauntings. To get to that part of the house she had to pass the doors leading into Venetia's suite, which was how she had come to end up in the North Octagon Room after turning in the wrong direction on her first evening in the house when she had run from the abuse the girl had shrieked at her.

As she drew near she saw that the doors stood open to the suite, the sunshine from its windows making a golden patch across the narrow carpet that stretched the length of the corridor ahead of her, bringing to life the deep colors of its Aubusson splendor. It was then that she paused, not with any reluctance to pass those open doors, but because the eerie feeling possessed her again of being watched by hostile, unseen eyes. She glanced about her, first back the way she had come and then ahead to the shadowed end of the long corridor where it branched in two directions, but unlike the moment when she had seen the reflected shine of the spyglass there was nothing to support her notion. Deciding that her imagination must be playing her tricks she continued along the corridor. When she drew level with the open doors she kept her eyes fixed ahead, but from the chaise longue in the salon within, Venetia sighted her.

"Where are you going?" she asked imperiously.

Juliette came to a halt and faced her. "I'm still sight-seeing in this magnificent house," she said, not intending to divulge her reason for it.

"Didn't you see enough yesterday?" Venetia retorted sharply.

Juliette guessed that jealousy spiked the question; Blake would have chatted about their tour of the house over tea with his ward. "We didn't visit the North Octagon Room. I only saw it briefly on my first evening here when I lost my way."

"Wasn't that enough for you? Isabelle scared you, didn't she?"

Juliette took a few slow steps into the room, intrigued that Venetia should have guessed the true reason for her scream and her sudden terror. "I hadn't heard about her then, but there was an eerie atmosphere that I found oppressive and extremely frightening."

"Nothing more?"

"A little sound that could have been—anything."

Venetia waved a hand towards a chair in invitation. "If it was Isabelle there's trouble stirring. She always makes herself known before any kind of catastrophe since Thomas Lockington called her back to West Thorpeby Hall on his deathbed. Doesn't that make you even more afraid?"

Juliette had seated herself, inwardly amazed that Venetia was prepared to talk to her. She supposed she had caught the girl in a mood of loneliness and boredom when any diversion was welcome. No doubt a sense of anticlimax had settled in after the dramatic impact she had made upon the assemblage the previous evening. Juliette decided that a unique opportunity had been put into her hands and if she used it wisely she might be able to make the first move towards helping Venetia to overcome that barrier which prevented her walking again. She had given Venetia's condition a deal of thought and had come to the conclusion that, since the doctors' reassurance that there was nothing physically wrong with her back or her limbs had failed to have any effect on Venetia, to say nothing of the kindly coaxing and persuasion the girl must have received from Blake and Lucy and probably from others equally concerned for her, some totally different approach must be used. Venetia had questioned her about being afraid, but what secret fear kept Venetia bound to a chair or chaise longue? Whatever it was, it must be located and conquered.

"How long is it since Isabelle last made her presence known?" she asked.

"I should think that was obvious. The eve of the accident that resulted in Elizabeth's death and my being left in the state you see me in today."

"Who saw her?"

"Elizabeth saw her. Twice, as a matter of fact. And she wasn't the first to see Isabelle by any manner of means. There are records and old documents in the house that tell of sightings from time to time, usually resulting in death by violence. At times the house gets restless with her presence, and people get frightened to look over their shoulder."

She thought Venetia was watching her closely as she spoke. Was the girl trying to frighten her or had she some idea of the eerie feeling that persistently possessed her. "I understand there was a house party being held at the time of the accident."

Venetia nodded. "Elizabeth was staying here with Lucy and another sister, who has since married and gone abroad." Her lips parted maliciously. "Do you want to know which room Elizabeth occupied?"

It was not hard to guess. She knew now why Blake had had the suite redecorated and refurnished for her coming. Nothing that Elizabeth had touched or known or handled was to be contaminated by a stranger's intrusion. "No doubt it was mine."

"It was. That's where Elizabeth saw Isabelle. Nothing was said at the time, but after her death Lucy, who had shared the room with her, disclosed that Elizabeth had woken in the night screaming that Isabelle had held back the bed hangings and looked down at her. Lucy told her she had had a nightmare, but it took her a long time to quiet her sister. She went as far as searching the whole suite to show her nothing was there, but after we had all heard that account I can tell you that none doubted Isabelle had come to gloat as she always does over tragedy to come." Venetia smirked. "Your maid, Cobbett, departed in a hurry, didn't she? What disturbed her in that suite? Neither Blake nor Gregory has said, but Caroline and I have drawn our own conclusions. Doesn't it make you afraid that one night you may wake and look full upon Isabelle's drowned visage as Elizabeth did?"

"I'd not be telling the truth if I said that such a grisly possibility would leave me untouched. We can all be scared by the unknown, something beyond the powers of our comprehension. Fear is part of our defense against danger, but when it gets out of hand it can break down and play havoc with our emotions."

Venetia twisted her mouth contemptuously. "Mercy

me! What blue-stocking talk is this? I'm in no mood to be fatigued by such tedious intelligence."

"I learned much about the subject of fear from my father," Juliette explained. "Being a soldier he was always interested to find out what it was that made a brave man and what made a coward, and whether there was really any difference. He used to expound his ideas to me many a time when I was with him at home at Rouen on vacations from the convent, telling me how often in battle he had seen the roles reversed."

"Military talk for a young girl's ears! Did you not fall asleep with boredom?"

"I was never bored in my father's company. My only regret is that he was away at war so much and precious time was lost that can never be recaptured."

Venetia bristled. "Don't mention the Napoleonic wars to me!"

"As you wish. You did well enough with your reference to them in your poem yesterday evening."

For a few tense seconds there was silence. Venetia's nostrils quivered and her red lips compressed together to a whiteness. With the sunshine from the window filling her copper hair with a fiery brilliance she looked to Juliette much like a voluptuous and dangerous wildcat.

"Does nothing bring you down, Frenchwoman?" The words were spat at her.

"Not fear of anything you can say or do. But I put it to you that you spend every day and night being afraid."

Venetia's eyes widened incredulously and she gave an angry laugh. "Of what, pray?" she taunted.

"Only you know that. You are as paralyzed with fright as a soldier looking in a cannon's mouth. That's why you're in the state you are! You want to move, to run, to ride, and to dance again—your secret attempt to walk proved that—but you can't break through your own fear!"

"That's not true!" She thrashed against the cushions at her back and drummed her fists at her sides in

helpless fury. "I'm in pain whenever my feet are put
to the floor! You don't know how many attempts have
been made to make me walk. Some of the physicians
brought nurses with them and forced me to walk until
I fainted in my agony! I've had my legs encased in
irons and bandaged from ankle to thigh in an attempt
to strengthen them, and I suffered so much that in the
end Blake drove away my torturers and would let no
more near me."

"I'm sure you were in terrible pain at first. But that
was long ago. You can't be in pain any longer. You're
imagining it. Why? What is it that so fills you with
fear that you want to stay helpless for the rest of your
life?" Juliette gulped, knowing she was taking a chance.
"Is it that it's the only way to keep Blake attentive
when you know he'll never marry you?"

It was the final straw. Venetia's fury reached such a
crescendo that she hurled herself forward with a shriek
that was part temper, part hysteria. She put one foot
to the floor and an unmistakable, high-pitched note
of terrible pain eclipsed all else in her shrieking, and
she fell headlong, knocking against the chaise longue,
which swung away on its castors to crash against a
small table, bringing that to the floor in a smashing
of the porcelain group of figures that stood upon it.

The din, combined with Venetia's screaming tan-
tram, brought servants running from all directions.
Caroline, arriving breathless on the scene, threw up her
hands at the sight of two maids and a footman in the
act of lifting Venetia from the floor to place her on the
chaise longue again while Juliette sat, white-faced and
straight-backed, in a chair, making no attempt to help
in any way.

"What happened? What have you done? What have
you been saying to her?" she cried to Juliette. When
no answer was forthcoming she darted over to the
sobbing girl on the chaise longue, putting her arms
about her, and demanding an account of what had occurred from the servants.

"We don't know, Mrs. Hazlett," the footman replied. "We arrived to see Miss Venetia on the floor,
all that smashed over there——" he gestured toward the

table lying amid the scattered porcelain fragments "—
and Miss Delahousse sitting where you saw her."

Juliette had risen and was making for the door. Caroline, sharp-tongued and agitated, called out after her.
"Blake shall hear of this! Stay out of this wing in future. You've no right to be in this part of the house.
Or in any of it, if it comes to that! This is our home,
not yours, you intruder!"

The shrill, upbraiding voice followed her as Juliette
went back the way she had come, all thought of returning to the North Octagon Room driven from her
mind. She had failed! She had failed miserably! She
had thought that by bringing Venetia face to face with
the truth on that uprush of wrath, the girl would forget all else in the desire to attack her for her goading,
and those first few important steps across the floor
would have been taken. From that point there would
have been no looking back for Venetia. Having walked
once, the barrier would have been broken.

Juliette clenched her hands together and lifted them
in pressure against her lips. What folly had she committed? What untold harm had she done? What on
earth had made her try to put into practice her father's battlefield method when a second shock, such as
firing a pistol close to a man transfixed with fright,
could get him moving again? The principle had been
the same, but the results disastrous beyond all measure!

She went down to luncheon, not because she did not
think that every mouthful would choke her, but because she knew she must face Blake sooner or later
with what she had done and she had no wish to delay
or evade responsibility. But as it happened he was
out, Gregory as well, and she was informed that Mrs.
Hazlett's luncheon had been taken up to Miss Venetia's suite. Juliette, thankful not to have to sit at table,
fetched her bonnet, put on her coat, and went for a
long walk.

She reached the cliff tops, which were no great
height, but stood like bulwarks against the sea. A
flight of steps, cut in the side of a cliff face, showed
that when the tide turned there would be a strip of
sand in the cove that lay below. She sat for a while on

the top step, watching a schooner, its sails taut and
full-blown, dipping its way northwards in a flurry of
spray. Tomorrow she would take out her water color
box, her brushes, and her easel, and start to paint from
the wide selection of scenes that this part of Norfolk
presented to her, its choice of sea and landscapes, its
rising cliffs and its low-lying marshes, its never-ending
range of colors, wild as well as serene, all subject to
its capricious weather. And always the sea birds with
their hoarse and raucous cries, which she hoped to
catch in flight with the curve of her brush in such a
manner that those very sounds would seem to echo
from her painting.

The best of the afternoon had faded when she
reached the gates of West Thorpeby Hall again and the
spiritual balm and refreshment that she had gained
from communing with nature for the past quiet hours
went from her at the thought of the ordeal which must
lie ahead, but no sooner had she started up the drive
when the gallop of hooves overtaking her caused her
to draw to one side to let whoever it was ride by. But
it was Blake who approached in the saddle, and she
knew the moment of confession had come sooner than
she had anticipated.

His face was very closed and contained, deeply withdrawn from her, even though no word of what had
happened could have reached him yet, but when he
saw her troubled expression his own changed to one of
concern and quickly he dismounted, taking the bridle
into his hand. "What's the matter? What's wrong?"

She told him, exactly as it had happened, keeping
back only that last sentence that she had spoken to
Venetia. If his ward's passion was a secret and not
known to him, it was not for her to reveal it or to put
Venetia in the embarrassing position of having him
discover it through another's words.

Rubbing his chin thoughtfully, he started to lead the
horse slowly forward, she keeping to his pace. "Venetia actually took a step, did you say?" he questioned.

"No, not a step. She just put her foot on the floor,
but when her weight went forward on to it she collapsed and the pain was obvious. Even then I hoped

she might scramble up and come forward to strike me."
Her face held a wan look. "How odd that sounds."

"What had you said at the last?" He eyed her keenly.
"Come along. There must have been some final challenge to make her throw herself from the chaise longue
in that manner."

She spoke firmly. "I prefer not to say."

He showed no surprise. "I may not be as much in
the dark as you seem to think. I can guess more or
less the point from which you made that final, well-
meaning attack upon her emotions. You're extremely
observant. I should have thought it would have taken
longer for you to sum up the situation, if at all."

"I knew right from the start."

"A woman's intuition?"

"Some might call it that."

They reached the forecourt where a groom took the
horse from him and led it away. As he walked with
her up the steps he said, "Don't regret what you have
done. You did it with the best intentions, and eventually Venetia will come to realize that. Some good
might come of it yet."

"I think she will need you more than ever after my
unhappy onslaught."

"I'm prepared for that."

In the house they went their separate ways, he to
see Venetia, she to her rooms. Later he told her that
his ward had sprained her ankle during the fall to the
floor, but it had been bandaged and she was comfortable, although still tearful, and would be staying in her
own suite for the next few days. Juliette was left with
a question in her mind: had Venetia felt pain when
she had put her foot to the floor or had it been the
twisting of her ankle in the same moment that had
caused the look of excruciating agony to pass across
her face as she fell?

That same evening Gregory invited Juliette to dine
alone with him in the North Wing, and she discovered that he had his own splendid dining room with
redpapered walls and mahogany furniture, where he
was accustomed to entertaining his own friends on occasion. Blake, respecting the privacy of those residing

in the house, had not shown her into any of the
rooms occupied or used by them during her tour,
and she was surprised to find how great a part of the
North Wing was entirely Gregory's own.

"You see how comfortable we shall be," he said,
throwing open more doors to show her into yet another room. "I thought this salon could be yours.
You'll be able to receive grandly here, because it's considered to be one of the most elegant rooms in the
house."

There was no denying it, but to her its icy blues
and silvered woodwork and circular carpet of shadowed grays was an echo of the North Octagon Room,
which could be no great distance away. Perhaps even
situated next to it. She summoned up her courage
to broach once again the subject of a house of their
own, which she knew to be anathema to him, but she
was forestalled by his action in picking up unexpectedly
a pink moiré silk covered box, ornamented with a bow,
which had been lying out of her sight on a sofa, and
handing it to her.

"A little gift. Something to remind you of the countryside of France."

She lifted the lid and saw folded within the box a
most exquisite cream silk stole embroidered with wild
flowers between dancing butterflies, a chain of bees in
flight making up the prominent border.

"It's the loveliest stole I've ever seen," she exclaimed
in delight. "I used to gather flowers like these on country walks around Rouen."

"I had it made specially for you." He whipped it
from the box and put the romantic offering about her
shoulders, keeping both ends in his hand so that she
was held within the loop of it, and his face was raptur-
ous with the words he spoke like a vow. "One day
the French lily will grow beside the English rose!"

She was touched by his strength of feeling and
counted again in his favor his heartfelt desire for peace
when so many others were crazed for war. "May that
day come soon!" she endorsed with equal fervor,
longing for men everywhere to lay down their arms
and for peace to be restored.

"It will! It won't be long before I'll have something of importance to disclose to you, but in the meantime we have much else to talk about—"

"I have something of utmost urgency to say now," she said quickly.

"What is it?"

"Since I have agreed to our wedding day being earlier than at first arranged, couldn't you defer to a wish of mine in return and let us begin our married life away from West Thorpeby Hall under another roof? Surely it would be possible to rent adequate property in East Thorpeby until such time as you wish to buy."

His amiable mood vanished and his face set in dark stubbornness. "No!" He spun away from her and took a pace or two across the circular carpet. "I've told you that we shall live here until such time—if ever!—I decide that we shall settle elsewhere."

"If ever?" she echoed frantically. "I'm at a loss to understand you."

"I like West Thorpeby Hall. It suits me exceedingly well. Later on we'll have a London residence, but our roots will be set in this place and no other."

"You were prepared to live at Ravensworth Hall!"

He rounded on her. "Not for any length of time. I didn't like the house, although I threw good money after bad and had it altered considerably. As you know, it was bequeathed to me and was not of my choosing. But I had hoped to keep it as an asset until such time as I was solvent again and would sell it without my creditors claiming whatever it fetched. I wanted to keep the amount of my debts from Blake's knowledge—a matter of personal pride—but I knew the game was up when he offered to raise a loan for me in London on my inheritance while fetching you. Had he not returned with you immediately he would have received the tidings before leaving that investigation had shown there wasn't a penny left to play with." He gave a sour laugh. "That's what I had to go through this morning in his study. Not that he preached at me! Hell's teeth! He's gambled more recklessly than I in his time and drunk more and womanized more and nicked more than one opponent in a duel. No, he wouldn't dare preach at me, but it's your welfare he's troubled about. He was angry that I'd allowed a false declaration of my financial position to go through when the contract was drawn up."

She shook her head impatiently. "Money is not important to me, but being independent of charity is! We have no right to continue living indefinitely under Blake's roof when there's no need for it."

"No right?" he echoed incredulously, his voice rising to a shout. "No right? I have every right to reside in the family home, and you—as my wife—will share that right! Only three years divide my age from Blake's, but it made me the younger son and made him the heir to this house, which means as much to me as it does to him. But I shall have it yet—and not only through the son that you shall bear me!"

His narrow eyes were blazing with a cold, black fire. He hates Blake! she thought with horror. He loathed with an insane jealousy his only brother! With this insight came the realization that, if it cost her life, she must never let him suspect that it was the brother whom he detested who had inadvertently won from her the love that by rights should have been his! The fact that Gregory didn't care whether she loved him or not didn't enter into it. Anything Blake possessed he wanted for himself. He would want her heart if he knew Blake had taken it from her. And God only knew what would happen to her should he discover it was lost for ever!

She drew away from him. "What do you mean? Not only through the hereditary rights of your son?"

He appeared to realize that in the heat of the moment he had said too much, and with that supreme self-possession of his, that cock-o'-the-walk arrogance, he shrugged off her question, letting his ill temper fall from him like a cloak, and indulged her with one of his dazzling smiles.

"Don't look at me like that," he coaxed, all his Lockington charm brought into play. "I mean him no harm. We are brothers."

She had to bite back the retort that so was Cain

brother to Abel. "It was a strange remark to make. You must explain it."

"Well," he said on a jovial, drawn out note, "if Blake should decide to travel or move away I'd be obliged to take charge of the estate and would be glad to do it." He drew her arm through his and began to walk her back through the open doors in the direction of the dining room, one room leading into another.

"Has he any intention of doing that?" she asked, taken by surprise.

"He wants to take Venetia to Italy one day. So far the war has prevented him taking her to a warm climate, but when peace comes—as come it must eventually—I believe he'll leave with her without delay. And do you know," he continued with a sardonic chuckle, "I shouldn't be surprised if Venetia recovers miraculously once she has Blake to herself. She'll make sure then that he doesn't return home, but resides permanently abroad. Then, my dear, you and I will have West Thorpeby Hall to ourselves."

She could not imagine Blake away from his wild and beautiful Norfolk for any length of time, but for Venetia's sake he was more than likely to do what Gregory had said. Perhaps she herself had been instrumental in bringing the two of them closer together than ever before through her actions that very day. The thought created a kind of numbness within her as if there came a point where the heart rejected momentarily any further pain.

Gregory put himself out to be an attentive host at dinner. A single footman waited upon them, and the round table at which they sat side by side created an informal atmosphere. Yet none of the niceties was skipped. When the damask cloth was drawn, another of finest lace was put in its place for dessert with fresh crystal goblets set ready for the decanters of sweet wine, which were placed before Gregory on wheeled coasters of silver. From the bowls of hothouse fruits, the preserves from India, and the comfitures, she chose a piece of sugared ginger, but before she could bite into it or Gregory pour the wine the footman, who had withdrawn to leave them on their own for the rest of the evening, returned with a sealed letter on a salver. He handed it to Gregory.

"This has just been delivered, sir. The person who brought it wished it to be put into your hands without delay."

"Person? What sort of person?" Gregory demanded, taking it from the salver.

"I don't know, sir. One of the housemaids took it in and brought it up." The footman left again.

"Please read it," Juliette said, gentle manners needing her permission. "It could be important."

"I expect it to be nothing more than a nasty note from one of my creditors," he declared, "but luck could decree otherwise."

He broke the seal with a quickness of fingers that did not wholly suggest he expected it to be a demand for payment, and there could have been very little written on the paper as a single moment of perusal took in its message. He folded the letter, frowning as he did so, and thrust it deep into his pocket. "It was important. A friend has sent for me. He's in trouble."

"What distressing news for you!" she said with an amused dryness that he did not seem to notice, for she was reminded of an occasion long ago when her father had failed to keep an assignation with a lady of whom he had tired. A letter, stained with tears, had been delivered in a similar fashion, and her father, afraid that the lady in question would arrive on the doorstep, had been compelled to go and settle the matter in person. "You must go at once."

With a fine show of remorse and reluctance he rose from the chair, his brow furrowed, his face set in deepest seriousness. "It's unpardonable of me to leave you in this fashion, but it could be a matter of life and death."

"Then don't delay another second."

He patted her shoulder almost benignly. "Take your time and don't hasten your dessert. Here! Let me pour you some wine." He took the decanter and the wine turned her glass rose-colored. "I'll send the servant back to attend you."

"There's no need. I'll sit a while longer and then retire."

He took her hand in his and kissed the palm of it, looked at her with genuine regret at having to leave her when the evening was still comparatively young, and then was away to whatever business he was about.

Left alone she tilted her head back and laughed quietly and a little wryly at being left high and dry at a table for two. How indignant her Gallic father would have been for her, he who would never have left the side of any beloved woman he was entertaining. But then Gregory did not love her. He had told her his views on love that night he had burst into her room. How different they were from Henri Delahousse's, who had considered love to be a glorious reason for living. She smiled again, letting her thoughts dwell on her father, setting her elbow on the table and her chin in her hand. How she missed him still! Missed his talk, his serious discussions. Missed his laughter, his wicked sense of fun. She would have liked him to have shared this little *contretemps* with her. She thought he would have complimented her on her composure, but—dear God!—how he would have regretted the bleakness of the marriage that lay ahead of her, he whose richly passionate nature she knew she had inherited.

But she would not sit at this table in thoughts that could turn to self-pity. That was not to be tolerated. Picking up the piece of ginger she popped it into her mouth, gasped at the unexpected hotness of it, and drank down the wine to cool her throat. She knew exactly how she would pass what was left of the evening. She would take a light and visit the North Octagon Room, which was near at hand. It fascinated and frightened her, but if needs be she must go back to it again and again until all terror of it had gone from her. Her father had always said that only by running the gauntlet of fear could it be conquered. Somehow she must conquer, or else a sense of shame left by her panic there on her first evening at the house would linger on and make a coward of her. That was a thought that a Delahousse could not tolerate.

Not trusting solely to naked candle flames again in

view of what had happened on her previous visit, she decided to take a lamp with her, at the same time deciding it would not go amiss to take a taper as well to light the wicks in the ancient iron corona that was suspended from the ceiling there, which would give extra illumination when she examined the murals in detail. Remembering the small study where Gregory's tobacco jars and pipes had been racked on the wall by the fireplace, she returned to it, took a taper from a container on the mantel and picked up from the desk a small, practical lamp, which was designed to give good light through clear glass. Trusting to her sense of direction she left the suite by way of the doors in the blue salon and, as she had expected, found herself in the corridor only a few yards away from the North Octagon Room.

She thought she must be a trifle flown with the wine she had drunk at dinner, that final glass having been a deal more potent than she had realized, because she felt no fear or nervousness, only a strange kind of excitement as if she might be on the verge of some discovery. Yet as soon as she entered the North Octagon Room the chill and heavy atmosphere of it closed about her as though it were a dungeon and silent, invisible doors had shut tight together after her; in spite of herself she became less sure and her heart began to thump. But there was nothing dungeon-like about the ice-gem colors of the room, which shone out in the light of her lamp as sharply as if the murals were a mosaic made up of chips of amethyst, crystal, chalcedony, opal, sapphire, onyx, and the darkly glowing mottled green of the bloodstone.

After putting the taper to the lamp flame she lifted a chair across to the center of the room, stood on it, and lighted the wicks of the ancient wax candles in the iron corona. They flared, melting away the cobwebs that the servants, no doubt spending no more time than they had to in that eerie place, had chosen to ignore.

Stepping down again she left the chair where it was for when she should extinguish the candles again, and went across to the panel that had a snow scene. She studied with interest the tiny figures of peasants dragging home firewood and huddled against the cold. She could not help contrasting the odd despair of this wintry room with the brightness and gaiety of the other three, for here no children played, none sliding on the ice or throwing snowballs, pastimes natural to children since time began, but those who were to be seen plodded dully in the wake of the adults. Even West Thorpeby Hall had been painted dark-windowed as though all life had stilled within, except for a tiny round spot of light, made with the finest of brush tips, which showed in one of the windows on the second floor. A shiver ran down the length of her spine. It was there that the spyglass had been leveled at her! But this could have been no spyglass, but a candle held to the glass as someone—Isabelle?—had looked out. Just as some unknown person had looked out at her on the castle ruins. Had that been Isabelle, too?

She withdrew from the panel with a rustle of her silken hem and put one hand to her ribs as if she could quiet the palpitation of her heart. The room was having an absurd effect upon her nerves. She must keep her senses and not harbor such foolish thoughts. Deliberately she turned and went across to the panel where the great storm raged, the wind lifting the first huge waves of the sea, which were later to sweep in, undermining the land, and the flooded marshes opened up to take down all that stood upon it.

She almost cried out, a pathetic little procession catching her eye. There they went through the rain, the band of strolling players with their broken limbs and battered faces, some carried on makeshift stretchers, some using branches as crutches, others being helped along, and with them their raped and weeping women with torn gowns and disheveled hair. And there at the head of them, in a rich, fur-sleeved gown that contrasted with the jester colors of their bedraggled finery, was Isabelle. There could be no mistaking her! She stalked bravely and shamelessly, with no looking back at the house where her husband had thought to imprison her for the rest of her life, carrying the babe of one of the players in the crook of her arm, its swaddling clothes a pathetically gaudy yellow, and by the hand she led another's child.

Swiftly Juliette crossed to the next panel where there was the scene of final destruction. As before, she was moved by the sight of the bobbing domestic debris that showed among the churning swathes of ugly water. And there was that tiny hand raised for the last time before disappearing for ever. Unless it was Isabelle's hand! It was certainly finely shaped, unmistakably a woman's hand. Wasn't that a ring on it?

Juliette held the lamp within an inch of it and was bending her head to examine it closely when she felt once again an unseen stare upon her, so strong as to be almost tangible, and although she tried to keep a hold on herself she was unnerved by it. Straightening up with a jerk, she pressed herself back defensively against the mural she had been examining and held out the lamp before her at arm's length, staring in turn towards each archway framing the blackness of the passage beyond.

"Stop skulking in the darkness!" she ordered with a fierceness born of a feeling of being cornered. "Come into the light, whoever you are!"

The silence surged back at her, thick and palpable, and she felt the roots of her hair prickle. There was one more challenge to make, and dreadful though a response to it might be, she had to utter it.

"Let me see you, whatever you are, no matter if you are a being of this life or the next!"

Then there came the sound that was a faint but definite hiss, and although barely audible it was to her as loud as a snake's rattle. And with it, horrifyingly, there came a damp, musty drift of air as malodorous as if it had been caused by the sweep of sodden skirts to which still clung the marsh mud gathered a full three hundred years ago. In the corona the candle flames spat in the hot wax and went out!

But this time she was not left in darkness. The lamp she held, although the wick fluttered dangerously low and caused a thread of smoke to curl around and upwards within the glass globe, stayed alight, but the ceiling candle holder had added a glow brighter than she had appreciated, and beyond the immediate limits of the lamp the shadows had returned. In a curiously stricken desperation she went on talking.

"If you are Isabelle come to portend a loveless marriage, you may leave again without delay. That knowledge was mine before I came to this house, but Gregory desires it and I am bound to it through the wishes of someone long gone from me."

She held her breath, listening acutely. Nothing to be heard but the thunder of her own heart. Warily she moved an inch or two from the wall, listened again, and then darted to the chair in the center of the room, sliding her hand along its back and one of its arms as she rotated against it, looking about her nervously. Summoning up her courage, she took one slow step and then another away from the chair, making for the archway between the snow scene and the blizzard. Her lamplight bounced off the stone walls of the circumferential passageway outside the octagonal room, and slowly she began to follow it round. At the inset door leading up into the dome above she put her hand on the cold iron ring and tried to open it, but it was securely locked as it had been for years. On and on she went, past each archway leading back into the room, trying not to think that perhaps the very presence she feared to see was retreating from her constantly beyond the range of the lamp or even—no, she must not think it!—stalking her from the rear.

With an almost tear-inducing sensation of relief she completed the circle and was back where she started. Once more she entered the room and stood in the middle of it. That curious, marshlike aroma had faded, but only because those swamp-soiled robe hems had settled into quiet folds for the time being, for evil still permeated that place; unseen eyes still watched relentlessly from the blackness. With a violently shaking hand Juliette again put the taper to her lamp, determined to relight the candles in the iron holder and show herself resistant to that awful hostility ranged against her. If she gave in to the mind-splitting terror that she was only just keeping at bay and fled from the North Octagon Room she knew her nerve would be broken and never again would she find the courage to return to it. Worse, she might release untold power to that evil force and never be free of its domination again.

She set down the lamp on the floor as she had done before and put her foot on the chair ready to step up on it, but suddenly spotted that she had pushed it a few inches too far under the line of the corona above, which would mean bending her spine at an awkward angle to put her taper to the wicks. She promptly stepped back off the chair again, intending to move it into place. In the same instant the heavy iron corona crashed down with a wild rattling of chains, splitting asunder the chair and landing at her feet, scattering splintered wood, wax candles, dust, cobwebs, and cutting through the carpet into the floor with its tremendous weight. The vibration of its falling echoed like clap upon clap of thunder within the surrounding passageway and went rumbling away through the house in all directions.

She stood motionless, staring at the frightful debris. That casual but split second decision to move the chair had saved her from terrible mutilation and death itself. Without a sound she crumpled to the floor in a faint.

She struggled back to consciousness to find Mrs. Harman reaching the point of anxiety, so deep and persistent had been her faint, and Caroline waving burning feathers by her nose, an assortment of vinaigrettes having had no effect.

"There! She's opening her eyes, Mrs. Harman!" Caroline exclaimed. "Nothing like an old remedy to do the trick!"

"That's as maybe," replied the housekeeper, thinking that nature taking its course had relented at last and released the girl from her oblivion.

Juliette saw she was lying in her own bed, still in her evening gown, but with the covers drawn warmly over her. For a few moments she could not think why she should be there or what had happened. Then it came flooding back to her, and she closed her eyes again on the shock of it.

Blake's voice this time, coming into the room. "How is she now?"

How worried he sounds, she thought. How good of him to be anxious about her when that beautiful carpet in the North Octagon Room had been ruined, to say nothing of the chair and even that ancient candle-holder itself.

"She's come round at last," Caroline's voice answered him.

"Are you quite sure she's suffered no injuries?" He was at the bedside now, leaning towards her.

"Not a scratch on her, Mr. Lockington," Mrs. Harman assured him. "A very fortunate young lady she is, and no mistake."

"You're quite sure she didn't suffer a blow on the head?"

"There's not a cut or a bump, sir. Rest your mind on that. It was nothing but shock that put her out, and it's no wonder at that. I had a fright myself hearing that great crash vibrate through the house. I thought at least a roof had fallen in."

He was still unconvinced that she had suffered no harm. "I do not doubt your diagnostic ability, Mrs. Harman—you've had enough experience in nursing the sick among the staff in this house, goodness knows— but I'll send to East Thorpeby for Doctor Barlow in order to make quite certain that all is well." His cool fingertips touched Juliette's face, his voice thickening anxiously. "You said she had come round, but her eyes are still closed—"

Although her lids felt heavy and her head still threatened to swim again at the slightest movement, she opened her eyes and managed a smile for him. Through her daze she saw his eyes flood with warmth and relief and a particular glow that showed for a second and was gone again. She tried to think when she had seen such a look in his eyes before, but in her confused state the effort defeated her.

"How are you feeling?" he asked at once.

She managed a lopsided smile. "I'm not hurt in any way. Please don't send for the doctor. The corona landed harmlessly at my feet."

He sat down on the bed, leaning his weight on one hand on the bedclothes beside her. "Can you tell me what happened?"

"I had gone to look at the murals and lighted the candles in the corona for extra illumination. When they blew out I stood on the chair to light them again with the taper I had." Her expression became agitated. "Did it set fire to anything when I dropped it?"

He shook his head. "It must have blown out as it fell. But there was no need to stand on a chair. The corona is suspended by an iron chain that runs over a pulley, and it can be raised or lowered by a ring handle attached to it, which hangs with clever concealment within one of the archways. This ring handle had been released from its hook, and it's that which made the corona come crashing down. I've just examined the corona chain and no link had snapped anywhere. Do you think you might have brushed against the ring and not noticed that you dislodged it? Did you feel anything catch at your sleeve and pull yourself free without paying attention to what it was? Anything at all like that?"

"No. Nothing." Deliberately she closed her eyes again. Mrs. Harman had withdrawn, but Caroline was still there, watching her from the foot of the bed, listening avidly. She wanted to say no more in that woman's hearing.

He rose from the bed. "I must let you rest. We'll talk about this in the morning. Try to put the narrow escape you had from your mind and sleep well. Nothing like it shall ever happen again. Every chandelier- and corona-hanging in the house shall be checked. Good night."

Through her lashes she watched him step down from the dais on which her bed stood and as he strolled slowly towards the door leading back through the anteroom Caroline moved quickly forward to leave with him.

"I don't know why she was in the North Octagon Room on her own," she said to him in low, confidential tones. "She was supposed to be dining alone with Gregory, but according to the servants a note came and he went out. Another of his women, I suppose. You would think that now he is betrothed—"

Blake cut her short with some distaste. "Who reached Juliette first after the crash was heard?"

"Well, I did, as a matter of fact. But I was only seconds ahead of one of the footmen, and other servants came almost immediately afterwards. Why?"

He ignored the query. "As I rode up the drive I heard the clock make an abortive clang. Not a struck note by any manner of means, but it must have been brought about by the reverberations caused by the corona's fall. It was deucedly odd to hear it, I can tell you."

They had passed into the anteroom. "That's not all that's odd in this house," Caroline insisted. "I think Isabelle is walking again. Oh, I know you don't like the subject mentioned, but . . ." Their voices, already little more than a murmur, became inaudible. In the salon the doors closed behind them.

Juliette lay still, looking up at the silken drapery of the canopy above her head. Had Caroline planned that she should overhear that remark about another woman? Was it a love note that had been delivered? She would not judge Gregory by anything Caroline said, and must dismiss it from her mind. There was something else to concentrate on: it had been a touch, unseen by her, that had slipped the ring handle off its hook at the precise moment when it had looked as if she was about to mount the chair. Why did Isabelle— or the force of evil that was Isabelle—want her dead? Had she disturbed once too often with her young and vital presence the North Octagon Room with its atmosphere of untold secrets and eerie solitude?

Hearing a door open, she hoped for one lightning moment that Blake had returned to see her again after getting rid of Caroline, but it was only Sorrel coming into the suite by way of the dressing room, and the girl brought with her a hot drink on a tray.

"Mrs. Harman sent you this, ma'am," she said,

putting it down on the bedside table. "Maybe you'd best drink it before I help you undress or it'll get cold."

Juliette decided on the reverse procedure, but when she lay in her nightgown against the pillows the milk was still quite warm and she discovered it was well-laced with brandy, which more than made up for any heat that had been lost.

"Thank Mrs. Harman for her thoughtfulness, Sorrel," she said when the girl had put everything away and was on the point of going again.

"Yes, ma'am. Good night."

Before going to sleep Juliette, in spite of Blake's advice, went over all that had happened that evening, even to everything that Gregory had said to her, but soon all thought faded, Mrs. Harman's brandy-and-milk having its desired effect.

From the following morning the days began to slip into a quieter pattern, keeping to a certain amount of routine, for which Juliette was extremely thankful, having had more than enough upsetting experiences since coming to West Thorpeby Hall. The only disturbing factor that persisted was the eerie feeling that came over her now and again of being watched. She would pause on the stairs and glance alertly upwards at the gallery that encircled the great hall or down over her shoulder to see if anyone lurked in the doorways below. In the shadows of the long corridors by day and night she would look sharply and look again, think herself reassured, and then know she was not when she walked on again. At these times she knew a very real fear of Isabelle, the horror of what she had already experienced having undermined her resilience to a certain extent.

The lists of wedding guests had to be compiled and given over to Blake's secretary, Mr. Tomlinson, a conscientious, scholarly man who had once been tutor to the Lockington boys in their early youth, but whose loss of hearing had put paid to his career in the teaching profession in his early forties. Blake had heard of his case, taken him into his employ, and given him a cottage on the estate. Juliette's list included several new friends made in London, but it was a small number compared with the many pages of names on Gregory's side. Within a few days of receiving the completed lists the invitations, written in Mr. Tomlinson's beautiful hand, were sealed and sent out for delivery. Juliette saw the one being sent to Aunt Phoebe before it was despatched.

Mr. Blake Lockington desires the pleasure of your company at the marriage of Miss Juliette Delahousse to his brother, Mr. Gregory Lockington, at West Thorpeby Hall on the twenty-second of June at twelve noon.

She thought how final it was, how absolute. The announcement of the end of her sweet days of liberty.

She had doubts as to whether all the guests could be accommodated in the private chapel of West Thorpeby Hall, but when she went into it she saw it was much larger than it had appeared from outside. It was as old as the house, an ancient edifice of much beauty with a magnificent hammered roof, fine carvings, and wooden pews dark with age, the air fragrant with the perfume of flowers set by the old font in which one day her children would be baptized. She spotted Thomas Lockington's tomb, his stone effigy neatly set out, his fine head on a pillow that must have been velvet, a dog at his feet, and the brocade of his robes picked out in detail by a skilled stone-mason's hand. Beside him was an empty space where she would have expected his first wife's effigy to lie, but Matilda Lockington had her own tomb nearby. So he had intended that Isabelle should lie with him through all eternity, and when she had betrayed him he had decreed that the space on top of his double tomb should remain bare for ever. She looked closely at his face. The Lockington good looks had been much in evidence even in those days.

Before leaving, her thoughts went to Thomas Lockington's final desperate and demanding shout on his last breath, which had had such eerie consequences. With a shiver she hurried from the church.

She did not return to the North Octagon Room to view the damage, having a natural reluctance to look

again upon the spot where she could so easily have
lain crushed to death, but Gregory went to see it and
so did everyone else in the house, even Venetia, being
pushed along in one of her wheeled chairs.

"Thank God you escaped injury—and worse!"
Gregory exclaimed soberly to Juliette. He appeared distracted and much shaken by what he had seen. "What
on earth possessed you to go looking at the murals at
that hour of the evening? You said you were going to
retire to bed shortly when I left you."

"It was just a whim," she said evasively. She had
said nothing to him of the errand that had taken him
away from her on that fateful evening, nor did he
refer to it.

On the morning she set up her easel in a sheltered
place he came sauntering along, apparently at a loss
to know how to pass the time for once, and sat down
on a low stone wall beside her to watch in silence
as her brush flowed the clear, soft water colors on to
the white paper and set in the view of distant ruins.

"You have talent," he said knowledgeably.

"Thank you, but perhaps you judge too soon. The
picture is only half-finished." She dipped her brush
into the little pot of water on its stand by her paintbox and then dabbled it in a pool of burnt sienna.

He had watched for a few minutes longer when the
crunch of wheels made him turn his head. "There
goes the North Octagon Room's carpet to be repaired,"
he commented idly.

Her brush halted in midair between paintbox and
paper. She saw a cart bearing away a long roll wrapped
in clean sacking.

"Where is it going to?" she enquired flatly.

"To carpet weavers in Norwich. It will look as
good as new when it comes back again."

It crossed her mind that, with the taking up of the
carpet, which was one of four that had been specially
woven to fit the octagonal rooms, the place where she
had narrowly escaped death would be looking now
exactly as it had done in Thomas Lockington's old age
when he had cried to Isabelle on his deathbed and
wrought such grisly havoc through it. How odd that he

had chosen to die amid those macabre scenes of destruction when he had had the other three brighter and equally beautiful rooms to choose from for his last days on earth! Was it that, having lived through the seasons of promise, love, and joy, he could only associate the end of his life with the betrayal of his land by the sea, the laying low of the earth by winter's chill, the apparent death of all nature, which altogether symbolized for him the misery and suffering inflicted upon him by the heartless Isabelle?

"Am I intruding upon you two lovebirds?" It was Caroline who spoke, a caustic edge to her voice. She was dressed for going out. Without waiting for an answer she addressed Gregory. "Blake has gone down to the dikes. He wants you to join him. I offered to deliver the message because I'm curious to see what the artist is painting." She stared at the half-finished landscape and damned it with faint praise. "Quite pretty. You're very much a beginner, aren't you? Never mind, it's a brave try. I paint myself, you know. I'll give you a few useful tips one of these days, particularly with regard to perspective. You've made those castle ruins look much higher than they are." She peered closer. "Is that blob on the battlements meant to be—er, meant to be there or has the paint run?"

Juliette was suddenly tense, remembering the spyglass at the window. Had Caroline been on the point of asking if it were she standing there? Or merely trying to find fault? Gregory, muttering against Blake's message, had risen to leave them, but he turned back again.

"Come with me, Juliette," he invited, not with any particular grace, his hackles always rising at any request from his brother that bordered on being an order, but with the thought that she should see something of the marshes since she was to live near them and with them to the end of her days, for he was determined that eventually he would be Master of West Thorpeby Hall. "Leave your painting and change into riding clothes. I want you to see the work that's in progress on the dikes."

"I'd like to." She rose from her painting stool. "I'll

be as quick as I can, but I must close my paintbox to stop the sun drying it out."

He nodded. "Don't be long. I'll meet you in the stable courtyard."

Caroline still lingered, watching Juliette take a rag to wipe the paintbox clean. "Did you hear about the escape?"

Juliette glanced at her in puzzlement. "What escape?"

"Half a dozen of the hundreds of French prisoners of war being housed at Norman Cross got away the other night and they haven't been found."

"Indeed? I suppose it will only be a question of time before the poor men are hunted down and recaptured."

"Recaptured and put in a noose!"

Juliette closed her paintbox with an angry snap. "It's no crime, but a duty for prisoners of war to attempt escape and try to regain their own lines. In this case the sea lies between freedom and the men of whom we are speaking, which surely makes their task all but impossible."

"These prisoners killed to make their escape! Not just two of the soldiers in charge of them, but they broke into a house to get food and murdered the occupants who tried to raise the alarm. The details are in the *Morning Gazette*, which has just been delivered. You may read it for yourself. On a farm near Thetford, an innocent family of husband, wife, two sons, and a servant girl all stabbed to death with the bayonets of the soldiers' rifles, which the prisoners stole and took with them."

Juliette had gone pale. "How dreadful! I can't believe that ordinary Frenchmen in the ranks would commit such a heinous crime. There are villians in the army on both sides, and I can only conclude that these were men given to crimes of violence in the first place."

"Naturally you would speak up in defense of your fellow countrymen as a whole!" Caroline sneered delicately. "You'll find that nobody else will share that theory of yours. It has roused such new feeling against the French that angry crowds gathered outside the jail and extra guards had to be put on duty to prevent any attempt to smash down the gates and get at the prisoners within."

"It's a most sorry affair!" Juliette left Caroline and hurried into the house. Knowing the newspapers were always left in the library she went in search of the *Morning Gazette*. She had no difficulty in finding the account of the escape and the murders that had followed. She did not have time to read it all, knowing that Gregory would be waiting for her, but she took in enough to see that Caroline had been right in all she had said.

In her suite she found the white-capped figure of Sorrel getting out the lemon silk gown that she was to wear that evening to the Rose-Marshall ball. "This is the one, is it not, ma'am? I thought I'd check in good time to see if it needs a stitch or a press."

Juliette nodded. "Put it aside for the moment and get out my dark green riding habit. I'm going to ride down to the dikes with Mr. Gregory."

Sorrel moved quickly and efficiently and in no time at all Juliette was arrayed in the habit, her feet laced into her ankle boots, and her plumed, military styled hat set jauntily on her head.

"Which stole will you want to wear this evening, ma'am?" Sorrel enquired in her solemn, impersonal way as Juliette flew for the door, imagining Gregory's growing impatience.

Juliette paused with a swirl of her heavy skirt. "Er —the new one, I think. That stole with the embroidered flowers, which Mr. Gregory gave me. I haven't worn it yet."

"Yes, ma'am."

In the stableyard Gregory was in the saddle of a chestnut stallion, a fiery brute with rearing head and rolling eyes. He was having trouble controlling it, for it was eager to be away, and he was wrenching on the reins while dealing out admonitory cuts of considerable force with his crop, swearing mightily as he did so. He glowered when he saw her come hastening through the ivy-covered archway from the direction of the house, showing himself to be reduced to as ill a temper as that of his mount, but managed to modify his language.

"Sooth! Does it take you so long to change from one garment into another! We're only riding down to some muddy dike banks manned by working scum—not to a drawing room at St. James's Palace!"

She flushed, thinking how easy it would be to quarrel with him in his present mood, but held her tongue as by way of the stone mounting block she took the saddle of the quiet bay being held for her by one of the grooms. Briskly she rode out of the stableyard after him, his stallion's magnificent tail wildly swinging like a length of fine silk, and brought herself level.

Together they rode side by side down the drive and out into the lane, he explaining to her that Blake was hoping that the new system of dikes he was having dug would drain the marsh land sufficiently to reduce the danger of it being swamped again as it had been in the past and eventually, if the method worked well enough, to make some of the land arable again. She glanced towards the rich fields and lush meadows and fine orchards that lay to the west of the lane following the hard escarpment as they cantered northwards, contrasting that good land to the soggy marshes beginning to spread out to the east of them and touched by the lips of the sea. Never had the growing of food been more important to England than at this time of the Napoleonic wars, when there was a compelling need to make every inch of land productive. No wonder Blake aimed to master the marshes and force a yield from that reluctant soil!

"There's Blake!" Gregory flung out an arm and pointed with his riding crop to a distant figure on horseback where a cluster of thirty laborers or more were at work. "I'll go ahead. Follow me and don't stray from the path. It's in this part that the village of East Thorpeby was lost without trace, and the swamps are treacherous."

Her bay trod daintily in the wake of the chestnut, which left a pattern of hoof marks in the soft mud. All around the coarse grasses rustled tall in the sea wind and once a wild duck, alarmed by the approach of the horses, flew up with a snapping of wings. Now and again the ground squelched, and clumps of tiny, wild flowers grew thick as moss out of the sodden ground.

Blake, in conversation with a foreman who stood looking up at him, arms akimbo, did not see that his brother and Juliette had arrived until they were within hailing distance. Then, when Gregory had made their presence known with a shout, he wheeled his horse about and came to meet them, doffing his hat to her. Always when they met, whether at table or by chance on the stairs or in the gardens, she found herself hoping that she might see again that warm, almost tender glow she had seen in his eyes when she had raised her lids after fainting and seen him looking down at her, but it was never there, his gaze as enigmatic and distant as it ever was. Each time she was dashed to disappointment, because she had thought that at last she might be becoming a whole person in his regard, and not just his brother's betrothed who bore a striking resemblance to a girl he had loved.

It was clear that on this occasion he had no time even to pass the time of day with her, being intent on showing Gregory some part of one of the other, older dikes, which had to be discussed. She was not invited to accompany them and the two brothers rode off together, leaving her feeling slightly at a loss. She dismounted and kept hold of the reins, allowing her horse to pick at the tender grass that grew among the roots of other, tougher growths, while she watched the workmen, knee-deep in water, at their slogging task. Like a small army moving in a disjointed rhythm they thrust in their spades, loosened a sodden clod, and heaved it up on the raw bank. When a spade's edge struck something in the soil she watched with interest as the foreman went to give the digger assistance and together they removed some mud-caked object. The foreman carried it up on the bank and set it down with a few other shapes that were impossible to identify.

She took a few steps forward and spoke to him as he moved away from the pile. "What have you there? Are they artifacts?"

The foreman gave a nod. "That's what the master

calls these 'ere things, but that weren't nothin' more than a bit of old wheel, I can tell you. No use to anyone. We don't find much, but when we gets a few bits together they get taken up to the 'ouse and what 'appens to 'em then I can't tell you." He took off his shapeless felt hat, scratched his head, and replaced its covering again. "You'd think 'e'd wanted the mud washed off, wouldn't you? But no. Pieces attached might be washed away, 'e says." He chuckled throatily. "Like old King John's treasure in the Wash not so far from 'ere all those 'undreds of years ago."

She gave a little laugh. "What a pity no bags of gold were dropped around here! They would make a better find than that piece of wheel."

"You're right there, miss. Now if you'll pardon me, I'll be getting back to work again."

Nothing more came to light during the next hour, but the time did not drag. She captured pictures in her mind's eye to set down later with her paintbrush. The sparkle of the sea where it lapped the bleak stretches of naked mud and the sight of an old woman picking marsh-samphire, which—in answer to her question to the foreman—she learned was used as a vegetable by local people. She recorded the misty sprouting of the sea-lavender, the sun-faded color of the upturned keel of a rotting boat cast up by a past tide, and the endless play of wings against the cloud-dotted Norfolk sky. A quiet contentment came upon her.

With the inspection of the dikes completed, Blake and Gregory turned their horses back to rejoin Juliette where they had left her close on a mile away. As they rode stirrup to stirrup they discussed the work that had been done and whether another dike should be dug to ease the land at another, less vulnerable point. It gratified Blake that Gregory, for all his daredevil ways, took a sober interest in the husbandry and protection of the West Thorpeby estate, and he never failed to give serious consideration to any suggestions his younger brother had to offer.

When they were boys they had been as close as twins, but gradually as the full realization had dawned

on Gregory that the Hall and its lands, which they
both loved and had roamed and explored and ridden
over until they knew every inch of it as well as their
own hands, would never be his, a terrible resentment
on his part had created a gulf between them. Over
the years that gulf had widened beyond all hope of
spanning it, changing Gregory's nature at the same
time; it was a source of deep regret to Blake, who had
always held his younger brother dear, and he felt
keenly the loss of their old companionship. Times such
as this present morning's inspection of work, when
they could talk amiably and be on good terms, were
prized by Blake, although he knew that Gregory gave
them no thought, indifferent to closeness once shared.
The conversation between them had swung to the
subject of cost and finance, which enabled Blake to
pick up another aspect of it.

"Have you reconsidered my offer to advance whatever sum you need towards the purchase of a residence
of your own?"

Gregory kept his gaze rigidly ahead, his jaw tightening. "I told you before. I'll have the house that I
want in my own good time."

"Your bride has a right to start married life in a
home of her own."

Gregory twisted in the saddle, his eyes blazing.
"Juliette has no more rights than any other woman.
She will do as I say and follow what I please as a
dutiful wife should. Her dowry will be mine to deal
with as I wish, and I don't intend to use any part of
it on bricks and mortar to humor her whim. I'll remind you that West Thorpeby Hall is my home and
birthplace too."

Blake's hand shot out and gripped his brother's arm.
"Does her happiness mean nothing to you?"

Gregory jerked himself free and pulled his sleeve
back into place, his mood easing as a lascivious grin
spread across his face. "Indeed it does. I'll make her
happy, have no doubt on that score. Oh, yes." He
gave a quiet laugh. "She'll not be able to fault me as a
husband, I can promise you that."

With that he spurred his horse forward to ride

ahead where the hard track across the marshy land
narrowed once again. Blake frowned as he followed
him, his face tight.

Juliette was back in the saddle, a bunch of wild
flowers in her hand, when they reached her, and she
greeted them, smiling. "I have had a splendid time.
What a wild and beautiful part of the country this is."

"You'll hear no argument from either of us there,"
Gregory replied good-humoredly as he and Blake
brought their stamping, restless horses abreast of hers.
She glanced at Blake, half-expecting him to endorse
the remark, and with a pang she glimpsed that special
depth in his eyes which she had come to call to herself
his Elizabeth look. Immediately she knew an anguish
that more than equaled his, especially when he turned
his face resolutely away from hers and dug in his heels
to lead the way back to the lane along the winding
path, his business for the day at the dikes being at an
end. It told her as clearly as if he had put it into words
that he had no wish to look upon her for the pain she
brought him and that he wished her far from his house
and from his sight.

The three of them dismounted at the steps of West
Thorpeby Hall, the two brothers to go indoors while
she strolled thoughtfully back to where she had left
her easel and painting equipment, one hand tapping
the end of her riding crop against her other palm. All
kinds of wild schemes to get Gregory to buy a home
of their own passed through her mind. She felt willing
to contemplate anything that could get her away from
Blake, but each idea was thwarted either by its impos-
sibility, such as borrowing on the strength of her own
dowry, which was not hers to dispose of, or by the
insurmountable barrier of having given her word to
marry Gregory, a vow doubly enforced by the promise she had made to marry him sooner than originally
arranged, which put paid to any idea of running away
and remaining hidden until Gregory complied with her
wishes.

Still wrapped in thought she came to her painting
pinned to its board on the easel. Then she stood
aghast at what she saw. Painted in the foreground by

a brush held in a hand with some ability was a guillotine, its decapitated victim in a dress of the color she was wearing that morning, and the head in the basket had her own light, fair hair! It was wicked, cruel, and terrifying to one who had only recently escaped death from a descending iron corona, which could have sliced off her unprotected head as easily as any guillotine blade, and her immediate reaction was to swing away from it and press herself against the tall box-hedge, her eyes covered by the fingers of her gloved hands.

After a few seconds she recovered and with averted gaze she tore the painting from the board and screwed it into a ball. The first thing she did when she entered the house was to throw it on to the burning logs in the hall's great hearth. It burst into flame at once and without waiting to see it reduced to ashes, fearful that it might uncurl in the heat and reveal its gruesome paint sketch once again, she hurried upstairs to her own apartments without looking back.

Chapter Eight

Sorrel fastened the last hook at the back of Juliette's gown. "That's it, ma'am." She gave her mistress no further glance, but proceeded to tidy up the clutter of scent bottles, cosmetic jars, combs, pins, and disarrayed trinkets spilled from the jewelry box on to the surface of the toilet table.

On the opposite side of the room Juliette regarded her reflection in the cheval glass, thinking that Sorrel had performed miracles with her hair, entwining its soft and slippery strands into a high-piled cluster of curls at the back of her head, which gave her the appearance of a shining-headed flower on a golden stem in her slender, highwaisted ballgown. The praise she had given the girl had been received as so much water running over a duck's back, but she had learned to accept Sorrel's detached, phlegmatic attitude and had long since decided it was preferable to Cobbett's endless clacking.

As Juliette swiveled around from her reflection Sorrel moved to take up all the accessories laid ready. The new stole was looped over Juliette's elbows, the gilt cords of the little silken reticule slipped over her white-gloved wrist, and the folded fan put into her hand. Finally her velvet wrap was placed about her shoulders.

"Thank you, Sorrel. If I'm not the best attired guest at the Rose-Marshall ball this evening it will not be your fault."

Sorrel eyed her critically from head to toe and replied with her usual candor. "You'll do well enough, ma'am, but no doubt others will do better." With that she gave Juliette no more of her attention and continued about her tasks.

Juliette said no more. Sorrel had deflected the compliment and turned it neatly into a cutting-down to size

of any inflated opinion she might be holding about
herself. So much for trying to praise Sorrel's work!
With anyone else it would have brought a smile to
Juliette's lips, but with Sorrel one trod carefully, it
being a matter of fierce pride to the maid that nothing
was allowed to bridge the gulf between mistress and
servant.

Downstairs Juliette did not find Gregory waiting for
her as she had expected and she strolled into one of
the salons to wait for him. When she heard some conversation on the stairs she glanced in the huge looking
glass above the marble fireplace, able to see through
the open doors into the hall and expecting to see Gregory and perhaps Caroline with him, although she was
being escorted by a widowed baronet from East
Thorpeby, and should have left by now. Then she
caught her breath.

It was Blake who had come down the great staircase, and in his arms he carried Venetia, her hands
linked lightly behind his neck, her expression triumphant, and her silver-gauze gown cascaded as delicately
as a spray dispersed waterfall. Venetia was breaking her
rule of never going to any place where dancing would
take place! Was it possible that the clash between them
when Venetia had attempted to rise from the sofa had
had some effect? Had one small bar of the barrier that
prevented her from walking been loosened and dis-
placed? Or was it simply that Venetia had made up her
mind that on no social occasion was Gregory's betrothed to outshine her, even if it meant overcoming
her natural agony at seeing others enjoying a pastime
in which she could only be an envious bystander unable to take part?

Neither of them noticed Juliette where she stood in
the salon. Blake, already cloaked, carried Venetia out
of the house as the footman on duty in the hall opened
the door for him and another sprang out with a lantern to light the steps for him down to the waiting
carriage. The clop of hooves carried them on their
way.

The house was silent with their going. She realized
that Blake must have thought she had already de-

parted as Caroline must have done. She went out into
the hall, thinking to send a servant to remind Gregory
of the passing of time, when his valet came hurrying
towards her.

"Mr. Gregory had to go out earlier this evening and
left word that, if he had not returned by this time, I
should convey his request that you depart for Hetherham House, the Rose-Marshalls' residence, without
further delay. He changed before leaving and will meet
you there."

In the carriage she fumed, tapping her foot. She was
exasperated with Gregory for his thoughtlessness. Had
he planned no attempt to return to West Thorpeby
Hall to fetch her she could have left earlier: as it was,
she was bound to arrive late. Perhaps Gregory intended
that they should make a grand entrance together, but
at least she should have been forewarned. In any case
it would all prove to be a sheer waste of effort on his
part since Venetia would have made the most spectacular of all entrances in her lovely gown and draped in
Blake's arms. No doubt Sorrel had known that Venetia
had made up her mind to attend, which was the reason for the remark that, however elegant she looked,
there were others who would look better!

The lights of East Thorpeby began to twinkle on
either side of the carriage. She had made a number of
short visits to the market town, visiting the library for
the latest novels from London and making a few small
purchases in the shops. It proved to be no more than
half a mile farther on to the gates of Hetherham House.
No other carriages were depositing guests at the doors
of the brightly-lit mansion, and she had the uncomfortable feeling that she was last to arrive. She hoped
that Gregory would have sent a servant to watch for her
coming and inform him, but he did not appear and she
went alone through the porch and into the house.
Again in the hall she looked for him in vain, there
being only one footman in best livery standing there,
all the guests apparently having congregated in the
ballroom which—to judge from the direction of the
music—was situated on the first of the upper floors.
A maidservant came forward to take her cloak and a

footman guided her to the foot of the huge central staircase. As she began to ascend she was dismayed at her own nervousness, but no matter how she tried to subdue her quaking, it persisted of its own accord.

She reached the top of the stairs. Ahead of her, beyond draped archways, couples were rotating in a flurry of color and a glitter of jewels, reflected more than a thousand times over in the looking glass panels that lined the walls, making the ballroom appear to be at first glance the largest and most populated room in the world.

Taking a deep breath, she adjusted her stole, flicked open her fan and walked through to find herself on a carpeted gallery with four shallow steps leading down to the polished dancing floor which was patterned with an intricate design of contrasting woods and inlaid with mother-of-pearl that shone as though pieces of the moon had been let into it. A butler stepped forward to take her name and announced her as the music brought the dance to an end in a little clash of cymbals.

"Miss Juliette Delahousse!"

It seemed to Juliette that her name, uttered in those stentorian tones, echoed and re-echoed about that enormous room. Those near at hand began to whisper, and the whisper gathered like the rustle of silk until all other conversation was stilled. To her consternation the stares on her became hostile; she felt herself scrutinized from head to foot, and the whispering grew in intensity until it reminded her of the awful hiss in the North Octagon Room, but magnified beyond all proportion. With despair she concluded that the company present, outraged at the murder committed by the French prisoners of war, had turned their fury against her as a representative of the nation that in the present state of war they abhorred in every way.

She stood as though rooted to the spot, her pride preventing her from fleeing, and apart from Caroline, who was turning away under the cover of her fan in a pretense at not seeing her, she could locate no one whom she recognized, although a shimmer of silver beyond the open door of an anteroom did show her where Venetia was sitting. It was the soft buzz of un-

broken conversation still coming from that room
which showed that in there at least nobody was as yet
aware that anything was amiss.

As the situation took on a nightmare quality, making her wonder wildly if she were destined to spend
all night like a statue being glared at, there was a
movement in the anteroom and Alex Rose-Marshall,
having been summoned at last, appeared in the archway. The whispering died to silence, all watching to
see what would happen. Then from behind him Lucy
appeared, and with running steps she darted ahead of
him and covered the full length of the ballroom floor,
her face smiling, her arms outstretched in welcome to
Juliette. Her clear voice reached every corner of the
room.

"Here you are at last! We've all been waiting for you.
And how kind of you to return my stole as you promised. It was quite foolish of me to take yours in mistake. Let us exchanged them without delay."

She had reached the steps and ran up them to whisk
the embroidered stole from Juliette's shoulders, whirled
it about her own, and then looped hers of gold tissue
around her bewildered guest. Tucking her arm through
Juliette's she led her down the steps and in the direction of the anteroom. Alex signaled to the musicians,
who had not dared to put bow to string in the moments of extraordinary tension that had ensued, and a
striking-up of the music for a polonaise brought an
immediate resumption of conversation as couples
moved to take their places on the floor.

"Please explain what is happening," Juliette implored.

Lucy, although her smile remained fixed for the
benefit of those watching them thread their way past
the dancing couples, gave her a pitying glance. "Don't
pretend. It doesn't become you. If it hadn't been for
Blake I would not have made any attempt to rescue
you from your predicament. Let us be thankful that
none here doubts the Rose-Marshalls' loyalty to good
King George or else I would never have got away
with that little deception."

"I swear I don't know what you're talking about!"

Juliette looked about her. "Where is Blake?" She hoped at least to get some explanation from him.

"When he heard that Gregory had sent a message that he would be late in arriving, Blake returned to West Thorpeby Hall to escort you here himself."

"My carriage must have passed his somewhere in the town or along the lane. Oh, Lucy! You must believe me when I say I'm completely in the dark!"

Lucy's over-bright smile would have been belied by the troubled look in her eyes if her lowered lashes had not kept them shielded to all but Juliette. "We'll talk about this matter later. Now you must dance with Alex."

He had come forward to meet them, his first words showing that he blamed the silence and unease that greeted her arrival on the recent grim event that was in everyone's mind.

"Forgive my other guests for their momentary lack of good manners in making you bear the burden of their enmity against France and shock at a certain local atrocity that has been committed in that country's name." He bowed to her. "Pray allow me the honor of this dance."

Juliette, letting him lead her on to the floor, looked towards Lucy rejoining those in the anteroom, her stole floating, and noticed how the border of bees on it stood out with an almost luminous quality, so skillfully had they been embroidered. In the same instant comprehension thudded home. The bees, creating that spectacular border, had been the innocent cause of the hostility directed towards her upon her arrival. Long before she had left France Napoleon had taken the imperial bee as his symbol, and she—foolish dimwit that she was!—had failed to see that by wearing Gregory's gift she was appearing to flaunt Napoleonic loyalty in the face of those whose one aim was to bring down the tyrant and all he stood for! Lucy's claiming of the stole as her own had removed the stigma from her, not even Alex suspecting that his sister had not been its true owner, and when the opportunity to explain that her wearing of it had not been deliberate she must hope that her new friend would believe her.

As she danced the swift, dipping steps of the polonaise with a lightness that did not match the heaviness of her heart, she tried to fathom out how she could have been so blind as not to see that the ornament of a bee in any shape or form would be associated with Napoleon. It was simply that in being away from France and feeling no bond towards the Emperor, it had not crossed her mind that in England it would hold the same significance. Never would she make the same mistake again! How careful she would be in future! Whatever would Gregory say when he heard of the mistake he had inadvertently made in giving her an innocent and beautiful article of apparel which had almost branded her as a Napoleonic agent in the eyes of the whole community?

Then with an unhappy start she recalled what he had said when he had given it to her. It was to remind her of France, he had said. He had known! And he had wanted her to wear it for him! Other things he had said came flooding back to her, references to the glory of France, his rage against the poem that Venetia had recited when he shouted of propaganda, and his wild promises that he and she would be instrumental in bringing peace. That he was a Francophile with such an aim had been the only point she had been able to mark up in his favor, but should he be a Napoleonist, that was a different and terrifying matter! Such admirers of Napoleon existed in England, she knew that well enough, and a handful of hot-blooded extremists wanted to see their own land, which had always symbolized freedom to less fortunate countries, dominated by Napoleon, with the British monarchy destroyed and dictatorship in its place.

She hardly knew how to answer the pleasant remarks Alex was making to her as the dance proceeded, but she managed it somehow, her smile feeling stretched upon her face. When the polonaise ended he asked for the next dance, which was a waltz, and as they spun round and round the floor it was obvious to her that, had she not been betrothed, she would have found a suitor in the kindly Alex Rose-Marshall for, as at Blake's dinner party, she could tell he was much taken with her and when the dance came to a fast swirling close he pressed her closer to him than he should otherwise have done, and was reluctant to relinquish her fingers. But the ice had been broken and others were waiting to ask her to dance, the seal of approval set upon her by the Rose-Marshalls had put into play the reminder that she was half-English and not quite a Frenchwoman, and in any case she wouldn't be marrying Gregory Lockington if she hadn't severed all connection with that war-mad nation on the other side of the Channel.

She saw neither Blake's return nor Gregory's arrival, but suddenly both men were present in the company and whirling past her with partners in another waltz. At the first opportunity she escaped the request of her next would-be partner for a cotrille and located Lucy, who immediately drew her away out of the ballroom and into a salon on the same floor.

"Now," Lucy said, closing the door behind them and hurling the stole, which she had worn ever since taking it, across the nearest chair, "I want the truth! What made you wear a Napoleonic favor from Paris into my home?" She was hurt and angry, two spots of high color in her cheeks. "I thought we were to be friends—good friends, but you brought this evening's ball to the brink of disaster! With everybody's feelings running so high after those dreadful murders, to say nothing of recent French atrocities in the Peninsula against our soldiers, had I not tipped the scales by protesting that the stole was my own, I doubt if a single person would have remained under the same roof with you, and in no time at all the ballroom would have been deserted."

"I wore the stole in all innocence. You must believe me! I did not bring it from Paris, I do assure you."

"Don't split hairs!" Lucy retorted contemptuously. "From France then!" She swept across and snatched up the stole again to handle it in demonstration, running it through a ring she made with finger and thumb. "See how fine it is! I know French silk when I see it. And I tell you that no patriotic British seamstress would embroider the tyrant's symbol in these days."

Juliette sank down in a chair and put shaking fingers to her temples. "You're right about its origins, I can see that. I suppose such articles are smuggled into England together with brandy and tea and lace and all else in that nefarious traffic. I wish I had never set eyes on the stole! This evening was the first time I had worn it and it shall be the last!"

Lucy regarded her uncertainly, not deaf to the ring of truth that had resounded in her words. "How did it come into your possession if you didn't bring it with you?" she questioned searchingly.

"It was a gift presented to me in England!"

"From whom?"

Juliette hesitated. She could not condemn Gregory without first challenging him with what she suspected. "From a gentleman."

"His name?"

"I prefer not to say."

With a sigh Lucy sat down in a chair near at hand. She could not disbelieve Juliette, so vehemently had the protestations of innocence been given. Moreover, she considered herself to be a good judge of character and had liked the girl with her quaint, Gallic mannerisms and lively, open looks, her lack of conceit in a beauty far beyond average. She pitied her being affianced to Gregory, who had always sought conquest and never love.

"I suppose it was someone you met in London before coming to Norfolk." Seeing Juliette's flash of surprise she misinterpreted the reason and shook her head in reassurance. "Don't be concerned. I'll say nothing about it to anyone. You were some time in Town with your aunt and much fêted, I am sure. I know that your marriage to Gregory has been arranged and I fear whoever gave you the stole thought to win your affections by hinting at his own Napoleonic sympathies. I know the last time I visited London it was common knowledge that Lord and Lady Holland have made their house in Kensington a center for those in favor of Napoleon and against the restoration of the Bourbons to the throne of France." She leaned across and put a hand on Juliette's arm. "Tell me honestly where your true loyalties lie, and whichever way you answer me I will never mention it again."

Juliette met her gaze steadily. "I love France. I will always love France, but I began to abhor Napoleon years ago when his wars took my father from me and I never knew if I'd see him again. Out of those childhood fears came my distrust of the Emperor and nothing that has taken place since has ever given me cause to change it. Do you believe me?"

Lucy dipped her head once. "I believe you."

"How would you have treated me if I had replied otherwise?"

"I should have been bitterly disappointed, but that doesn't mean I couldn't have understood how Napoleon had bewitched you as he has done thousands of others with the force of his personality. For Blake's sake I would have tried to convert you from that blind faith in the Emperor who longs to bring England under his heel."

"For Blake's sake?" Juliette raised her eyebrows delicately. "Not Gregory's?"

"No, not Gregory's," Lucy replied levelly. "Blake is important to me. I must admit to harboring a deep affection for him. No, more than that. I love him. I have always loved him. Indeed, I know I love him more than Elizabeth ever did, because she—sweet, gentle, lighthearted creature that she was—loved the world and everyone in it, and Blake had to be content with as much of her heart as she could spare him."

"Did he know that?"

"He knew it, but it made no difference. He was enchanted by her, just as everyone else was. That's why there was so much bitter feeling against him when she was killed. I'll not have him suffer further cuts and rebuffs if I can help it. That's why I intervened as quickly as I did when you arrived wearing that hateful stole. My one thought was to protect Blake. Had I not tipped the scales you would have been ostracized forevermore, not one person would have accepted Blake's invitation as host to your wedding, and much of the old resentment of the past would have been brought up again to hurl against him for having you as guest and future sister-in-law in his house."

Juliette clenched her fists together on her knees, her face taut. "Tell me how Elizabeth died. Nobody will talk about the accident to me. I heard gossipy accounts in London and Aunt Phoebe was vague about the details, and—now that I come to think about it—never particularly eager to talk to me about West Thorpeby Hall and those who live in it. Why was Blake blamed?"

Lucy's face saddened. "It is grossly unfair. Because he happened to have been drinking—not to excess, but more than he does at social occasions these days—it was said that he was too far gone in his cups to know what he was doing and for that reason it was his blundering that brought about the crash. You see, Blake had come home from London with a crowd of people for a house party, and that year the summer weather was particularly fine and dry and steady, which is unusual on this stretch of the coast, and at Elizabeth's suggestion he agreed to hold a grand ball out of doors. With everything neoclassical being the current mode, it was her idea that sections of the grounds should be made to look like Grecian temples and gardens with pillars and statuary. From that moment forth no expense was spared. She demanded that chariots be made so that races could be held like those in the days of the ancient Olympian games, and the estate carpenters built a special one for her and Venetia with their initials on the sides, because they intended to compete as partners in a special ladies' race."

"Wasn't that highly dangerous?"

"Not in these parts. Norfolk women of quality are brought up to know how to handle horses. They ride to hounds a great deal and it's long been a custom at my own home and one or two others to hold driving competitions during house parties as a little *divertissement*." Lucy got up and went slowly across to the window where she gazed out unseeingly at the darkness, showing that it distressed her to recall the events of that particular evening. Juliette twisted in her chair and rested an arm on the low back of it, watching her, but remaining silent.

"You should have seen how splendid West Thorpe-by Hall and the grounds looked that evening. Garlands of flowers were hung everywhere, inside the house and out, and long tables had been set out on the lawns for dining under the stars, the illumination provided by flaring torches. It was a romantic notion of Elizabeth's that the chariot races should be run when the moon had risen, and so it was after supper that we moved across to that section of the grounds where they were to take place, it having been decided that the ladies should race first and the gentlemen with their faster horses afterwards. To come from the lawn by the stables, which was where the chariots were lined up, the competitors had to drive past the north side of the house under the limes and follow one of the wide, graveled paths between the box-hedges. Elizabeth and Venetia were first to take the route, and because they were well ahead of the rest nobody knows exactly what happened. But it was the strangest thing. Their horse suddenly took fright and bolted, and because of the spot where it happened, the old tales of Isabelle's hauntings were revived and blamed as the cause of the accident. For myself I don't know what to believe."

She parted her linked hands indecisively and folded them together again. "I know Elizabeth had no doubts as to Isabelle's spectral existence." She turned about and retraced her steps slowly. "Anyway, the horse came bolting out of the hedges at a mad pace some little distance from where the rest of us were thronging about as we waited, everyone excited and in a merry mood. Some actually began to raise a cheer at the sight of the horse until with horror we saw that Elizabeth had lost the reins and she and Venetia were clinging to the sides of the chariot to save themselves from being hurled out. Blake acted first, throwing himself into the saddle of one of the horses which were to be used by the umpires, and went galloping after them. Others followed, most on foot, but by the time I saw the chariot again it was lying smashed against the gate-pillar at the way out of the drive—Venetia was unconscious and Elizabeth had died in Blake's arms."

Juliette rose to her feet. "But why was he blamed? He was the first to try to save them as you said yourself."

"Any good horseman should have been able to stop that runaway, and normally Blake would have managed it with ease. But those on horseback who reached the drive in time to see what happened said, when he drew level with the bolting horse, he caught hold of the reins, but swerved with it, causing the chariot to swing out and crash against the pillar with such tragic results." She gave a long, deep sigh. "Those who knew Elizabeth and loved her were shattered. The whole county grieved for her, and all the way from Hetherham House to the churchyard townspeople and farming folk from miles around stood five or six deep and threw flowers in the path of the cortège."

"You and Alex never condemned Blake, and yet you were the two most grievously bereaved," Juliette said emotionally.

Lucy turned and looked at her across the room. "Never had he needed friends to stand by him more than at that time. There were even those who whispered that he had seized the opportunity to be rid of her, and other such slander."

"How wicked! How could people be so cruel and evilminded!"

Lucy shrugged and came to Juliette again. "Blake has enemies like all rich and powerful men. Moreover, he has never suffered fools gladly, and there's many a grudge held against him. Even one jealous woman can create a whole tissue of lies, and we all know how mud will stick."

"But to say he wanted to be rid of Elizabeth when all speak of his great love for her!"

"He was devoted to her, but you must remember that the Lockington brothers have long had a reputation for being heartbreakers, never constant in love, and ruthless in their living, and this old score was turned against him. That Elizabeth had brought Blake to the brink of marriage when he had always eluded the snare before was a wonder to everyone. After the accident some said he had tired of her frivolousness long since, but that's not true. We who know him saw how the tragedy struck him down. He changed from that time, relinquishing his wild London friends and taking up his life in Norfolk, which had always absorbed him whenever he was away from those hard-drinking, hard-gambling companions of his. Now you see why it was so important this evening that I should step in and absolve you from the conclusions being drawn. For Blake to have a whisper of Napoleonism muttered against him would undo all the good that has been done."

Juliette bit deep into the inside of her lower lip. Whatever madness Gregory was about she must do her best to turn him from it, but she would give her mind to that later, for there was more that she wished to learn from Lucy. "What caused the horse to bolt in the first place?"

"Nobody knows."

"But it must have been frightened by some unexpected sight or noise. What explanation did Venetia give?"

"She remembers nothing that happened. She was unconscious for several days, and her memory remains a blank."

"That I had not heard." Juliette pondered for a few moments on the possibility of that blankness of memory being linked with the girl's inability to walk. "Was Venetia in love with Blake before he came to care for Elizabeth, do you think?"

Lucy stared at her incredulously. "Venetia has never been in love with Blake. It's Gregory whom she loves. Didn't you know?"

Juliette stood dumb. Suddenly any number of small incidents and events were slotting into place, Venetia's venom towards herself clearly explained. And Blake had thought she was referring to his ward's love for his brother and not to any affection directed towards himself when she had talked to him on the day she had returned from her walk to the clifftops.

"Have I upset you?" Lucy looked concerned.

"You have nothing to worry about, I do assure you. Whatever there was between them is finished on Gregory's side."

"But—but he told me that Venetia hoped to marry Blake."

Lucy compressed her lips in wry amusement. "I imagine she's playing the old, old trick of trying to make him jealous, thinking she might revive his passion for her that way. She's an artful minx, you know. She plays on Blake's compassion to get anything she wants from the latest gee-gaw from London to that magnificent Chinese chair. But don't be misled. Gregory is the Lockington brother on whom she set her heart, and Blake will never marry anyone else now that Elizabeth has gone." She gave a rueful little twitch of a smile. "Not that I have completely surrendered all hope."

Together the two girls moved towards the door to make their return to the ballroom. "What was Elizabeth like to look at?" Juliette asked tentatively.

"Have you never seen a likeness of her? Then you shall. There's an excellent portrait of her in the next room." Lucy led the way through communicating doors into it. "I'll leave you to look at her by yourself. I must get back to the guests before the supper dance."

The room was softly lit, no doubt for the pleasure of any couples choosing to seek out a quiet place, but there was sufficient light for her to see the face of the girl within the gilt frame above the marble fireplace. Then, believing her eyes to be playing her tricks, she picked up a three-branched candlestick and held the flames' glow closer. The pretty, smiling face of Elizabeth was round and merry-cheeked, her hazel eyes large and guileless, her chestnut hair a tumble of curls. Juliette stared in incredulous disbelief. In no way did she and Elizabeth resemble each other. Not in coloring or bone structure or in expression! Why had Gregory said there was a resemblance between them? And why then had Blake looked at her so many times with that deep, anguished look, which to her had spoken of a love cherished for someone else?

Behind her the door of the room opened as somebody entered, and was closed again. Every sense in her told her who it was. Slowly she put the branched candlestick down again, but did not turn her head towards him. "I was looking at Elizabeth," she said huskily.

"She was exactly as you see her in that delightful portrait," Blake's voice replied.

She held her breath. "Do you see any likeness between us? Perhaps my voice or my mannerisms remind you of her?"

He sounded surprised. "No, not at all. I would say that you are as different from her as you could be, except that you in your own sphere can captivate as she did. The world is a poorer place without her as it would be without you."

"I know you loved her very much." Still she did not look at him. What he had said gave a new explanation for those guarded, anguished glances of his that had settled on her down by the dikes and at other times, but she must not give thought to what that might mean.

"I did. Not only was she lovely, as you can see in the portrait, but her gaiety was infectious. She was kindness itself to everyone, whatever their station in life. A gentle person too, and tenderhearted. The like of Elizabeth is not easily found again."

"No wonder everybody says that nobody can take her place."

"She loved everyone and everybody loved her, but she was incapable of passion."

Now she did look at him, but warily and out of the corner of her eye, her head at an angle. He had perched his weight against the edge of a writing desk, arms folded, his face in the shadows. "Are you saying that she loved you no more than anybody else?"

"I've had many long hours to think things over since I lost her, and that is what I have come to believe. I can see she was more in love with the idea of marriage and tripping up the aisle to me in her finery than anything else. A child dressing up. I doubt if her pretty head ever gave a thought to what lay beyond it. The deep relationship that should exist between a man and a woman in all spheres would never have been fulfilled. She would have played at living until the end of her days. She would never have become adult. Always the enchanting, beguiling girl even when her hair was gray."

"Yet you would have gone on loving her."

"Yes. It would have been impossible not to. She awakened the desire to protect and to indulge in all whom she gathered about her. My feelings for her have not lessened in any way, and my part in her passing is a burden I shall carry with me until I die, but her spell bewitched, and now it is gone I'm able to see things clearly."

She was also able to see what he would never say. Such cloying sweetness without depth would have been hard to live with. In the end Elizabeth would have made his life more barren than if he had never known love at all.

"What was it that alarmed the chariot horse so much that it bolted that night?" she asked.

"Nobody will ever know for sure. Venetia can remember nothing."

She faced him, the candlelight behind her creating a nimbus about her hair. "Could it have been Isabelle?"

Briefly he put his hand to his brow and rubbed it with his fingers as if uncertain how to answer her, his ruby ring creating a little blaze of winking, crimson fire. "What is Isabelle? A rustling branch? A whispering draught? A flicker of candlelight across shadow? A force of personality stamped on West Thorpeby Hall as perhaps we all leave some part of ourselves behind when death takes us from a place we love or hate?"

"A tormented soul seeking vengeance?"

"Vengeance—or the peace of eternal rest."

She had not thought of Isabelle in that light before. "Has West Thorpeby Hall ever been exorcized?"

"During the past three hundred years at least six times according to records."

"All to no avail."

"Perhaps by passing the tale of Isabelle from one generation to another we Lockingtons recreate the turbulence that heralds every disaster that befalls." He thrust himself away from the writing desk and took a few steps towards her. "Elizabeth spoke of Isabelle to me before she died. It was difficult to catch her words, but she said, 'Isabelle . . . not her . . . take care.' I could make nothing of it, except that with her last breath she was giving thought to me. It was natural that I could speak of it to no one else."

"But you have told me."

"I have told you in this room what no other has ever heard from me or will hear."

"I'm honored," she said, low-voiced, "and what I have learned will stay only with me from this time forth."

"How much have you learned?"

It was a question she did not dare to answer recklessly. She had learned that it was not through any physical likeness to Elizabeth that he looked at her as he did. And she had discovered that his love for Elizabeth had not been that for which such a man as he should have been destined. It had been revealed to her that, contrary to local opinion, Elizabeth had not been the one love to end all loves for him, but had only paved the way. She saw that the reason he had spoken out was due in no small part to the quiet intimacy of the room and their being alone and away from the bustle and activity of countless people dancing and conversing in the ballroom, from which the music drifted to make romantic undertones to their talk. She deliberated carefully before she gave him a reply.

"I think enough to try to persuade you not to resign yourself to bachelorhood."

"I'll not marry for the sake of marrying. Not even for an heir."

Her head jerked. "How fortunate men are! They can pick and choose what to do with their lives, but not women. Our path is set for us. Out of a loveless match I must provide that heir."

"I cannot believe Gregory feels no affection for you. When he saw the miniature he declared you were the most beautiful young woman he had ever seen and he loved you already."

"Were you the only witness to that proclamation?"

"No, I was not. Venetia was present, so was your aunt, and Caroline too."

Only too clearly she saw that Gregory could have been taking a sadistic delight in tormenting Venetia with that extravagant statement. She knew only too well from the way Nicolaus had behaved towards her at the door of Marianne's boudoir that men could be fiendishly cruel to women they no longer wanted.

"Nevertheless," she said with a catch in her voice, the awfulness of that occasion having returned all too vividly, "it is not love that Gregory feels for me." She straightened her shoulders. "You returned to West Thorpeby Hall this evening to fetch me in Gregory's absence. That was chivalrous of you. Now I had better go and find him."

His next words brought her to a standstill before she was halfway to the door. "If it lies in my power to change your fate I will do it."

Her eyes, startled and glistening, met his. "How?"

"I'll persuade him to tear up his half of the marriage contract. That will set you free."

"He'll never agree!"

"Then he does care for you."

"No, he does not!"

"I can replace your dowry from my own coffers. He needn't fear being the loser in that respect."

"He'll take nothing more from you! That was why he borrowed on the strength of his inheritance. But it's more than that. Reasons I can't explain to you."

She darted for the door, but he reached it before her, setting his clasp on the handle and holding it, barring her way. "What reasons? I can only imagine that you feel you might yet fall in love with him!"

The retort was out before she could stop it. "Never! You know that's impossible!"

"How do I know it?"

Shivering, she looked into his ardent face and stayed quite still. Her only movement was to place one hand lightly against the necklace that she wore. It was as if she drowned in his eyes, and as he had once looked at her across a wide room in a London house it was with passion that he communicated with her in their silence. He moved forward and put his arms about her, drawing her with him further back into the room. He whispered her name, bent his head and kissed her bare shoulder, said her name softly again. She made no answer, but it came to him through the involuntary, amorous trembling of her young body pressed to his, and then of her own accord she lifted her lips to his, her arms going about his shoulders. His mouth took hers in an onslaught of longing and pentup desire, and she responded with a wildness over which she had no control, kissing him back ardently, her hands pressing into the nape of his neck.

Neither of them heard the door open. It was the beam of light falling on them through the widening aperture that made them realize they were observed. In a last sweet, careless moment of ecstasy they did not start or react with anything other than mild amusement at the intrusion of the outside world upon their discovered joy in each other, and she turned her head just before he did to see who stood in the doorway. Then the hot, unhappy color suffused her cheeks. It was Lucy who stood stricken as though she might never move again.

Lucy spoke first. "It's the supper dance," she said faintly. "I thought you'd like to know."

"Lucy—" Juliette stammered, cold reason having returned and with it an awareness of the extent of her unguarded behavior.

Lucy ignored her and addressed Blake. "Count yourself fortunate that it was I and not Gregory who discovered you. Brother or not, he would have called you out."

He answered grimly. "It may well come to that."

"No!" Juliette cried, looking from one to the other of them. "That must never happen!"

Lucy regarded her coolly. "Then I suggest you remember which brother it is to whom you are betrothed. It wouldn't be the first time that one Lockington shot another dead in a tasteless quarrel over a fickle woman."

"That's mightily unjust of you, Lucy," Blake stated fiercely, but Juliette did not wait to hear any more.

She rushed from the salon, leaving Blake and Lucy on their own. They faced each other and Lucy made a quick little movement with her hands.

"Unfair, perhaps," she admitted, "but necessary. I was outspoken then, but I do not regret it. It will do Juliette no harm to be reprimanded. She cannot—and she must not—forget that she is betrothed to Gregory, least of all when alone with his own brother. You know Gregory better than I, but even so our respective families have been friends for enough years for me to know that he is hotheaded, jealous, and possessive of anything he owns. And, in this case, he owns Juliette by mark of his betrothal ring on her finger."

Blake walked across to look up at the portrait of Elizabeth. "Are you telling me that the Lockingtons could not survive another scandal?"

"You would survive. Throughout the centuries the Lockingtons have survived sieges and the Black Death and the flooding of their land by the sea and attack by fire and storm, to say nothing of scandals both old and comparatively new. You and those who bear your name will always survive, but should you come between your brother and the girl he has chosen to marry you will bring down not only yourself, but Juliette as well into the mire. She is a stranger in an alien land, young and lovely and ripe for living and enjoying herself. Would you have her cold-shouldered by all she met? Would you reduce her to misery and homesickness and shame?"

"No, you know I would not. But if Gregory should release her—"

"Oh, Blake." Lucy shook her head sadly. "Have you seen how he looks at her?"

He swung round on his heel and answered her harshly. "Yes, as he looks at other women whom he intends to bed!"

She came towards him and rested her palms against the silk facings of his coat. "Don't delude yourself. Gregory will always be that way, but something tells me—I don't know what, intuition, I suppose—that Juliette has a special quality in his eyes. He'll never let her go."

He put his hands over hers, looking down into her face. "Lucy, you are a good friend. You always have been. I shall be in your debt for the rest of my life for all that you and Alex did for me. I'll not expose Juliette to scandal, but I cannot change my feelings towards her."

Lucy's sensitive face was full of gentle understanding. He did not have to tell her that feelings towards one person could not be changed at will. Love was tenacious. Even when cut to pieces, however unwittingly done, it still lived and soared and was as it had ever been. Blake, not quite knowing why, bent his head and kissed her lips softly. She drew back, smiling at him.

"We must get back to the ballroom, or else you and I will start tongues wagging."

He smiled, sharing the absurdity of her little joke. Together they went out of the room. Elizabeth's portrait glowed in the candlelight.

Upstairs Juliette had sought the sanctuary of the bedroom that had been set aside for ladies to titivate during the evening. It was deserted, due to the supper dance being in progress, except for a lady's maid in attendance, who took one look at her face and pushed a chair forward.

"Sit down, ma'am. I'll fetch you a drink of water."

Juliette sipped it automatically, stunned by her own foolishness. Not only had she thrown herself at Blake, setting into motion innumerable complications that she had not given a thought to, but Lucy—of all people!—must needs discover them in each other's arms. There was no one whom she would have wanted to hurt less than Lucy who had shown her nothing but kindness from the start, and who only that evening had saved her from an intolerable situation. The only part of all that had happened which she could not regret was the knowledge of Blake's mouth on hers, its tender violence, its eager possessiveness. At the mere thought of it a flame leapt in the pit of her stomach and a glorious, sensuous wave of pleasure seemed to engulf her from head to foot. But that kiss had been the begin-

ning and the end of it. A few jeweled minutes to remember privately, but which could make no difference
to the pattern that events must follow. Gregory would
never let her go and at all costs Blake must never ask
him, or else the bitterness which would result could easily lead to bloodshed. Why hadn't she extracted a
promise from Blake to say nothing, instead of dashing away? Lucy, out of personal pain and love for
Blake, could be relied upon not to reveal what she
had seen. At least Lucy and she shared the same urgent desire to prevent a rift between the brothers that
could reach to limits far more deadly than the mere
difference of opinions which divided them at the present time.

"Feeling better, ma'am?" the lady's maid inquired,
seeing her rise from the chair to tidy herself before a
looking glass.

"Yes. Thank you for looking after me."

Juliette's feet twinkled downstairs in her haste to
rejoin Blake and beg him to keep silent, but when she
took the curve of it her heart sank. Gregory stood waiting for her at the foot of it, his face taut, his eyes narrowed and flint-bright. He knows already! she thought
on a crescent of sudden panic. But his first words made
her realize that his wrath sprang from another
source.

"What on earth possessed you to wear that French
stole this evening?" he demanded in an anger-thick-
ened voice. She had reached him and he seized her
arm to pull her roughly to the side of the staircase
where they would not be seen, although with everyone
having gone in to supper there was little chance of it.
"I had a full account of what happened from Caroline. Fortunately, not having seen the stole before, she
assumed Lucy had loaned it to you and even suspected
her of having had a little joke at your expense. A little joke! God's teeth! Where is it now? Does Lucy still
have it?"

"We talked about it in that salon over there." She
indicated the door several yards from them. "As far
as I know it's still where she left it on a chair."

"What did you say to her?"

"Very little. She knows it was a gift, but not who the donor was."

He relaxed, less angry, and stroked her arm. "I can understand your eagerness to wear it, but the time is not yet. I—"

She interrupted him. "Why did you once say I was like Elizabeth Rose-Marshall?"

He looked puzzled. "Did I say that? It could only have been the way you looked at me when we first met. Wary and watchful. She was the same whenever—"

A footman came into sight and Gregory stopped what he had been about to say and substituted a reminder that they should be going in to supper together.

"Whenever?" she persisted.

"Oh, I don't know," he said vaguely. "Whenever she was at West Thorpeby Hall. A look of being inwardly on guard as if she never quite trusted the house or anybody in it." Then he grinned at her with great charm, his eyes twinkling with that uplift swing of mood which she had come to recognize as characteristic of his buoyant nature. "But it was I of whom you were wary that night. You were afraid I might ravish you, were you not? How you trembled! I've never seen a prettier sight or been more sorely tempted."

Taking her hand and tucking it into the crook of his arm, he chuckled over his teasing of her, but she did not smile and could not, there being too much truth in his words. Obviously proud of her, looking to the right and left when they entered the ballroom, he led her down the length of the floor to the supper room, which opened out of the anteroom where Venetia had been sitting.

Juliette saw her the moment they entered the supper room. She had half a dozen young men attending her but, alerted to where her true love lay, Juliette noticed how her eyes darted to Gregory and followed him before one of her gallants spoke to her and brought her attention back to himself.

After supper Juliette danced with Gregory, a number of other partners, and then Blake. To converse without the risk of being overheard by other couples was impossible, but she did manage to say, "Please say nothing."

It was enough for him to understand what she meant. He gave her fingers in his a small, reassuring squeeze. "We'll discuss it tomorrow."

She had to be content with that for the time being, but there was no promise in his tone, only a light dismissal as though the whole matter were already settled in their favor. What dear, foolish optimism! What utter disregard for the danger that would threaten him! Her steps followed his, and her skirt swung out like a long, slender bell as they rotated together under the embellished, pink ceiling and the crystal chandeliers. Being so close to each other with the memory of their wild kissing uppermost in both their minds made it impossible to converse on any other level, and both of them said no more for the whole of the lilting, whirling dance, although the pressure of his hand on the back of her waist was a declaration of love, his fingers on hers a caress, and whenever their eyes met she read messages in them that she had no right to receive.

When the waltz ended Alex was waiting to partner her and Blake had no choice but to surrender her, not knowing she had made up her mind not to dance with him again that evening, fearful of giving her heightened emotions away to the eagle eyes of dowagers and chaperons, who watched from gilded chair and gallery, swift to whisper behind their fans and set gossip or scandal aflame at the slightest sign of amorous interplay or impropriety. For Blake's sake, not her own, she must guard against that whenever she was with him. Once again she felt herself ranged with Lucy, albeit they were now estranged, against the world for love of Blake.

Alex, however, showed a careless disregard for any gossip he might bring down on his own head. He put her hand to his lips as he led her on to the floor and took hold of her eagerly when the music commenced. It was another waltz.

"I've been waiting ever since our last dance to take you in my arms again," he said, laughing in his throat, his eyes sparkling at her. "Gregory doesn't deserve his good fortune. I'd give half my life to be in his shoes."

She could tell that where he had been bold before he would be even bolder now. He had consumed a deal of wine since he had partnered her previously, and it had loosened his basic shyness, making him ready to say and do anything in an uninhibited wooing of her favors. She knew she could check him neatly and with charm, leaving him scarcely aware that he had been rebuffed; only conscious that he had gone so far and must go no further. But an idea stirred and she merely smiled, neither encouraging nor discouraging, her mind distracted, her feet following almost of their own volition the dance that surely had been created for lovers, wishing in spite of everything that it was Blake with whom she waltzed.

She came in contact with him again when she and Alex, breathless from a gavotte, were served glasses of wine and found themselves drawn into a group seated in an alcove. Hardly had they taken their places when the conversation happened to turn to Venetia.

"It's wonderful to see her here this evening," one lady remarked. "Time and time again we have all invited her to such occasions and been disappointed, but now that Lucy and Alex have been successful in persuading her to attend I hope we may expect to see her at all future balls and dances."

"I'm sure her decision to come this evening is due as much to Juliette as to our mutual friends," Blake remarked, making everyone look at her.

"Is that so?" the lady said inquiringly.

"Juliette is sweeping the cobwebs out of West Thorpeby Hall like a fair wind from across the sea."

"From France," sniggered somebody *sotto voce*.

Blake twisted in his chair to address him deliberately. "No, sir. From Sweden, where Juliette was resident before coming to England. Her father was in the service of Bernadotte, the Crown Prince who has shown friendship to us in refusing to support Napoleon's trade blockade against Britain."

After that they eyed her in a new light. The matter

of the stole with the border of the Bonaparte bees had
been settled once and for all. Had she not made up her
mind how to silence Blake completely on the matter
of her marriage to Gregory she would have given him
a grateful glance, but as it was she could no longer look
at him because the way she must deceive him for his
own good caused her so much pain that she scarcely
knew how to bear it. Desperately she concentrated on
the talk around her, which had turned to the treaty of
alliance Bernadotte had signed with Russia, setting his
face once and for all against his former Emperor. The
news had come fresh that day, and Juliette had not
heard it before. In the midst of her dejection she
felt proud that Bernadotte had made a stand, which
all free thinking Frenchmen everywhere could look to
as an example, showing full opposition to the tyrant's
bloody rule. At the first opportunity she intended to
draw from Gregory the extent of his Napoleonic lean-
ings, it being obvious to her now that he imagined that
she shared them, and for no other reason than that she
was French-born and must be expected as a woman to
have no mind of her own, being thus molded to follow
without question the way that the Emperor led. Proudly she raised the glass she held in her hand.

"Long life to Bernadotte!"

They all drank with her. Afterwards Alex led her
into the dancing again and she began a frenzied flir-
tation with him. For the second time that evening people stared at her, but this time she welcomed it, knowing that it meant none had spotted her passion for her
future brother-in-law, and he was absolved from all
harms. What effect her behavior was having on him
she did not know, not daring to look in his direction,
although several times she caught a glimpse of him
out of the corner of her eye. Lucy's face she saw once,
an oval of shock and consternation at the sight of her
brother being beguiled by someone whom she had already condemned as fickle, and Juliette knew sadly
that she had lost beyond all chance of recall the
friendship that would have meant much to her by this
third and final offense of the evening. She thought
Gregory had departed, because he was not to be seen

dancing or chatting on the gallery, and she was becoming used to his comings and goings without thought for her when the mood took him, but later she was to discover that in this case she had misjudged him, for he had settled down to play for high stakes at Faro with some other gentlemen in another part of the house.

As she had expected, it was only a matter of time before Alex became more urgent in his persuasion that they should seek a quieter place than the ballroom floor in which to follow up this special interest they had discovered in each other, but she played for time until she saw Blake lift Venetia up in his arms and knew he was on the point of leaving. Only then did she acquiesce.

"I'll go ahead to the salon where Elizabeth's portrait hangs," she whispered, teasingly, to Alex, her coquettishness delighting him. "You may follow a few seconds after. We mustn't be seen leaving the floor together."

Her plan worked perfectly. So perfectly that she almost wept. Not appearing to notice Blake with Venetia, while making sure they saw her, she ran lightly across their path into the salon, leaving the door ajar. As she had expected, Alex had to stop and receive thanks for his hospitality and exchange good nights. She opened the door a little wider.

"Alex," she called softly. She had time to see Blake's face rigid and white-boned as she slipped an arm about Alex's neck and drew him into the room with her, closing the door.

Her immediate explosion into tears had the same effect upon Alex as if ice cold water had been thrown over him. He had her in his arms, but as hers about his neck fell away and she covered her face with her hands he stood at a loss, showing part annoyance, part exasperation, and part a certain sweet gentleness, there being nothing vindictive or brutal in his nature, for all that he was a healthy young man with strong and normal desires, and his disappointment was acute.

"What is it? What's the matter? I thought—but I'd no intention of abusing you—come, Juliette, you've no need to be afraid of me."

Because she liked him and because she had hated using him for her own ends, his considerate tones exacerbated her unhappiness and her tears flowed faster than ever. Quite expertly he drew her to him and she buried her face in his shoulder. Having grown up with three sisters he was not unused to tearful displays, although it was some time since he had had to witness any, for if Lucy cried over being twenty-five and on the shelf she did it in the privacy of her own quarters and never showed any sign of it.

Another possible cause of Juliette's distress occurred to him, and he turned her face tenderly and tilted it upwards. "Gregory is not going to lose his temper over—well, over nothing." He pulled his fine linen handkerchief from his pocket and dabbed the tears flowing down her cheek with it. "Everybody flirts. It's *à la mode.*" His eyes went to her soft, tremulous mouth and the creamy swell of her breasts pressed against him within the lemon silk frill of her low-cut bodice, causing his blood to beat hot for her again and with it came the knowledge that he was more than half in love with her. He saw little joy for her in her marriage with Gregory who—if the cards had turned against him or if he was deep in his cups—could well lose his temper most vilely should he learn that they were alone together, in spite of the reassurance he had given her to the contrary in order to quiet her tears. Yet nothing of any consequence could be achieved in a room with an unlocked door. But what of other times when they could be alone together in more favorable circumstances? No one expected fidelity in a marriage of convenience, and she was surely not naive enough to expect it from Gregory, who could never leave a woman's skirts alone. He could give her the love and comfort that she would need. She might even come to love him in return. Damn Gregory to hell! Had she not been betrothed he could have wooed her honorably —and won her.

"You're most kind, Alex," she said appreciatively, drying her eyes with a corner of the handkerchief that he still held. "I behaved badly to you and yet you forgive me. Do believe me when I say I had good reason."

He thought he understood. She had been trying to punish Gregory for his poor treatment of her that evening. Firstly, he had let her arrive by herself and then, after no more than a dance or two with her, he had taken himself off to the Faro tables. Well, she would learn that such tactics were a waste of time. Perhaps she had learned that already.

"I believe you, and don't apologize." His good-natured face split into a grin, his eyes wicked and mischievous. "I enjoyed the greater part of our time spent together."

She responded with a dawn of a smile, thinking that there were few people she had ever liked as much as him. It was a great pity she had alienated his sister, because she set high value on the friendship of each of them.

"I do not feel inclined to return to the dancing," she said, fussing her fingertips at her eyelids, certain they must be red and swollen, "or of facing the company again. Would you have my carriage called?"

He went right to the carriage with her and before it departed he entered it with her and sat on the opposite seat, having a final word with her in private. "This evening has meant much to me. I hope it has created a bond between us."

She was touched by his warm words and regarded him fondly. "It has set you in a special place in my affections."

"I would that it was to Hertherham House you were to be a bride."

He had not intended to say it, but the words had come of their own accord, propelled by his heart. Briefly she closed her eyes and shook her head.

"That can never be, and you must never think of it again." She leaned forward and although he turned his mouth eagerly she avoided it and kissed him on the cheek. "Good night, Alex. You must return to your guests and I must go home."

She waved to him from the carriage window. He

did not go back into the house until the last gleam of
the carriage lamps had vanished from sight.

At West Thorpeby Hall she was halfway across the
hall when she saw Blake come to stand in the doorway
of the library where he must have been awaiting her
return. She slowed to a standstill, thinking she had
never seen a man with such a look compounded of
anger, hurt, and accusation stamped upon his face,
his hands balled at his sides. Neither of them spoke.
Then deliberately she laughed, the merry little sound
seeming to tinkle in that area of marble pillars and great
looking glasses, much as if a draught had disturbed the
pendants of the crystal chandelier suspended above her
head. With the most Gallic of shrugs, a high up-pulling
of shoulders and a flicking out of lifted hands, her
head impishly on one side, she laughed at him again,
conveying a visual message that he had been mad to
suppose that what had passed between them in the
salon at Hetherham House had been unique in her
experience, for had she not shown him the error of
his supposition almost immediately afterwards?

He blanched, his mouth so tight that it was as if he
did not dare to allow speech to come from him for
fear of what he might say, and his dark, wrathful eyes,
slashed with the anguish of his loving, followed her as
she tripped lightly up the stairs, humming to herself a
snatch of a waltz that she had danced with Alex, her
lifted hem revealing glimpses of her slender ankles
in the cross-ribbons of her silk slippers. For the second
time that night a man watched her out of sight. But
this time her face, which he could not see, was stricken.
This time her cheeks were hollow and her face whiter
than his own.

On the threshold of her bedroom she paused abruptly, her lack of color becoming even more pronounced,
and Sorrel, who was waiting to help her undress,
came forward quickly with a rustle. "Do you feel
faint, ma'am?" she enquired.

Juliette entered the room cautiously, looking about
warily. "How long have you been waiting for me?"

"In here, ma'am? Only since I heard your carriage

arrive. I've been pressing your dresses in the linen room."

"Has—has anything strange happened?"

Sorrel frowned at her as if she thought her mistress was half out of her head. "Goodness, no."

"Open the window."

"The moths will come in to the candlelight."

Swiftly Juliette went across to the window herself, throwing it wide and gulping in the night air. When she felt that sufficient draught had circulated in the room she left the window, waving aside the vinaigrette that Sorrel had snatched up in the belief that she was indeed about to swoon.

"I have no need of that."

"Yes, ma'am." Sorrel's expression remained dubious, but Juliette said no more. Let Sorrel think she had taken too much wine if she liked. Juliette knew she would never forget the eeriness of being greeted at the door of her own bedroom by the faintest aroma of that dankness she remembered all too clearly from the North Octagon Room. Isabelle had come trailing her awful, mud-encrusted skirts through this part of the house. For what evil purpose? It did not bear contemplation.

Chapter Nine

Returning from a ride out across the countryside, Juliette dismounted by the stable entrance. When the groom came to take the bridle and lead the bay back to its stall she had a question to ask him.

"Can you show me whereabout the chariots led off from on the party night when the fatal accident occurred?"

"That were over a year ago, miss. 'Fore I came to these stables. I'll fetch someone else to you." He led the bay, its hooves clipclopping daintily on the cobbles, away under the ivy-covered archway and shouted to another groom who was polishing some harness in the sun on the steps of the tackroom. " 'Ere, boy! Attend the lady! She 'as something to ask you."

The second groom was able to give her the information she sought. "They lined up there, miss," he said, pointing with the hand that held the rubbing cloth towards the lawn on the far side of the stableyard drive. "Real pretty they looked, shining gold in the moonlight and all the torches flaring. Miss Venetia and the other young lady, the one who was killed, took off first. All the young ladies had dressed up in Grecian costumes for the race, and them two were in white with scarlet ribbons in their hair. There was to be a parade first around the course, and no allotted space was to be allowed between each chariot. I was standing right here with a watch in me hand, timing the seconds until the second one should follow, but just as I gave the signal we heard this commotion down that path beyond the trees within the shelter of the tall box-hedges. For no reason anyone can make out the horse which was drawing the chariot in which Miss Venetia was standing with Miss Rose-Marshall, who held whip and reins, took fright and bolted." He put

212

his head on one side with polite enquiry. "Getting acquainted with everything concerned with the Lockington family, are you, miss? Seeing how you're soon to be a Lockington yourself."

"That is right."

He became even more cooperative, thinking her a right pretty young woman and worth better than Mr. Gregory, but then he always did get the good-looking fillies who could see no deeper than whatever their eyes showed them. A man who was brutal to a horse would treat a woman the same way, and no doubt many of them had come to discover that. He could name one for a start. There were some women, of course, who would like the kind of treatment Mr. Gregory would mete out to them as though they were savage, unbroken mares, although they surely had a streak of cruelty in their own natures to match whatever it was that the younger Lockington brother needed to suit his pleasure. But there was no hint of that darkness in the young woman who was concerning herself over the tragedy, unaware that her clear, direct-looking eyes were softened by sadness over it.

"Would you like me to show the exact place where the horse took fright?" he offered.

"Yes, please."

She looked about her as they went along the path under the branches of the lime trees. To the left lay the north wing of the house and the corner of the block in which on an upper floor the North Octagon Room was situated, and for the first time she noticed the oaken door in the base of it which led down to the dungeons where once Isabelle had been incarcerated and then rescued. She turned with the groom into the shade and shelter of the box-hedges, and ahead lay a leafy arbor created by a cultivated copse, which formed a tunnel of soft foliage.

"It were right on this spot that the horse reared, judging by the way the gravel of the path was gouged and scattered, and it took off down through the arbor, continued in a straight line across the rose garden, galloped between other hedges, and came out close to the lawn where the race was to be run. That's when Mr. Lockington gave chase on horseback, but he was too late to stop the horse reaching the drive and only came level with the chariot when it was going through the gates. I suppose you know the rest, miss."

"I do," she said gravely. "Tell me, have you any ideas of your own as to why the horse should have taken fright at that particular spot?"

"Well, miss, I have given thought to it many a time since." He set one fist on his hip and stood in the relaxed stance of countrymen since time immemorial, and rubbed his chin with finger and thumb. "All the chariots had smaller flares attached to them in iron holders, and it could be that sparks landed on the horse or flew in front of his eyes."

"Did the horse have any burn marks on him?"

"No, but they didn't have to be big sparks to make him jump."

"Agreed. What else have you thought of?"

"Maybe it didn't care to be hitched to a chariot. All the horses were excited and restless that night. They always know when something different is up. Sometimes it takes no more than a trick of the light or an unexpected movement or sound to make a nervous horse up and go. You, being a horsewoman, miss, would know that."

"Yes, indeed."

"I must say that I did wonder if one of the guests strayed away from the company waiting to see the chariots appear and stepped into the horse's path by chance, causing the trouble, and afterwards not dared to admit to it. But I came to the conclusion that it was impossible. The foliage is too thick for anyone to have gone pushing through and ruining any of the fine clothes they were all decked out in that night."

"Then it appears we are left with the one generally accepted explanation as to what actually caused the horse to bolt."

He knew what she meant and was made uncomfortable by it, rubbing the loose gravel with the toe of his riding boot while he looked up and then down, but not at her. "I admit this is an ill-fated patch of ground. There's none I know who'll come this way by night."

It seemed he would have left the subject there, but she continued to wait expectantly, giving him no choice but to continue. "Yes?"

He squinted past her up at the north wing where the windows level with the octagonal rooms at either end blinked in the sun. "It's said that when old Thomas Lockington threw the lute player from one of those windows up there—" he pointed to the row "—the poor fellow landed to break every bone in his body on that spot." His finger followed dramatically the arch of the fall and indicated a place at Juliette's feet. So vivid was the picture conjured up in her imagination that it was all she could do not to draw back a step.

"Are you saying that the horse sensed or saw the lute player lying in its path?"

"No, it wouldn't have seen him, but *her,* the Lady Isabelle." He drew a deep breath. "Now I'm not saying I believe she appeared that night. It's far more likely that it was nothing more unusual than what I've already put forward, but there's some what say ghosts walk and some what say they don't. All I know is that the tales have been handed down about this part of the house and grounds for donkeys' years. The Lady Isabelle cries her tears over the place where the lute player died. There are folk who say they have heard her."

She searched his face keenly with her gaze. "Have you?"

"Trees make strange sounds at night, squeaking and rustling their branches. And owls hoot, and hares squeal. I can't say I've heard her."

She saw he would not admit to fear, but she could guess that in his room in the stable loft when the wind blew wild and savage from the sea, making the trees moan, nothing in the world would induce him to look from the window in case he saw that pale, grisly wraith from the marshes.

"Thank you for all you've told me," she said. "It was most interesting."

Interesting, she thought, as she strolled away from

the arbor, leaving the groom to go back to work, but
not enlightening. She had learned nothing new about
the cause of the tragedy, except perhaps that the horse
which pulled the chariot had been in a singularly nervous state, but more ready to shy, rear, or bolt than
anyone, even the groom, had appreciated, or else
the two girls would never have set off with that particular animal in the shafts.

"There was one small thing I've just remembered,
miss!" The groom had swung back from the direction
of the stables and had taken a few running steps after
her.

"Yes?" She slewed round to face him.

"I don't even know if I ought to mention it, the
family's personal affairs being none of my business, but
Miss Venetia was right upset by something that had
taken place just afore the race. Miss Rose-Marshall
had to persuade her to take part, 'cos she was all for
going off and throwing herself in the nearest dike—
or so she said in the heat of the moment, and she
looked as if she was right ready to do it. I heard more
than I should have done 'cos, as I said, I was waiting
to time the taking off, and neither of them noticed
me."

"Have you told anyone else about this?"

"No, miss. At the time we were all questioned it
had gone right out of my head. I suppose we were con-
centrating on what could have frightened the horse
at the arbor. It never came to me until much later that
Miss Venetia could have done something in the state
she was in to make it rear as it did, but what that could
have been I've no suggestion to offer, since, as I mentioned, Miss Rose-Marshall had both reins and whip.
By then the funeral had been over for a month or
more, and it was generally understood that the less said
about the whole business the better, seeing that Miss
Venetia had been left crippled by it. I must say we
all thought it a blessing that she couldn't remember
anything that happened, because I tell you Miss Rose-
Marshall had a terrible death. The whole of the lower
part of her body was crushed between the chariot and
the gate-pillar."

Juliette's hand fluttered to her mouth and she pressed her fingertips against it in distress. "That's the first time I've heard the details. Dear God!"

He shook his head sadly. "You can just tell how we all felt. Many of us shed a tear right there, and I'm not ashamed to say it. If only Miss Rose-Marshall had let Miss Venetia drop out of the race as she wanted to and stayed with her, instead of thinking she was doing the best thing for her by making it look as if her pride hadn't been hurt and all that over— well, over what it was, then the accident would never have happened."

Juliette had no intention of questioning him about that private conversation between the girls, but it was not hard to draw her own conclusions as to what the catastrophe was that had made Venetia talk of suicide. "I feel I must commend you on your discretion in not discussing Miss Venetia's emotional upset with all and sundry."

The man looked shyly pleased by her approval, shifting his weight from one leg to the other. "I can't abide gossip and never have. What's more, I'm proud to serve the Lockington family. I've been at the stables at West Thorpeby Hall since I was a nipper, and my father and my grandfather afore me."

She smiled. "Have you children to follow in your footsteps?"

"Yes, miss." He grinned proudly. "Two sons, and both of them are showing that they have a way with horses."

"I'm very glad to hear it."

Once more she turned her steps towards the house. Suppose she sought an opportunity to talk to Venetia about all that happened? If the girl could be brought back to the scene, not necessarily in a chariot, even if any were still left in the stable storerooms, but in her dragon chair at the same hour as she had driven to-wards the arbor and with the same kind of moon above, wasn't it highly likely that her memory would be jogged, everything would come flooding back, and with it the ability to walk again?

But it would be difficult to find an opening for any

kind of conversation with Venetia, who made a point
of answering in abrupt monosyllables any remark Juliette addressed to her. It created a deal of unpleasant
atmosphere when they both dined at the same table,
and Caroline did nothing to ease it, always ready with
a snide comment, except when her baronet was invited
to dine at West Thorpeby Hall and then she was like a
young girl instead of her thirty years, agreeable to all,
excited, and happy to be the object of male admiration
again. Juliette hoped that the baronet, Sir Humphrey
Howlett, a well-built, ginger-headed man, would come
up to scratch and offer for her, it being obvious that it
did not suit Caroline to lie alone in bed, much frustra-
tion as well as grief festering the wound of bereavement which otherwise would heal quite normally and
healthily. But Sir Humphrey showed himself to be a
cautious man, his late wife—so it was said—having
been something of a shrew, and it was obvious he was
not going to leap into matrimony without the most
careful cogitation as to whether the lady he was con-
sidering would prove to be as sweet-tongued after his
ring was on her finger as before.

Since the ball Juliette was only too aware that Blake,
although still the most courteous of hosts, had lapsed
back into that distant attitude towards her; whereas
previously his guarded attitude had sprung from the
knowledge that he loved his brother's future wife and
must in no way reveal it, he now believed himself utterly rejected and would not suffer her to humiliate and
torment him further. Yet like all lovers, whether they
acknowledge themselves to be or not, they were acutely
sensitive to each other the whole time; she had only
to enter the same room and it was as if their bodies
communicated by electric currents and without turning
his head or even hearing her footsteps he knew she
was there. It was the same if he rode along the drive
when she was at her easel in the garden at work on a
painting of the house, her brush faltering long before
his shadow passed across her paper; he never reined
in to enter into conversation with her, taking his cue
from her careful avoidance of being on her own with
him at any time, and he would merely raise his hat

and sometimes pass a comment on the weather. It was a bleak and distressful time for both of them, each shut away in a private cocoon of anguish, and to hers was added the pain of having him believe that she had not loved him after all, but had played a cruel game for the triumph of conquest. Daily the acceptances to her wedding poured in, but his secretary dealt with them and it was with difficulty that she managed a smile when asked to view the list and see how many names had been ticked off.

Her thoughts dwelt on Gregory as she turned the corner of the house and made her way up the steps to the entrance. His session at the Faro tables had left him a thousand guineas richer for the night's play, and the next morning he had taken himself off to Norwich for purposes of his own, giving no word of when he expected to return. When they met again she intended, without further ado, to make it clear to him that she was no supporter of Napoleon and nothing could sway her mind on the matter. She feared he would be in for something of a shock to discover that his future bride, although able to give him prestige in the eyes of fellow Napoleonists through the gallant surname that was hers, had a will equal to his and would not be easily subdued on any score.

As she passed from the sunshine into the house a servant on duty by the door addressed her. "Mr. Gregory has come home, miss. He is in his apartments in the north wing and would be vastly obliged if you would join him at your earliest convenience upon your return from your ride."

So Gregory wanted to see her. Well, she certainly wanted to see him, but the meeting would bring neither of them any joy. In her bedroom she rang for Sorrel, who came with her usual calm mien and untalkative efficiency to help her out of her riding habit and into a day gown of white sprigged strawberry silk. Since becoming her lady's maid Sorrel wore a far more flattering mobcap with a lace frill, a dark crimson ribbon threaded through it to match each of the three daily dresses that Juliette had chosen for her to wear, thinking she would find the color more pleasing and better suited to her coloring than the black she had worn before. But Sorrel, although immaculate and starched-crisp at all times, seemed to take no interest in her own looks, and continued to hide every strand of hair under the cap, preventing it from enhancing in any way her quaintly goblin features. Juliette had come to see that this subjugation of all personality most surely sprang from the girl's early and intense ambition to advance herself from humble beginnings to a position of considerable standing in the hierarchy of domestic service. With time she hoped the girl would realize she was established and, feeling secure at last, would emerge from that hard, protective shell as a full person in her own right, a blooming from closed bud to full flower, but so far there was no sign of it.

To test herself once again and make sure she had not lost her courage, Juliette decided to go by way of the North Octagon Room into the wing which Gregory had made his own. Her heart began to palpitate as she drew near, but she did not slow her purposeful pace and like a swimmer plunging into the cold sea she took in a deep draught of breath before she left the window-bright corridor and entered the ever dim, ever gloomy North Octagon Room where dusk seemed permanently to linger in the absence of any direct daylight. The carpet was still in the hands of the weavers, but carpenters had been at work and the damaged floor where the corona had crashed down had been repaired. The corona itself, its dents and bent candle-holders put right by a blacksmith, was again suspended from the ceiling. She peered upward and was able to follow with her gaze the molding which cleverly concealed the chain that enabled the corona to be lowered for cleaning or for the lighting of wicks until her eyes reached one of the archways where she saw the chain with the ring attached set into a groove in the stonework.

With a rustle of her skirt she moved across to the ring and looped her fingers into it, gingerly prepared to feel the hard pull of the heavy corona when she took it from its hook, but to her surprise it moved easily and was so well weighted that she was able to

raise and lower it without effort. Only the sharp releasing of the ring from the moment of it being taken from
the hook would bring it crashing down. She shuddered
again at the memory of how near death she had been,
and made sure that she replaced the ring securely.

Emboldened by the way she had so far asserted
herself in that eerie room she promenaded in a complete circle, keeping close to the walls, and came to a
halt again where she had started, right by the mural
where Isabelle's hand stretched for the last time above
the surging waters, a red-stoned ring on her finger. An
unusual ring with gold claws like those of an eagle.
After studying it closely she came to the conclusion
that it was identical to the one that Blake wore. How
odd!

She glanced through the arched aperture into the
blackness of the encircling passageway from which
night darkness never lifted. Was she brave enough to
walk the few steps across it to the recessed door that
led up into the dome? It was like playing the children's
game of missing the lines of the flagstones or else the
Devil would pounce. Only in this case it was Isabelle!

She moved swiftly, giving herself no time to think
further about it, and with a little burst of speed she
landed her palms flat on the door's ancient oaken surface. Then she froze, inhaling the faint, faint aroma of
dank marsh-mud. She stared fixedly at the door, the
shape of which was only just discernible. Isabelle must
be on the other side of it! And she needed no lock
to turn, no opening gap to come through, but could
waft out and materialize wherever she would!

Juliette gulped, terror possessing her, and dreading
what she might see she closed her eyes tightly and slowly backed away. When she knocked against the opposite wall of the passageway a gasp escaped her and her
eyes flew open. She saw nothing, but it seemed to her
that the dankness hung in her nostrils. She felt for the
edge of the nearest aperture, whirled herself through it,
and ran full speed across the octagonal room and
through the archway that led her in turn away to the
corridor in the north wing. She did not slow her pace
until she came to a bow-fronted Adam commode of

satinwood under the windows, on which stood a bowl
of flowering daphne, plucked from the garden and arranged in sweet-scented, pink profusion. She buried
her nose in their fragrance, wanting to dash the last
trace of the pungent marsh-mud right away from her.
Taking a sprig of the daphne from the rest she held it in
her hand as she hurried along the corridor, almost as if
she feared that the aroma would pursue her, and she
was reminded of the judges who took posies into the
courtrooms to guard themselves against the odors and
plagues of the prisoners in the dock.

To her surprise Gregory was not alone, but had a
guest with him, a gentleman of some elegance, and
both of them rose sharply to their feet at her entrance.

"How are you, Juliette?" Gregory greeted her amiably, showing himself to be in high good humor.
"You look a little pale. Your fingers are quite cold
and you're trembling." He had taken her hand pos-
sessively into his. "Is anything the matter?"

Although still shaken by what she had experienced
in the octagonal room she shook her head, looking past
him at the stranger. She knew one of her own countrymen when she saw one. There was no mistaking
the leanness of feature, the olive tint of the skin, the
exceptional blackness of hair brushed forward in the
windblown style. Gregory followed her gaze and
smiled broadly.

"Allow me to present Monsieur Jean-Louis Brousais.
Sir, my betrothed, Mademoiselle Delahousse."

"Enchanté, mademoiselle."

She curtsyed to his bow, but answered him in English, suddenly filled with distrust. "How do you do,
sir."

"Très bien, merci. Permit me." He offered her the
chair on which he had been sitting, and when she had
seated herself, her whole attitude wary and alert, he
took a chair beside her.

Gregory remained standing, feet apart, and hands
behind his back. "Before we start to talk I want your
word that you will be honor-bound not to repeat a
single word of what you hear to anyone."

She was puzzled by his request, but she gave him a direct answer. "You have it."

"Capital!" He grinned at her. "Monsieur Brousais has brought splendid news. Very shortly we may expect to hear that Napoleon has issued a declaration of war against Russia."

"So the rumors and the speculation have not been false," she said with disquiet. "How do you have this information, monsieur? Are you newly come from France?"

He exchanged an amused, conspiratorial glance with Gregory before looking back at her. "There are some questions I cannot answer. Let us say that I have spent a short time on English soil and now that I have completed my mission I shall be departing again."

He was a spy! And Gregory was in league with him, aiding and abetting him! She had meant to discover the extent of Gregory's Napoleonic interests, but never had she suspected that he would go to the lengths of acting traitor to his own land!

"Is it not dangerous for you to be in this house, monsieur? If you should be discovered it would lead to immediate arrest."

"I know myself to be among friends." He smiled complacently from her to Gregory and back again. "And it was the purse of your betrothed that provided the gold which has shipped to safety on barges along the waterways to a schooner waiting at King's Lynn half a dozen of our fellow countrymen, who will even now be half way back to France."

She gave a gasp. "Do you mean the escaped prisoners of war who committed those murders?"

His hooded lids moved in a half-blink. "Ruthless times merit ruthless measures. It was unfortunate, but if the alarm had been raised they would have been recaptured."

"Instead, those innocent people lost their lives!"

"It becomes you to be tenderhearted, mademoiselle, but I must remind you we're at war."

"I could scarcely forget it. It has been a background to my whole life."

"Indeed it has, and all honor to you, who bear the name of one of France's heroes. It was a sad day when we heard of your father's death. I was present on one of the several occasions when Colonel Delahousse was decorated by Napoleon." He smiled at her again. "Your father would have been proud had he known how courageously you displayed the Emperor's symbol of the bee at a local social event of the year quite recently."

"No, no!" she cried, aghast. "I did it entirely in error!"

"No matter. Jumping the gun is better than hanging back, and no harm was done. Your enthusiasm and loyalty do you credit. You shall be commended to the Emperor when I return to him to make my report."

"Never! I forbid you to mention me to him!"

"Modest as well as charming. Nothing delights the Emperor more."

Before she could make any reply Gregory shook his head apologetically at her. "I spoke sharply to you over the wearing of that stole. I was alarmed. I wanted no questions asked and no suspicion stirred. Even now we must bide our time for a little while longer. The reason I was late arriving that evening was because I had received an urgent message from a fellow agent to meet and arrange the final stages of Monsieur Brousais's journey to the coast. It was a similar rendezvous that took me from you on the evening we dined alone together. I trust that when you hear the nature of the glorious purpose that inadvertently caused my neglect of you, you will forgive me."

"Glorious purpose?" she repeated with cool inquiry.

He seized a straight chair, swung it about to set it in front of her and straddled it, resting his arms together along the back of it. "I've wanted to tell you before. You have known that I had something of importance to disclose to you when the moment was right. I had to wait until I had been in personal contact with Monsieur Brousais, but now the plan is set and I may take you into our confidence. It has been the undercover work I have been doing in this area which prevented me from going to London to meet you more than keeping the bailiffs out of Ravensworth Hall. It was a ruse to divert suspicion. I had to find some good reason to show why I was content to stay in Norfolk for far longer than normal when luck at the gaming tables had gone against me. The three gentlemen keeping me company in that house when the bailiffs came knocking on the door were French agents like Monsieur Brousais and until the hour for them to meet a French ship putting into a nearby cove we kept the doors bolted and played cards. When I left that night, tossing the key to the bailiff, they rode off with me as if they were three local gentlemen departing for their own homes. Clever, was it not?"

"Magnifique!" Monsieur Brousais commented with a chuckle.

Gregory did not seem to notice that she had said nothing, and he continued exuberantly. "It will not take Napoleon long to defeat the Russians. He confidently expects to capture Moscow by late August or early September and then the war will be won. That's when he can again turn his eyes to England, and all will be ready for him!"

"Aren't you forgetting the British fleet?" she pointed out, shocked by the blazing fanaticism she saw in his eyes. "Napoleon can do nothing against it in direct attack. Since Nelson's victory at Trafalgar French ships have been able to do little more than prevent merchant vessels from these shores trading with the Continent."

"It will not be long before many British warships have to be diverted to patrol another coast! Invasion by the United States against British North America is imminent. Regiments will be sent to strengthen the defense there, leaving this country the weaker for it. A plum ripe for the taking!"

"You misjudge your own people—our people," she argued. "Admittedly I know myself to be more French than English in many ways, but I believe that, should Napoleon attempt to invade, whatever regiments are left would not stand alone. Every man and woman would take up picks and staves and fowling pieces to stand shoulder to shoulder with the soldiers to prevent one French foot being set down on British soil."

"Agreed—if the throne of England were set against Napoleon's coming." He tilted his head and gave her a cunning, sideways glance, his grin wide. "But suppose the Sovereign went down to the shores to welcome Napoleon? That would create a different situation altogether, would it not?"

"You know full well that the poor old King has lost his reason and would not know Napoleon if he saw him," she retorted impatiently. "But the Prince Regent is the Emperor's sworn enemy and would take a pistol to him himself."

"I'm not talking of the King or the Prince Regent," Gregory replied. "I'm thinking of a woman who is more than ready to take her rightful place. The Princess Caroline."

Juliette stared at him in sudden comprehension. Through pressure exerted on him by Parliament the Prince Regent had gone through a marriage of convenience with Princess Caroline of Brunswick, but they disliked each other so much that he had had nothing to do with her for many years and she was bitter and vindictive towards him, doing everything she could to ingratiate herself with the people, winning sympathy from many and drawing to her side all those who condemned her errant husband for his profligate and extravagant ways. Should the opportunity be presented, there could be little doubt in anyone's mind that Princess Caroline would snatch at it to become Regent and eventually Queen, rejoicing in seeing the father of her only child ignominiously demoted to a humbler position in life.

"Has the Princess Caroline been approached with the proposition?"

"She has. This was Monsieur Brousais's mission. It has been accomplished."

"Successfully, of course."

"Of course."

She looked at him steadily. This man she was to

marry was everything she despised. A man ready to betray his country and its Crown. A man entirely without principles. A man who abused his brother's house and hospitality by bringing a spy into it in the guise of an honest acquaintance being entertained overnight or longer. His winnings in the home of a friend and patriot had greased palms to allow murderers to escape the course of justice. Was there no end to the deceit and evil to which he was prepared to go in his fanaticism towards his cause!

"I admit to being enormously astonished," she said levelly, awaiting the moment when she would disillusion him utterly as to where her loyalties lay. So far both he and the Frenchman had arrogantly accepted her arguments as intelligent expressions of question and curiosity, and not as condemnation of their purpose. "I believed your interests to be on a par with those other British Napoleonists who think that the rule of the Emperor is right for France and that on no account should the Royal House of the Bourbons be restored. But that you should wish to see this island ruled by a Bonapartist puppet is in total opposition to what they would condone and far beyond anything I ever visualized."

"Perhaps it would surprise you to know how easily many of them can be persuaded to our point of view—and have been over the past weeks and months. You must remember that the prospect of having Princess Caroline as Regent is enforced by the fact that she is mother of Princess Charlotte, a child who has endeared herself to everyone in the land, and who will one day be Queen."

"How do you intend to set about persuading the Prince Regent to step down in his wife's favor?" she asked. "He would laugh in your face and declare it would have to be over his dead body."

"That can't be ruled out."

She thought at first she had not heard right. Then she saw from the grim, sardonic expressions on the faces of the two men that if what they had planned did not go their way there was nothing they would not do to bring it about. Instantly she knew she must not shout out her own abhorrence of all that they had in mind. Not because she feared being silenced in her turn, but because if it lay with anyone to persuade Gregory away from those plans it could be she alone who might do it. She must not antagonize him at the present time when he was so proud and exalted over it all, or else all chance would be lost for ever.

"Not bloodshed!" she implored hoarsely.

He reached out across the chair and patted her on the side of the arm, smiling in a reassuring manner. "That's the last thing we want. A peaceful coup is planned. Princess Caroline expressed that same condition. I meant only that, with his corpulence and self-indulgence in eating and drinking and philandering, the Prince Regent could well have an attack of apoplexy at any time, and then all paths would be clear."

All except that barred to Napoleon by the British people themselves. No matter what happened, they would stand stolidly against the advance of any foreign invader or dictator, but Monsieur Brousais—like Princess Caroline, who came from a Prussian duchy—did not understand them well enough to comprehend that fact, and Gregory was blind to all but the mad dream that he cherished.

"What of those who refuse to support your coup?" she asked, wondering what he would say.

"When a dam bursts it only needs that first trickle of water to bring a torrent after it. Your dowry will help to open up that dam. A payment here and a payment there will unlock doors and bring forth necessary documents and put pens into the hands of men to sign them. In that manner the Prince Regent will be brought down without a hair of his head being harmed."

Now she understood his eagerness to bring their wedding day forward. Her dowry was to bribe and corrupt and undermine. How he must have laughed to himself when she had begged him to spend one small part of it on buying whichever grand house took his fancy.

Monsieur Brousais smiled at her indulgently. "The

Emperor will show his gratitude towards all those who have served him in this great cause. You and your husband, as Mr. Lockington will be by that time, may have any house of your choice and an income to go with it."

She flashed a glance at Gregory and he met it with a deep nod, his expression laughing and knowing. "So West Thorpeby Hall is to be yours without any great deal of waiting," she said without expression.

"I told you that one day you would be a princess in your own right with a magnificent home to live in." He could have been drunk, so intoxicated was he with excited anticipation of all that was to come.

The Frenchman spoke again. "Without a doubt a title will be yours, mademoiselle. After all, the Emperor made princesses of his sisters by his own decree. Should you wish to be known as the Princess of Norfolk I'm sure there is nothing the Emperor would deny you." His worldly, sensual gaze flickered over her. "I shall see that you are presented to him second only to Princess Caroline."

His unconscious insolence almost took her breath away. Already he had picked her out as suitable for the Emperor's bed, and Gregory had taken no offense, seeing her as an asset to forward his greed and his aims. Only to his brother would he deny her. Only towards Blake would his hatred and jealousy flare.

She felt she could endure neither his company nor that of Monsieur Brousais a moment longer, and rose to her feet. They stood with her. "I'll leave you now. I'm sure you have plenty to discuss, and I have much to think over."

"But we shall have the pleasure of your company at dinner later," Gregory said, the undertone of an order in his request.

She had no choice but to accept. It would be folly to let either of them suspect that a white-hot coal of anger against them burned within her. "I'll return at eight o'clock."

Gregory went with her out into the corridor and drew the door shut behind him. "I'm pround of you,"

he said, taking her face with unexpected gentleness between his hands. "No man could wish for a better partner during the days that lie ahead."

Her expression became torn with appeal. "Don't go
through with this venture! Think again, I beg you!"

He misinterpreted her reasons and smilingly silenced
her with a fingertip against her lips. "There's no need
to be afraid for my safety. All will go well. Now we
must not talk any more here where we might be overheard and I cannot neglect my guest any longer."
With another smile at her he went back into the room.

Wearily she leaned a shoulder against the paneled
wall and put a hand to her head. Gregory had the
true fanatic's inability to see anything beyond his own
goal. Would there be any way to get through to
him?

Reluctant to face the North Octagon Room again
she left the north wing by a roundabout route in the
opposite direction and came eventually into the entrance hall. Through the open door of a drawing room
her footsteps were heard and Blake came out into the
hall, his attitude courteous as always but restrained and
distant as it had been since the night of the ball.

"Can you spare a moment?" he inquired. "I'm
showing Venetia and Caroline the latest artifact that
has come to light. I know you will be interested in it.
It was uncovered yesterday."

She could not answer him, her eyes swimming suddenly and unexpectedly with tears. He looked so dear
to her, so admired and beloved, and after all she had
experienced in the past hour she wanted nothing more
than to throw herself into his arms. He saw her distress
and came forward to take her hands.

"What is wrong?" he asked, concerned.

She could hardly speak. "I cannot bear that we
should not be friends still. My folly at the Rose-
Marshalls' ball took many forms, but let us not be
enemies over it."

"Enemies?" He shook his head and his voice deepened. "How could we ever be enemies? You took a
hard way to set me in my place. I was angered, but I

understood. I feel anger still against circumstances, but not against you."

"You must set yourself free of it, because nothing can be changed." A tear spilled over and trickled down her sad but inexorable young face. "But I'm thankful to hear you harbor no animosity towards me."

"None, I assure you."

She withdrew her fingers from his and took a handkerchief from her pocket, which she used quickly to dry her eyes. "I have said what I have longed to say. At least I have your friendship still."

"Call what lies between us friendship if you will. Remember what another Juliet said? *That which we call a rose, by any other name would smell as sweet.*"

She turned her face from him that he might not see the effect his words had on her. "Please let us go and see the artifact you mentioned. The others will wonder what has become of you."

It seemed to her as they moved simultaneously towards the door of the drawing room that there was a rustle like swishing petticoats away from it, but when they entered they found a quiet scene with Venetia composed and relaxed in her chair, handling the artifact, which was small and appeared to be made of silver. In equal repose was Caroline, one hand on the back of Venetia's chair, the two of them studying the object together. Both of them looked up as Blake and Juliette entered, and Venetia held out the artifact to him.

"What a pity a pair was not found. I should like to have displayed them on my black velvet shoes."

Blake took it from her and put it into Juliette's hands. It was a silver shoe buckle of exquisite design and workmanship. "It's beautiful!" she exclaimed in wonder, turning it about. "It must have belonged to some person of quality."

Venetia spoke in affectedly grisly tones. "Perhaps to Isabelle herself."

Juliette felt herself start at the words. Had Venetia intended that? She raised her eyes from the buckle to look questioningly at Blake. "Do you think it could have been hers?"

He gave a nod. "It's quite likely, but that's something we shall never know for certain."

As he held out his hand palm uppermost to take the buckle from her again she withheld it and turned his hand over to put her fingertip lightly on his ruby ring.

"Surely that ring was once Isabelle's?"

In the background Caroline shuddered exaggeratedly and murmured, "Heaven forbid!"

He clenched his hand, the better to show off the ring, and shook his head. "It was Thomas Lockington's. Admittedly he brought it back from London as a gift for Isabelle, but in view of what he discovered upon his return she never received it."

"But in the mural in the North Octagon Room it is on her finger in those last moments of her life."

He nodded seriously. "Yes, I know it is, but that must have been artist's license. Thomas had the ring on his finger when he died. Since then it has always been handed down to the eldest son."

Venetia, obviously feeling left out, broke into the conversation. "Let me have another look at that buckle."

Juliette left them all then and made her way upstairs, her thoughts dwelling on the heirloom ring. One day her son would wear it if things went as Gregory planned. Then her mind took another turn, recalling with faint disquiet the whisper of sound caught when she and Blake approached the drawing room from the hall. Had Venetia or Caroline been eavesdropping? Could they have overheard the quiet words that had passed between Blake and her? With all her heart she hoped not!

Chapter Ten

"Sorrel," Juliette said hesitantly, buffing her nails at the toilet table, "have you at any time noticed anyone following me or watching me from a window?"

"No, ma'am." Sorrel went on smoothing out the fringe of the pelisse that matched the gown Juliette was wearing.

"Mrs. Hazlett has never asked you questions about where I intend to spend the day or what my plans are at all?"

Sorrel hooked the pelisse over the back of a chair. "No, ma'am. Why should she? She sees you each morning at breakfast." On her quick feet she went to fetch a bonnet from a shelf in the cupboard.

Juliette put the buffer down on the toilet table and looked with an abstracted gaze at her own reflection. Was she wrong to suspect Caroline of spying on her? Why should the woman do it? It was all so pointless. Unless Venetia, who liked to pretend a complete lack of interest in her, wanted all her comings and goings reported for some obscure reason of her own. Did Venetia fear that Gregory might truly care for her and want to know of any hand holding or embracing and kissing, suffering her own torments in any such accounts that might reach her? Well, there would be little enough for Caroline to carry back on that score. Although Juliette knew he found her desirable, making that plain enough, they were rarely alone together, and when they were, she found herself comparing him constantly with Nicolaus, who had also desired her, but as shallowly and with as little love.

Caroline lost no opportunity to hint that Gregory might have romantic diversions elsewhere, wiping out all doubt in Juliette's mind that the remark let fall by

Caroline in the bedroom after she had escaped death
from the corona had been intended for her ears. Outwardly Juliette ignored these innuendoes, pretenting to
let their significance pass her by, but inwardly she was
forced, from what she had observed herself, to accept
that it did give reason for Gregory's comings and goings
at unusual hours and the amount of time he spent away
from her. Whenever they were at any gathering it was
impossible not to notice how he was drawn to flirt
wickedly with any pretty woman who caught his fancy, his purpose thinly disguised, and such is the power
of a dangerous man to attract that he was rarely if
ever spurned, and later, doubtless with some assignation made, he would return to Juliette and be at
his most charming, his most attentive, his most irresistible Lockington self.

Once, while she was shopping in East Thorpeby,
his carriage passed her with its blinds down, hiding
the identity of the passenger with him, and another
day he came in from riding with grass on his jacket,
a sprig of blossom tucked in his cravat, and a well-
satisfied expression on his face. It was only a few days
afterwards that Juliette had cause to go to the north
wing to ask him about an invitation to a social event
that they had both received, and there was the unmistakable scurry of feminine heel taps disappearing
into another room before he opened the drawing room
door to her. As there was a side entrance into the
north wing he could receive visitors without any intrusion into the rest of the house, and Juliette thought
the unknown lady must have slipped away by that
same route, because Gregory was in no hurry that she
should leave, insisting that she drink a glass of wine
with him, discussing the invitation at length, and then
engaging her in a long conversation about a district
in France that they both knew. He would scarcely
have done that had the lady's toe been tapping a
silent but impatient tattoo in the next room. Afterwards she had tried to analyze her feelings and knew
only a relief that for the time being he was content to
lie in another's arms, but it stirred thoughts of how her

wedding night might be when he would deal with her
as he wished, a time she did not care to dwell upon.

Shutting her mind quickly to that side of her forthcoming marriage, she again pondered over the feeling she had of forever being observed. Surely the painting of the guillotine on her water color had been proof
enough of Caroline's pettiness and spite? It followed
that she could be watching daily for some further
opportunity to strike out at her, even if Venetia were
not involved at all. She could accept that at times it
was some eerie notion that Isabelle's presence was
again near at hand which gave her that chilly feeling
down her spine and the dank and gruesome aroma
that trailed after those ghostly skirts could not be denied, but it had been no spectral hand that had held the
spyglass in the window and it was a human being who
withdrew from sight behind a quietly closed door or was
lost in the shadows of a long corridor whenever she
turned sharply to try to locate the malevolence that
seeped out towards her.

The thought of spying and the slyness involved
caused her mind to recall Monsieur Brousais and the
dinner party that evening when the three of them had
talked round the circular table with no further mention of the ill purpose that had brought him to the
house. No mention of France came into the conversation, and to the servants waiting on them Monsieur
Brousais chose to appear as an émigré long established
in England, a role he no doubt had adopted in London,
for in no way could she fault his knowledge of current
affairs, both Parliamentary and social, and it was obvious he knew how to get around as well in London as
in Paris.

In the morning he was gone. Whether he had actually slept in a bed at West Thorpeby Hall or, within
an hour or two of her leaving the north wing, had
gone to board some waiting vessel along the coast she
did not know and did not ask. At least she could be
sure that no great action would be taken by the Napoleonist extremists in England against the Prince Regent
until the Emperor was well on the way to victory in

Russia. The final proof that nothing could stand in Napoleon's path would be their rallying cry to treachery and insubordination. But although there was time in hand there, the days leading up to her wedding day were running out like beads from the thread of a broken necklace. Only ten of them left, to be precise. Ten short, fleeting days. Then the dreaded gold band would be placed on her finger.

"Are you taking your water paints with you this morning, ma'am?"

Juliette turned to take the bonnet Sorrel was holding out to her and shook her head before putting it on. "It's such a bright morning I'm going to walk. There are parts of the grounds I haven't explored yet, and I thought I'd go through the orchards."

Sorrel put the pelisse about her shoulders and handed her the parasol, which she put up a few minutes later as she emerged from the house into sunshine. Coming round the corner of the house she paused, seeing ahead of her on the flagged terrace Venetia reclining on a long, cushioned garden seat, and several chairs were set out in a semicircle to face her as if company was expected. Venetia spoke first.

"A fine day, is it not?" Her tone was lanquid and not openly hostile for once as if, like a cat lying in the sun, she felt warmed and comforted, lulled by it into an unusually benevolent mood.

Juliette, encouraged to think that this might be the opening for which she had been waiting, mounted the steps of the terrace and went across to her. "I've something most important to disclose to you," she said, sitting down on one of the chairs nearest the girl. "I think I've discovered a way to get you walking again."

Venetia rolled up her eyes wearily. "More talk about my wanting Blake to marry me, I suppose!" she exclaimed with delicate scorn.

"No. I realize I named the wrong brother."

Venetia looked at her fiercely. "I don't wish to discuss my private affairs with you."

"I wouldn't dream of attempting it. I only wanted to tell you that I've been to the spot where the chariot horse took fright, and found out all I could about it. Whether it was Isablle or something else that alarmed the horse we may never know, but I think you should go back to that place at the same hour on a similar night when the moon is on the wane as it was on that occasion, and try to relive what happened in your mind."

Venetia's expression was still resentful. "What good would that do?" she taunted.

"It could lift that blockage of memory from your mind."

"What a fanciful idea!"

"Isn't it worth trying?"

Venetia adjusted the shady brim of her hat worn to protect her complexion from the sun.

"For what purpose?" she asked idly.

"By remembering all that happened you may well find that the power to walk will return to you. I said before that you were a prisoner of fear and I still believe it. My father told me that to be afraid before battle is natural to every man, but he always found that when the first shot was fired his fear was destroyed in the fighting charge against the very cause of fear, and his courage was as it had always been. I want you to destroy your fear by facing up to the source of it. You were so frightened at the time that shock took your memory from you, which is Nature's way of healing sometimes, but somehow you are associating whatever happened with the agony of your broken leg, which prevented you walking then as it still does through your not wanting to remember what took place."

Venetia gave an exasperated sigh. "You weary me with all this foolish talk of battles and fear and such nonsense." She put a forefinger to each temple, a gesture that could be interpreted as an indication of it being all beyond her ability to comprehend, or that Juliette was more than a little mad, to say the least.

"Won't you try what I have suggested?" Juliette urged.

Venetia gave an involuntary little shiver. "I'd be

too nervous. It's creepy in that part of the garden at night."

"I'd come with you."

Venetia's face set determinedly. "No! I will hear no more about it. Now you had better go. The visitors I'm expecting will soon be here, and it is I they are coming to see—not you."

In view of such a peremptory dismissal Juliette had no choice but to leave the terrace. Deeply disappointed by her failure to persuade Venetia to take the course she had suggested, she went with haste away through the gardens, past the fountains and along paths that she had never taken before.

Barely was she out of sight when Gregory appeared going in the direction of the stables. He looked back over his shoulder when Venetia called to him, and swiveled about on his heel.

"Yes? What is it?" He showed impatience as he came towards her.

Venetia leaned back against her cushions and smiled lazily at him, patting a chair beside her. "Stay and talk for a little while. Lucy should be here soon, but I'm so bored with my own company."

With little grace he snapped open his watch fob and looked at it. "I suppose I can spare five minutes." He threw himself down in the chair, scraping it back along the flagstones as he crossed one ankle over the other of his outstretched legs, and he folded his hands across his waistcoat. "Well?" His tone was uncompromising. "What do you want to talk about?"

It was a question designed to quell the start of any verbal interchange, but Venetia merely tilted her head to one side and regarded him coolly. "Your marriage."

His eyes snapped and he lowered his lids warily. "What about it?"

"If you go through with it you will be making the biggest mistake of your life."

He smiled slowly. "Indeed? I happen to think otherwise."

"Why?" she flashed bitterly. "Because she can walk and run and dance—?"

He leaned forward swiftly to the edge of his chair. "Your accident had nothing to do with everything ending between us. I have told you that before. Many times. But you will not listen."

He had come within reach and she snatched at his hand and held it between both her own, her clasp frantic and nervous.

"Juliette does not love you, and I know you don't love her."

Again he smiled with a hint of cruelty. "What makes you think I don't care for her?"

Briefly she was taken aback, and then she swept his words aside as though it were impossible for her to branch on any thought that diverted from her full conviction. "You have never really loved anyone except me. You told me so at times that neither of us can forget, and I know in your heart you still love me. But you cannot face life with a wife who is immobile. So you pretend it is over between us—"

"Venetia." He spoke her name with a sharp irritation he could not control, always finding distasteful the persistence of women who could not accept the end of an affair gracefully, and through her various attempts to win him back she had long since driven from him the compassion he had originally felt for her after the catastrophe that had laid her low. "You must not harbor these foolish illusions."

She ignored what he had said. "Nothing could be as it was with that Frenchwoman between us. Tear up that hateful marriage contract. My dowry can more than match hers. You can have my whole fortune to spend as you will. You know my parents left me everything."

He pulled his hand away. "Don't beg," he said coldly, rising to his feet. "It does not become you, and your attempt to sell yourself offends me."

"Wait!" She threw out both arms in a plea to stay him as he made to turn away. "Answer me one question and I'll tell you who would make Juliette his own tomorrow if the chance came his way."

He halted uncertainly, a suspicion once considered and dismissed rearing again in his mind. In spite of

himself he wanted to know what Venetia would say.
"What is your question?"

Her response astonished him. She cast aside her hat
and tore the pins from her hair, shaking her glorious
tresses free in a blaze of red-gold as she snatched at
the bodice of her gown, pulling it down over her
shoulders and exposing the voluptuous swell of her
white breasts. "If I ran into your arms now, could you
turn from me?"

His mind was filled with remembered moments of
her passion, the dark fire and fierceness of it that had
matched a streak in his own character, which had
made their mating that of tigers, but his feeling for her
had waned and, sated and suddenly desperate to be
free of her cloying demands, he had made an end
to what had been with a kind of pentup hatred that
had never quite left him. Now she had revived it
again.

"I'll give you my answer when you have told me
what you know," he said, half-smiling.

She lifted her chin in anticipated triumph, burying
her fingers sensually in her hair. "Blake has forgotten
Elizabeth at last. I have observed more than either he
or Juliette have ever realized. When that silver shoe
buckle was found he had some words on his own with
Juliette, but Caroline listened at the door and told me
what passed between them. Do you know what he
said to her? He called her Juliet to his Romeo, and
comforted her when she wept over some estrangement
between them. It is your own brother who will take
Juliette from you when you tear that marriage contract into pieces. Now tell me! Tell me your answer!"

What she had revealed to him had not angered him
in any way. Juliette he trusted, knowing her standards
of honor, and whatever little upset she had experienced would have been harmless enough. As for
Blake, he knew his own brother well enough to know
he would not overstep the mark towards a woman he
respected, and he was convinced that the Romeo-Juliet
nonsense was nothing but one of Venetia's lies. Moreover, it pleased him to think that Blake wanted some-

thing he could not have. It would make marriage with Juliette all the sweeter. He had been resolved since their moment of meeting that nothing should part them, and had that vow needed strengthening Venetia's words would have done it.

"On the day you find you can run to me," he said enigmatically and unmercifully, "you will discover whether or not my arms will be waiting for you."

"That's no answer!" she cried wildly.

"It depends which way you look at it. In the meantime I stay bonded to Juliette no matter whether Blake wants her or not. Have I made myself clear? Good day to you, Venetia."

"Gregory!" she cried hoarsely. But he had already left her, on his way again to the stables along the path from which she had diverted him. He did not look back.

She crouched back against her cushions, her face a mask. With shaking fingers she began to fasten her bodice, and then, unable to find the hairpins she had scattered, she put on her hat again and thrust her tresses under it. With her appearance comparatively tidy, she picked up the little silver bell always at her side and rang it. She would not wait for Lucy. It was impossible to suffer normal everyday conversation with all she had on her mind.

A manservant appeared and she addressed him. "Fetch my pony and trap. When Miss Rose-Marshall comes, give her my apologies. I'm going for a drive."

In a distant part of the grounds Juliette was realizing that in her haste to get away from Venetia she had taken a wrong direction somewhere and was far from the cherry orchards in among box-hedges. Wandering past fountains she had never seen before she took the fork of a path that brought her out from the hedges to the lakeside among the willow trees, the surface of the water a waxen pink carpet of water lilies. And standing with his back to her, one hand resting against a tree trunk, the other thrust deep into his pocket, was Blake!

She came to a standstill, but he must have heard

the whisper of her skirt hems, for he straightened his
back and half-turned his face, the sun highlighting the
strong bones of cheek and jaw. He uttered her name on
a catch in his voice, showing that she had been the
subject of his thoughts. "Juliette!"

Her heart contracted with a spasm of adoration for
this man who could never be hers. "I'm on my way to
the orchards. I didn't expect to find you here."

He turned fully and faced her. "Don't marry Gregory, I beg you! Put an end to the betrothment while
there is still time. I know you don't care for him in any
way."

She could not deny the truth of it. In fact, there
was no more pretense left between them. Her feelings
were naked in her face and she could no longer hide
them. "I wish I had never had to come to West
Thorpeby Hall!" she burst out. "Another bride could
have been found for Gregory. Why—oh, why—did I
have to be his choice?"

His anguish grooved his cheeks. "I did my part in
promoting this marriage of convenience between you
and my brother, thinking you would make him an
ideal wife, having the strength of will and character to
stabilize him and help him to achieve something worth-
while with his life. I still think you could do it. I still
believe that I learned enough about you from Sir Duncan, your aunt, and the letters that came from Sweden,
to see you as the perfect partner for Gregory—except
for one factor that I didn't take into account. Your
happiness! And now mine, too. I'm tortured by the
knowledge that I turned down the chance to take you
for my own before Gregory's name was even mentioned. I had no idea that I was going to fall in love
with you myself!"

Before she could move he had stepped forward to
crush her to him and kissed her with such passion that
she was powerless to resist him. They were locked together in embrace and swayed with the tumult of their
kissing.

When at last he let her draw breath she thrust his
arms from her, not because she did not wish to stay

within them, but because she knew despair at the folly of having lost all the ground she had gained in keeping him at a distance. His declaration of love still seemed to hang in the soft air. Those tender words which he should never have spoken and which she should never have listened to, no matter how she had longed to hear them. But it was done. Now they must try to salvage what was left of their lives.

"I knew Sir Duncan asked you first," she said shakily. "Aunt Phoebe told me. But there can be no looking back. My fate has been decided, and there's an end to it. I cannot—even if it should cost me life itself—retract my promise to your brother!"

He made a move towards her, ready to hold her to him once more, but again she withdrew, sharply this time, shaking her head desperately, eyes brimming with tears.

"No!" she cried. "No! No! No!"

Then she spun on her heel and ran away from him along the lakeside. Blindly and frantically, although she knew he was not following her, realizing that any further persuasion at this time could not thrust a deeper wedge between them, she kept on running, and she came at last to the new-cut lawn where the archery butts were situated, the row of circular targets forming bright blobs of color against the green banks. Passing the little baroque pavilion in which all the sports equipment was stored, she began to slow her pace, aware that she had drifted far from her original destination of the orchards, but no longer caring. Ahead of her were more hedges and she had passed through a shaped archway in one and wandered a little distance before she realized that she had entered the maze. Only then did she become alert to her surroundings and began to suspect that the beguiling simplicity of the straight and narrow paths probably formed a trap in themselves.

Quickly she retraced her steps, as she thought, but it was only to find that those enclosing, ten-foot high yew hedges appeared to have blended together on all sides. She was already lost! In fuming exasperation at her

own foolishness, being in no mood for the light
divertissement of finding her way out of a maze, she
set off to get out of it as best she could. Holding her
parasol high, she hoped that somebody might see it
from the upper windows of the house and notify others
that the owner of it was trapped in the maze. But it was
a fruitless attempt to get noticed. Her arm soon began
to ache, and even if she had not been forced to lower
the parasol to its usual height the chance of being
sighted before the maze swallowed her up completely
had been extremely slim. Wryly she thought it was a
pity that the owner of the spyglass had not been on the
watch to turn it to good use and have rescue sent to
extricate her. Then the less pleasant thought followed
that perhaps she had been seen and that unknown person was taking a malicious satisfaction in knowing she
was trapped like a fish in a net.

It was soon obvious that it was indeed a most tan-
talizing puzzle in which to be caught. Some of the paths
were long and straight, appearing to offer a direct way
out, but when she hurried along them it was only to
find yet another foliaged arch leading into a new coil of
the intricate pattern that had been laid out. She had lost
all sense of direction, the domes of the house quite hidden by the height of the hedges, and it gave her an
extraordinary sensation of loneliness such as she had
never experienced before, not even in solitary walks
across the most deserted countryside. Another curious
aspect of the maze was the way in which all sound
seemed cut off, reminding her of the heavy silence that
lay on the North Octagon Room, and although she
strained her ears she could hear nothing of the country
sounds that drifted into her bedroom at the house
when the windows stood open. No barking dog could
be heard. No cattle lowed. No distant shout of farm
worker reached her, or rattle of cart or wagon. Not even
the faint lash of waves against the cliffs, which could
often be heard when the wind was in the right direction. Only then did she realize that within the closeness of the hedges the wind could not penetrate to
bring with it those comfortable, everyday noises.

She began to feel extremely tired, her eyes wearied by the monotonous greenery that enclosed her. The width of the paths was narrow, and the hedges, although closely trimmed, had plenty of sharp-ended little twigs to catch the wafting muslin of her gown and snatch at the dancing fringe of her parasol, holding her captive until she untwined the offending material and released herself again.

Midday came and went. She gave up using patience over the snagging of her skirt and resorted to wrenching herself free, tearing the flimsy muslin. Those who happened to be in the house would be sitting down to luncheon. She would be missed, but that was no guarantee that anyone would be alarmed for her; in any case, Blake would think he knew the reason why she had absented herself. On and on she walked, wondering wildly if she was ever going to find the way out.

With relief she came to a stone seat and she flopped down on it for a welcome rest, relaxing against its carved back, her parasol angled to give shade. It was then that it dawned on her that she was not alone in the maze any longer. It had been no more than a faint squeak of gravel under a shoe's sole that had reached her, but in the stillness she had caught it with hearing acute and tuned.

Her first instinct was to cry out joyfully, thinking that someone had come to her rescue, but alerted as she was by all the strange events which had happened since she had first arrived at West Thorpeby Hall, caution immediately took over on the observance that whoever it was had moved as though with secrecy and stealth. Surely she was letting her imagination run away with her! Probably it was simply that someone had wandered into the maze to pass away an hour or two in the quiet and harmless amusement usually accorded with trying to find one's way out again. Or perhaps two of the servants had chosen the maze as a secret trysting-place away from the prying eyes of his fellow workers and hers. But—it could be more than that. Someone could have been following her for a considerable length of time without her suspecting it.

"Who's that?" she called out sharply.

Instantly the unknown person became as still as a statue, as though with breath held, and no reply was forthcoming. She listened, her head tilted expectantly, hoping to hear a scurrying away which would tell her that she had been right in her supposition about the servants. But there was no movement of any kind.

She closed her parasol and sprang to her feet, filled with a sense of danger and no longer certain that the unknown person was from the house. Suppose an intruder had got into the grounds, a rogue bent on robbery perhaps, and having seen her go into the maze had trailed her until she was sufficiently enmeshed and out of anybody's earshot to strip her of her rings and brooch. Or worse! Deliberately she gripped the handle of her folded parasol, holding it at an upward slant, ready to use the pointed ferrule of it as a weapon in self-defense if need be, and slowly backed away. Somehow she must escape from the maze before the intruder caught up with her!

As quietly as she could she slipped through one gap and took another, harassed by the snagging of her gown, but thinking that she would soon shake off the intruder if he blundered on after her, because each path always presented alternative outlets and the odds were entirely against whoever it was making the right choice every time. Once that error was made the whole maze would have to be circumambulated before any meeting could take place.

She drew breath some little time later and stood listening confidently, certain she would have thrown off any pursuit. Then she froze. There had been a faint snap of a dried twig-cutting on the other side of the hedge by which she was standing. It was no stranger to the maze who was following her, but someone familiar with every twist and turn!

Quickly she looked in one direction and then the other. She was in one of the long, straight paths, with outlets at either end. She decided to turn left and sped the several yards along it, the tearing of a dangling frill of snagged muslin proclaiming the direction she

was taking to her pursuer. She had reached the far end
and was about to dodge through the arched opening
when something that shone hissed through the air and
buried itself in the thickness of the hedge beside her,
striking home in a hidden branch, its feathered shaft
trembling. It was an arrow!

A cry of alarm burst from her, and she swung her
head round in time to see a shadow vanish out of sight
at the opposite end. Somebody had stepped out, aimed
even as she had been running, and tried to bring about
her death with an arrow in the back! And it had been
no man whose hand had held the bow. She had caught
the white flick of a petticoat!

She raced on again, terrified afresh when she found
herself in yet another long path in which she was
uniquely exposed to danger, but in the same instant
came hope. It had been two such paths running parallel
to each other which had led her into the maze in the
first place. She must have reached the way out! Yes!
There was the exit to freedom!

She hurled herself through it and discovered she
was on the far side from the house and in a formal
garden of flower beds. Some distance away among the
flower beds a gardener and two gardener's boys, both
stalwart lads, were busy planting.

"Help!" she cried, not slowing her pace, but they
were too far from her to hear.

Again there came the deadly zing of an arrow. Her
would-be murderess had come to the maze's exit to
take aim at her again. With a thud the arrow bit into
the trunk of a tree she was flashing past. She screamed.
This time the men did hear her. Seeing her flying towards them in an obvious state of distress they sprang
from their work into a run to meet her.

She half-collapsed in the arms of the lad who reached
her first. "Someone tried to kill me in the maze!" she
sobbed. "With an arrow. You'll find another in the tree
trunk back there."

The lad who held her and helped to steady her on
her feet stared at her incredulously, both he and his
companion stunned to disbelief at her extraordinary ac-

cusation, but the gardener frowned with bushy brows and gave an indignant nod of understanding at what he believed to have been the cause of her fright.

"It must have been a poor marksman at the butts, miss. Them arrows fly in all directions there sometimes. I've said more than once to the master that I thought them targets were set up too near the maze, but Miss Venetia won't have them moved. There's shade and shelter for her there, d'you see?" He turned to the two lads. "Jimmy, you nip along and tell whoever it is at the butts what's been happening to their arrows, and you, Barney, escort the young lady back to the house. She's real shook up, I can see that."

She was staring at him. "Does Miss Venetia practice archery?"

"Yes, miss. Not that she's down to the butts more than once or twice a week on the average, but soon she and her young lady acquaintances will start practicing in earnest for the tournaments held at the end of the summer."

"But how can Miss Venetia shoot when she is so handicapped?"

"The master had a chair specially designed for her, and she can sit and shoot away to her heart's content. Quite independent she is, too, once the chair is set out for her. When the mood takes her she even comes and goes in a little pony-trap. Ain't you never seen her in it?"

"No, I haven't," Juliette answered almost inaudibly.

The gardener chortled jovially. "Well, don't you fear. It wouldn't have been Miss Venetia's arrows what came ricocheting into the maze, because she shoots true and only Miss Rose-Marshall shoots better, having an eye straight as a hawk's."

"Miss Lucy Rose-Marshall?"

"Yes, miss. She's the only one left now, seeing that her sister married." He looked past her with a jerk of his turkey-red neck. "Here comes Jimmy back. Now we'll hear who it was at the butts."

The lad gave the answer that Juliette had expected. There was no one there. No, not in the pavilion either.

The door was padlocked as it always was when not in use.

"Funny," the gardener said, but he did not say it in any sense of being amused. "I'll take a look in the maze. If there's a practical joker in there I'll have him out quick as a terrier with a rat."

She sank down on the grass to wait, glad of the two lads' company, although they were too shy to talk to her and hung about awkwardly, but she had no wish to be left there on her own. When the gardener returned he had the arrow from the maze in his hand and compared it with the one he had removed from the tree trunk. Both were from a stock kept in the pavilion, but gave no clue as to who might have shot them. The gardener came to the conclusion that one of the stable-boys or perhaps one of the other gardeners' assistants had come across them lying with a forgotten bow somewhere and let fly.

"Not knowing the danger of it, you see," he explained patiently to her. "I'll make inquiries, miss. I'll root out the culprit and give him a flea in his ear."

She let the lad named Barney escort her back until she was in sight of the house and then she bade him leave her, which he did at a bolt, thankful to be rid of such a duty. No culprit would be found in the stables or the potting sheds. A female had tried to kill her, and she no longer believed that Isabelle had been responsible for trying to bring about her death with the corona in the North Octagon Room. It had been a human hand that had released it in an attempt to kill her! And now a second attempt had been made.

She had two suspects. Caroline never stopped talking of wanting personal revenge against the French for her husband's demise on the battlefield, but was she so unhinged by a festering grief that she would be prepared to kill in order to release the poison within her? It was hard to accept that she would, but there was the evidence of the painted guillotine that had appeared after she had been left alone with the water color, which could have been threat, warning, or sheer exultation at the vengeance that would eventually be

carried out. There was also the admittance in her own
words that she had been first on the scene in the North
Octagon Room after the corona fell. Moreover, having spent much of her childhood at West Thorpeby
Hall, she would know the pattern of the maze and be
able to find her way about in it.

Venetia would also know every twist and turn of
the maze, but she, to all intents and purposes, was unable to put one leg in front of another. But suppose she
could? Suppose the shock of being surprised in her
solitary attempt to walk on that first evening had been
enough to break down the slender barrier that lay between full activity and self-imposed immobility? Her
suite was not far from the North Octagon Room, and
she could easily have slipped back into it unseen within a matter of seconds. Again, it was difficult to accept
that she would murder to rid Gregory of his betrothed
and open the way again to a reconciliation when it was
safe to reveal that she was as she had been before,
ready to run to him, ready to dance with him, ready to
be wife to him in the place that had been left vacant. It
could also have been Venetia with the spyglass.

Juliette went slowly up the steps to the house, thinking that in spite of all she was turning over in her
mind there was nothing positive she could present as
evidence. Nothing at all.

As she stepped over the threshold her attention was
riveted by a few shreds of fresh grass dropped from
someone's heel, which lay on the polished floor. There
was none on her own shoes, for she had kept to the
paths all the time, but she recalled that the lawn where
the butts were situated had been freshly cut.

"Miss Rose-Marshall left this for you, miss," said
the footman on duty in the hall, handing her a package wrapped in soft paper from where it had lain on a
side table.

She opened it. Lucy had returned the French stole.
Folding the paper over it again she half-turned and
looked at the servant. "How long is it since Miss Rose-
Marshall was here?"

"It's no more than half an hour since she left in her

carriage. Before that she was quite a time in the garden, looking for Miss Venetia, but couldn't find her."

"Where has Miss Venetia been?"

"She took a ride in her pony-trap. She came in not five minutes ago."

"Was Mrs. Hazlett in attendance?"

"No, miss. She returned about the same time as Miss Venetia, but she had been to try to sight a new bird that's nesting on the marshes."

"Tell me, apart from those three ladies mentioned, has anyone else been into the hall during the past hour?"

He looked faintly surprised by her cross-questioning. "No, miss."

"You're quite sure?"

"I'd back my life on it, miss."

"Thank you." Juliette continued on her way. It could have been either Caroline or Venetia in the maze. Both of them had time entirely to themselves unobserved by anybody. But did she have a third suspect to add? With the Rose-Marshall family being old friends of the Lockingtons, a friendship dating back two or three generations, Lucy could be as familiar with the layout of the house and the maze as either Venetia or Caroline. No. She could not believe that Lucy would use violence against her! Not even when she had inadvertently destroyed Lucy's hopes that one day Blake might turn to her in love. Desperately she shook her head and drove all suspicion of Lucy from her.

One thought stayed with her: the spying on her had not been a haphazard process, but a careful vigilance kept for the right opportunity to bring about her death and make it appear to be caused by an accident of some kind. Such cold-bloodedness seemed almost inconceivable, but someone was hiding behind an apparently innocent visage, content to bide her time to avoid all chance of being suspected.

Should she go to Blake with all that had happened and seek his advice and protection? But that would mean being alone with him, something that had to be

avoided at all costs. Better to wait and be on the alert to
see what next move her unidentified enemy would
make, and by night she would keep the doors into her
bedroom well and truly locked.

But when she reached her suite she received a fresh
shock. Someone had removed the keys from every
door!

Chapter Eleven

The next day the weather changed, banishing the cool but balmy days as though winter had returned in full force to give summer no chance to break its hold again. Juliette had never seen such rain. It made the whole landscape gray. As the days continued with fierce, buffeting winds and a range of wetness from light drizzle to torrential downpours the growing crops suffered, and with the exceptionally high tides the dikes reached danger level and spilled their banks. Blake was constantly on the watch, riding down to see what progress the men were making to prevent all the earlier work being lost to no avail, and discussing new precautions with his overseers. Occasionally Gregory accompanied him, the two of them riding their horses at a gallop away down the drive, their eyes screwed up against the lashing rain, the tails of their shoulder-caped coats flying out. Several times Juliette braved the weather herself, sometimes to watch the great waves throwing spray hundreds of feet into the air against the cliffs, at others to see the insidious gleam of water seeping into the marshes and Blake watching from a distance, a dark figure in the saddle against the turbulent skies. She had the impression he almost welcomed the crisis, which was helping him to be concerned with something other than the steady approach of her wedding day. At times he looked quite gaunt, and she sensed there was so much anger and outrage in him against her union with his brother that he was stunned to the brink of insensibility and was like a man moving in a nightmare. For herself, it was as if her heart were numb, shedding its own desperate tears.

In contrast to his wretchedness and hers, as well as the violence of the inclement weather sweeping the

wild, torn Norfolk coast, preparations went ahead in the
house for the wedding as though outside the sun shone
and nobody had a care in the world. The women servants were taking a particular pleasure in all that was
going on, giggling and whispering together in a high
state of excitement and peeping in at the display of
presents, which grew daily with frequent deliveries by
coachmen and grooms from the other great houses.
One afternoon Sorrel unpacked the wedding gown, the
slippers, and the veiled, rose-trimmed bonnet, and went
to great pains to eliminate each tiny crease from everything. To Juliette the sight of her finery caused a
deep and painful shock. It seemed to symbolize the
inevitability of what awaited her, and from that point
time began to run out at lightning speed, bringing her
far too swiftly to the very morning before her wedding
day was due to dawn.

She was in her salon writing to acknowledge the
gift of a pair of Swedish silver candlesticks which her
stepmother had sent, when the housekeeper came into the room, carrying a package wrapped in canvas
and sealed with red wax. At first Mrs. Harman made
no reference to what she held, but exclaimed instead
at the wedding gown which she could see on a stand
through the half-open doors of the bedroom.

"What an exquisite outfit, Miss Delahousse! Is that
a touch of pink around the neckline and hem?"

"Yes, it is." Juliette looked vaguely in its direction
and made a motion towards it with her hand. "Sorrel
has been making a minor alteration on it, which is not
quite finished. By all means take a closer look at it
if you wish, Mrs. Harman."

"I should like to very much. I feel privileged to see
it before any of the others. All the servants are being
allowed to line up in the hall tomorrow, whatever
their rank, to see you come down the grand staircase
and leave for the chapel, ma'am. I understand a titled
gentleman is giving you away."

"Yes, Sir Duncan Berry, a Scottish acquaintance."
He who arranged this whole charade, she added silently to herself.

Mrs. Harman, about to go through to the bedroom,

remembered the business she was about and paused to deliver the information. "I have had the suite next to yours prepared for Mrs. Colingridge," she said. "It's not as large as this one, which is the grandest in the house, you know, but exceedingly comfortable. I thought you would like her near you, seeing as she will be your only relative staying for the wedding."

"That was thoughtful of you. She should arrive this afternoon. She was allowing plenty of extra time for bad weather."

"I remember there was rain and wind when she visited before." She glanced down at the package she held before handing it over. "This was delivered when I was on my way to come and speak with you."

It was another wedding gift, addressed this time to Gregory as so many of them were, but he had asked Juliette to deal with everything. She broke the seals and took a pair of scissors to cut through the thick thread that kept the canvas fold stitched together. From the bedroom Mrs. Harman went into raptures again over the wedding gown.

"I don't know when I've seen prettier bridal attire! Each of these pink embroidered roses has a pearl in the heart of it, I see. It reminds me of old Granny Nutfield's work. She could embroider like that when she was sober, but unfortunately that wasn't often, so she didn't get the high grade work that she should have done, except from this house."

"Who was Granny Nutfield?" Juliette asked, snipping another length of thread. Whatever the gift was, it was contained in a plain, polished, wooden box.

"Sorrel's grandmother. She had a cottage on the estate, the Nutfields having been long in the service of the Lockingtons. Sorrel came to live with her when she was no more than five or six. Looked like a gypsy child she did, and there's some that say it was a Romany who fathered her. Her grandma taught her well. The stitching on this unfinished seam is far superior to that done by professional hands."

"I'm very pleased with her standards of work," Juliette answered, "and I—" Her voice trailed away. She had pulled the canvas completely away from the box and lifted the lid. A pair of pistols lay on a bed of purple velvet. Dangerous and purposeful-looking weapons with no decoration or ornamentation such as might have been expected from a gift of some importance, and with them an accessory kit including everything from powder flask to ammunition. She supposed Gregory would be pleased with them and hoped he would know who the donor was, no card or letter being enclosed. She closed the lid again.

"Do you know if Mr. Gregory is at home?" she asked the housekeeper, who had come back into the room.

"I don't think so. He went down to the dikes again with the master. There was bad flooding last night. Unless this wind drops before the exceptionally high tide due tonight there could be an end to the master's hopes to reclaim the marshland for many years to come."

She left the room, and Juliette went across to look out at the driving rain. She was still standing there a few minutes later when Sorrel came with a message from the housekeeper.

"A bright blue carriage is coming up the drive. Mrs. Harman recognizes it as belonging to Mrs. Colingridge."

Aunt Phoebe had come! She had arrived ahead of time. Dear, dear Aunt Phoebe to come early when she was needed most. "Thank you! Go and tell Mrs. Harman I'll be in the hall to meet my aunt."

Juliette flew into the bedroom to check her appearance and flew out again. Out of the salon she dashed, slowing her pace only when she reached the head of the stairs. Below in the hall the housekeeper waited, two footmen behind her to carry baggage, and a maidservant in attendance. All of them were looking towards the door which the butler was about to open, timing it to the moment when the carriage slowed to a halt at the steps. Watching the door herself she set her hand on the banister and took the first stair. It was then that two hands came behind her and she received a violent thrust in the back, went toppling forward, and it was only her instinctive grip on the banister that saved her. She swung painfully against the balusters, striking her hip, her knees buckling, and half-fell, half-slithered down several stairs. Those in the hall ran up to her, but before they reached her she flung a glance back over her shoulder at the shadowed landing, but whoever had tried to make her break her neck in a fall had vanished from sight.

Aunt Phoebe entered the house to find Juliette, who had refused offers of assistance, declaring herself to be unharmed, running to embrace her. "I'm so glad to see you, Aunt!" she cried between joyfulness and tears.

"And I to see you, child."

"You must have left London in good time."

"I did. I was not going to risk any delays to prevent my being at your wedding." She held her niece back from her. "I declare! You're thinner. You've lost weight." She laughed merrily. "That is what being in love does for you."

Juliette looked beyond her. "Where's Sir Duncan? Isn't he with you?"

"He's been north on some parliamentary business, but will be at West Thorpeby Hall by dawn tomorrow, driving through the night."

Still talking, arms about each other's waists, they went up to the rooms Aunt Phoebe was to occupy. When her aunt had taken time to tidy and freshen up after the journey, as well as changing from traveling clothes into an elegant gray silk gown, Juliette had tea served in her salon, where they sat down together to resume their chatter more freely now that they were alone without Aunt Phoebe's lady's maid or any of the other servants being present.

"Now are you not excited about your wedding day?" Aunt Phoebe exclaimed happily over the teacup she held. "When I heard that you had brought the day forward by six weeks I knew—I just knew!—you had fallen in love with Gregory. Was I not right? You found him to be as fine-looking and as wickedly fascinating as I told you he would be."

Juliette, not fully recovered from the fright she had had on the stairs, had been sipping the hot tea thankfully, needing something to quiet her nerves. Now she lowered her cup and gave her aunt a direct look.

"He's a spendthrift and a gambler and a womanizer."

Aunt Phoebe looked completely taken aback, her rosy mouth dropping open. Then she recovered herself, stammering effusively. "B-but not any longer. Oh, he was. I know he *was*. Both the Lockington brothers have been quite notorious in their time, but it's easier for an ugly man or a plain woman to be virtuous than for those with beauty, male or female, for they are fêted and pursued and offered temptations denied to those with lesser looks and no charm." Her smile became deliberately bright and cheerful, and she tapped her niece on the arm in a knowing way. "Remember! Reformed rakes make the best husbands. Everyone knows that."

"In Blake's case I would agree with you, but Gregory is bent on—" she could not reveal his political activities—"leading the same kind of life as before. He does not love me and makes no pretense, and I don't care for him."

Aunt Phoebe's face crumpled. It was what she had feared in the innermost recesses of her mind and refused to acknowledge, telling herself that her womanly intuition had been no match for Sir Duncan's male wisdom on the matter.

"Life is never perfect, child," she said distractedly. "I'd hoped you would not discover that for a while." Determinedly she brought her optimism into play, drawing a blind with it over the unpleasant prospects Juliette's statement had conjured up. "Gregory will settle down once he's married if you'll prove a good wife to him in *every* way." She put a delicate emphasis on her words, hoping the girl understood what she meant. For herself the pleasures of the bed were inexhaustible, but then she had never taken a lover for whom she did not care. But Juliette would come to care for Gregory, too. She must. And then everything would be all right. Wedding night fright was all that was troubling the girl. Aunt Phoebe's smile lifted again. "It's no good telling me that Gregory is not in love with you, because I do not believe it. I do not! I remember when I came to West Thorpeby Hall with your miniature how he exclaimed over it to me, and even

Blake declared you were just the girl to be wife to his brother!" She put forward her cup and saucer. "Is there more tea in the pot?"

Juliette poured it and said no more. It was pointless. Aunt Phoebe was no help, no help at all. As for the miniature, it was obvious to her that Blake, although he had not realized it, had fallen a little in love with her through that likeness, and he had thought that any man would consider the world well lost for such a bride. It had not occurred to him that his brother would not share his feelings, the cause of which he had not recognized himself.

She had hoped to confide in Aunt Phoebe about the attempts that had been made on her life, but she saw that would be useless, too. Aunt Phoebe, dear as she was, would be incapable of appreciating how deadly and determined those attempts had been. Better to turn the conversation to something better suited to her aunt's intelligence.

"What are you wearing to my wedding?" she inquired.

Thankful that the unpleasant subject had been dropped and her niece set no blame on her for disappointment in the bride-groom-to-be, Aunt Phoebe leaped into a description of her outfit from the bonnet plumes to the lattice-ribbons of her silken shoes. There then followed all the latest gossip and scandals from London and Juliette listened to her patiently and with affectionate indulgence, seeing how much her aunt was enjoying herself, and thinking that little did Aunt Phoebe know that Gregory's Napoleonist activities could form the most unsavory scandal of all under her very nose if ever the news leaked out.

Aunt Phoebe did not have her niece to herself as long as she had hoped, for an hour later some other guests arrived to stay for the wedding and during the rest of the day more came from long distances to be accommodated in the great house, all with servants in tow. By teatime Alex and Lucy had come, Blake having invited them to stay overnight for fear that the appalling weather would make the road from East Thorpeby impassable on the wedding day, and Alex was to be Gregory's best man. For the same reason Gregory fetched the priest himself in his own carriage, and the bridal posy was delivered and left in the cellar where it was most cool. When evening came, no less than thirty people sat down to dine. Alex sat on one side of Juliette and Gregory on the other. Lucy was placed some little distance away. Earlier Juliette had thanked her for returning the stole.

"It's your property," Lucy had replied coolly. Then she had turned away to speak to someone else, having rebuffed any attempt at a renewal of friendship firmly and politely.

At dinner Alex mentioned Lucy. "She's a trifle uppish over my behavior towards you at the ball," he confided with a twinkle. "Didn't approve. You being betrothed and all that."

There's more to it than that, my dear Alex, Juliette thought. He gave her no chance to speak to Gregory until his attention was finally engaged determinedly by the lady on his other side, and then she did mention to Gregory that a pair of pistols had been delivered, but he silenced her quickly on the matter with a sudden drawing of his brows together in a frown, glancing to the left and to the right to make sure she had not been overheard. A heavy feeling of dread settled in the pit of her stomach. Those pistols had been sent to him for no good purpose, but from whom? And how was he to use them?

"I've been expecting that package," he said to her in a low voice under cover of a wineglass. "Where is the box?"

"In my rooms."

"I'll collect it when everyone has retired to bed." Then he seemed to reconsider. "No, it would be better if you bring them to me."

"Very well." It occurred to her that he had never set foot inside her suite or come anywhere near it since the occasion of their first meeting. Was it fear of Isabelle that kept him away? He had had no doubt that Cobbett had seen her that night. Did he avoid the North Octagon as assiduously?

He grinned at her suddenly with his peculiar arrogance and raised his glass a little higher to her in a privately spoken toast for no one else to hear. "Here's to tomorrow, Juliette. May it bring fulfilment to all our hopes."

She knew what those hopes were, and could not lift her glass. He did not appear to notice.

"I have some news to please you," he continued amiably. "We're to leave for London as soon as the wedding reception is over."

For that she was grateful and her expression showed it. "I'm glad." Then she looked anxious. "But what if the road becomes impassable as everyone fears?"

"There are plenty of flat-bottomed boats kept in the stable buildings for such emergencies, but let's hope it doesn't come to that, because it's not the most comfortable mode of transport even for a short distance." He put down his glass to have it refilled. "There's another matter. Don't bring your lady's maid with you. I've arranged attendance where we are to stay."

"But I must take Sorrel," she protested. "I could not find a better personal maid anywhere."

"You can't appear in London attended by a gypsy," he stated derisively. "In any case, my mother never believed in taking country maids to London. It turns their heads. Leave your maid at West Thorpeby Hall until we come back again."

"I do not understand what you are talking about," she answered impatiently, "and I will not let you talk disparagingly about Sorrel. Her dignity and grace stem from having Romany blood in her veins. In any case, nothing could turn her head."

"Don't you believe it. She is a country wench like all country wenches. Once in London they succumb to its temptations. She would soon be after bigger fry than a footman or a groom, and would start soliciting payment for what she gave free in the country hay. Her work would deteriorate and you would have to get rid of her anyway."

She was indignant, but she continued to keep her voice low as he had done in order that their discussion should not be overheard. "You must not slander Sorrel. You have no cause to cast aspersions against her.

I know her to be a most proud and moral young woman, who in truth thinks herself much above the rest of those below stairs."

He laughed, having been enjoying his goading of her, and unnoticed by anyone else he slid his arm about her waist and gave it a little squeeze. "All servants are immoral, my little innocent. How do you think the adolescent sons of gentlemen learn the facts of life?"

"Gregory!"

Grinning widely, he chuckled again, and peered into her face. "Hasn't it occurred to you that I might want to have you entirely to myself away from everything and everybody connected with West Thorpeby Hall? The house where we are to stay will be fully staffed. You and I will be able to go anywhere and do anything we wish."

She took a chance. "Perhaps we could even look for a London residence? To rent," she added hastily, not wanting him to think she was being too demanding on the dowry that he had earmarked for his Napoleonic cause. Alone with him in London she was certain she would find a way somehow to win him away from his mad scheme.

He cocked an eyebrow at her in mock weariness at her eternal wish to reside anywhere other than at West Thorpeby Hall, but in his present good humor he gave a nod. "I promised you that we should find ourselves a *pied-à-terre* in Town. If it amuses you, you may look for a suitable house, but don't expect to spend much of the year in it, although we can avoid the worst of the Norfolk winter by attending the best of the Season's social functions when the time comes." He nodded towards the curtained windows and curled his lip. "I must say I'll not be sorry to turn my back after tomorrow on this local rain for a week or two."

A week or two! No longer? In disappointment she felt she could eat no more of the turbot on her plate with its lobster sauce, and set down her fork. To see Blake daily was so much worse than not seeing him, or was it? Which was the greater anguish? She could not tell. Her gaze went to him at the head of the table, and as if he saw the movement of her head out of the corner of his eye he turned his head and held her look before she could avoid it with lowered lids. He had caught her unawares, and she hoped she had given nothing of her innermost feelings away. She took care not to glance again towards the head of the table for the rest of the sixteen courses.

Being the bride of the morrow she was very much the focus of attention that evening, although Venetia did her best to capture as much of it as she could for herself, being in a curious, half-truculent, half-exhilarated mood, which made some people suspect she was more than a little flown with the wine. Juliette knew better; to Venetia the wedding day was to be a special torture, and on the eve of it she was at a loss to know how to assuage the pain which racked her. If it were she who had tried to rid Gregory of his betrothed, how galling it must be for her to see them together and he in an extremely buoyant and good-humored mood as though in high anticipation of the next day.

When all the good nights were said, Juliette and Aunt Phoebe went together along the corridor that led to their apartments, but when they reached the first door her aunt made a little theatrical exclamation of dismay. "I've left my fan in the drawing room. Do fetch it for me, child."

"Yes, of course. I expect it's on the sofa where you were sitting."

A clock struck somewhere as she retraced her steps to the drawing room. She paused, pressing a hand against her chest. Midnight. It was her wedding day. With her throat choked she pushed open the door and entered. Most of the candles had been extinguished, but there was enough light to show her that the fan lay on the sofa's striped silk upholstery. As she reached out to pick it up she heard the key turn in the lock of the door. She swung about, startled, and saw Blake leaning against it.

Taken completely by surprise, all emotion heightened, such a gush of love engulfed her at the unexpected sight of him that her face was transfigured by it, but only momentarily, for she was instantly aware of having foolishly lowered her guard. She tried to assume a nonchalant air and made an unconsciously graceful little gesture with her hands.

"I came down for my aunt's fan."

"I know. I asked her to conspire with me."

She was at a loss. "You had no right to do that," she said helplessly.

"How else could I get you to myself for a little while?"

"We have nothing more to say to each other," she said, looking away from him. But it was too late. He was undeceived.

"My love," he said quietly.

She knew she should shake her head, cry protest, rush from him. Anything to prevent what would otherwise come. But she could not. He had touched her with that soft utterance and melted away every shred of resistance in her. Slowly she lifted her head and his eyes were waiting for hers. She saw all love there, all passion, all yearning, and knew her own held the same melting eloquence. He came forward and took her hands into his, and drew her by her fingertips to him, her elbows folding, and they stood close, she looking up into his face and he looking down.

"I love you," he said, low-voiced. "I loved you when I looked across the room in your aunt's house and saw you turn your face towards me. It was as if all my life I had been waiting for that moment without realizing it."

"That was how I felt, too," she whispered. "Only I thought you were the man I had come to England to marry."

"I knew that. I could tell when your aunt presented me. You have expressive eyes, my darling."

She smiled sadly. "I thought I had hidden my feelings so well."

"The only time you managed it was at the Rose-Marshalls' ball. Then it was not that I believed you loved me any the less, but that you had overcome it with some superior strength that I did not possess, and would never allow me to catch a fragment of what you felt for me again."

"I managed it—until the day by the lake."

He smiled. "And again this evening at dinner. I knew in that single look we exchanged that all defense was gone."

"That's not what I intended."

"I understood that, too."

"Was I so transparent in my loving?"

"Only to me."

"I never suspected that you observed me so closely," she answered wonderingly.

"I was hard put to take my eyes from you at any time."

Her lips parted on an indrawn breath of rapture, and he was unable to resist her any longer. His arms went about her, their mouths came together with a desperate, joyous frenzy, and with her body arched to his they sought in their impassioned kiss to assuage the longing for closer union that each felt for the other.

When their kiss melted and their lips parted she leaned back against the support of his arms to look into his face and, dazzled and breathless and pulsating with her own deeply sensual response, she wondered at the love she saw there, which was directed only towards herself. She brought her hands from his neck to trace her fingertips over his features as though to register with touch as much as sight the passion in him.

"I love you," he said again with such overwhelming tenderness that she closed her eyes on the joy of it and swayed against him, surrendering once more to the tempest of his lips.

She was lost to his loving. On the silken couch where he drew her down there was nothing for her beyond the circumference of his arms, no candle-shot darkness, no walls, no house, no world, no universe. Only his mouth, his touch, his worshipping body against hers. She learned what it meant to be a woman adored by a passionate man, and answered him with love-words of her own, tender and ardent, aroused to an amorousness that knew no bounds.

Eventually it was the clock, striking loudly in the quiet room, which jolted her back to awareness that although everything had changed, it was true at the

same time that nothing was changed. She was still ir-
revocably bound to Gregory and within a matter of
hours would be marrying him.

As if Blake read her thoughts, his lips against her
hair, she lying within the circle of his arm, he said,
"There'll be no marriage today."

She twisted round to face him, a forearm resting
against his chest. "How can you say that? Nothing
could stop it at this late hour."

"I have thought of a solution. It would not be the
first time a bride and groom by mutual agreement decided amicably at the very last moment that the ceremony should not take place. Invariably Society ap-
plauds their courage and gives approval." Then he
added with a grin, his eyes dancing, "Particularly if
the wedding presents are promptly returned to the
donors."

"Don't joke," she exclaimed in loving, half-exas-
perated tones. "I'm in no mood for it. That Gregory would agree to an amiable parting is as impossible
now as it was at the beginning."

"I disagree. I've thought of a solution."

She tried not to let hope filter through, keeping a
check on herself. "What could that be?"

"I shall offer him West Thorpeby Hall and all its
estates in exchange for your freedom."

She was completely overwhelmed. "You would
make such a sacrifice for me?" she whispered incredulously.

He touched her cheek, his eyes warm and tender.
"Did you not believe me when I said I loved you?"

"Yes, but I know how much West Thorpeby Hall
means to you."

"You mean far more to me than anything else on
earth. Gregory shall receive my proposition this night,
and I cannot believe he will surrender this chance to
gain from me what he has always wanted."

She shook her head and turned her face from him.
"He'll never agree. I know. It will not be through
love of me, but to deprive you in turn of your heart's
desire."

And more, she thought. Gregory believes it to be

only a matter of time before he receives West Thorpeby through the munificence of a conquering Napoleon, and therefore he has no need to give up the bride of his choice.

"Do you seriously believe that my brother hates me so much that he will refuse my offer and destroy your happiness as well as mine to such a cruel end?" he questioned in disbelief.

"I fear so." She swung back to him in panic. "Don't put the proposition to him, I beg you! No good can come of it. Lucy warned you on the night of the ball that Gregory would call you out if he suspected that we cared for each other in any way. He could—could—"

"Kill me?"

She nodded dumbly, too choked to speak, her head bowed.

He tilted her chin, making her look at him. "What makes you think he is the better shot?" he inquired dryly.

Her eyes were full of tears. "I don't know that he is, although I've heard more than one person praise his aim with a pistol. But I know you! I know you would never shoot to kill in a duel, and with your own brother you would turn your weapon harmlessly at the last second."

He pursed his lips in a smile. "Would you have me do otherwise?"

"No. But Gregory has no such principles. Gregory would aim to put a bullet through your heart."

It was then that outside in the garden there came a terrible scream. For a second they stared at each other in bewildered astonishment at the sound. Then, as it came again, he leaped to his feet. "That sounds like —but it can't be—Venetia!"

He did not attempt to leave the room by the door, but threw on his coat as he made for the window, intent on taking a short cut to reach the girl. He sent the curtains rattling back on their rings, threw open the casement, and jumped out. The screaming continued like a din out of Bedlam. Juliette, buttoning her bodice with shaking fingers, ran to the window after him. Upstairs there came the sound of doors opening and closing and the first thud of hurrying feet, the whole house roused by the screaming which still had not stopped.

Blake, having used his initiative, had lost no time in getting to the scene with a minimum of delay, and Juliette, from the vantage point of the open window, was able to see by the moonlight under the branches of leaves into the arbor. Venetia's wheeled chair lay tilted against the hedge as though she had leapt out of it, and she stood screaming at the very spot where the chariot horse had taken fright on that long ago night of the party. As soon as she sighted Blake, Venetia broke into a shaky, unsteady run towards him, her hands pressed to her head, screaming as she came, and when he reached her she threw herself against him. With a stinging slap he stunned the hysteria from her, and after a second or two of gulping and gasping she became coherent.

"I remember! I did what Juliette told me to do, and I remember!"

He wasted no time in questioning her, but scooped her up in his arms and swept her across to the open window, tipping her into the room feet first, where Juliette took hold of her and steadied her. "Don't let anyone into the drawing room," he said quickly to Juliette. "She's in no state to face a crowd of people and a deal of cross-questioning. I'll quiet down the rest of the house."

He pushed the casement closed, and she heard him reassuring stable hands and house servants alike, who had arrived at a run, that there was nothing to be alarmed about. Probably it had been no more than an owl that had frightened someone taking the night air before retiring. Those in the house proved to be more obstinate to pacify, but when Blake knocked on the door to be let into the room again he was alone.

"Caroline was clamoring to come in, but I've told her to await Venetia upstairs."

He closed the door determinedly and came hurrying across to where Venetia sat leaning back in a wing chair, her face ashen. Juliette had poured her a brandy and she had taken a few sips of it. He pulled up a tapestry stool and seated himself on it by the chair, taking Venetia's hand into his.

"Now tell us slowly and in your own time exactly what happened."

"I waited until I thought everyone had gone to bed," she began hesitantly. "Then I had two of the servants carry me down to my chair and push me out to the stable lawn. There they left me. I wheeled myself down the path under the limes, following the route that Elizabeth and I took in the chariot. Juliette thought that if I could relive that night, I would be able to remember what happened and perhaps walk again." Her voice faltered. Juliette gave her another sip of the brandy, and then she continued. "My chair bumped several times—that path is quite uneven, and gradually I remembered how the chariot had begun to dip in a strange way as it approached the arbor."

"How did it dip?" Blake questioned keenly.

Venetia frowned. "It was as if something was the matter with one of the shafts or the wheel, I'm not sure. I remember Elizabeth being alarmed, and said something about it feeling as if the chariot was broken. Then—as we reached the arbor—" Her hands flew to her face and covered her eyes as though to shut out the sight she recalled, and she began to sob in the high-pitched tones that preluded a return to hysteria.

Firmly Blake took her wrists and jerked her hands down from her tear-stained face, compelling her to keep control. "Go on," he said levelly. "What did you see?"

She answered him in a moan, closing her eyes. "Isabelle! We saw Isabelle! It was only for a second—her awful white face in the blackness and the hissing sound she made. The horse reared and bolted. Elizabeth and I were both screaming. I remember people shouting and running, and then the open gates out of the drive lying ahead." With tears streaming down her face she turned to look at Blake. "I know now what happened when you reached us. The horse would have stopped when you pulled at the reins, but the chariot broke! It broke! That's what tossed us against the pillar. It was nothing you did, Blake. Nothing!"

She threw herself forward into his arms, sobbing uncontrollably. He held her, and over her head he and Juliette looked at each other, she seeing that a great load had been lifted from him by this clearing at last of the guilt he had carried. She smiled at him to show she shared that relief with him, and he reached out a hand and took hers in a brief, warm moment of physical contact. Then he spoke to Venetia again.

"You ran to me from the arbor. Are you aware of that? You did more than walk—you ran!"

Slowly she lifted her head, eyes still flooded. "I did, didn't I? But it's no use! No use!"

"What do you mean?"

"I always thought that if I could walk again it would be possible to win Gregory back to me. I knew he had loved me right up to the time I became immobile, and thought it was only that which had made him turn from me, and I knew I had to make the effort tonight, because it was now or never with the wedding tomorrow, and I was so afraid to face the darkness, knowing I should do it on my own." She shook her head in utter dejection. "What a foolish dream to cherish! I know that now I can recall all that took place that night. Shortly before the chariot race was due to begin he told me it was finished between us and said many cruel and terrible things to me. I wanted to die. It was only Elizabeth, seeing that I was in a kind of trance of suicidal misery, who saved me from it. How she did it I don't know, but you know how sweet and good she was, and nobody else would have been able to make me carry on as I did. Then it was she who was killed. Oh, how much better if it had been me!"

Blake let her cry for a little longer, and then he raised her to her feet. "Now walk to the foot of the stairs with me. That will be all you can manage tonight, but tomorrow you shall come down them. It will not take you long to get your strength back, and then the ballroom shall be opened up again and we'll invite everyone for miles around to come and watch you lead the first dance of the evening with any man of your choice!"

In spite of her tears, some part of her distress went from her, and she pressed herself affectionately against him.

"Dear Blake. It shall be you."

Slowly he led her to the door. When they reached it Blake looked back to see if Juliette was coming with them, but she smiled and shook her head, indicating that it was best to remain where she was.

She waited until she could be sure that he had gone as far as Venetia's suite to hand the girl into Caroline's charge, and then she slipped up to her own rooms and closed the door. She saw the box containing the pistols where she had left it, but she could not face going to the North wing at this late hour. Gregory must wait until morning. She felt emotionally exhausted and intensely weary. The warmth Venetia had shown towards Blake suggested that one brother might well replace the other in her affections, and if he were eventually to find consolation there Juliette knew she should be thankful that he at least would not yearn for her throughout the rest of his life as she would for him.

Almost aimlessly she crossed to the box and lifted the lid to take one more look at the weapons as if they might provide a clue as to why they had been sent and why Gregory had awaited them so eagerly. Then she gave a gasp. One of the pistols was missing! The imprint in the velvet where it had lain was showing bare.

Holding the box she hastened through into the bedroom. Sorrel, white-capped and neat, sat in one of the chairs waiting for her, and she sprang to her feet, dashing sleep from her eyes. "Oh, ma'am! I didn't hear you come in." She made to come forward and help Juliette out of her evening gown, but was stopped in her tracks by the query put to her.

"One of the pistols in this box is missing. Do you know what has happened to it?"

Sorrel stared hard at her as if daring her mistress to accuse her in any way of stealing it. "I touch nothing that's no affair of mine, ma'am."

Juliette hastened to make amends. "I'm not suggesting you put it anywhere. But has anyone been in my salon?"

"No, ma'am." Sorrel relaxed slightly, but her eyes still smoldered at the affront.

Knowing that the presence of servants was often ignored to the point where a lady or gentleman would declare a room empty even if a dozen footmen stood in it, and that the servants themselves adopted the same attitude when replying to such a question as she had just asked, Juliette phrased it another way.

"Are you quite sure that nobody from above or below stairs has entered this suite during the time you have been waiting for me to come to bed?"

"Nobody at all, ma'am. If anybody did come it was when I left the suite after putting away your afternoon clothes and before I came back a while ago to await your coming up from the drawing room."

That was no guarantee that somebody had not slipped into the salon while Sorrel had been busy in the bedroom and hanging clothes away in the dressing room closets. The theft of the pistol held a new and deadly significance. She did not doubt that it was to be used against herself!

As Juliette went about preparing for bed she gradually began to formulate a definite idea as to whose hand it was that had removed the pistol. For the first time she began to gather in a tiny point of evidence here and there which previously had come to her notice, but on which she had placed no significance. Her mind dwelt on the guillotine which had appeared on her watercolor as she climbed between the sheets that had been folded back for her. When dressed in bridal finery she would challenge her enemy and force her into the light. But first she would have to go back to the North Octagon Room!

Chapter Twelve

She had fallen asleep on blissful thoughts of Blake and all that had passed between them during that short spell of enchantment in the drawing room when she heard someone trying to open the door of her bedroom. Since the disappearance of the keys she had had bolts put on all the doors leading out of it, determined to give her enemy no chance of creeping up on her in the darkness of the night. She sat up, startled.

"Juliette! Open this door!"

It was Gregory. She slipped from the bed, put on a robe, and ran across to unbolt it. He entered with a candle.

"Why didn't you bring the pistols to me? I expected you to come when you had dealt with Venetia's squealing hysterics."

"I thought it could wait until morning." She took the box up from her bedside and held it out to him. "Unfortunately one of the pistols and the accessory kit have disappeared since I opened the package."

"What! Hell's devilment! Let me see!" He snatched the box from her and threw open the lid. Slamming it down on the toilet table he swung round to her. "It has to be found! These are no ordinary pistols. They have the truest aim at the longest distance yet known. There are no others in the country."

She shuddered inwardly. A ball from such a weapon could reach her even as she sat in her wedding carriage and the assassin be away before there was a chance of pursuit or discovery. Then the significance of the pistols' unique power and Gregory's panic-stricken fury at its disappearance came home to her. She recalled his totally unexpected announcement at the dinner table that they were to travel alone to London. London! Where the Prince Regent rode daily in his carriage or on horseback. There would be countless opportunities for an assassin to set his eye along the barrel of a pistol at that corpulent target!

"You swore that no harm would come to the Prince Regent!"

His piercing look was enough to tell her she had scored a bull's eye of her own, and he made no attempt to deny the accusation that revealed she had guessed the truth of his purpose. "That was what I had hoped, but it's not to be. There's no other way." He seized her by the arms. "Today is our day! Not only the beginning of our married life, but the beginning of everything. The date is the twenty-second of June, as I need not remind you. A day that will be remembered for ever more. The day of Napoleon's declaration of war against Russia! I received a secret communication with instructions as to what to do when the pistols came. We'll raise the great cry here and make it ring throughout the land—*Liberté, Egalité, Fraternité!*"

He is mad, she thought. Or else his brain is so turned with a secret addiction to some drug, common enough among those who led a dissolute life, that he can no longer reason logically. It could be that he was being thus used as a pawn by those who simply wished to set Princess Caroline up as Regent without any thought of Napoleon taking true power through her, for her Royal husband had many enemies who would like to see him replaced. She remembered her distrust of Monsieur Brousais, who could well be a double agent, working for both those very people and for France. It was all she could do not to shriek out her total opposition to all he believed in and her absolute determination to destroy his plans, but then he would slip away to London without her and all would be lost.

"I think I know who took the pistol," she said to distract him from her lack of endorsement to his crazy boast.

"You do? Tell me. I'll get it back!"

She shook her head. "You don't want to show your interest in it. Leave it to me. I'll find it."

He saw the sense of her argument, but was uneasy. "Don't you want any help?"

She managed to persuade him that she did not, and he left again, taking the single pistol in its box with him. She looked at the clock. She had had no more than an hour's sleep, but it would have to suffice.

Taking a lamp, she went on slippered feet from her suite and crept through the dark and silent house until she reached Blake's study. He had shown it to her on their tour of West Thorpeby Hall shortly after her arrival, and she had seen the row of keys in a glass-fronted cupboard. Holding her breath, she opened it and it did not take her long to discover that four of the largest keys were those to the doors leading out of the octagonal rooms to the domes above. She took the one she wanted, and departed with it.

As she hurried along the corridor towards the North Octagon Room her heart began to thump painfully against her ribs, but she knew she could not turn back now. When she reached it she took a quick glance around, and it seemed to her that the colors of the painted ceiling had dulled and darkened as though a tangible shadow had taken possession of the room, but she shook the thought from her and went across to the recessed door in the outer wall. She set in the key and turned it. Well-oiled, the lock made no sound, but the door, as she swung it open, hissed on its hinges, making her recoil sharply until she realized what it was. At the same time the musty, dank aroma which had terrified her before in the same place, rushed out to meet her on a strong, cold draught.

Her courage might have failed her at that point had not the rays of her lamp revealed that the stone walls of the stairway, which curved upwards out of sight, were covered with mildew, and trickles of moisture glinted amidst the green of it, showing her that she had located the source of that curious odor she had associated with marsh mud clinging to the hem of Isabelle's gown. Now she could confirm that the hiss, followed by the gust of that curious smell, had been due to the door being opened by a human hand to allow her unknown enemy either to enter or depart. And that day when she had put her palms against the door the aroma had not come from a spectral presence on the other side, but from a whiff drifting from those mildewed walls through the keyless lock of the door.

Telling herself that she had nothing to fear at the moment and that her enemy would think her in bed and asleep, she set her foot on the first of those slimy, green, stone steps, thankful that she had brought a lamp, for the strong draught would have extinguished any candle flames, as it had done when the door had been opened unknown to her and the candles in the corona had been extinguished; whether that had been the case with the candelabrum when she had been left in darkness the first time in the octagonal room she did not know, but she could not shake off the conviction that she had sensed the presence of Isabelle on that occasion.

Halfway up the flight she noticed a tiny grating set into the wall and she paused to dip her head and peer through it, discovering that it looked right into the octagonal room below. Continuing up the spiral curve she reached the top and came into the dome room, her robe and nightgown billowing out in the draught, and she saw in the pale glow of her lamp that it was almost as large as the octagonal room below and the floor was awash with rain, which was dripping through cracks in the domed ceiling, as well as through a broken aperture, part of which must have been torn away by the wind long since, and upwards through it she could see the wet and glistening moonface of the huge clock that topped the dome, its black hands closed together at the figure twelve. She could tell that the aperture had been constructed originally to give access to the clock and to accommodate the viewing of the naked sky through the ancient telescope which stood with some other rusty equipment in the middle of the floor.

Her lamp did not reach far, and blackness reigned beyond its range, but she was able to see that the room had been constructed with tall, narrow, wooden pillars, delicately grooved, and alcoves set against the walls corresponded with the archways in the North Octagon Room below. Mildew covered everything. Years of being shut up and the penetration of rain and damp weather due to roof damage impossible to see from the ground below outside had resulted in slow but extensive damage to the whole dome. She shuddered at its decay and the bleak eeriness of the place, longing to be gone from it. Warily she looked about her. Then the lamp rays caught the bright sheen of polished brass. Avoiding the pools of rainwater, dismayed at the sponginess of the floorboards, she went cautiously over to a cupboard and looked at the spyglass lying there. It was surely the one that had been turned on her many times more than she could estimate. She no longer had any doubt that the pistol and ammunition would be in the dome room, too, and she began to search for them, her nerves strained, tense and afraid.

Her lamplight danced over dark shapes in black alcoves, and gleamed on the wooden pillars which partly supported the dome. Skirting another wide rainwater pool, which she now realized had been seeping through over the past spell of bad weather to stain the painted ceiling and soak down into the murals of the room below, she backed a few steps, holding up her robe and nightgown hems to keep them clear, and turned again nervously. Then she screamed piercingly with all the power of her lungs. Her lamp was shining full into the gaunt and awful hollow-eyed, green-stained visage of Isabelle!

In panic-stricken terror she hurled herself away, knocking against a pillar, which creaked and shook loosely, bringing some plaster down in a cloud of choking dust, and she plunged through it to reach the steps. Down the flight she flew, her mind stunned with the horror at what she had seen, not daring to look back or knowing how she saved herself from falling on the treacherous surface of the slippery steps. She reached the passage-way and whirled about to slam the door shut and lean against it as she locked it, her breath sobbing, and she seemed to have no strength left in her limbs.

Yet, propelled by fright, she pelted back along the corridor, clutching to her the key she had withdrawn from the lock, giving no thought in her panic to the futility of locking any door against a spectral being. Reaching her suite she flung herself into it, and only then did she stop, her lungs tearing, to press the hand that clutched the key against her pounding heart. How long she stood in the salon getting her breath back she did not know, but at last, feeling as weak as if she had risen from a sick bed, she stumbled into her bedroom and dropped the key out of sight into a drawer.

Then summoning up her strength she moved into action, pulling off her robe and nightgown, which she rolled into a bundle and shoved deep into a silk-covered box kept for laundry. Then she poured water from the ewer on the washstand into the bowl and bathed herself from head to foot, shivering, but wanting to rid herself from any taint of that musty aroma in the dome room. When dry, she threw on a frilled peignoir and brushed her hair hard with a brush to make sure all trace of her encounter in Isabelle's abode had gone from her. Outside dawn was lighting the windows.

She peered out. The wind had died down and the rain had dwindled to a gray drizzle under heavy clouds. The sun would not shine on her wedding day, but it was of no importance. She had other, more dreadful things to think about. To pass the time until Sorrel came early as instructed, she lay down on the bed. Sleep came instantly.

She had forgotten to rebolt her bedroom door, and she awoke to find that Sorrel had brought in her breakfast on a tray and the housemaids were pouring hot water into the dressing room's hip bath. She drank one cup of coffee, and forced herself to eat a little of the food.

"What news of the flooding?" she inquired. "Did the sea take over the marshes?"

"No, ma'am. There is some flooding, but not as bad as the master feared, and the road is still open for the wedding guests to get here. Your bath is ready."

After her bath, which was a deal more pleasant than

her earlier cold douche, Juliette put on her wedding lingerie and sat at the toilet table to allow Sorrel to dress her hair. It was like any other day with no conversation passing between them, and Juliette sat, heart-heavy, watching the maid's skillful fingers comb her hair into a shining cap with an adornment of finger-ring curls to cascade down the nape of her neck beneath her veiled bonnet. So were virgins prepared for sacrifice in ancient times, she thought. At what point would the pistol be turned on her? She had failed to find it, but in no way had she changed her belief as to the identity of the person in whose possession it was. The moment of confrontation must come when the pistol was being handled and pointed in her direction. Pray God she would see it in time!

"It's early to put on your wedding gown, ma'am."

"No matter. The bonnet can wait until later."

She stepped into the filmy gown and stood to have it hooked up for her. Sorrel gave her no praise for her appearance, seeing only the pristine state of the garment as made ready by her hands.

"I'll go and fetch your bridal posy from the cellar, ma'am."

Sorrel departed. Juliette opened the drawer where she had hidden the dome room key and weighed it absently in her hand, almost as though weighing evidence, and thinking over what she had seen. Suddenly she heard Aunt Phoebe's voice crying out in agitation, her footsteps pattering in haste from the corridor and across the salon floor.

"Juliette! Mercy me! Where are you, child?"

She darted through to her. "What is it, Aunt?"

Aunt Phoebe, breathless and white-faced, already arrayed in the bright blue gown she was to wear to the wedding, threw up her hands with a wail. "They're going to fight a duel! Blake and Gregory. Over you. I should never have sent you to get my fan—"

Every vestige of color had drained from Juliette's face and she shook her aunt to silence her. "Where are they, Aunt? Where?"

"I don't know. Sir Duncan has just arrived and he's acting as Blake's second. Alex is Gregory's—"

Juliette was already on her way. She reached the head of the stairs. In the hall below Venetia sat on a chair being comforted by Lucy, and Caroline, glancing up and sighting Juliette coming at a run down the stairs, shook her fist.

"This is all your fault! You wicked, wicked creature!"

Juliette ignored her and spoke direct to Lucy. "Where can I find them?"

Lucy answered without preamble. "They're on the stretch of lawn beyond the arbor."

That ill fated place! Juliette tore out of the house into the gray drizzle, the dark and lowering clouds creating a somber gloom. Blake had said there would be no marriage that day and he had meant it. How could there be when the blood of one Lockington brother or the other would stain the grass! He must have told Gregory the reason why he would have an end to the mockery of the betrothment and the sham of marriage due to follow either that morning or last night after Gregory had collected the pistol box from her.

Breathless, she reached the limes and there, in the gloom at the far end of the arbor, a girl stood pressed into the hedge for concealment while slowly she raised the pistol she held to aim at one of the two duelists, who had already turned their backs to each other and against the blackness of the oaks beyond and the silhouetted figures of their seconds, had begun to pace out the distance on the rain wet grass until that fatal moment when each would turn and fire.

"No!" Juliette shrieked, as much to the two duelists as to the girl who aimed to fell one of them. "Stop! Don't!"

Neither of the men heard her, and if they had done they would not have stayed their pacing, but the girl with the pistol threw her one wild look over the shoulder and then turned, unnerved by discovery, to press the trigger even as both men swung around and fired. The deafening noise seemed to echo far across the lawn and within the arbor. Juliette had time to see that Gregory and Blake were still on their feet even as she hurled herself after the girl, who had slipped away through the arbor. A twig caught the lace frill of the escaper's cap and whipped it from her head, releasing a flow of luxuriant blue-black hair. She did not stop, but went dipping and diving under branches and between the limes and was lost from sight beyond them, making for the house.

One of Juliette's running feet squashed the cap into the wet ground as she pursued her quarry, and she made for the nearest side entrance, which she guessed the girl had taken. Through it she went, coming into a little used part of the house, and darted up a minor staircase. She dashed along into her bedroom to snatch up the key to the dome room where she had left it, and with her pace unchecked she went on flying feet along the corridor to the North Octagon Room.

She had expected to find the recessed door locked against her, but it had been left slightly ajar. Thrusting it wider, she entered and started up the slimy steps, which were illuminated now by daylight showing from the dome room. Cautiously she came round the curve of the wall and stood on its threshold. Although she had known whom to expect she gave a gasp. Facing her, panting as much as she from the running they had both done, the hand with the pistol pressed into the side folds of her skirt, was Sorrel. But what a different Sorrel, with her cap gone and with it the false image she had presented for so long. The tumbled magnificence of her hair flowing down her back and over her shoulders gave her a wild and wanton look, a she-devil of dark, erotic desires, her features so contorted with hatred that her mouth was pulled into a satanic grin.

Fighting to get her breath back, Juliette gulped out her accusation. "You were aiming at Blake!"

Sorrel spoke in gasping tones, her chest still heaving, but less swiftly. "Did you think I'd risk letting him kill Gregory?"

Juliette took one step into the room and leaned a shoulder in exhaustion against the damp wall. Through the aperture in the roof the drizzle-laden draught revived her. "How long have you and Gregory been lov-

ers?" she asked wearily, understanding at last why he
had always avoided the suite at any time the girl was
on duty. At least he had had the doubtful grace to do
that.

"Since before you came to West Thorpeby Hall!"

"How long?"

"I wanted him and meant to have him from the
time I left childhood behind, but my grandma saw the
way I looked at him when he rode by and packed me
off into service at Hetherham House because the Lockington brothers had a reputation for their lecherous
ways from early manhood. That's when I concentrated on working my way up to lady's maid. I saw
him sometimes at Hetherham House, but he never saw
me. Then he and Miss Venetia were always together,
and rumor had it that he would marry her. I had to put
a stop to that, and my chance came when the eldest
Miss Rose-Marshall, to whom I was lady's maid, took
me with her to West Thorpeby Hall on the eve of the
open air ball. I had heard that Miss Elizabeth and
Miss Venetia were to race a chariot together."

"Was it you who stood by Elizabeth's bed that night
and frightened her?"

Sorrel shook her head and her cheeks hollowed as
though inwardly she shuddered. "No. That must have
been Isabelle. But it was I who managed to scare that
stupid Cobbett before slipping out into the corridor
and returning by way of the door from there into the
dressing room to watch what happened."

"I felt someone was watching me when I went to
fetch the vinaigrette!"

"The master wanted you to have that suite when
you came because it's the grandest of all the guest
apartments, but I wove spells of my own to keep Isabelle at bay when I came to work there. She must have
known what was going to happen to Miss Elizabeth
and came to warn her, but it was Miss Venetia I wanted
dead."

"What did you do?" Juliette asked in a whisper,
aghast.

"I have a way with horses and other animals—a pow-

er that's always been in me. I can talk to them as my
Pa did, and I can coax them as easily as I can frighten
them. I had only to stand in the darkness of the arbor
in my black dress and with my black hair loose and
covering my face to be almost invisible, and I gave a
special high-pitched sound that terrifies any horse when
theirs drew level with me."

"Elizabeth must have seen you and recognized you!"

"No. She couldn't have done. I drew back through
the branches quickly and they were already past."

"Nevertheless, she must have caught the barest
glimpse and it was enough. In her last words she gave a
warning, and now I understand its meaning. 'Isabelle . . .
not her.' She was trying to say that it wasn't Isabelle,
but you whom she had seen, but she was not spared
long enough to get all the words out."

"I never thought the horse would get as far as the
gates. I expected the chariot to crash against one of
the great oaks."

"How could you be so sure they would crash?" Juliette's voice was low with horror.

"I didn't grow up on this estate for nothing. I knew
where all the tools were kept and how to use what I
needed. I sawed that chariot through in two places. As
it happened, Venetia did survive, but Gregory saw her
then as an object of pity and I knew I had triumphed."

Juliette burst out at her furiously. "He was already
tired of her! You had no need to resort to such terrible lengths."

Sorrel was unmoved. "So I discovered afterwards,
but it was too late then. I soon managed to establish
myself at West Thorpeby Hall. Miss Venetia couldn't
bear me near her, and I believe that, without knowing
why, she connected me with that accident, but I took
care never to show my hair, which could have given me
away." She put up a hand to it and rumpled it sensually
through her fingers with an intensely voluptuous
grace. "But I let Gregory see me with it down. I know
the effect it can have on men. He wanted me from that
moment forth as much as I wanted him. I've spent
many nights in the north wing and we've met in the

woods and other quiet places. When I discovered that he was to enter into a marriage of convenience I knew I must get rid of you, too."

"But why? Surely you know Gregory's character well enough to realize he would have tired of you as he has tired of all the other women who have come in and out of his life."

"No!" Her eyes narrowed curiously. "I have enough Romany in me to know how to cast a spell over a man. He can never have enough of me, and he'll lust after me until the end of his days. When you have gone I'll make his thoughts turn to setting me in your place. He means to have West Thorpeby Hall for himself. What he doesn't know yet is that I intend that he shall make me mistress of it!"

Juliette straightened up from the wall warily, ready to take flight back down the steps. "But I haven't gone. And I don't intend to go."

Sorrel brought out the hand she had kept at her side and pointed the pistol at Juliette. "I gained enough time on you to reload. Even after the shot is heard it will take them some time to locate where in the house it was fired. I'll be right back on my duties by then, waiting with the bridal bouquet, which I was on my way to fetch when I heard everybody crying out about the duel. None will be more surprised than I when they tell me the bride won't be needing those flowers after all!"

"You dare not kill me!" Juliette bluffed desperately. "They'd find out it was you."

"No, they won't. Nobody saw me come in the side entrance and I know you followed me that way. Nobody knows yet that you're back indoors. They'll be looking for you in the grounds. When they do find you, you'll be lying here with the pistol placed in your hand. They'll think you couldn't face your wedding after all."

It was true that enough people knew she had not welcomed the day for that conclusion to be reached, and Gregory would remember that she had declared the pistol stolen and think she had kept it for one reason only. But now she must play for time.

"I knew it was you who had taken the pistol!" she lashed out. "You weren't as clever as you imagined yourself to be."

Sorrel's eyes gleamed. "I thought you suspected me this morning. But how?"

"It was a combination of tiny facts that suddenly slotted together. Yesterday Mrs. Harman mentioned that you had lived on the estate, something that I hadn't known before, which meant, when I came to think about it, that you could be as familiar with the maze as any other child growing up in the vicinity of the house, whether you were officially allowed in the grounds or not. No doubt that's when you learned some skill with a bow and arrow. The gardener immediately thought of mischievous youngsters letting fly with arrows from a bow left forgotten by the butts, which suggested to me that it was no unusual occurrence."

Juliette gained confidence, seeing that, in spite of herself, Sorrel was intensely interested, perhaps to make sure she had made no errors she might unwittingly make again. "Gradually I became convinced you had been watching me since that first evening when I set foot in the house and found myself in the North Octagon Room."

"You're right on one point, but not on another. I did watch you. I had to watch for opportunities to bring about your death when there was no chance of suspicion falling on me. That's why I kept to my duties without fault. I wanted all to accept me as the perfect lady's maid. But I wasn't in the North Octagon Room that evening. I was with Gregory at Ravensworth Hall. We lay together while the foreign gentlemen staying there prepared themselves for their journey. I returned to West Thorpeby Hall with him on his horse." Her lips parted, showing her white teeth in a grimace that was no smile. "He gave you your betrothal ring that night, didn't he? I didn't care. It was not his choice for you. The master had purchased it in London, thinking it a disgrace that his brother had no ring to give you and nothing in his pockets to buy one." The grimace widened. "Gregory found it waiting for

him in his rooms in the north wing. He laughed and
tossed it in the air and caught it again, treating it like a
worthless bauble. He tried it on my finger for size and
took me while he did it." She gave an odd, gloating
chuckle in her throat.

Juliette chose to ignore it. "Then it *was* Isabelle I
heard in the North Octagon Room on that first evening—but it was you who released the corona, you
who shot the arrows, and your hands that tried to push
me down the stairs!"

Sorrel's tones mocked her. "Isabelle must have
been warning you of what was to come, but most of all
she must have been trying to tell you that death would
finally take you in this quarter of the house."

"I never thought of Isabelle coming to warn, only to
threaten. You have given me a different picture of her.
But surely you were afraid sometimes that you would
meet her in her domain?"

Sorrel's face tautened. "I've kept her at bay with
my own powers. With everybody else reluctant to come
near the North Octagon Room it meant there would be
no intrusion. I had the key to the door below copied
and returned the original to its place with nobody being
any the wiser. I would have had the keys of your
room duplicated if I had realized how difficult it was
going to be to dispose of you, and when I did take
them you tricked me by having bolts put in their place."
She flicked a hand casually. "They are here somewhere. A perfect hiding place for anything. When I
took the pistol yesterday I knew I had only to bring it
to this room and it would be safe. Fear and aversion to
this part of the house keep all at bay."

"Perhaps you haven't kept Isabelle at bay!" Juliette
challenged. "Perhaps she has simply decided to let
you come and go as you will, choosing not to warn
you of retribution to come."

"Enough!" Something close to fright showed in Sorrel's eyes.

Juliette pressed on. "It was your coming to this room
yesterday evening to hide the pistol that gave you
away to me!"

"How? Tell me how!" An urgent note resounded.

Instantly Juliette realized that she held an answer Sorrel needed to have in order to protect herself in the future. She moved further into the room, taking one pace and then another. The pistol cocked threateningly, but she had gone far enough. She rested her hand on the wooden pillar against which she had knocked when flying from the spectral image of Isabelle, and she felt it vibrate even to her light footsteps on the rotten boards.

"Tell me first where you hid the pistol, and I'll tell you what you want to know."

Sorrel jerked her head, unconsciously setting her glorious hair into wild ripples. "Behind that figure. Now you give me your answer."

Juliette followed with her gaze the direction which Sorrel had indicated and she gave a violent start that was not without a first reaction of fright even though in the very same instant she realized that it was only a lifesize stone effigy of Isabelle which stood propped upright in the shadows of one of the alcoves where Thomas Lockington must have had it placed long centuries ago. No wonder it had looked so curiously alive when her lamplight had shone full in its face, for moisture gave a sheen to the features, which were green-stained with mold as though it had indeed risen from some foul, watery grave. Now she knew why Thomas had chosen to die in the North Octagon Room below. He had wanted to be close to a likeness of the woman he loved, to link his death with hers depicted in the murals when the end came.

"Isabelle!" she whispered hoarsely.

"Don't call on her!" Sorrel shrieked, brought close to panic, and the pistol in her hand shook.

"You chose a cunning hiding place," Juliette said quickly, afraid that some involuntary pressure by the girl's finger on the trigger might set it off.

"Yes, yes! Now tell me what I want to know!"

Outwardly appearing calm, although the rate of her pulse was increasing with suspense and tension, Juliette tightened unobtrusively her hand into a hard grip on the pillar, ready to exert further pressure on it.

"You were always so spick and span," she said

mildly. "Your clothes were always scented by the lavender bags you keep amongst them, and never once did I see you with a creased apron or a spot of dirt under a fingernail. But last night when you helped me to bed there was a musty aroma about your clothes, which—although I didn't know then what its origins were—I associated immediately with what I knew to lurk behind the recessed door in the North Octagon Room. What is more, it was the second time that the dank, mildewy smell had been in my room—the first time was after the ball when I opened the window. I suppose that was one of the occasions when you had come from returning the spyglass to its hiding place, and I remember thinking it strange that you had not noticed that lingering trace hanging in the air, not realizing that you had become so accustomed to it you would not be aware how it clung to you. Oh, how well you have known this fearsome place, Sorrel! How cruelly you have used it!"

Without warning she cast all her weight against the pillar and threw herself towards the effigy, sprawling full-length at its feet. The pistol exploded, but harmlessly, in Sorrel's split-second of surprise as instinctively she dodged the falling timber that crashed down, striking another as it fell, and with it came a terrifying crack of plaster and the jingling of the clock's machinery.

Sorrel, looking up in terror, saw the roof collapsing above her and she screamed, dropping the pistol and flinging herself back. But she was too late. With horrified eyes Juliette saw the great clock above the domed roof beginning to tumble through it, and it was as though all motion had slowed and every detail was being implanted into her mind, even to the flying of splintered wood. Screaming herself, she scrambled as far into the alcove as she could get, shielding her face against the effigy, which was rocking and trembling violently. Down through the floorboards the clock crashed, taking with it the ancient telescope, pillars, slates, beams, bricks, and half the alcove in a great cloud of choking black dust. The effigy trembled dangerously, but held.

The great din thundered away to an odd tumbling of bricks and the clatter of one more piece of rotten board. Slowly Juliette raised her head, choked with dust, her eyes stinging, and she looked across at the spot where she had last seen Sorrel. She was gone. Nothing was left of the floorboards on which she had stood. Overhead the roof was completely open to the sky. With dread Juliette lowered her eyes, seeing that she herself was left on what amounted to no more than a crescent-shaped rim of floor with three alcoves left only half in place, and below in the North Octagon Room lay an enormous mountain of rubble that bore no resemblance to anything.

She sat paralyzed, clinging to Isabelle's effigy as though to life itself, the dust settling on her like a veil. She lost all sense of time. When her rescuers called to her she had no voice to answer them. Her pulse did not seem to beat again until she saw Blake reaching his arms to her from a ladder that others were holding. She swayed to him, choked out the words that Sorrel lay buried beneath the rubble, and closed her eyes. She was lifted and taken down and borne away.

It was Lucy and Aunt Phoebe who between them removed her tattered bridal clothes and bathed her free of dust and dirt while she stammered out an account of all that had happened, holding back only the intimate details that Sorrel had given her and Gregory's involvement with the pistols, which amounted to a task that had yet to be done. All the time Caroline was doing what she could to help the two attending to Juliette, fetching and carrying as though seeking to make amends. Once she made to open her mouth, but was silenced by a warning frown from Lucy, and wept again. Outside carriages departed, bearing away guests who knew there would be no wedding that day. A reprieve, Juliette thought, but through what a terrible and ironic twist of fate.

Curtains were drawn and Aunt Phoebe and Caroline sat with her while Lucy went to fill in details to Blake, who was in charge of operations in the North Octagon Room. Juliette slept, and awoke, emerged from shock, to find Lucy had returned. She assured them that she felt much better, and only then, while Lucy helped her to dress, was Caroline allowed to speak out what was on her mind.

"I painted that guillotine on your water color, Juliette—but I didn't really want you dead. Then you nearly were! I feel I wished an omen on you, and I never meant to. Do say you forgive me! Please!"

Juliette smiled and warmed to the offer of a truce and friendship that had come at last. "It's forgiven and forgotten. Never think of it again."

"Oh, I'm so thankful!" They embraced, and each kissed the other's cheek.

Juliette turned to Lucy. "May I ask your forgiveness? You thought I played with your brother's affections as well as Blake's, but I never wished you or anyone else harm through it."

Lucy nodded, her face gentle, her smile a little self-mocking. "I was taken by jealousy when I saw you with Blake, but it was my folly. He loves you, and he will always love you."

Juliette colored. "He shouldn't have told you. Honor was settled by that duel, and what passed between the two brothers is over and done with. Gregory and I—"

Lucy spoke very quietly. "Gregory is dead."

Juliette stood statue still, while behind her Aunt Phoebe gave a sob into her handkerchief. "No!" The word was torn from her. "Gregory did not fall! Blake would never have shot his own brother! Neither of them fell!"

"Not at first. Blake aimed wide. It was Sorrel's wild shot that gave Gregory his fatal wound. He stayed on his feet for several minutes, insisting that he wasn't badly hurt. Then he collapsed and died half an hour later."

Juliette dropped her face into her hands. "I distracted Sorrel as she pressed the trigger."

Lucy put an arm about her shoulders. "You did what you could to save both men. Gregory had sworn to kill Blake. Had Sorrel's bullet not caught him a fraction of a second before he fired, it would have been Blake we would all be mourning."

Slowly Juliette lowered her hands. "Where is Blake now?" she asked almost inaudibly.

"In the other room. Waiting for you."

She left the bedroom, Lucy closing the door after her to withdraw with Aunt Phoebe and Caroline by way of the dressing room. Through the anteroom she walked and came into the salon. He stood by the window and their eyes met. For several seconds neither of them moved. Then with a desperate little cry she ran to him and he caught her and held her to him, her face resting against his shoulder, his hand cupping her head and his lips against her hair. After a few minutes of immediate comforting he led her by the hand across to a sofa where he sat down with her.

"Gregory called me out as soon as I told him that I loved you. My offer of West Thorpeby Hall and all its lands he turned down with ridicule. I had no option but to meet his challenge, for he would not have it otherwise."

"I am the cause of all that has happened," she said brokenly.

"Through no fault of your own, and there's none who would think otherwise, least of all Gregory."

She looked at him through her tears. "What do you mean?"

"At the end Gregory shouldered all the blame. In those last minutes of his life after his collapse he was again the brother I once knew and he spoke to me as if all the differences between us had never been."

"I'm most thankful to hear that," she whispered heartfeltly.

"There is more to tell you. His feelings for you had become love over the past weeks and he asked me to let you know of it."

"Oh, Blake." She wept again, overcome by his disclosure. "What a complex person he was with the many different facets to his character. I have something to tell you that you never suspected." Her breath shuddered as she drew it in. "He was a Napoleonist and, more than that, he was plotting against England and the Crown." Suddenly she rose to a realization of danger that had to be averted. "There was a plot hatched

for Gregory to assassinate the Prince Regent. Another
assassin could take his place when the news gets out
that he is dead. His Highness must be warned!"
Quickly she told him everything she had learned of
Gregory's treacherous aims and of the spy who had
come to the house.

"I'll send a fast messenger to Carlton House at
once!" Blake jumped up and went swiftly across to
the rosewood bureau where he sat down, drew a
sheet of paper towards him, and began to write, his
nib flying in and out of the inkpot. He acquainted the
heir to the Throne, who would remember him from
meetings in the past, with all details recounted to him
of the Napoleonist plots, withholding only his brother's name. Gregory was dead, and in all fairness Blake
wanted to give him the benefit of doubt that at the last
moment he might not have pressed the trigger, no matter that the evidence against him suggested that there
would have been no change of heart. After adding his
signature Blake dashed sand on the letter and sealed
it. Five minutes later it was on its way to London,
carried in a leather satchel worn by the best rider
among the grooms and borne on the swiftest of all the
horses.

Gregory's funeral took place the day after Sorrel
was laid to rest, and their graves were no great distance
from each other. In the North Octagon Room the rubble
was cleared away, and on scaffolding men were at work
rebuilding the dome-roof in order that the graceful
symmetry of the house should not be spoiled. The
room itself was to be restored as near as possible to its
original condition. This was Juliette's wish. She explained why to Blake on the afternoon he took her
to the museum room where the artifacts from the
marshes were displayed on the shelves in a gleam of
copper and pewter, the richness of primitively-colored
pottery, and in the dark hues of ancient woods. The
effigy lay supported by four stout trestles, and he
wanted her to see how he had cleaned a small patch,
no bigger than a half-penny, on the brow and had discovered that beneath the green stains there was the
pure white of the finest Carrara marble.

When she had admired what he had done she leaned over the effigy to look down into its face. "I know now there was hope and forgiveness in those winter murals. The bleakness depicted there in the North Octagon Room was only the darkness before the dawn. Thomas wanted Isabelle to know that he loved her still, and that's why he had the ruby ring, which she never received, painted on her hand stretched above the water."

"You're very sure," he said, smiling.

She nodded seriously. "More sure than I've been about anything, except how much I love you." With gentle fingertips she touched the effigy's face. "Isabelle loved Thomas, too. Maybe she did betray him and maybe she didn't. We'll never know. But she loved him enough for her spirit to reject the grave and wait until he called her to him. But he died before he could speak his wish to those left behind that the effigy should be laid beside his. He had longed all the time for a reconciliation. Why else would he have had this likeness made of her in her youth and beauty, as he remembered her, unless it was in the hope that one day they would come together again?"

Blake put an arm about her waist and drew her to him. "When the effigy has been cleaned and restored it shall be laid in its rightful place next to Thomas on his tomb."

She kissed him on the lips. "They shall be reunited forevermore."

The work took two months, and during that time Thomas Lockington's effigy and his whole tomb was cleaned and restored to the full beauty of its gleaming marble. Then invitations were sent out to the marriage of Blake and Juliette, which was to be held at noon on a mid-September day, but the guest list was extremely short and included only those closest to them. The wedding ceremony was to be preceded by another to sanctify the effigy of Isabelle, which had been laid at last beside that of Thomas Lockington.

In soft, autumnal sunshine Blake and Juliette arrived together at West Thorpeby Hall's private chapel, having covered the short distance on foot from the house, hand in hand like simple country lovers. Still talking softly to each other they paused in the porch while she tidied one breeze-blown tendril of hair, tucking it into her veil-trimmed bonnet. They smiled again at each other with their lips and with their eyes, and then she held her nosegay before her with both hands. With a swish of azure silk she entered the chapel at his side.

In the gloom of the church, lightened by candle glow and shafts of stained glass sunlight, Isabelle's effigy gleamed at her husband's side on the large tomb, which had been bedecked with garlands of sweet smelling flowers. Waiting by it was the kindly-faced Rector, and gathered about him were those whom Blake and Juliette had wanted most to be there. Aunt Phoebe, accompanied by Sir Duncan, was nodding and smiling in a new bonnet, a lace handkerchief clasped in readiness for the tears she would inevitably shed during the marriage ceremony, and beside them Alex and Lucy Rose-Marshall stood side by side. Caroline had her hand tucked into the crook of Sir Humphrey's arm, he having proposed some days previously, and their own marriage was already arranged. Venetia, long since returned to full health and strength, was the only other person present, the arrival of the bride and groom distracting her from daydreams of a young officer in the Dragoons, home from the Peninsula, who was quite the favorite of her current beaux and with whom she intended to dance every dance at the grandest ball ever to be held at West Thorpeby Hall, which Blake was giving in honor of his bride that evening.

The Rector waited until the wedding couple had taken their places beside him, and then he stepped forward to commence the prayers for Isabelle's soul and the sanctification of her effigy. The tiny congregation made their responses to the prayers with bowed heads. Then he raised his hands and pronounced the blessing. It was done. Thomas and Isabelle would be together for all time.

"Thank you, Rector," Juliette breathed, and Blake expressed his own thanks.

The Rector smiled at them. "Now I have another happy duty to perform." He glanced at the guests and motioned them to take their places in the front pews. When they had settled themselves he took his place on the chancel steps. To the glorious thunder of the organ Blake took Juliette up the aisle.

Throughout the ceremony they barely took their eyes from each other, and when he slipped the gold ring on her finger she thought her heart must burst with happiness. After signing their names in the chapel register under countless Lockington names before them, Blake gave Juliette his arm, and joyously they went back down the aisle, the opened chapel doors showing them that the tenants and workers of the estate had gathered to line the path outside and wish them well.

"Wait, Blake," Juliette said when they drew level with the tomb.

He watched her take a crimson rose from her nosegay and tuck it into the effigy's hand. "Well done, my love," he said.

The chapel bells had begun to ring. Far from West Thorpeby Hall, thousands of miles beyond the shores of England in Moscow, Napoleon was facing the first shadows in a deserted palace, not yet aware that victory bells would never ring for his armies again, his dreams, like those that Gregory had cherished for him, doomed to come to nothing.

Cheers went up on all sides as Blake and Juliette emerged into the sunshine. Laughing under showers of rice and rosepetals they hurried towards the carriage waiting to transport them home to West Thorpeby Hall. In the wake of the guests preparing to follow in their own carriages, a little breeze wafted into the chapel through the open doors. The crimson petals of the rose trembled in the draught, giving out a sweet fragrance, its stem held securely by the marble hand.

ABOUT THE AUTHOR

BARBARA PAUL lives in England with her Norwegian husband, Inge Ovstedal, and their two children, a son and a daughter. Before settling in Sussex, the Ovstedals lived in Norway and Canada; their present interests include restoring a centuries-old cottage in Ovstedal, Norway, and collecting Norwegian legends. Barbara Paul's previous works of romantic suspense include *The Seventeenth Stair* (featured in *Good Housekeeping* as "Reach for Tomorrow") and *Devils Fire, Love's Revenge*.